VOICES IN A HAUNTED ROOM

VOICES IN A HAUNTED ROOM

PHILIPPA CARR

G. P. PUTNAM'S SONS
NEW YORK

PRINTED IN THE UNITED STATES OF AMERICA

Contents

The Family Tree

William Farland m Dulce

Damask m Bruno

Catharine m 1) Felipe Gonzales

m 2) Jake Pennlyon

Roberto

Linnet — Damask

Linnet m Colum Casvellyn

Connel — Tamsyn m Fennimore Landor

Fennimore — The Twins

Bersaba m 1) Luke Longridge

Lucas

Bersaba m 2) Richard Tolworthy

Angelet m Richard Tolworthy

Richard

Arabella — Richard — Angelique — Fennimore

Arabella m 1) Edwin Eversleigh 2) Carleton Eversleigh

Edwin

Priscilla — Carl

Edwin m Jane Merriden

Carl

Priscilla m Leigh Main

Carlotta (by Jocelyn Finton) — Damaris m Jeremy Granthon

Clarissa (by John Field) m Lance Clavering

Sabrina m Richard Frenshaw

Zipporah m Jean Louis Ransome

Charlotte (Lottie) by Gerard d'Aubigné

Richard (Dickon) m Isabel

Jonathan — David

Charlotte m Charles de Tourville

Charlot — Claudine

A Birthday Party

On my seventeenth birthday my mother gave a dinner party to celebrate the occasion. At that time I had been living at Eversleigh for three years. Little had I thought when I had left my grandfather's *château* that I should never see him again. Of course I had known that there was great anxiety throughout France. Even a girl as young and ignorant of the world as I had been, could not be unaware of that, especially as my own grandmother had met a violent death at the hands of the mob. That had had a devastating effect on everyone around me.

Afterwards my mother, my brother Charlot and I had left our home at Tourville and had gone to live in my grandfather's *château* of Aubigné in order to comfort him, and Lisette, my mother's friend, and her son, Louis Charles, had come with us.

I had loved Aubigné and my grandfather had seemed a splendid gentleman, though a very sad one, unlike the man I had known before the death of my grandmother. Yes, no one could help being aware of a brooding menace; it had been everywhere—in the streets, in the country lanes, in the *château* itself.

Then my mother had brought us to England—myself, Charlot and Louis Charles—to visit her relatives, and there everything was different. I was fourteen at the time and adapted myself quickly. I felt it was my home. I knew my mother felt like that too; but that was understandable because she had lived there in her childhood. There was a certain peace —indefinable—for it was by no means a quiet household. No household could be with Dickon Frenshaw in it. Dickon in a way reminded me of my grandfather. He was one of those dominating men of whom everyone is in awe. Such men don't have to ask for respect; it is freely given them, perhaps because they take it for granted that it must be there. He was tall, quite handsome, but what one was most aware of was that sense of power which emanated from him. I think we were all aware of it—some resented it, like my brother Charlot, and I fancied on some occasions that Dickon's own son Jonathan resented him as well.

So through those June days we rode, we walked, we talked, and my mother spent a lot of time with Dickon, while I was delighted with the company of his children, David and Jonathan, who both showed an interest in me and teased me because of my imperfect English; and Sabrina, Dickon's mother, looked on benignly because Dickon liked to have my mother there, and Dickon's slightest wish was law to Sabrina.

She was turned seventy then, but she did not look her age. She had a great purpose in living, and that was anticipating and granting the wishes of her son.

It was clear to us all even then that Dickon would have liked my mother to stay. If ever two people were attracted by each other, those two were. They seemed very old to me and it was a source of wonder that two such mature people could behave like young lovers—and one's own mother, at that, made it more surprising than ever.

I remember the time when my father had been alive. She had not been the same with him; and I think she did not mind very much when he had gone to fight with the American colonists. That was the last we saw of him for he had died in the fighting, and it was soon after that when we left Tourville and went to my grandfather at Aubigné.

Then came this holiday. My mother had refused to leave my grandfather and he had promised to come with us but he had been too ill right at the last moment when it was too late to cancel our arrangements—and I had never seen the *château* since.

I remembered well that day when my mother received the message that he was very ill and prepared to return to France. There had been hurried consultations and at length she had decided to leave us children —as she called us—with Sabrina, and had travelled back with one of the grooms who had brought the message from Aubigné.

Dickon had been in London at the time and Sabrina had tried to persuade my mother not to go because she knew how upset Dickon would be by her departure when he returned to find her gone. But my mother was adamant.

When Dickon returned and discovered that she had left for France, he was frantic and lost no time in setting out after her. I did not fully understand why he should have been so disturbed until I heard Charlot talking with Louis Charles and Jonathan.

"There's trouble over there," said Charlot, "big trouble. That is what Dickon is afraid of."

"She should never have gone," said Louis Charles.

"She was right to go," retorted Charlot. "My grandfather would want to see her more than anyone when he is ill. But she should have taken me with her."

I joined in then. "You would, of course, fight all the mobs in France."

"What do you know about it?" asked Charlot witheringly.

"If I knew what you knew, that wouldn't amount to much," I replied.

Jonathan grinned at me. I always felt that he was amused by me. He provoked me, but in a special sort of way—not in the least like Charlot, who was contemptuous.

"You're an ignoramus," said Charlot.

"You're a swaggering braggart."

"That's right, Claudine," said Jonathan. "Stand up for yourself. But there's no need to tell you to do that. She's a bit of a firebrand, our little Claudine, eh?"

"A firebrand?" I asked. "What is this firebrand?"

"I'd forgotten Mademoiselle's imperfect knowledge of the language. It is one who is always ready for trouble, Claudine . . . and very energetic in pursuing it."

"And you think that describes me?"

"I *know* it. And I'll tell you something else, mademoiselle. I like it. I like it very much indeed."

"I wonder how long they'll stay in France," went on Charlot, ignoring Jonathan's banter.

"Until our grandfather is better, of course," I said. "And I expect we shall be going back soon."

"That was the idea," said Charlot. "Oh I do wonder what is happening there. It was so exciting . . . in a way . . . but awful that people are hurt. One wants to be there when something important is happening in one's country." Charlot spoke earnestly and it occurred to me then that he did not feel as I did about Eversleigh. This was an alien place to him. He was homesick for the *château,* for a way of life which was different from that of Eversleigh. He was French. Our father had been French and he took after him. As for myself, I was like my mother, and although she had had a French father, her mother had been English, and it had not been until she was well past her youth that she had married my grandfather and became the Comtesse d'Aubigné, presiding over a *château,* living the life of a lady of the French nobility.

Ours was a complicated household, and I suppose that accounted for many things.

I shall never forget the day they came home—my mother and Dickon. News was filtering into England from France, and we were realizing that the long-awaited revolution had broken out at last. The Bastille had been stormed and the whole of France was in turmoil. Sabrina was beside herself with anxiety to contemplate that her beloved Dickon was caught up in the holocaust.

I never doubted for one moment that he would not emerge triumphant. And he did, bringing my mother with him.

When they reached the house one of the grooms saw them and shouted: "He's here. Master's here." Sabrina, who had been watching and waiting during those days of anxiety, ran out and I saw her in the courtyard, laughing and crying at the same time.

I went out too and was caught in my mother's arms. Then Charlot and all the others came. I thought Charlot was just a little disappointed. He had been planning to go and get them out of France. Now he no longer had an excuse to return there.

And what a tale they had had to tell—how they had escaped death by inches, how my mother had actually been taken to the *mairie* and the mob were round the place screaming for her blood. She was after all the acknowledged daughter of one of the leading French aristocrats.

My mother was in a strange mood of shock and exultation which I supposed was to be expected from one who had narrowly escaped death. Dickon seemed more powerful than ever; and for some time I think we all shared Sabrina's view of him. He was magnificent; he was unique; he was a man who could ride into the midst of the mob and come through unscathed and triumphant.

There was a shock for poor Louis Charles, as his mother had been yet another victim of the revolution. She had never been much of a mother to him and I think he cared more for my mother than he ever had for his own, but it was a blow nevertheless.

My mother had such tales to tell—tales which would have seemed incredible had not wild and fearful happenings taken place across the water. We heard about Armand, the Comte's son, who had been imprisoned in the Bastille, and whom we all thought had been murdered when he disappeared. But he had come back to Aubigné when the Bastille had been stormed; and he was still at the *château* with his poor sister Sophie, who had been so badly disfigured during the disaster at the fireworks display which had shocked the whole of France at the time of the King's wedding.

When my mother had arrived in France she had found my grandfather dead, and she had come to think of that as a blessing, for he could never have borne to see the mob ravaging his beloved *château* and destroying that way of life which he and his family had known for centuries. No wonder my mother was torn between a bewildered grief and that exultant exhilaration which Dickon always inspired in her. She had always had such spirit; she was so beautiful—one of the most beautiful people I have ever known. I was not surprised that Dickon wanted her. He always wanted the best of everything. Sabrina would say he deserved it. As for her, she was supremely happy. I believed that what was happening in France meant little to her. She wanted my mother to stay in England and marry Dickon, and she had wanted that as soon as she had heard that my father had died in the colonies. She wanted it fiercely because it was what Dickon wanted, and in her eyes his wishes must always be gratified. And if these terrible things had happened to bring to Dickon what he wanted, she accepted that calmly enough.

So my mother and Dickon were married.

"This is our home now," said my mother to me tentatively. I was always closer to her than Charlot had been, and I remember how anxiously she had looked at me. I knew what she was thinking.

I said: "I should not want to go back, Maman. What is it like . . . at the *château?*"

She shivered and lifted her shoulders.

"Aunt Sophie . . ." I began.

"I don't know what is happening to her. They came for us and they took Lisette and me. They took us away and left the others. Armand was in a sad state. I don't think he can live long. And Jeanne Fougère was looking after Sophie. Jeanne seemed to understand the mob. She showed them Sophie's poor scarred face. It stopped their desire to harm her, I think. They left her alone. Then Lisette jumped from the balcony of the *mairie* . . . and the mob were at her."

"Don't talk of it," I said. "Dickon brought you safely home."

"Yes . . . Dickon," she said, and the look which illuminated her face left little doubt of her feeling for him.

I clung to her. "I'm so happy you're back," I told her. "If you hadn't come back, I should never have been happy again."

We were silent for a few moments, then she said: "Shall you miss France, Claudine?"

"I'd hate to go back," I told her truthfully. "Grandfather is not there. It must be quite different. Grandfather *was* France."

She nodded. "No. I don't want to go back either. It's a new life for us, Claudine."

"You'll be happy with Dickon," I said. "It is what you have always wanted . . . even when—"

I was going to say "even when my father was alive," before I stopped. But she knew what I meant and that it was true. I knew it had always been Dickon for her. Well, now she had him.

When they were married she seemed to throw off her melancholy. She seemed young . . . only a few years older than I . . . and Dickon went about breathing contented triumph.

I thought: Now it is to be "happy ever after."

But when is life ever like that?

I adapted very quickly and soon I was feeling that I had always belonged to Eversleigh. I loved the house. To me it was more homely than either my father's or my grandfather's *château.*

Every time I approached it I had a feeling of excitement. It was partly hidden by the high wall which surrounded it, and I found great pleasure in glimpsing, from some little distance, the gables just visible beyond the wall. There was that sense of coming home when I rode or drove in through the wide-open gates. Like so many big houses which had been constructed during that period in England, it was built in the Elizabethan style—E-shaped, in honour of the Queen, which meant that there was a huge main hall with a wing on either side of it. I loved the rough stone walls adorned by armoury which had actually been used by my ancestors; and I spent hours studying the family tree which had been painted over the great fireplace and added to over the decades.

I enjoyed galloping through the green fields; I liked to walk my horse through the country lanes; sometimes we rode to the sea—which was not very far from Eversleigh—but then I could not resist looking across that expanse of water and thinking of my grandfather—who had died just in time—and wondering what was happening to unfortunate Uncle Armand and sad Aunt Sophie of the scarred face and constant melancholy. So I did not go to the sea often. But I believe Charlot did.

I was with him once and saw the look of frustration in his eyes as he gazed across to France. . . .

There were undercurrents of emotion in the household. I did not pay much attention to them because I was so absorbed in my own affairs. A governess had been engaged and I had lessons with her; but I mainly studied English. I think it was Dickon's idea that I should, as he said, "speak properly," which meant that he wanted me to be rid of my French accent. Dickon seemed to hate everything French, which I was sure was due to the fact that my mother had married Charles de Tourville. Not that he dominated my mother completely. She was not of a nature to be dominated. They sparred together in a way which is really lovers' talk; and they could scarcely bear to be out of each other's sight.

Charlot did not like that. There was a great deal that Charlot did not like.

I was really more concerned with David and Jonathan, for both of them had a very special interest in me. David, the quiet and scholarly one, liked to talk to me and told me a great deal about the history of England; he would smilingly correct me when I mispronounced a word and used an incorrect construction of a sentence. Jonathan's attentions were no less obvious but quite different. There was the jocular banter for one thing; and he was constantly putting his hands on me in a protective proprietorial way. He liked to take me riding; we would gallop along the beach or across meadows, and I always tried to outride him—something he was determined I should not do. But he enjoyed my attempts. He was constantly trying to prove his strength. It occurred to me that when his father had been his age he must have been more than a little like Jonathan.

It was an interesting situation. The brothers made me feel important and that was very pleasant for me, particularly as Charlot kept up the big-brother contemptuous attitude, and Louis Charles, although he was a little older than Charlot, looked up to him and took his cues as to how to behave from my brother.

When I was fifteen—that was about a year after we had settled in Eversleigh—my mother had a serious talk with me.

It was clear that she was anxious about me. "You are growing up now, Claudine," she began.

I did not mind that in the least. Like most young people I was eager to escape the bonds of childhood and to live freely and independently.

Perhaps living in such a household was a kind of forcing ground. I was aware of the dynamic attraction between my mother and her husband; one could not live in such an atmosphere without being constantly reminded of the powerful effect one person can have on another. That my stepfather was a man of immense physical powers, I was sure, and that he had awakened my mother to an understanding of such a relationship I was subconsciously aware even then, although I did not see this clearly until later. My father—whom I remembered vaguely—had been a typical French nobleman of his age. He must have had numerous love affairs before his marriage, and I was to have proof of that later. But this bond between my mother and Dickon was different.

My mother was watchful of me, and no doubt because she was growing more and more aware of the power of physical attraction, she saw what was brewing round me.

She had suggested we walk in the gardens and we sat in an arbour while she talked.

"Yes, Claudine," she said, "you're fifteen. How the time flies. As I said . . . you're growing up . . . fast."

She had not brought me here to tell me such an obvious fact, so I waited somewhat impatiently.

"You look older than your years . . . and you are in a household of men . . . and brought up with them. I wish I could have had another daughter."

She looked a little wistful. I think she was sad because this great passion which she shared with Dickon had so far been unfruitful. It seemed strange to me too. I thought they might have started a brood of sons . . . lusty sons, like Dickon himself . . . or Jonathan.

"As you grow older . . . they will realize that you are becoming an attractive woman. That could be dangerous."

I began to feel uneasy. Had she noticed Jonathan's way of trying to be alone with me? Had she seen the way in which he watched me with that look in his eyes which made them glow like two intensely blue flames?

Then she surprised me. "I must talk to you about Louis Charles."

"Louis Charles!" I was amazed. I had not thought very much about Louis Charles.

She proceeded slowly, and rather painfully I imagined, for she hated talking about her first husband. "Your father was a man who . . . liked women."

I smiled at her. "That does not seem so very unusual."

She returned my smile and went on: "And in France they have a slightly different code of morals. What I am trying to tell you is that your father was also the father of Louis Charles. Lisette and he were lovers at one time and Louis Charles is the result of that liaison."

I stared at her. "So that is why he was brought up with us!"

"Not exactly. Lisette was married off to a farmer and when he was killed . . . that fearful revolution again—she came to us, bringing her son with her. I am telling you this because Louis Charles is your half brother."

Understanding dawned. She was anticipating a love affair between Louis Charles and myself. She stumbled on: "So you see you and Louis Charles could never—"

"Dear Maman," I cried. "There is no danger in any case. I would never want to marry a husband who looked down on me. Charlot has taught him to do that and he follows Charlot in every way."

"It is just a brotherly feeling," she said quickly. "Charlot is really very fond of you."

I was relieved. I had thought she was going to talk about Jonathan—but my relief did not last long, for she continued immediately: "Then there are Jonathan and David. With a household of young men . . . and one young woman among them . . . there are bound to be complications. I think both David and Jonathan are very fond of you, and although their father is my husband, there is not a close blood relationship between you."

I flushed and my confusion seemed to answer her question.

"Jonathan is so like his father. I knew Dickon when he was Jonathan's age. I was even younger than you are . . . and I was in love with him even then. I would have married him, but my mother stopped it. She had her reasons . . . and perhaps she was right at that time. Who shall say? But it was long ago. It is the future which concerns us." She wrinkled her brows. "You see, there are two brothers—twins. They say twins are very close. Would you say that Jonathan and David are very close?"

"I would say they are poles apart."

"I agree. David is so thoughtful, so serious. He is very clever, I know. Jonathan is clever too . . . but in a different way. Oh, he is so like his father, Claudine. I . . . I think they are both getting fond of you . . . and that could present a problem. You are growing up so quickly. Dear child, always remember that I am here to talk to . . . to confide in . . ."

"But I know you are."

I felt that there was so much she wanted to say and that she was not quite sure of my ability to understand. Like most parents she saw me as a child, and it was hard to change that image.

What she was really doing was warning me.

—

There was a great deal of activity at Eversleigh. The running of the estate was not all that occupied Dickon and his sons. Dickon was one of the most important men in the South East; and he had many interests in London.

David loved the house and the estate, so Dickon had wisely made that his province. He spent hours in the library, to which he had added considerably; he had friends who would ride out from London and perhaps stay with us for a few days. They were all very erudite and as soon as meals were over, David would conduct them to the library, where they would sit for hours sipping port and talking of matters which were of no interest to Jonathan and his father.

I liked to listen to their conversation at dinner and when I joined in—or tried to—David would be delighted and encourage me to air my views; he often showed me rare books and maps and drawings—not only of Eversleigh but various parts of the country. He was interested in archaeology and taught me a little about it, showing me what had been found at various sites and how a picture of ancient days could be built up through artefacts. He was passionately interested in history and I could listen to him for hours. He gave me books to read and we would discuss them, sometimes walking in the gardens, sometimes riding together. We would stop now and then for refreshment, perhaps at some old inn, and I would notice how much people liked him. They showed him a certain deference, and I was quick to realize that it was a different kind of respect than that which was given to Dickon or Jonathan. They demanded it—not in so many words, of course, but by their attitude of superiority. David was different; he was gentle, and respect was given him because people responded to his gentleness and wanted him to know it.

I enjoyed being with David. He stimulated my interest in so many subjects, and matters which might have been dull became exciting when he explained them to me. I could see that he was advancing my education far more rapidly than my governess was doing, and I was beginning to cast off that French accent, and it was only occasionally that it showed itself. I was growing very fond of David.

I sometimes wished that Jonathan had not been there to complicate matters.

The two brothers were diametrically opposed in almost everything. They looked different—which was rather odd, for feature by feature they were alike; but their entirely different characteristics had set their stamp on their faces and nullified their resemblance.

Jonathan was not the man to settle down to look after a country estate. He was concerned with interests in London. I knew that banking was one of these; there were others. My stepfather was a man of very wide interests—rich and influential; he was often at Court, and my mother accompanied him there, for he never went away without taking her with him. It was as though, having come to happiness late in their lives, they were determined not to miss one hour of each other's company. That was how my grandfather and grandmother had been. Perhaps such are the ideal marriages, I thought—those to which people come when they are mature in judgement and knowledgeable in the ways of men and women. The fires of youth blazed forth and could burn out; but the steady fire of middle age, stoked with experience and understanding, can burn brightly for life. My mind was stimulated and enriched by my sessions with David; with Jonathan I experienced different feelings.

His attitude was changing and I sensed a certain impatience. Sometimes he kissed me and held me against him, and there was something very meaningful in his manner towards me. I knew, in a way, what that meant. He wanted to make love with me.

I might have had a romantic feeling towards him. I could not pretend to myself that he did not arouse new emotions in me such as I wanted to explore; but I did know that he had dallied with some of the serving girls. I had seen them look at him and I had watched his answering response. I had heard it whispered that he had a mistress in London and that he visited her when he was there—which was frequently.

All this I would have expected of Dickon's son, and if I had felt indifferent towards him it would not have bothered me; but I thought about it a good deal. Sometimes when he helped me down from my horse, which he did whenever he could, although I was quite capable of dismounting on my own, he would hold me closely and laugh up at me, and although I quickly wriggled free I was rather alarmed to discover that I did not really want to. I had an inclination to smile at him invitingly and let him proceed with what he was planning to do—because I knew how much I wanted to experience it.

At Eversleigh there were portraits of our family—men and women—and I often studied them. The men were of two kinds—I mean of course in one respect only, for their characters were quite diverse and they could not be neatly divided; what I mean is that there were those who were physically demanding and others who were not. I could pick them out by a certain expression in their faces—the sensuous and the austere. There was one ancestress—her name was Carlotta—who embodied all the former; I believe she had had a colourful life with a leader of the Jacobite faction; and there was her half sister Damaris, mother of Sabrina, who was in the second category. My mother was a woman who understood passion and needed it in her life. Jonathan made me feel that I was the same.

So there were many times when I felt weak and ready to respond to his invitation. It was only because of who I was that he did not hustle me into a physical relationship. He could not treat his new stepmother's daughter as he would some friend in London or any of the servants in our or other households. Even he would not dare to do that. My mother would have been furious and she would have made sure that Dickon was too; and Jonathan, bold as he was, would not wish to incur his father's wrath.

Right up to the time of my seventeenth birthday we played our tantalising game. I used to dream about Jonathan—that he came to my room and into my bed. I even locked my door when the dream became too vivid. I always took great care never to meet his eyes when he practised little familiarities, the meaning of which I was fully aware. When he went to London I used to imagine his visits to his mistress, and I would feel angry and frustrated and jealous, until David soothed me with his interesting discoveries of the past. Then I could forget Jonathan in just the same way as I forgot David when I was with his intriguing brother.

It is all very well to play these games when one is growing up to sixteen, but when one has reached the mature age of seventeen—which is a time when many girls are considered to be ready for marriage—it is a different matter.

I became aware that my mother—and I suppose Dickon, too—would like me to marry either David or Jonathan. I was sure that my mother would prefer David because he was quiet and serious and his fidelity could be relied on. Dickon regarded David as a "dull dog," and I imagine he thought that a lively girl such as I was, would have a more exciting time with Jonathan. However, he would certainly give his blessing to either match—and so would my mother.

It would keep me with them, and my mother—to whom the only fly in her marriage ointment was that fertility was lacking—would have grandchildren under her roof.

"In a few weeks you will be seventeen," said my mother, eyeing me with a sort of wonder, as though for a girl to reach that age was a feat of extreme cleverness. "I can't believe it. Seventeen years ago . . ." Her eyes clouded as they always did when she thought of those years in France. She did often, I knew. It was impossible not to. We were always hearing of the terrible things which were happening over there, how the King and Queen were now the prisoners of the new régime, and of the terrible humiliations to which they were submitted. Then there was the bloodshed—the guillotine with its horrible basket into which the severed heads of aristocrats dropped with appalling regularity.

She, too, often thought of poor Aunt Sophie and Armand, and wondered what had become of them. The subject would now and then be raised at the table, and Dickon would wax fierce about it, and there were often arguments between him and Charlot in which Louis Charles joined. Charlot was a problem. He was becoming a man and had to decide what he was to do with his life. Dickon was for sending him to the other estate at Clavering—and Louis Charles with him. That, Dickon thought, would get them both out of the way. But Charlot declared that he did not intend to manage an *English* country estate. He had been brought up in the belief that he was to have charge of Aubigné.

"The principle of management is the same," Dickon reminded him.

"Mon cher Monsieur." Charlot often introduced French phrases into his conversation, particularly when he was talking to Dickon. "There is much difference between a great French castle and a little English country estate."

"Indeed yes," said Dickon. "One is a ruin . . . overrun by rabble; the other is in perfect working order."

My mother, as she always did, interposed between her husband and her son. It was only because he knew that these altercations distressed her that Dickon did not carry on the battle.

"Seventeen," she went on now. "We must have a real celebration. Shall we have a dance and invite the neighbours, or would you like just a dinner party with a few selected friends? Then we might arrange for a trip to London. We could go to the theatre and do some shopping . . ."

I said certainly that appealed to me more than the dance and the neighbours.

Then she was serious. "Claudine, have you ever thought about . . . marriage?"

"I suppose most people give it a thought now and then."

"I mean seriously."

"How can one unless one is asked?"

She frowned. "There are two, I believe, who would be ready to ask you," she went on. "In fact I think they are waiting for the all-important birthday. You know who I mean, and I know you are fond of both of them. Dickon and I have talked of it. It is something we should be very happy about. There is something unusual about twins. We had twins in the family some years ago—Bersaba and Angelet—and do you know, eventually they each married the same man . . . Angelet first, and after her death, Bersaba married him. That was before the family were at Eversleigh. It was Bersaba's daughter Arabella who married into the Eversleigh family—that was at the time of the Civil War and the Restoration. So you see it goes back a long way. But why am I telling you this? Oh . . . twins. Although they are so different—as Bersaba and Angelet were by all accounts—they both fell in love with the same man. I think it is rather like David and Jonathan."

"You mean they are both in love . . . with me?"

"I'm sure of it, and so is Dickon. You are attractive, you know, Claudine."

"Oh, I am not beautiful like you, Maman."

"You are very attractive, and it is obvious that you will soon be called on to make a choice. Claudine, tell me, which is it to be?"

"Isn't it rather unseemly to choose between two men when one has not had a proposal from either?"

"It is only for my ears, Claudine."

"Dear Maman, I hadn't thought . . ."

"But you have thought of them."

"Well—in a way . . ."

"David loves you steadily . . . wholeheartedly. He would be a very good husband, Claudine."

"You mean that if I were asked by both of them you would prefer me to take David?"

"I would accept your choice. It is your decision, dearest child. They are so different. It is a situation fraught with difficulties, for whichever one you choose, the other will still be there. It worries me quite a lot, Claudine. Dickon laughs at me. He has his own ideas of these matters and I don't always agree with him." She smiled reminiscently. "In fact," she went on, "I hardly ever agree with him." She made disagreement sound like the ideal state. "I am concerned though. I wish it could have been different. But, Claudine . . . I am so selfish. I don't want you to go away."

I put my arms round her and held her close to me.

"There was always something rather special between us, wasn't there?" she said. "You came when I was a little disillusioned with marriage. Oh, I loved your father and we had some wonderful times together, but he was never faithful to me. To him that was the natural way of life. I suppose I had been brought up differently. My mother was so English. You were such a comfort to me, my little Claudine. I want you to make the right choice. You are so young. Talk to me. Tell me. Let me share your thoughts."

I was bewildered. Certainly I hadn't thought of having to make a choice. But I could see what she meant: the growing seriousness of David and his obvious delight in my company against the impatient gestures of Jonathan. Yes, I could see that the time of indecision was coming to an end.

I was glad my mother had prepared me for this.

I said to her: "I don't want to choose. I want everything to go on as it is. I like it this way. I love being with David. It is exciting to listen to him. I have never heard anyone talk as he does. Oh, I know he is rather silent in company, but when we are alone . . ."

She smiled at me lovingly and said: "He is a good young man. He is the best of young men . . ."

And that seemed significant. But I could not bring myself to talk to her of the emotions which Jonathan aroused in me.

I was to have a new dress for the party, and Molly Blackett, the sewing woman, who lived in one of the cottages on the estate, came to make it for me.

She cooed over the yards of white satin and blue silk which were to make up the dress. I was to have paniers of blue which would part to show a white satin petticoat; and the bodice was to be decorated with tiny white and blue flowers embroidered in silks; the sleeves stopped short at the elbow, from which flowed cascades of fine white lace. It was a style which had been introduced by Marie Antoinette, and when I saw it I could not help thinking of her in her prison waiting—and no doubt longing—for death; and this dampened my pleasure in the dress.

Molly Blackett made me stand for what seemed a very long period while she knelt at my feet with a black pincushion beside her into which she would jab the pins with a ferocious joy when she discarded them.

She chattered all the while about how beautiful I was going to look in my dress. "The white is so suitable for a young girl and the blue will match your eyes."

"They aren't that shade at all. They're dark blue."

"Ah, that's the point, Miss Claudine. The colours will make you eyes look a darker blue . . . in contrast, you see. Oh, these colours are just right for you. My word, time passes. I remember when you first came. It seems like yesterday."

"It is three years ago."

"Three years! And your dear mother now with us. My mother remembers her well. She sewed for *her* mother. That was before she went away to France . . . and after that she sewed for the first Mrs. Frenshaw. Things have changed now."

I was standing there only half listening. She had taken off the bodice, having rearranged the set of the sleeves, which had not pleased her, so I was left with the skirt about my waist and nothing but the shift at the top.

She laid the bodice on the table and was saying: "I'll have this right in a jiffy. Sleeves is so important, Miss Claudine. I've known a badly set sleeve ruin a dress, however handsome the rest of it . . ." when the door opened. I gave a little gasp because Jonathan was standing there.

He did not look at me but said: "Oh, Molly, the mistress wants to see you at once. It's urgent. She's in the library."

"Oh, Mr. Jonathan," she turned flustered to me; she looked back at the table. "I'll just—er—see to Miss Claudine . . ."

"The mistress said immediately, Molly. I think it is important."

She nodded nervously and with a little giggle ran from the room. Jonathan turned to me and the blue flames were in his eyes as they swept over me.

"Charming," he said. "Very charming. All glory below and sweet simplicity above."

"You've delivered your message," I said. "Now you'd better go."

"What?" he cried indignantly. "You'd ask me to go now?"

He put his hands on my shoulders and bending his head swiftly kissed my neck.

"No," I said firmly.

He just laughed and pulling my shift down over my shoulder put his lips against my skin. I gasped and he lifted his head to look at me mockingly.

"You see," he said, "the top does not suit the skirt, does it?"

I felt exposed, unprotected; my heart was beating so fiercely that in my state of undress he must be aware of it.

"Go away," I cried. "How dare you . . . come in here . . . when . . . when . . ."

"Claudine," he said. "Little Claudine . . . I was passing. I peeped in and saw dear old Molly with her pins, and you there in a certain degree of nudity . . . and I had to come and tell you how charming you looked."

I tried to pull my shift back into place but he would not release it, and I could not escape from his hands or his lips.

It was wildly exciting. It was like one of those fantasies during which I had pictured his coming into my bedroom. It was over very quickly, for I heard Molly Blackett coming back. She burst into the room just as Jonathan had slipped my shift back onto my shoulders.

Her face was flushed. "The mistress was not in the library," she said.

"Was she not?" Jonathan turned to her, smiling easily. "I expect she had to go away. I'll find her, and if she still wants you, I'll let you know."

With that he bowed to us both ironically and went out.

"Well, I never," said Molly Blackett. "The impudence. He had no right to come in here. I don't believe the mistress wanted me urgently."

"No," I said. "He had no right."

Her head shook and her lips twitched. "Mr. Jonathan and his tricks . . ." she murmured.

But I noticed later that she glanced at me speculatively and I wondered whether she thought I had encouraged him.

That scene in the sewing room affected me deeply. I could not get it out of my mind. I avoided him for all the rest of that day, and an hour or so before dinner I went into the library to talk to David. He was excited about some Roman remains which had been uncovered along the coast and he wanted to go down to see them at the end of the week.

"Would you like to come with me?" he asked. "I know you'd be interested."

I said enthusiastically that I would.

"They could be important. You know we are not far from the spot where Julius Caesar landed and the Romans seem to have left quite a lot of evidence of their residence. They used this area for fuelling their ships. The remains of a villa have been unearthed and there are some very well-preserved tiles. I must say I am greatly looking forward to seeing it."

He had blue eyes and when they sparkled they looked remarkably like Jonathan's.

I questioned him about the discovery and he brought down books to show me what had been found in the past.

"It must be a most satisfying profession," he said a little wistfully. "Imagine the satisfaction when great discoveries are made."

"Imagine the frustration when after months and perhaps years of work, they find nothing and learn that they have been searching for something which is not there!"

He laughed. "You're a realist, Claudine. I always knew that. Is it the French in you?"

"Perhaps. But I seem to be getting more and more English every day."

"I'd agree with that . . . and when you marry you will be English."

"If I marry an Englishman. But my origins will be unaffected. I have never understood why a woman should take her husband's nationality. Why shouldn't a husband take his wife's?"

He pondered that seriously. That was one of David's characteristics which I found so comforting; he always gave consideration to my ideas. I suppose that living in a household dominated by men, I had become aware of a certain patronage—certainly from my brother, Charlot, and Louis Charles followed him in all things. While Jonathan, although showing a great interest in me, made me feel that I was entirely female and therefore to be subdued by the male.

That was why being with David was so refreshing.

He went on: "I suppose there has to be some ruling about this. For instance, there would be some confusion if a wife did not take her husband's name. What name should the children be given if she did not? When you look at it that way there is some reason in it."

"And to preserve the myth that women are the weaker sex."

He smiled at me. "I never thought that."

"Well, David, you are different. You don't accept every argument that is put before you. It has to be logical. That is why it is so reassuring to be with you in this community of men."

"I'm so glad you feel like that, Claudine," he said earnestly. "It's been so interesting since you came. I remember your arriving with your mother and I have to say that I did not realize in the beginning what a difference it would make—but I soon did. I began to see that you were different . . . different from all the other girls whom I had ever met."

He hesitated and seemed as though he were making up his mind. After a while he continued: "I am afraid it is very wrong of me, but sometimes I am glad of everything that has happened simply because . . . it has made Eversleigh your home."

"You mean the revolution—?"

He nodded. "Sometimes I think of it at night when I'm alone. The terrible things that are happening over there to people you have lived amongst . . . and the thought is always there . . . Yes, but it brought Claudine here."

"I daresay I should have come at some time. My mother would certainly have married Dickon sooner or later. I think she only hesitated while my grandfather lived, and when she married Dickon I would naturally have come here with her."

"Who knows? But here you are and sometimes I think that is all that matters."

"You flatter me, David."

"I never flatter . . . at least not consciously. I mean it, Claudine." He was silent for a few seconds; then he went on: "Your birthday will soon be here. You'll be seventeen."

"It seems a sort of milestone."

"Isn't every birthday?"

"But seventeen! Stepping from childhood into maturity. A very special milestone, that one."

"I always thought you were wiser than your years."

"What a nice thing to say! Sometimes I feel quite foolish."

"Everybody does."

"Everybody? Dickon? Jonathan? I don't think they ever felt foolish in all their lives. It must be gratifying to know that you are always right."

"Not unless it is universally agreed that you are."

"What do they care for universal opinions? It is only their own that count with them. Always to be right in one's own eyes does give one a tremendous panache, don't you think?"

"I'd rather face the truth, wouldn't you?"

I considered. "Yes . . . on the whole, I think I would."

"We always seem to think alike. I want to say something to you, Claudine. I'm seven years older than you."

"Then you must be twenty-four if my arithmetic does not betray me," I said lightly.

"Jonathan is the same."

"I have heard that he put in an appearance slightly ahead of you."

"Jonathan would always be first even at such a time. We had one tutor who was always urging me to assert myself. 'Go in,' he used to say. 'Don't stand on the edge looking in. Don't wait for your brother always. Go in ahead of him.' It was sound advice."

"Which you did not always take."

"Hardly ever."

"It must be a little disconcerting sometimes to have a twin."

"Yes, there are the inevitable comparisons."

"But there is supposed to be a special bond."

"Jonathan and I have long ago released ourselves from that if it ever existed. He is indifferent towards me. Sometimes I think he despises my way of life. And I am not exactly overcome with admiration for his."

"You are quite different," I said. "The fairies at the christening dealt out the human qualities—this one for Jonathan, that one for David . . . so that what each possesses, the other doesn't. . . ."

"The qualities," he said, "and the frailties. There is something I am leading up to."

"I gathered that."

"I should like to marry you, Claudine."

"What!" I cried.

"Are you surprised?"

"Not really . . . only that you bring it up at this time. I thought—after my birthday."

He smiled. "You seem to think there is some magic about the actual day."

"That's foolish, isn't it?"

"Both your mother and my father would be pleased. It would be ideal. We have so much to interest us both. I wouldn't have asked you if I hadn't thought you liked me. I believe you enjoy our talks and everything . . ."

"Yes," I said, "I do. And I'm very fond of you, David, but—"

"Have you never thought of marrying?"

"Oh yes, of course."

"And . . . with someone?"

"One can't very well think about marriage without including a bridegroom."

"And did you ever consider me?"

"Yes . . . I did. My mother talked to me about it. Parents always want to see their offspring married, don't they? But my mother wants it to be right for me . . . she wouldn't wish it otherwise."

He came to me then and took my hands in his. I was reminded how different he was from Jonathan, but I knew that he would be kind always, and understanding and interesting; oh yes, it would be a wonderful life with him.

There was something missing though, and after my encounters with Jonathan, I knew what. I did not feel that overwhelming excitement when David took my hands, and I kept thinking of Jonathan in the sewing room slipping my shift from my shoulders; and I knew in that moment that I wanted them both. I wanted the gentleness, the reliability, the sense of security, the absorbing subjects I could share . . . all that came from David; and on the other hand, I wanted the excitement of that sensual allure which Jonathan brought me.

I wanted them both. What a quandary, for how could one have two husbands?

I looked at David. How pleasant he was. There was an earnestness about him—an innocence in a way. I believed I could enjoy a life spent at Eversleigh, discussing with him the affairs of the estate, looking after tenants on the Eversleigh land, delving into matters which absorbed us both.

If I said Yes, my mother would be pleased. Dickon would be too, although he would be indifferent as to whether I chose David or Jonathan. But Jonathan had not asked me. Yet I knew that he wanted me. . . . He lusted after me, as they put it in the Bible. And because of who I was he would have to marry me to get me into his bed.

I came very near to saying Yes to David, but something held me back. It was the memory of Jonathan, and the stirring of hitherto unknown emotions which he had aroused in me.

"I'm so fond of you, David," I said. "You have always been my very good friend. But just now, I feel I want to wait."

He understood at once.

"Of course, you want to wait. But think about it. Remember everything we could do. There is so much in the world to absorb us." He waved his arms, indicating the shelves of books. "We have so much to share, and I love you very dearly, Claudine. I have from the moment you came here."

I kissed his cheek and he held me against him. I felt pleasantly secure and happy; but I could not shut out the memory of Jonathan; and when I looked in David's clear blue eyes I thought of the startling blue flame in those of Jonathan.

I couldn't sleep that night. Perhaps that was understandable. I had had a proposal of marriage which I had almost accepted; I had also had the experience in the sewing room and I did not know which had affected me more deeply.

One thing I had done before getting into bed was to lock my door. Coming to the sewing room as he had, Jonathan had shown me clearly that he was capable of rash actions, and my response had taught me that I had to beware of my own feelings.

I spent the morning as I always did with my governess, and in the early afternoon I went for a ride. I had not gone very far when I was overtaken by Jonathan.

"Hello," he said. "What a surprise!"

Of course I knew that he had watched me leave and had then come after me.

"I should have thought you would have been ashamed to show your face," I said.

"I was under the impression that you rather liked it; and if it pleases you, that is all I ask."

"What do you imagine Molly Blackett thought of your behaviour in the sewing room?"

"I must first ask a question of you. Does Molly Blackett *think?* I believe her mind is completely taken up with pins and needles and ladies'—er—is there such a thing as a placket? It would be most appropriate if there is, because that rhymes with her name."

"She was shocked. You know very well that my mother did not wish to see her."

"But *I* wished to see *you* more closely in that delicious state of undress."

"It was very foolish and decidedly ungentlemanly."

"The best things in life often are," he said ruefully.

"I dislike this flippant talk."

"Oh come! You know you find it irresistible . . . as you do me."

"I knew you always had a high opinion of yourself."

"Naturally, for if I don't, who else will? They take their cue from me, you know."

"I don't want to hear any more glorification of your character."

"I understand. It does not need glorification. You are wise enough, chère Mademoiselle, to see it as it really is, and that pleases you. I believe it pleases you mightily."

"You are absurd."

"But adorable with it."

My answer to that was to whip up my horse. I turned into a field and galloped across it. He was beside me. I had to pull up, as I had come to a hedge.

"Let me make a suggestion," he said. "We could tether our horses and sit under yonder tree. Then we could talk of many things."

"It is hardly the weather for sitting out-of-doors. I believe it could snow in a moment."

"I would keep you warm."

I turned away again but he laid a hand on my bridle.

"Claudine, I do want to talk to you seriously," he said.

"Well?"

"I want to be near you. I want to touch you. I want to hold you as I did yesterday. That was wonderful. The only trouble was that dear old Molly Blackett would come blundering in."

"What do you want to talk seriously about?" I asked. "You are never serious."

"Rarely. But this is one moment when I am. Marriage is a serious business. My father would be quite pleased if you and I married, Claudine, and what is more important—so would I."

"Married to you!" I heard a pitch of excitement in my voice. I went on scathingly: "Something tells me that you would not be a very faithful husband."

"My chère Mademoiselle would keep me so."

"I think I should find the task too onerous."

He laughed aloud. "Sometimes you talk like my brother."

"I find that rather a compliment."

"So now we are to hear of the virtues of St. David. I know you are rather fond of him—in a special sort of way."

"Of course I'm fond of him. He is interesting, courteous, reliable, gentle . . ."

"Are you, by any chance, making comparisons? I believe Shakespeare once commented on the inadvisability of that. You will know. If not, consult Erudite David."

"You should not sneer at your brother. He is more . . ."

"Worthy?"

"That is the word."

"And how it fits. I have an idea that you are more favourably inclined towards him than I like."

"Are you by any chance jealous of your brother?"

"I could be . . . in certain circumstances. As no doubt he could be of me."

"I don't think he has ever aspired to be like you."

"Do you think I have ever aspired to be like him?"

"No. You are two decidedly different natures. Sometimes I think you are as different as two people could be."

"Enough of him. What of you, sweet Claudine? I know you respond to me. You like me, don't you? You liked me very much when I came into the room and routed old Blackett and I kissed you. True, you put on your mask of properly-brought-up-young-lady. 'Unhand me, sir!' which really meant I want more of this . . . and more . . ."

I was scarlet with mortification.

"You presume too much."

"I *reveal* too much which you would prefer to hide. Do you think you can hide the truth from me? I know women."

"I had gathered that."

"My dearest little girl, you don't want an inexperienced lover. You want a connoisseur to direct you through the gates of paradise. We would have a wonderful time together, Claudine. Come, say yes. We'll announce it at the dinner party. It's what they want. And in a few weeks we'll be married. Where shall we go for our honeymoon? What say you to Venice? Romantic nights on canals . . . the gondoliers singing love songs as we drift along. Does that appeal to you?"

"The setting would be ideal I am sure. The only thing I should object to is that I should have to share it with you."

"Unkind."

"You asked for it."

"And the answer is?"

"No."

"We'll make it Yes."

"How?"

He looked at me intently; his expression changed and the set of his lips alarmed me faintly.

"I have ways . . . and means," he said.

"And an inflated opinion of yourself."

I turned sharply away. He fascinated me and I had to overcome a desire to dismount and face him. I knew that would be dangerous. Beneath the light banter there was a ruthless determination. I was very much aware of it and it reminded me strongly of his father. It was said that men wanted sons because they liked to see themselves reproduced. Well, Dickon had reproduced himself in Jonathan.

I started to gallop across the field. Ahead of me was the sea. It was a muddy grey on that day with a tinge of brown where the frills of waves touched the sand. The tang of seaweed was strong in the air. It had been a stormy night. I felt a tremendous sense of excitement as I galloped forward and let my horse fly along by the edge of the water.

Jonathan pounded along beside me. He was laughing—as exhilarated as I was.

We must have gone a mile when I drew up. He was beside me. The spray made his eyebrows glisten; his eyes were alight with those blue flames which I was always looking for; and I thought suddenly of Venice and gondolas and Italian love songs. In that moment I would have said: "Yes, Jonathan. It is you. I know it will not be easy; there will be little peace . . . . but you are the one."

After all, when one is seventeen one does not look for a comfortable way of life. It is excitement, exhilaration, and uncertainty which seem appealing.

I turned my horse and said: "Home. I'll race you."

And there we were once more pounding along the beach. He kept beside me but I knew he was choosing the moment to go ahead. He had to show me that he must always win.

In the distance I saw riders and almost at once recognized Charlot and Louis Charles.

"Look who's there," I cried.

"We don't need them. Let's go back and do that gallop again."

But I called: "Charlot."

My brother waved to us. We cantered up to them and I saw at once that Charlot was deeply disturbed.

"Have you heard the news?" he said.

"News?" Jonathan and I spoke simultaneously.

"It's clear that you haven't. The murdering dogs . . . *Mon Dieu,* if I were there. I wish I were. I wish . . ."

"What is it?" demanded Jonathan. "Who has murdered whom?"

"The King of France," said Charlot. "France no longer has a King."

I closed my eyes. I was remembering the tales my grandfather used to tell of the Court, of the King who was blamed for so much for which he was not responsible. Most of all I thought of the mob looking on while he mounted the steps of the guillotine and placed his head beneath the axe.

Even Jonathan was sobered. He said: "It was expected . . ."

"I never believed they would go so far," said Charlot. "And now they have done it. That vile mob . . . They have changed the history of France."

Charlot was deeply affected. He reminded me of my grandfather at that moment, of my father too. Patriots, both of them. Charlot's heart was in France with the royalists. He had always wanted to be there to fight the losing battle for the monarchy. Now that the King was dead—murdered like a common felon on that cruel guillotine—he wanted it more than ever.

Louis Charles looked at Jonathan almost apologetically. "You see," he said, as if he needed to explain, "France is our country . . . he was our King."

We all rode back together quietly, subdued, in mourning for a lost régime and the death of a man who had paid the price for the excesses of those who had gone before him.

The news had reached Eversleigh. As we sat at the table, the execution of the King of France was the only topic of conversation.

Dickon said he would have to leave for London and Jonathan must go with him. He guessed the Court would be in mourning.

"It is alarming to all rulers when one of their number is treated like a common criminal," commented David.

"Yet this death comes as no great surprise," said Jonathan.

"I always believed that it could never happen," added Charlot vehemently. "No matter how powerful the revolutionaries became."

Dickon said: "It was inevitable. When the King failed to escape and join the émigrés, he was doomed. If he had been able to join them, the revolution might have come to an end. And he could so easily have escaped! What an example of idiotic ineptitude! Travelling in style . . . the grand carriage . . . the Queen posing as a governess! As if Marie Antoinette could ever be anything but Marie Antoinette! One could laugh if it were not so tragic. Imagine that cumbersome and very, very grand carriage riding into the little town of Varennes, and the inevitable questions. Who are these visitors? Who is this lady calling herself a governess? No marks for guessing! What a charade!"

"It was a brave attempt," said Charlot.

"Bravery counts for little when folly is its companion," said Dickon grimly.

Charlot was sunk in gloom. Never had I realized how deeply his feelings were involved.

Dickon was very well informed. We were never quite sure why he spent so much time in London about the Court; he was a friend of Prime Minister Pitt, and at the same time on excellent terms with Charles James Fox and the Prince of Wales. It was rare that he talked openly of what we thought of as his secret life, though I daresay he confided to some extent in my mother. She went with him everywhere, so she must have had some notion of what his business was. But if she had, she never betrayed it.

On this occasion he did talk a little. He said that Pitt was an excellent Prime Minister, but he wondered how he would shape up to war.

"War?" cried my mother. "What war? Did not Mr. Pitt say that England was assured of peace for some years to come?"

"That, my dear Lottie, was last year. A great deal can happen in politics in a very short time. I am sure William Pitt regarded all that turmoil on the other side of the Channel as a local matter . . . no concern of ours. But we are all realizing now that it is of concern to us . . . of the greatest concern."

Charlot said: "And it is right that it should be so. How can the nations of the world stand aside and let an outrage like this pass unavenged?"

"Quite easily," retorted Dickon dismissively. He always showed a faint contempt for Charlot, which I think would have been more than faint but for the fact that it upset my mother. "It is only when events affect us tangibly that we act. The revolutionaries, having ruined France, now seek to see others in a similar plight. The success of the French debacle was assured by its agitators. They are the real provokers, those who pointed out to the people how wrongly they had indeed been treated, who stressed the differences between the aristocrats and the peasants, and who, where there were no grievances, created them. Now we shall have them here. The dog who has lost his tail cannot bear to see those who have retained theirs. The agitators will be here. That is one thing. I can tell you this: societies are being formed in London and as far as Scotland. They are seeking to bring about in this country that to which they have so successfully contributed in France."

"God forbid!" said my mother.

"Amen, my dear Lottie," replied Dickon. We will not allow it here.

Those of us who know what is going on will do everything possible to prevent it."

"Do you think you will be able to?" asked Charlot.

"Yes, I do. We are aware of what is happening, for one thing."

"There were some who were aware of it in France," said my mother.

Dickon snorted. "And they involved themselves with the American colonists instead of cleaning out their own stables. Perhaps now they see the folly of their ways, for those young fools who were screaming for liberty, and for the elevation of the oppressed, are now seeing what the oppressed are offering them—the guillotine!"

"At least Armand tried to do something," insisted my mother. "He formed a group of real patriots who wanted to see justice. Oh I know you thought he was incompetent . . ."

"He thinks everything is incompetent which is not done in England," said Charlot.

Dickon laughed. "How I wish I did! I should like to see this country act wisely, which I admit to you, my young Monsieur de Tourville, it does not always do. But perhaps we are a little more cautious, eh? That little bit more likely not to act rashly . . . not to excite ourselves unduly over matters which are not to our advantage. Shall we leave it at that?"

"I think," said David, "that it would be wise."

Dickon laughed at his son. "I see troubles ahead," he went on, "and not only for France. Austria can hardly stand aside while its Archduchess follows her husband to the guillotine."

"Do you think they will kill Marie Antoinette too?" I asked.

"Undoubtedly, my dear Claudine. There will be more to gloat over her death than those who have done so over that of poor Louis. They have always blamed her, poor child . . . which was all she was when she came to France, a pretty little butterfly who wanted to dance in the sun—and did so most charmingly. But she grew up. The butterfly became a woman of character. The French liked the butterfly better. *And* she is Austrian." He grinned at Charlot. "You know how the French hate foreigners."

"The Queen has been much maligned," said Charlot.

"Indeed it is so. Who is not maligned in these ferocious days? France will be at war with Prussia and Austria. Holland too, most likely, and it will not be long before we are drawn in."

"Horrible!" said my mother. "I hate war. It does no good to anybody."

"She is right, you know," said Dickon. "But there are times when even peacelovers like Mr. Pitt see the necessity for it." He looked at my mother and said, "We must leave tomorrow for London. The Court will be in mourning for the King of France."

My mother looked at me and said: "We must be back in time for Claudine's birthday."

Dickon smiled benignly at me. "Nothing—wars, rumours of wars, revolutions proved and planned—nothing must stand in the way of Claudine's coming to maturity."

My parents, with Jonathan, were away for the greater part of a week. Charlot went about in a mood of bleak depression; he and Louis Charles were often deep in earnest conversation. The entire atmosphere had changed; the death of the French King seemed to have opened up fresh wounds which brought us nearer to that state of unease which existed beyond the Channel.

David and I visited the Roman remains and I caught his enthusiasm for them. He told me about Herculaneum, which had been discovered early this century, followed by the discovery of Pompeii—both of which ancient towns had been destroyed by a volcanic eruption from Vesuvius.

"I should very much like to see those places," he said. "I believe they are most revealing of how life was lived all those hundreds of years ago. Perhaps we could go there together one day."

I knew what he meant. When we were married. A honeymoon perhaps. It sounded most exciting. Then I thought of Venice and a gondolier with a tenor voice singing love songs in the darkness.

We talked a great deal, naturally, about the revolution in France. It was never far from our minds. David was quite knowledgeable—far more so than he appeared to be during the mealtime conversations which Dickon naturally dominated and where Jonathan also gave a good account of himself.

I went round the estate with David. That was another side to him. He was a businessman, and eager to do everything he could to improve the lot of the tenant farmers and others who lived on the estate. He was very efficient in a quiet way and I saw again how greatly he was respected, which made me feel gratified.

I was beginning to think that I could have a very happy life with him —but that was because Jonathan was absent.

They came back two days before my birthday. I knew that my mother would not allow anything to interfere with that.

So the great day arrived. Molly Blackett wanted to be present when I put on my dress.

"Just in case I'm not satisfied, Miss Claudine. Perhaps a little stitch here, a touch there. You never know."

I said: "You're an artist, Molly." And she was pink with pleasure.

Guests began to arrive in the late afternoon, for a few had to come from a long distance. The Pettigrews, whose country estate was some thirty miles from Eversleigh, were staying the night. They visited us now and then, as Lord Pettigrew was a banking associate of Dickon's. Lady Pettigrew was one of those domineering women who keep a very sharp eye on what is going on; and I believed she was looking for the best possible match for her daughter Millicent.

Millicent was a considerable heiress, and like most parents of such well-endowed offspring, Lady Pettigrew was eager that she should be matched by a partner of equal financial worth. I visualized the rather plump Millicent seated in a balance with a possible husband on the other side to be weighed with her while an eagle-eyed Lady Pettigrew made sure that the scales tipped in Millicent's favour.

Our neighbours from Grasslands—one of the two big houses in the vicinity—had had to be invited; we were not very friendly with them in spite of their being our nearest neighbours.

They were Mrs. Trent and her two grand-daughters Evalina and Dorothy Mather. Mrs. Trent had married twice and both husbands had died. The first had been Andrew Mather, from whom she had inherited Grasslands; and on his death she had married the estate manager, Jack Trent. She had been unfortunate for, besides losing both husbands, she had also suffered the death of her son Richard Mather and his wife. Her consolation was her grand-daughters—Evie and Dolly, as she called them. Evie was about seventeen years of age, I supposed; Dolly was a year or so younger. Evie was quite a beauty but Dolly was a sad little thing. She had sustained some injury when she was born and her left eyelid was drawn down somewhat so that she had some difficulty in opening that eye. It was only a slight malformation but it gave a certain grotesque look to her face and I had the impression that she was very much aware of this.

The other nearby house, Enderby, was vacant. It seemed to be unoccupied most of the time, for it was one of those houses which over the years had collected an unsavoury reputation. Certain unpleasant events had taken place there. Sabrina had lived there for a time—in fact, I think she had been born there—but her mother had been that Damaris whose virtuous looks I had noticed in the picture gallery and her influence somehow suppressed the evil which returned after she had died. However, Enderby was vacant, so no one came from there.

Our hall was beautifully decorated with plants from the greenhouse, as we should dance there later. The dining room table had been opened to its full size and seemed to fill the room, which looked charming in the light from the fire and the countless candles. There was one large candelabrum in the centre and smaller ones on either side.

I was seated at the head of the table—the hostess for the occasion—and on my right hand sat my mother, and on my left, my stepfather Dickon.

I felt grown-up at last and very happy—yet at the same time I had a strange feeling that I wanted to catch at these moments and make them last forever. I must have understood even then that happiness is just a transient emotion. Perfection may be reached, but it is elusive and there are forces all about which will surely snatch it away.

Everyone was laughing and talking. Very soon Dickon would rise and propose a toast to me, and I must stand up before them all and thank them for their good wishes and tell them how happy I was to see them here before asking the members of my family to drink the health of our guests.

Sabrina sat at the end of the table. She looked very young for her years and supremely happy. She watched Dickon most of the time, and I was sure she believed that all her dreams had come true. Lottie, my mother, was Dickon's wife, where she had always belonged; if only Clarissa, my great-grandmother, and Zipporah, my grandmother, were here, Sabrina would have asked nothing more.

Jonathan was next to Millicent, and Lady Pettigrew watched him with a certain dazed expression which I believed I construed correctly. Dickon was a very rich man, so Jonathan, presumably, would match up to Lady Pettigrew's requirements for a son-in-law. Of course it was a way parents had, especially with the female members of their households. As soon as a girl became nubile, they started to plan for her. Wasn't my own mother the same? Hadn't she planned for me? David or Jonathan? she was asking herself. I must not be too hard on Lady Pettigrew. It was only natural that she should want the best for her daughter.

The musicians were already in the gallery and as soon as the meal was over they would play for dancing. Dickon whispered to me that he was going to make the toast now.

He stood up and there was silence.

"My friends," he said, "you all know what occasion this is, and I want you to drink a toast to our daughter, Claudine, who this day has left her childhood behind her and become that most delectable of beings . . . a young lady."

"To Claudine."

As they raised their glasses I noticed that my mother's attention had strayed and I realized that something was going on in the hall. Then I distinctly heard the sound of rather shrill raised voices. Was it guests who had arrived late?

One of the servants came in and going to my mother whispered something to her.

She half rose.

Dickon said: "What is it, Lottie?"

There was silence round the table. This was the moment when I should get to my feet and thank them all for their good wishes and propose the toast to our guests which my family would drink. But it was my mother who stood up. "You must excuse me," she said. "Friends have arrived . . . from France."

Dickon went out with her and everyone was looking at each other in amazement. Then Charlot said: "You will excuse me, please." And he, followed by Louis Charles, left the dining room.

"Friends from France!" said Jonathan. "They must be émigrés."

"How exciting!" That was from Millicent Pettigrew.

"Those dreadful people," said someone else. "What will they do next? They say they will kill the Queen."

They were all talking now. It was an excited buzz. I looked along the table to Sabrina. Her face had changed and she looked like an old woman now. She hated any sort of trouble and no doubt she was thinking of those terrible days when Dickon had been in France and she had suffered agonies of fear for her son. But that was over and Dickon had come back triumphant—as if Dickon could ever do anything else!—and he had brought Lottie home with him. We had reached the happy-ever-after stage, and Sabrina did not want to be reminded of what was happening on the other side of the Channel. We were in our cosy corner, apart from strife; she wanted to wrap her family in a cosy cocoon and keep it safe. Any whisper or suggestion of horror should be shut right away. It was no concern of ours.

Dickon came back into the dining room. He was smiling and I noticed that Sabrina's anxieties faded away as she looked at him fondly.

He said: "We have visitors. Friends of Lottie's . . . from France. They have arrived here on their way to friends in London. They have escaped from France and are in a state of exhaustion. Lottie is arranging beds for them. Come along, Claudine, say your piece."

I stood up and thanked them all for their good wishes and proposed the toast to our guests. When it was drunk we sat down and the conversation was all about the revolution and how terrible it must be for those aristocrats who went in fear of the mob and had to flee their country.

"So many are getting out," said Jonathan. "There are émigrés all over Europe."

"We shall insist that they put the King back on his throne," said Lady Pettigrew, as though it were as simple a matter as finding the right husband for Millicent.

"That might be rather difficult, considering he has lost his head," Jonathan pointed out.

"I mean the new one. Isn't there a little Dauphin . . . King now, of course."

"Young, very young," said Jonathan.

"Young men grow up," retorted Lady Pettigrew.

"A statement of such undeniable truth that I cannot challenge it," went on Jonathan.

I felt laughter bubbling up within me in spite of the subject. Jonathan always amused me, and I imagined his being married to Millicent and having a lifetime of verbal fencing with his mother-in-law. Almost immediately I was appalled by the thought of his marrying Millicent. I could not imagine her in a gondola listening to Italian love songs. Nor did I want to think of her in such a situation.

Charlot and Louis Charles did not immediately return. I guessed they were with the new arrivals. It was much later when we were dancing in the hall that they joined the company.

I danced with Jonathan, which was exciting, and I danced with David, which was pleasant, though neither of them danced well. My brother Charlot danced far better. They paid more attention to such matters in France.

I sought out Charlot and asked about the visitors.

He said: "They are in such a sad state. They could not face all those people. So your mother took them into the solarium while fires were lighted in their bedrooms and the warming pans put in the beds. There they were given food and as soon as the rooms were ready they went to bed."

"Who are they?"

"Monsieur and Madam Lebrun; their son and his wife and the son's daughter."

"Quite a party."

"They have had some hair-raising adventures. They almost did not get away. Do you remember them?"

"Vaguely."

"They had that big estate not far from Amiens. They had left their *château* some time ago and had been living quietly in the heart of the country with an old servant. But they were discovered and flight became necessary. They have been helped by some. There are a few worthy people left."

Poor Charlot! He was deeply moved.

The party was over and the guests had left, except those who were staying the night. I lay in my bed, too tired to sleep. It had been an exhilarating evening and everything had worked out as smoothly as my mother had planned—except for the untimely arrival of the Lebruns. And even that had been handled with the utmost discretion.

I had come to a turning point in my life. There would be pressure on me now to make up my mind. David . . . or Jonathan? What an extraordinary choice for a girl to have to make. I began to wonder how much they loved me. Was it because of who I was, or because it had been expected and was what the family hoped would happen? I had a notion that they had been cleverly manoeuvred towards this situation.

Jonathan undoubtedly wanted to make love to me. But he might have had the same feelings for a milkmaid or any of the servants. It was because of who I was that he wanted marriage.

And David? No, David's affection was solid. It was for me only, and when he offered marriage it was for the sake of true love.

David . . . Jonathan! If I were wise it would be David; and yet I had a feeling that I should always hanker for Jonathan.

I should have to decide . . . but not tonight. I was too tired.

I slept late next morning, for my mother had given instructions that I was not to be awakened. When I went downstairs most of the overnight guests had left, and those who had not were on the point of doing so.

I said my farewells and when we stood waving to the departing guests I asked about the French people.

"They are sleeping," said my mother. "They are quite exhausted.

Madeleine and Gaston Lebrun are too old for this sort of thing. How sad at their age to be driven out of their country."

"Worse still to be driven off the earth."

She shivered. I knew all this had brought back to her mind that terrifying experience when she herself had come close to death at the hands of the mob. She understood as none of us could—except perhaps Dickon, and he would always be certain that he was going to get the better of whoever attacked him—the horror of what they called the Terror in France.

"We must do all we can to help," she said. "They have family connections over here north of London and when they are sufficiently rested they will go to them. Dickon is sending a message to them today to tell them that the Lebruns have safely arrived in England and are staying with us for a few days. He will help them make the journey. Perhaps he and I will accompany them to their friends. Poor things, they must feel lost in a strange country. They haven't much English either. Oh Claudine, I am so sorry for them."

"So are we all," I said.

"I know. Charlot is incensed." She sighed. "He feels so deeply. I don't think he will ever adjust himself to living here. He is not like you, Claudine."

"I feel this is . . . my home."

She kissed me. "And so do I. I have never been so happy. It is such a pity all this has to happen. . . ."

I slipped my arm through hers and we went into the house.

We were at supper the following night and with us were the younger Monsieur and Madame Lebrun with their daughter Françoise, who was about my age.

They were very grateful for the hospitality they were receiving, and when Dickon said that he and my mother would accompany them to their destination and that they would spend a night in London on the way, they were overwhelmed with relief.

Conversation, rather naturally, was all about their escape and the state of affairs in France; and it was conducted in French, which shut out Sabrina, Jonathan and David somewhat. David could read French quite well but he did get lost in conversation. As for Jonathan I doubted whether he had ever bothered to learn much of the language. Dickon's French was a good deal better than he allowed it to be thought and he always spoke it with an exaggerated English accent which suggested that he was determined no one should mistake him for a Frenchman. The rest of us, of course, were fluent.

We learned a little of what it was like to exist under the Terror. People such as the Lebruns lived in perpetual fear of it. They could never be sure of their safety from one moment to another. They had lived with a faithful servant who had married a man who had a small farm; and they had pretended to be relations of hers. But they could so easily betray themselves and it was when Monsieur Lebrun had tried to sell a jewelled ornament he had managed to salvage from his possessions that he was suspected and flight became imperative.

They had disguised themselves as labourers, but they were well aware that one gesture, one lapse from the patois they had adopted, could betray them.

My mother had found some clothes for them, which, if they did not fit very well, were better than the stained and tattered garments in which they had arrived.

Madame Lebrun said: "There are so many people who are kind to us. To see the mob . . . to hear those who have been one's servants and whom one has treated well . . . turn against one . . . is so depressing. But it is such a comfort to learn that the whole world is not like that. There are many in France who help people like us. We shall never forget what we owe to them, for we could never have escaped but for them."

Charlot leaned forward and said: "You mean . . . our own people."

"Most of our kind would help if it were possible," replied Madame Lebrun. "But we all have to help ourselves. We are all in danger. Yet there are those who have given themselves up to the task of helping such as we are out of the country and remaining there themselves for this purpose when they could escape. There are houses of refuge. You can imagine how dangerous it is. There has to be perpetual watch for the enemy."

"Their unselfishness is very heartening," said Charlot vehemently.

"I knew there would be such people," echoed Louis Charles.

"I wonder what is happening in Aubigné," said my mother.

"I saw Jeanne Fougère in Evreaux when we passed through."

We were all alert now. Jeanne Fougère had been Aunt Sophie's faithful maid and companion—an important person in the household because she had been the only one who could manage Aunt Sophie.

"When was that?" asked my mother eagerly.

"Oh . . . several months back. We were a long time there. We stayed at one of the houses I spoke of managed by people who help others to escape."

"Months ago!" echoed my mother. "What did Jeanne say? Did you ask about Sophie—and Armand?"

Madame Lebrun looked at my mother sadly. "She said that Armand had died in the *château.* At least the mob had left him alone. I think she said that the young man who was with him recovered and went off somewhere."

"And what of Sophie?"

"She was still at the *château* with Jeanne."

"At the *château!* They didn't destroy it then?"

"No, apparently not. They took the valuables and furniture and such. Jeanne said it was a shambles. But she had some chickens and there was a cow and they managed to live in a corner of the place. That was how it was then. People did not seem to bother them. Mademoiselle Sophie was an aristocrat, daughter of the Comte d'Aubigné, but she was almost a recluse . . . badly scarred. In any case they were living at the *château* unmolested. Jeanne was uneasy though. She kept lifting her eyes to the skies and murmuring: 'How long!' Perhaps even now the mood has changed. Now the King is dead, it will become worse, they say."

"Poor Sophie," said my mother.

The following day the Lebruns departed and, true to his word, Dickon went with them as their guide; naturally my mother went too.

After they had gone the whole mood of the house seemed to have changed. The Lebruns had brought into it a threat of what could happen to disrupt people's comfortable lives. We had known, of course, what was going on over there, but this brought it home to us forcibly.

I soon discovered what was in Charlot's mind.

It was naturally at the dinner table that we all gathered together and there the talk as usual turned to France and the plight of those refugees who were left behind.

The guillotine was claiming more and more of them every day. The Queen was in prison. Her turn would soon come.

"And our aunt is there," said Charlot. "Poor Aunt Sophie! She was always so pathetic. Do you remember her, Claudine, in that hood she used to wear to cover one side of her face?"

I nodded.

"And Jeanne Fougère. She was a bit of a dragon. But what a treasure!

What a good woman! She would not let us in very often to see Aunt Sophie."

"She always liked you to go and see her though, Charlot," said Louis Charles.

"Well, I do think she had a special fondness for me."

It was true. Charlot had been a favourite of hers, if she could have been said to have favourites. It was a fact though that she had actually *asked* Charlot to visit her on one or two occasions.

"Those people who are helping aristocrats escape the guillotine are doing a wonderful job," went on Charlot.

He looked at Louis Charles, who smiled at him in such a way that I knew they had discussed this together.

Jonathan was attentive too. He said: "Yes, it is a great adventure. My father went over there and brought Claudine's mother out. It was a marvellous thing to do."

Charlot agreed, though he had no great love for Dickon. "But," he went on, "he just brought out my mother. Just one person because she was the only one he was interested in."

I defended him hotly. "He risked his life."

It was a good thing that Sabrina was not present; she would have grown hot in her defence of Dickon; she often did not come down to the evening meal when Dickon was away, but had something in her room. Yet if he was there she usually made the effort to join us.

"Oh yes, he did that," said Charlot lightly. "But I think he enjoyed doing it."

"We usually do well what we enjoy doing," said David, "but that does not detract from the virtue of the act."

The others ignored him.

Jonathan's eyes were shining. They blazed with that intense blue light which I had thought I aroused in him. Obviously other matters than the pursuit of women could make it shine forth.

"It must be exciting," he said, "rescuing people, snatching them from prison at the last moment, depriving that hideous guillotine of another victim."

Charlot leaned across the table nodding and they started to talk about the escapes which the Lebruns had mentioned. They talked with great animation; they seemed to have created a bond between them from which David and I were excluded.

"What I would have done in those circumstances," Jonathan was saying; and he went on to outline some adventurous stratagem. They looked boyish in their enthusiasm.

Jonathan explained in detail how my mother had been taken by the mob to the *mairie,* where she was kept while the people screamed outside for her to be brought out that they might hang her on the lanterne.

"And my father, disguised as a coachman, was in a carriage at the back of the *mairie.* He bribed the mayor to let her out and he drove the carriage right through the mob in the square. At any moment something could have gone wrong."

"He never believed anything could go wrong," I said.

There was silence at the table. They were all lost in admiration for Dickon. Even Charlot seemed to think he was rather splendid in that moment.

Then he said: "But he might have brought others out at the same time."

"How could he?" I demanded. "It was difficult and dangerous enough to get my mother out."

"People *are* being brought out. There are brave men and women who are giving their lives to this. *Mon Dieu,* how I wish I were there!"

"I too," echoed Louis Charles.

And so they talked.

I continued to be concerned with my own problem. Jonathan or David? This time next year, I thought, I shall be eighteen. I shall have decided by then.

If only I did not like them both so much. Perhaps it was after all because they were twins—in a way like utterly opposite sides of one person.

I thought frivolously that when one was attracted by twins one should be allowed to marry them both.

When I was with David I thought a good deal about Jonathan. But when I was with Jonathan I must remember David.

The day after that conversation I went riding and I expected that Jonathan would come after me as he usually did. He knew what time I left.

I rode rather slowly to give him time to catch up, but he did not appear. I made my way to the top of a small incline where I could get a good view. There was no sign of him.

I finished my ride and went back considerably piqued. As I entered the house I heard voices in one of the small rooms which led from the hall and I peeped in.

Jonathan was there with Charlot and Louis Charles. They were deep in conversation.

I said: "Hello. I've been riding."

They hardly seemed aware of me . . . even Jonathan.

I came away distinctly annoyed and went to my room.

That night at dinner the conversation took the usual trend: the events in France.

"There are other places in the world," David reminded them.

"There are ancient Rome and ancient Greece," said Jonathan rather contemptuously. "You're so steeped in past history, brother, that you are losing sight of the history which is being made all around you."

"I assure you," retorted David, "that I am fully aware of the significance of what is happening in France at this time."

"Well, isn't that more important than Julius Caesar or Marco Polo?"

"You cannot see history clearly while it is happening," said David slowly. "It is like looking at an oil painting. You have to stand back . . . some years. That particular painting isn't finished yet."

"You and your metaphors and similes! You're only half alive. Let's tell him, shall we, eh, Charlot, Louis Charles? Shall we tell him what we propose to do?"

Charlot nodded gravely.

"We are going to France," said Jonathan. "We are going to bring out Aunt Sophie . . . among others. . . ."

"You can't!" I cried. "For one thing, Dickon would never allow it."

"Do you know, little Claudine, I am no longer a child to be told do this . . . do that." He was looking at me with a teasing indulgence. "I am a man . . . and I will do what I will."

"That's true," agreed Charlot. "We are men . . . and we are going to do what we think fit, no matter who tries to stop us."

"Our father will soon put a stop to those plans," said David. "You know very well he would never give his consent to your going, Jonathan."

"I don't need his consent."

Charlot smiled complacently at Louis Charles. "He has no jurisdiction over us."

"He will prevent it, you see," said David.

"Don't be too sure of that."

"Well," I said practically, "how are you to set about this great adventure?"

"Never trouble your head," replied Charlot. "You wouldn't understand."

"Oh no," I cried, "*I* am quite stupid . . . but not so stupid as some who indulge in wild fantasies. Remember the stories of Uncle Armand. How he made some plan to descend on the agitators? What happened to him? He was sent to the Bastille . . . and there a strong and healthy man was turned into a pitiable invalid. And . . . according to the Lebruns he is dead now. He never recovered from his incarceration in the Bastille."

"He must have been careless. He made mistakes. We should not do that. This is a noble thing to do. I refuse to stand aside any longer while these things are happening to my people . . . my country."

David said: "It is indeed a noble idea, but a great deal of careful planning is needed."

"Of course it needs planning," retorted Charlot. "But how can we plan until we get there . . . until we know what we shall find?"

I said: "I believe you are serious."

"Never more so," answered Charlot.

I looked at Louis Charles. He nodded. Of course he would go where Charlot went.

I forced myself to look at Jonathan, and I saw the blazing blue of his eyes, and I felt hurt and angry because that flame was there for a project which did not concern me . . . and he could so impulsively risk not only his own life but those of Charlot and Louis Charles.

"You would surely never go with them," I said.

He smiled and nodded.

"But you are not French. It is not your problem."

"It is the problem of all right-thinking people," said Charlot a little sententiously.

He was motivated by love of his country; but it was different with Jonathan, and he had wounded me deeply. He had shown me clearly that I was only of secondary importance to him.

He wanted this adventure more than he wanted me.

All the next day Jonathan was absent and Charlot and Louis Charles with him. They returned in the evening and did not say where they had been; but there was a certain smug satisfaction about them. The next day they went out riding again and did not return until late.

I talked to David about them and he expressed some anxiety as to what they were planning.

"It must be all talk," I said. "They could not possibly go to France."

"Why couldn't they? Charlot is a zealot and Louis Charles would always go along with him. Jonathan . . ." He shrugged his shoulders. "Jonathan has often made wild plans and I can assure you that many of them never materialized. He likes to imagine himself on a magnificent charger riding into danger and riding out again victorious. He has always been like that."

"He is very like his father."

"My father would never have quixotic ideas about rescuing strangers. He always said the French brought the revolution on themselves by their own folly—and now must pay the price for it."

"But he went over there magnificently and came out victorious."

"He would always have a purpose. He went solely to bring out your mother. He would plan coolly and efficiently. These three appear to be allowing their emotions to get the better of their common sense."

"That is something you never do, David."

"Not willingly," he agreed.

"What are we going to do about them? I feel they are reckless enough to attempt anything."

"My father will soon be home. He will deal with it."

"I wish they would return."

David took my hand and pressed it. "Don't worry," he said. "There is so much going on. We are almost at war with the French. They wouldn't find it very easy to get over there in the first place. They would find the obstacles . . . insurmountable."

"I hope you are right," I said.

I was greatly relieved when the next day Dickon and my mother returned home.

"All is well," said my mother. "We have delivered the Lebruns to their friends. It was a happy reunion. They will find the refuge they need, but it is going to take them some time to recover from their terrible experiences."

The storm broke at dinner.

We were all seated round the table when Charlot said almost nonchalantly: "We have decided to go to France."

"You couldn't possibly do that," said my mother.

"Couldn't? That's a word I don't accept."

"Your acceptance of the English language is immaterial," put in Dickon. "I know you have an imperfect understanding of it, but when Lottie says that you could not possibly go to France, she means that you could not be so foolish as to attempt to do so."

"Others have done it," Charlot pointed out.

He looked defiantly at Dickon, who retorted: "She means it is impossible for you."

"Do you imply that you are some superhuman being who can do what others can't?"

"You may have a point there," said Dickon aggravatingly. "I'll have a little more of that roast beef. They do it well in the kitchen."

"Nevertheless," said Charlot, "I am going to France."

"And I," put in Jonathan, "am going with him."

For a moment father and son stared steadily at each other. I was not sure of the look which passed between them. There was a certain glitter in Dickon's eyes, something which made me think, fleetingly, that he was not altogether surprised. But perhaps I thought of that after.

Then Dickon spoke. He said: "You're mad."

"No," said Jonathan. "Determined."

Dickon went on: "I see. So it is a plan. Who is going to join this company of fools? What about you, David?"

"Certainly not," said David. "I have told them what I think of the idea."

Dickon nodded. "It is a pleasant surprise to find that a little sanity remains in the family."

"Sanity!" retorted Jonathan. "If sanity is devoting oneself exclusively to books and mathematics, then the world would not have progressed very far."

"On the contrary," contradicted David, "ideas . . . thought and education have done more to advance it than rash adventurers."

"I would contest that."

"That's enough," said Dickon. "I suppose you have all been moved to this by the arrival of those refugees. You should have heard some of the stories they have been telling us. France has become a land of savages."

"There are fine people there still," said Charlot, "and they are doing all they can to save the country."

"They'll have a hard task. I warned them years ago that they were heading for disaster."

"It's true," said my mother. "You did, Dickon."

"Then they were preaching against us . . . joining the American colonists. What fools! Who can be surprised at the state they are now in?"

"I can," said Charlot. "But it is no use trying to make you understand."

"I understand well enough. You are not very profound, you know. You're just a little band of idiots. Now that's an end of the matter. I want to enjoy my roast beef."

Silence fell on the table. Sabrina, who had come down for the joy of having Dickon at the table and seeing him enjoy his roast beef, looked a little strained. She hated conflict.

My mother was anxious too. It was such a pity. After being away, even for such a short time, she wanted to enjoy her homecoming.

Dickon said he wanted to see Jonathan in his study after the meal. When I went upstairs I heard them talking quietly there.

My mother came to my bedroom. She sat on my bed and looked at me sorrowfully.

"How did all this come about?" she asked.

I told her how they had talked and become so absorbed in their plotting that the rest of us did not seem to exist for them.

"It was Charlot who started it, I think," I said.

"Charlot was always a patriot. He is his father's son. It is a pity he and Dickon cannot get on."

"I don't think they ever would. They have a natural antipathy."

She sighed and I smiled at her.

"Dearest Maman," I said, "you cannot have everything in life, can you? And you have so much."

"Yes," she agreed. "I have, and Claudine, remember this when you grow older: one of the best things in life is to have your happiness when you are mature enough to enjoy it."

"Well, that is the way you have had it."

She nodded. "Don't worry about these foolish young men. They'll realize their folly. Dickon will make them see it."

But he did not.

They went off secretly the next day and nobody thought anything about them until evening when they did not return.

We spent an uneasy night and the next morning a letter arrived for Dickon from Jonathan.

They had arranged their passage in a boat calling at the Belgian coast and by the time Dickon received the note, they should be about to land.

A Wedding at Eversleigh

Our household was disrupted. Dickon raged and my mother was plunged into melancholy. Although she had never been so close to Charlot as to me, and they had grown farther apart since her marriage to Dickon, he was her son, and I realized during the weeks which followed how his flight saddened her. She knew Charlot had never really wanted to stay in England, and she felt a certain guilt because she understood how frustrated he must have felt. He had come for a holiday—as we all had—and to have been forced to stay in England had angered him.

I had often heard him say that he wished he had gone back that time with my mother. He would never have come away if he had. He would have stayed behind to fight. David said: "You would not have been there long to fight. You would have been just another in the long march to the guillotine."

One remembered these conversations now; one remembered so much. Rides had lost their savour. There was no fear, no hope, of Jonathan's springing out on me. He had gone. What if he never came back?

My mother mourned secretly; she did not want to upset Dickon more than he already was. After a while he ceased to show a great deal of distress even though Jonathan, his son, had gone away and into danger so acute that it was hard for any who had not experienced it to imagine. I supposed that Dickon was not very emotionally involved with either of his sons; but they were his heirs, and like most men he had wanted sons. I wondered whether he considered the possibility of Jonathan's not coming back. Perhaps he consoled himself that he still had David.

During the first weeks we looked out for them. I would find myself at the top of the house, watching the road; and sometimes my mother would creep up to watch with me. Then she would grip my hand and I knew that she was seeing herself once more in the *mairie* with the mob below her. Such experiences are never forgotten; and at times such as this, naturally they became more vivid.

Once she broke down and cried: "This terrible revolution. What good can it possibly bring compared with the evil it has wrought! My father lost his only son. Just think of it! He went out one day and he only came back all that time after when my father was dead. You wouldn't have known him, Claudine."

I pressed her hand; then I kissed it.

"Thank God I have you," she said.

"I will always be near you."

"Bless you, dearest child. I believe you will."

I would have done anything at that moment to bring her comfort.

I think what Dickon felt most was anger. He had never liked Charlot, and I am sure would not have minded his going in the least. He was angry because it had upset my mother.

I doubted he had ever been so flouted in his life.

Sabrina became ill. I was sure it was with anxiety, and in a way this turned our thoughts from what was happening to them in France.

I would sit and read to her, which was what she liked, and she talked a great deal about the past. She remarked what a fortunate girl I was. I had been loved all my life; and she threw a little light on her own childhood, which made me see her differently.

She told me how when she was a little girl she had been forbidden to skate on a frozen pond because a thaw was setting in. She had disobeyed and fallen into the water, to be rescued by her mother, who caught a chill which shortened her life. Her father never forgave her. It was a shadow which had hung over her life. Only my great-grandmother, Clarissa, who was her cousin, had understood her. And then she had married the man whom Clarissa had loved.

I looked at her frail body, her white hair, and her thin but still-beautiful features, and I saw that her life had been overshadowed by guilt. She had shared Dickon with Clarissa and they had found their consolation in the son of the man whom they had both loved.

What happens in our young days must surely shape our natures. Dickon was arrogant, aggressive, seeing himself inheriting the earth as his right. Well, those two admiring women had helped to make him what he was. And Charlot . . . he had been brought up in France. It was his country and he would never tear himself away from it.

I prayed that he would never be caught by those who were making revolution. It would be a martyr's death for him if he were. Louis

Charles had always been something of a disciple. And Jonathan? No, I could not imagine anyone's getting the better of Jonathan. He had that quality which was Dickon's and somehow I felt he would always survive. I fostered that belief because it cheered me.

I was spending a great deal of time with David. I could discuss this alarming situation with him much more easily than I could with my mother.

I said: "I'm afraid for them. How I wish they would come home."

"Jonathan will come, you'll see. I don't know about Charlot and Louis Charles. Charlot has been serious about this for a long time, and he carries Louis Charles with him. It is a new adventure for Jonathan. I fancy he will tire of it though. He does lose his enthusiasms rather quickly."

The trip to London which was promised for my birthday was postponed. No one really felt in the mood for such frivolities.

"Perhaps," said my mother pathetically, "when they come back we can all go together."

Dickon, however, did go to London and my mother accompanied him. I wondered whether Jonathan had walked out on certain business commitments as well as his home.

The days passed quickly when the first shock was over. These consisted mainly of daily lessons for me. I spoke English fluently enough to satisfy even Dickon; and it was only rarely that a faint French accent could be detected.

David would often read passages to me from books which interested me, and I was learning something of the subjects which fascinated him. He liked me to ride round the estate with him and I was getting to know the tenants in the outlying districts. I took a great interest in the state of the cottages and when the young people were having babies. David was delighted and often commented on how popular I was with these people. He said that on those occasions when I was not with him they asked after me.

"The other day one of them said, 'She's one of us—Mistress Claudine is. No one would ever think she was aught else.' "

"It looks as though they have forgiven me for having a French father."

"A great concession, I do assure you," said David.

"Why are people so insular?"

"Because their horizons are as narrow as their minds."

"Charlot was the same."

I wished I had not said that. We were always trying to avoid any mention of what had happened.

"Charlot is so much a Frenchman that he cannot accept anything that is not French. My father is the same about England."

"It seems to be a masculine failing."

"Well, perhaps. Your mother, it seems, could be French or English . . . whatever is demanded. So can you, Claudine."

"Home is where those whom you love are. It is not a house or a piece of land surely."

"So this is your home, Claudine."

"My mother is here. I suppose home would always be where she is."

Then he said: "And others . . . perhaps."

I looked at him steadily and replied: "Yes . . . and others."

"Myself, for instance?"

"You, of course, David."

"You will marry me, won't you, Claudine?"

And I said: "Yes, David, I will."

Afterwards I wondered why I had answered so promptly, for although since Jonathan left I had been more and more drawn to David, in my heart I was still unsure.

Looking back, I think I wanted to escape from this slough of despond into which we all seemed to have drifted. I wanted something to happen, anything which would lift us out of it. Since Jonathan had gone so lightly, so eagerly abandoning me for the sake of a new adventure, I had been telling myself that it was really David whom I loved, because I was sure that with David, I came first. And having promised, I tried to convince myself that I had done the right thing—that which in my heart I had always known.

David was jubilant, and almost at once the atmosphere in the house lightened. The gloom lifted and for a while I too felt quite joyous. The change in my mother was amazing and Dickon was so delighted that it appeared that what he wanted more than anything at this time was our marriage.

My mother threw herself into preparations with an almost feverish energy. When should the wedding be? There should not be too long a wait. Summer was the time for a wedding. Of course the summer would soon be over. This was August. There must be some time for preparation. What about the end of September? Or the beginning of October? It was finally decided that it must be October to give us the time we needed for preparation.

It had been late February when the young men had left for France. Somehow it seemed like years.

As the days began to pass I was telling myself twenty times a day that I had done the right thing. I was very happy. David and I had everything in common and we would be happy all our lives in the heart of the family.

"It is true," I would say to myself. But why should I have to tell myself so insistently?

I was happy, however, to see my mother so absorbed. She was almost her old self wondering whether Molly Blackett was capable of making the wedding dress or whether she should risk hurting her by engaging a court dressmaker. While she concerned herself with such a matter at least she was not brooding about what might have happened to Charlot.

At length she decided that fashion must be sacrificed to human kindness and Molly set to work with yards and yards of pure white chiffon and delicate lace. And there was I standing, while she knelt at my feet, with the pincushion beside her, and my thoughts went back to another occasion when Jonathan had burst in on us and lured Molly away on a false pretext while he held me in his arms.

The dress turned out to be quite a triumph, and the joy of Molly Blackett's life. It hung in my bedroom cupboard for a whole week before the wedding, and every night, before I got into bed, I would look at it, and very often I thought it was like a ghost standing there—not a ghost from the past, but the ghost of what was to come. Once I dreamed that I was wearing it and Jonathan came and slipped the bodice from my shoulders and kissed me.

I supposed that every girl felt a little apprehensive before her wedding. I often pondered on those marriages which were arranged in highborn families. How did the bride feel going to an unknown bridegroom? At least I knew David for a kindly, interesting person, someone who really loved me, and, I said almost defiantly to the ghost in the cupboard, "whom I love."

During the days I was less fearful. Riding with David about the estate I felt contented. This was what our life would be. I should grow into it graciously. I should help him when he had little worries about something on the estate; we should take trips to London. Indeed we had planned to do so on our honeymoon. I often thought of the one we had planned in Italy, visiting Herculaneum or Pompeii—but that would not be easy now that we were at war with France. I often wondered what would happen to an Englishman found in France at this time. Dickon said that the country was in such a turmoil that they would pay little attention to foreigners; they were too intent on killing each other. But I feared for Charlot and Louis Charles as well as Jonathan.

We decided we would go to London . . . just for a week, say. We would sail up the river as far as Hampton; we would go to the theatre; and we would stay in the family house, which would be like home in a way.

I could not help thinking of Venice and Italian love songs as the gondoliers swept their way over darkened waters.

One day we came home past Grasslands, which belonged to Mrs. Trent, and as we were passing she came out and called to us.

I had never really liked her. There was a certain slyness about her. When I had visited Eversleigh the very first time—and I was quite young then—I had thought she was a witch and had been rather afraid of her.

Why I should have felt so I was not quite sure, for she must have been rather pretty when she was young; but there was a certain wariness about her which put me on my guard.

She called a greeting and said: "So it is our young bride and groom. Come and drink a glass of sloe gin . . . or if you would prefer it, the elderberry wine was very good this year."

I wanted to refuse, but David was already thanking her and accepting the invitation. I guessed he did not want to go any more than I did, but he was too kindhearted to refuse.

Grasslands was a very small estate compared with Eversleigh. There were only two farms, but I had heard it said that Mrs. Trent had a very good manager.

We went into a hall—a lofty place with some magnificent oak beams—but small compared with ours at Eversleigh, and she led us into a parlour and called out for the serving girl to bring the elderberry wine and sloe gin.

Mrs. Trent was beaming her satisfaction. I knew that she did not have many visitors. I gathered that for some reason she had never been accepted in the neighbourhood. There was some scandal about her. Her mother had been housekeeper to my distant relative Carl Eversleigh—in fact she had been his mistress and the story was that she had robbed him right and left. There was some scandal, which was discovered by my grandmother Zipporah, and the lady had disappeared, but not before her daughter had gone to work for Andrew Mather at Grasslands, and so insinuated herself into his life that he had married her, and when he died shortly afterwards leaving her with a baby son, she had become the owner of Grasslands.

Rumour had branded her an adventuress, and soon after the death of her first husband she married Jack Trent, her manager—who was said to have been her lover—and had lived in outward respectability ever since, but such a past was not easily forgotten.

"Everyone is most excited about the wedding," she said. "I reckon your mama is really pleased—and your step-papa too. It's always nice when things turn out the way people want, don't you think?"

David said we were also delighted about the coming marriage.

"Well, if you weren't that would be a nice kettle of fish, wouldn't it? I expect Mr. Jonathan's nose will be put out of joint when he comes home and finds his brother has stolen a march on him."

I felt myself flushing. Yes, that was what I remembered about Mrs. Trent. She seemed to be aware of one's weaknesses and to find a pleasure in letting one know it—and to set one wondering how much she really knew. It was that witchlike quality.

The wine had arrived and she poured it out.

"Good ones this year—both sloe and elder," she commented. "There now. Let's drink to the wedding."

We did. Then she went on: "And to the safe return of Mr. Jonathan."

Her eyes glittered as she looked straight at me. I could almost feel her probing my mind.

She said: "I like things to happen. That's one thing about the country . . . it can be a bit quiet. I started my life in London, you know. What a difference! Then my mother came to Eversleigh and it was the country life for me and has been ever since. There's some that say I've been lucky, and in spite of everything I'd say I've much to be thankful for."

Her bright eyes seemed to be looking back into the past and she was smirking at memories.

"I saw your step-papa out riding the other day. What a fine gentleman!" There was a special glitter in her eyes now, as though she knew something about Dickon which she would dearly love to tell.

I wondered whether I was imagining that certain slyness, this harbouring of secret knowledge, because in my childhood I had thought of her as the witch.

When she spoke of Jonathan and Dickon there was a note in her voice which seemed to suggest that she knew them very well indeed and was greatly amused by them.

I had a great desire to get away; she was depressing me. I wondered if she had the same effect on David. I caught his eye and tried to indicate that we should finish the wine and get out. There was something claustrophobic about Grasslands.

Mrs. Trent cocked her head as though listening. Then she called out: "I can see you . . . peeping in. Come and meet the happy pair."

The two girls came in. They were dressed in riding habits. Evie looked very pretty, which made the contrast with her sister very noticeable.

"You know my Evie and Dolly," said Mrs. Trent. She looked at Evie with pride, and I immediately felt sorry for Dolly, who hung back a little, for I guessed she was very much aware of her deformity.

The girls dropped a curtsy, and Mrs. Trent went on: "They think it's lovely . . . you, Miss Claudine, and Mr. David, don't you, girls?"

They nodded.

"Where's your tongues?" demanded Mrs. Trent. "Haven't you got something to say?"

"Congratulations, Miss de Tourville and Mr. Frenshaw," said Evie.

"Thanks," we replied simultaneously and David went on: "I saw you riding the other day. I must say you manage your horses well."

"Oh yes," said Mrs. Trent, "I've had them brought up in the right way, both of them. I was determined my girls should be as good as anyone else."

"I'm sure you succeeded, Mrs. Trent," I said. "I do agree about the wine being especially good this year. Thanks for letting us try it, and now I think we really ought to be going, don't you, David?"

"I'm afraid so," he said. "There is so much to do round the estate."

"Don't I know it," said Mrs. Trent. "In my own little way, of course. Grasslands is no Eversleigh, but my goodness there's enough to keep us busy. It was very gracious of you to call. We do appreciate that, don't we, girls?"

Evie said: "Oh yes, we do."

"And I'll come and dance at your wedding. You girls will have to wait a bit for yours. But I've a feeling Evie won't have so long. Well, we'll see."

We rose and thanked her for the wine, and she came out with us to our horses. Evie and Dolly came with her and stood looking at us while we mounted.

Mrs. Trent slapped the flanks of my horse affectionately.

"I'll be at the wedding," she said. "I have a special interest in your family."

I don't know why it was—perhaps because of the mood she aroused in me—but I thought the words sounded ominous.

As we rode away, David said: "She is rather ill-bred, but I don't think she means any harm."

So he must have felt the same as I did. I agreed that she was ill-bred, but I was not so sure of the harm; but my apprehension did seem rather foolish so I pressed my horse into a gallop. I felt I wanted to put a distance between myself and Grasslands.

We slowed down as we came to the road. "They must have been at Grasslands for a long time," I said.

"Well, Mrs. Trent went there as housekeeper, and married old Andrew Mather."

"Yes, I heard that. The girls' father was her son."

"Yes, by her first husband. He managed the estate very well until his death. Now she has quite a good manager."

"Grasslands is very different from that other house . . . Enderby."

"Very. Always was. It's odd about Enderby."

"Do you believe that houses have an effect on people? They do say that Enderby is unlucky."

David laughed. "How can a house be? It's only bricks or stone. They can't change luck, can they?"

"Let's go and look at the old place. Just a glimpse. It's up this way, isn't it?"

I turned off the road and David followed me. As we rounded a bend, there was the old house. I have to admit that even in broad daylight it sent a shiver through me. It looked dark and menacing, as neglected houses will sometimes. The shrubs about it were thick and untended.

"It looks very dejected," said David.

"And at the same time defiant," I replied.

He laughed. "Can a house look so?"

"Enderby does. Come on. I want a close look. Do you think anyone will ever buy it?"

"Not in the state it's in. It's been empty for years. Because of its reputation probably."

"David, I want to look closer."

"Hasn't Grasslands been enough for one morning?"

"Perhaps because of Grasslands."

He looked at me puzzled. Then he smiled and said: "All right. Let's go."

We tethered our horses to the post which was set there conveniently for the use of visitors and went to the front door. It was silent, eerie. There was a rusty bell which I pulled, and we stood listening to the jangling which echoed through the house.

"No use ringing the bell," said David. "Whom do you expect to answer it?"

"Ghosts," I said. "People who have lived in the house and can't rest because of their sins. Wasn't there a murder here once?"

"If there was it's ancient history."

"It's ancient history that makes ghosts."

"Claudine, I believe there's a side to your nature which I have not discovered. You believe in evil spirits. Do you, Claudine?"

"I don't know, but I should if I were made aware of them. In fact, David, I would believe anything in the world if I had evidence of it."

"Well, that is the crux of the matter. Are you going to believe without proof?"

"Standing here . . . in the shadow of this house . . . I could."

"We can't get in because there is no one to let us in."

"Is there a key somewhere . . . just in case of a prospective buyer?"

"I believe it is with Mrs. Trent. She's the nearest neighbour. You're not going to propose that we go back and ask for it, are you?"

I shook my head emphatically. "Still, I should like to explore a bit."

David, ever willing to please, followed me round the house. We fought our way through overgrown weeds in the long grass. When I found the window with the broken latch, I pushed it open and looked into the hall.

"David," I said excitedly. "We could climb through here. Do let's."

He did, and standing in the hall turned to help me in, and soon we were there, looking up at the vaulted ceiling and the minstrels' gallery and the wide staircase at one end of the hall.

"That," said David, "is said to be the haunted spot. It all started when someone in financial difficulties, I think, tried to hang himself with a rope suspended from the gallery. The rope was too long and he landed on his feet suffering terrible agonies. Ever since then the house has been cursed."

"Sabrina lived here in her childhood."

"Yes. But even when she was well she avoided coming here. The house was quite normal then because her mother, who was a very good woman, made it so. And after she died her husband was heartbroken and it reverted to its gloomy aspect. That shows, does it not, that it is people who make the house what it is—not stone and bricks?"

"You win," I said.

And he laughed. He put an arm about me. "There you are, Madam. An undesirable property. But one which could be made desirable . . . by the right people."

"Who in their right minds would want to live in such a place? Think of all the work which would have to be done."

"Nothing that a few gardeners could not alter in a month. To my mind it's the darkness. It's all that growth outside."

"Come and look at the haunted gallery then."

We mounted the staircase. I parted the curtains. They were thick with dust. I went in and stood looking down on the hall. Yes, there was an eerie atmosphere. The house seemed silent, watchful.

I shivered, but said nothing to David. He would not notice. He was too practical.

We looked down to the other end of the hall, to the screens with the kitchens beyond. I could imagine the people who had danced in this hall; and I wondered what it would be like here when darkness fell. It really was ghostly, and one's imagination might play tricks. No one would ever want to come and live here and the house would crumble and decay.

We went up the staircase, our footsteps echoing through the house. We looked into the bedrooms. There were many of them, and some of the furniture must have been there for years—such as the old court cupboard in one room and the four-poster bed in another.

I had a feeling that I wanted to be alone here—just for a few moments. David was too prosaic, too unimaginative to feel the atmosphere as I did. Of course, I was fanciful and was allowing myself to pretend I felt something which I had probably worked up within myself.

I slipped into one of the rooms. I could hear David's footsteps in another and I guessed he was examining the old court cupboard.

Silence! Just a faint murmur in the trees which grew so thickly round the house. I heard a sound. It must have been the swaying lattice of the broken window downstairs, but it startled me.

Then suddenly I heard a sibilant whisper. It seemed to fill the room. It was: "Beware . . . beware, little bride."

I felt myself go cold with horror. I looked quickly round. Someone had spoken. I had distinctly heard those words. I ran to the door and looked along the corridor to the staircase. There was no sign of anyone.

David emerged from the room in which he had been.

I said: "Did you hear someone?"

He looked surprised. "There's no one here," he said.

"I thought I heard . . ."

"You're imagining things," he said.

I nodded. I now had a great desire to get away. I had known there was something malevolent about the house.

We went quickly down the staircase to the hall. All the time I was looking about me to see if there was any sign of anyone's being in the house.

There was nothing.

David helped me through the window. I tried to stop my hands trembling as he helped me into the saddle.

"Can you see anyone's trying to make a home of that place?" said David.

"I can't really. I think it is full of evil ghosts."

"And cobwebs and spiders' webs doubtless."

"Horrible."

"Never mind, my dearest. It makes you appreciate Eversleigh all the more."

Eversleigh . . . My home forever . . . surrounded by love, the love of my mother and my husband. And if Jonathan ever came home . . . ?

I tried not to think of that but I could not stop myself. I kept hearing those words: "Beware, little bride."

The days which followed were very busy and I forgot our visit to Enderby. It was only occasionally—and in dreams—that those words kept coming back to my mind.

It was to be a moderately quiet wedding. The absence of Jonathan, Charlot and Louis Charles could not be lightly brushed aside. However much we tried to forget it, and while we were in doubt as to where they were and what was happening to them, ours must be an anxious household. It was seven months since they had left and that seemed a long time.

The hall was being decorated with plants from the greenhouses and there was an atmosphere of bustle everywhere; savoury smells emerged from the kitchen and the cook was making an enormous wedding cake over which she seemed to be puffing and groaning every time I went into the kitchen.

We should have a few people staying in the house—those who came from too far to be able to get home on the evening of the wedding day;

those in the not-too-distant neighbourhood could attend the ceremony and the reception which was to follow and then start the journey home.

The marriage was to take place in the Eversleigh chapel, which was reached from the hall by a short spiral staircase. It was not small—as chapels in country houses go—but on the other hand it was not large and would therefore, I was sure, be overcrowded. My mother had said that the servants could sit on the staircase if there was not room for them inside the chapel.

The day after the wedding David and I would leave for London and would spend a week there before returning to Eversleigh.

"The honeymoon proper is temporarily postponed," said David, "but only until life settles down more peacefully on the Continent. Then for us it will be the Grand Tour. We may go through France if that is possible and perhaps visit some of the people and places you once knew. And then . . . on to Italy. In the meantime we shall have to be satisfied. Will you accept that?"

"Needs must," I said laughingly.

I began to thrust aside my doubts. My mother was so pleased. I knew she had always favoured David. Why was it that she, who had chosen Dickon, the wildest of adventurers, and one least likely to be a faithful husband, should have chosen serious David for me? Perhaps for the very reason that she herself had chosen Dickon. I believed my own father was a man whom she had shared with many women. So perhaps that was the very reason why she preferred the steady one for her daughter.

It was the night before my wedding. I opened the cupboard door and looked at my dress. Before the candles were lighted it looked like a woman standing there. Soft chiffon! The pride of Molly Blackett's life. It was beautiful. I should be happy ever after.

I undressed and brushed my hair, braiding it neatly into two plaits. I went and sat by the window and I asked myself if everything would have been different if Jonathan had not gone away. Suppose I could go back to the days before my birthday. It was on my birthday, with the arrival of the refugees, that everything changed. It was they who had fired Jonathan and Charlot with the idea of going to France. Charlot had always wanted to go back.

Suppose those refugees had not escaped. Suppose they had never come to Eversleigh. . . . Would this then be the eve of my wedding?

I looked out into the distance. How often had I stood there straining my eyes to the horizon looking for a rider who might be Jonathan returning from France.

But he had not come. Perhaps he never would come. Perhaps he would disappear as my Uncle Armand had—although he came back . . . when it was too late.

Would Jonathan?

I got into bed. It was difficult to sleep. I kept thinking about the future, sometimes fearfully. But what was there to fear? David loved me and he was the kindest of people.

And if Jonathan ever came back . . . ? Well, what if he did? I should be married then. His coming and going would be no real concern of mine.

At last I slept and I awoke to find my mother standing by my bed.

"Wake up, little bride," she said. "It's your wedding day."

I was coming out of my sleep and as I smiled at her I seemed to hear another voice, strange and ghostly: "Beware, little bride."

So I was married to David in the chapel at Eversleigh. It was a simple ceremony performed by the priest who lived on the estate and officiated on all such occasions. I felt a sense of fatality standing on the red tiles where generations of Eversleigh brides had stood before me.

The chapel was so hot and the overpowering odour of so many flowers made me feel a little faint; but perhaps that was the excitement.

David was smiling as he put the ring on my finger and said the words required of him in a resolute voice. I hoped I sounded equally determined to do what was expected of me.

Then we were walking out of the chapel and I was aware of all the people there: Lord and Lady Pettigrew with their daughter Millicent; friends from the neighbourhood; and at the back of the chapel—suggesting to me a certain false modesty—were Mrs. Trent and her two grand-daughters.

I could feel their eyes on me. But this was natural, for was I not, as the bride, the focus of attention?

The servants who had been seated on the stairs hastily pressed themselves against the wall to make a passage for us, and so David and I, now husband and wife, came into the hall.

My mother was right behind us. She was flushed and looked very beautiful; with her dark blue eyes and luxuriant dark hair, she was still a strikingly handsome woman.

There were tears now in her lovely eyes. She whispered to me that it was so moving. "I kept thinking about the day you were born and all the funny little things you used to do."

"I believe that is how mothers are on their daughters' wedding days," I said, "so, dearest Maman, you only acted true to form."

"Come," she said. "They are all returning now. We shall feed them right away."

Soon they were assembled in the hall and there was a buzz of conversation. Dickon looked very pleased and I could hear his hearty laughter above the conversation. My mother was at his side and I thought: She is happier than she has been since the day Charlot left.

I cut the cake with David's help and I smiled to note the cook's anxious eyes on us while we performed this ceremony, for the servants had gathered in one corner of the room.

I nodded towards her to imply that it was perfect. She closed her eyes, and opening them, rolled them to the ceiling in ecstasy. David and I laughed together and went on cutting the cake.

Mrs. Evalina Trent was talking to Millicent Pettigrew, rather to Millicent's consternation, for her mother would most certainly not approve of Mrs. Trent. I think Evalina Trent knew this and was rather maliciously keeping Millicent in conversation although it was clear that she wanted to escape.

"It'll be your turn next, my dear," I heard her say. "Oh yes it will. Take a piece of cake and put it under your pillow, my dear. Then tonight you will dream of your future husband."

Millicent looked over Mrs. Trent's head and Mrs. Trent went on, indicating her two grand-daughters, who were close by. "Now my girls will put that cake under *their* pillows, won't you, girls? They're determined to see their future husbands tonight." She turned to Millicent: "You'll be staying the night, I daresay."

Millicent admitted that she would be.

"Too far to travel back by night," went on Mrs. Trent. "Dangerous, too. I wouldn't want to travel after daylight. Those gentlemen of the road are getting bolder. They're not content with taking a lady's purse. . . . They want something else besides, so they tell me."

Millicent murmured: "Excuse me!" and went over to join her mother.

People came up to congratulate us; toasts were drunk and there was a great deal of laughter. Dickon made a speech saying how happy he and my mother were, and he stressed what an unusual state of affairs this was when a man's son could marry his wife's daughter and it could be the most perfect union imaginable.

Everyone applauded, and the servants cleared away the food and dancing began. As was customary I opened the dance with Dickon, followed by David with my mother; and the others fell in behind us.

I was tired and a little apprehensive, half relieved and half fearful, when the guests began to depart, leaving only those who were staying in the house.

Mrs. Trent came to say goodbye to me before they left.

"I reckon you're glad to see the back of us," she said, her eyes sparkling as she almost leered at me. "Now," she went on, "the real wedding can begin."

I watched them leave and felt quite glad because they were no longer under our roof.

The carriages started to leave and we stood at the door waving to them as they clip-clopped off into the darkness.

Then David slipped his arm through mine, and together we went to the bridal chamber in which so many of my mother's family had spent the first night of their married lives.

The Return

I was happy. My doubts had disappeared. David was so kind, so tender and considerate, so eager to do everything which would please me. We slipped from a long and companionate friendship to a more intimate relationship, as though it was the most natural thing in the world. I had left my innocence behind me and I was glad.

When I awoke on the morning after my wedding day, David was sleeping. He had changed subtly as I supposed I had. He had ceased to be the quiet young man absorbed in serious matters. He was passionately in love with me, and I was very happy that he should be. We had always been the best of friends, but this new closeness was a comfort to me. I felt happy and secure. I believed that I was learning to know David as I had never known him before; and I daresay he felt the same about me. I had always been intrigued by that phrase in the Bible which I think says: "He came unto her and knew her." I understood now what that meant. David came unto me and I knew David and he knew me, and we were miraculously united.

When David awoke and found me studying him, he returned my gaze with a kind of wonderment. We embraced. I knew that he felt the same as I did, and that we did not need words to express our thoughts. That was part of the new relationship which was springing up between us.

My mother studied me anxiously. I must have looked radiant for her fears vanished immediately. She held me very closely and said: "I am so glad, my dearest. Now you are going to be happy."

She looked very like her old self as she stood waving us off.

What happy days they were! London had always excited me; the bustle, the carriages with the fine ladies and gentlemen riding in them; the shops full of exciting merchandise; the link boys when it was dark; the vitality of it all.

And now to be here with David, making plans as to how we should spend the day, seemed absolute bliss.

We stayed at the family house in Albemarle Street, so in a way it was like being at home; but it was the first time we had ever had the house to ourselves. I felt very grown-up and fancied the servants treated me with a very special deference because of my newly-entered-into marital state.

Then began one of the happiest weeks of my life—which is what a honeymoon should be, of course. I was determined to enjoy every moment, and during that time all my doubts had disappeared. I was sure I had made the perfect marriage.

There were so many interesting things to do. We liked to wander through the streets, to stroll through the market listening to the street traders; we went for trips along the river to Hampton and we rode into the interlying villages as far out as Kensington, coming back across the bridge over the Westbourne at Knightsbridge. As we passed Kingston House David told me of the recent scandal concerning the late Duke and his mistress Elizabeth Chudleigh, who claimed to be the Duchess. It had been a *cause célèbre* some years before.

He had many interesting stories to tell me, and I felt I was seeing London as I never had before. I loved our leisurely walks through the streets of the City when he would point out those historic spots which had been the scene of much of our country's history. There was that spot in what had been Pudding Lane, where the great fire of London had broken out in a baker's shop at one o'clock in the morning of a Monday and raged through the City until the following Thursday. David could talk vividly, and he made me see the raging furnace and the terrified people running from their houses, the craft on the river and finally the experiments with gunpowder which had demolished the houses straight ahead of the fire and so stopped its progress. We visited the new St. Paul's, which had replaced the old one—a magnificent example of the work of Christopher Wren.

To be with David was like reliving history.

We strolled past Carlton House, and paused to admire the colonnade of single pillars—one of the houses of the Prince of Wales, and which had previously been the residence of Frederick Prince of Wales, who had died before he could reach the throne. Here was a link with Kingston House because the notorious Duchess had been maid of honour to the Princess of Wales—so she, too, had lived in this splendid Carlton House.

Dickon had many associates in London and some of them were eager to entertain members of his family while we were there; but because we were so newly married they guessed, quite rightly, that we would prefer to have a few days to ourselves—and they respected this. So for those first few days of that week we were alone, and I think they were the most enjoyable, which delighted me because they confirmed that I had been right in marrying David. The more we were together, the more at one we seemed to become. He was, of course, moulding my tastes to fit his; but it was gratifying that I had no difficulty in accepting his guidance. I was very happy during those days. "The days of my innocence," I called them later; that was when I would be overcome by a passionate desire to escape from what I had become and go back to them. Very few people must have wanted to turn the clock back more than I.

But to return to those idyllic days, I remember that evening at Ranelagh which seemed such magic. The pleasure gardens, the river at dusk, the magnificent temple with its painted ceiling, the Rotunda in which could be heard the finest music executed by the greatest musicians throughout the world. Mozart himself had appeared here. I remembered hearing my grandmother talk about that. We sat there entranced, listening to the orchestral music of Handel and Pleyel and the exquisite voice of Signor Torizziani.

There was a fireworks display of the utmost magnificence when we gazed in wonder at the scintillating rockets as they burst in the air, and were most impressed by the bombshell which exploded to release what looked like myriads of stars and comets.

"No one would think we were a country at war," said David sombrely.

I pressed his hand and answered: "Forget war and everything unpleasant. I am so happy tonight."

We took one of the vehicles which was run by the management of Ranelagh to pick up people in various parts of London and bring them with the minimum of discomfort to the pleasure gardens. These were imitation French diligences. I wondered why we imitated the French in so many ways, and they did the same with us, when we seemed to be such natural enemies and even now were at war with each other.

David always seriously considered my lightly made observations. So he pondered this one all the way from Ranelagh to Hyde Park Corner, where we alighted from the diligence.

Then he said: "There is an antipathy between our two countries. I think it is because we have so much respect for each other's skills—both peaceful and warlike—and we are, at heart, afraid of each other. If we admired each other less, we should hate each other less. So we have this animosity and these occasional outbreaks of imitation when the desire to be like each other is irresistible. Remember imitation is the greatest form of flattery."

I laughed at him and told him that he was so solemn that he made an issue out of everything.

"Really," I said, "I do believe you should be in Parliament with Mr. Pitt, Mr. Burke, Mr. Fox and the rest."

"A career for which I should prove most unsuitable."

"Nonsense. You could do anything you set your mind to, and as the affairs of the country seem to be in a certain disorder, surely we need clever men to put them right."

"You overrate my cleverness," he said. "Politicians have to be single-minded. They have not only to *think* they are right, they must know it. For one thing, I doubt myself all the time."

"That is because you are clever enough to know that there are two sides to every question."

"Which would damn me as a politician."

He laughed, and arms entwined, we walked the short distance to Albemarle Street.

Looking back, I am surprised by how much we did in those few days. We visited the piazza at Covent Garden and David told me how Dryden had been assaulted there because of some verses in his *Hind and Panther;* and how a soldier had been shot dead on the spot. He had stories to tell of so many people: Steele, Dryden, Pope, Colly Cibber, Dr. Johnson and famous names of the theatre such as Peg Woffington and David Garrick; and painters, Sir Peter Lely and Sir Godfrey Kneller—all of whom used to frequent the piazza in their day.

I marvelled at his knowledge. I said to him: "And to think I shall be able to draw on it for the rest of my life!"

We went to Covent Garden to hear the marvellous voice of Elizabeth Billington, which was thrilling—particularly as the glittering audience included the Prince of Wales with Mrs. Fitzherbert. I was drawn to them because they seemed—as David and I were—very much in love.

I often thought afterwards of the way in which life deals with us all. It seems that even when we are at the height of our bliss, evil lurks, waiting to strike. That was one of the last performances Elizabeth Billington gave, for the next year she left the country and retired to the Continent because of scandalous publications about herself. And the royal lovers had their vicissitudes to face in the years to come, as all know now.

As for myself—I was so young, and innocent enough to believe I was going to live happily ever after.

The next day friends began to call on us. I enjoyed meeting them, but it was not quite the same as those idyllic first days.

Of course we could not shut ourselves away from events for ever. We had to face reality. There was a great deal of talk at dinner parties about what was happening in France, and there was no doubt that the people in the centre of things were very uneasy. David was deeply interested to hear the views expressed. He listened with great attention. I supposed that was why he was so clever. He never missed any piece of information, any point of view.

When we returned to the house he would sit on the bed and talk while I lay back on my pillows watching him.

"What does this mean to us?" he said. "That is what we have to decide. How is the revolution in France going to affect us here in England?"

"It already has," I answered. "It has killed my grandmother; it has taken my grandfather's estates; it has ruined the family, for who knows where my Aunt Sophie is? And now it has taken my brother Charlot, Louis Charles and your brother Jonathan."

"Yes," he agreed. "But that is personal . . . our family tragedy. What effect is it having on our country? And that, Claudine, can have every bit as much effect on us in the future as purely personal trials. Have you noticed that no one seems to be certain . . . even the politicians. Who are our leading men just now? I'd say Pitt, Fox and Burke, wouldn't you? Yet they seem to me from what they say and do in Parliament to be at variance with each other. Fox is too trusting; he believes in freedom and that a country should be ruled by its majority—which he takes to be the revolutionaries. I think Burke sees it differently. He knows that what the people of France want is equality . . . but they do not want liberty. Not for their enemies certainly. How many have gone to the guillotine completely innocent of anything but being born aristocrats? Burke is aware that revolution—and that means anarchy—could erupt all over Europe. And Pitt . . . he does not share Fox's sympathy with the will of the people. He is a great upholder of peace, and I am sure he believes that in due course France will settle down. It is with great reluctance that he goes to war. With three diverging views, where does that lead us?"

"I don't know," I said yawning, "and I do believe you are not sure either. And even if you were . . . what could you do to help?"

I held out my arms to him and laughingly he came to me.

But if the subject was dismissed for that night, it reared its head again the very next day. An entertainment was given in our honour. I had always known that the family had vast interests in London. Whenever I came up with my mother and Dickon, there had been a great deal of social activity from which on account of my youth I had generally been excluded. Now I realized the extent of Dickon's connections and the desire of certain people to show friendship for Dickon's son and my mother's daughter.

I enjoyed meeting these interesting people who seemed so poised and knowledgeable. I liked to listen to their conversation, but I did notice that it revolved round one subject at the moment.

As we sat at table on this occasion, the talk took the usual trend. Someone said something about Charlotte Corday. It was just over three months since she had been executed for stabbing Jean Paul Marat in his bath but it was still talked of as though it had happened yesterday.

"I don't think," said the man next to me, "that anyone has much sympathy for Marat."

"No," I agreed, "but many have for Charlotte Corday."

"A brave woman. She knew she was signing her own death warrant. That takes courage."

I agreed with that too.

Our host said: "I wonder who will be next. Danton perhaps."

"Do you think it will come to that?" said the lady on his right.

"These people always turn against each other," replied our host.

David said: "I feel sure that the leaders of the revolution like Danton and Robespierre will in due course be brought to the guillotine. They are all jostling for power; they are envious of each other. That is what it is all about. Better conditions for the people? Of course not! Power for Messieurs Marat, Danton and Robespierre . . . and the rest. And each one in his turn will be the downfall of the others."

There was a murmur of agreement round the table.

Our hostess said: "I trust you will be able to forget these disagreeable men when you listen to Ludwig Blochermund, who is shortly going to entertain us on the piano."

"Blochermund!" cried a fat fair lady. "My dear, how did you manage to get him? I hear he is in great demand."

"Yes. He was performing at the Rotunda recently."

"I did have the pleasure of hearing him there and I look forward greatly to hearing his performance tonight."

"Wonderful," murmured several of the guests.

After the meal we went into the drawing room in which was a grand piano and there Herr Blochermund performed to our delight.

I sat in blissful contemplation until the recital was over and just as the pianist had risen from his stool and was receiving the congratulations of his audience, the butler came in and announced that a gentleman had come to see our host, and it appeared that the matter was somewhat urgent.

Our host went out and it was ten minutes later when he returned, looking very disturbed.

He addressed us all in a tone of melancholy and said: "I know you will all be made aware of this sad news soon enough. I am sorry to spoil the evening with it, but you will not wish to be kept in the dark. The Queen of France has followed her husband to the guillotine."

There was a hushed silence.

"So they have dared . . ." whispered someone.

"Both are dead now . . . the King and the Queen . . . murdered by a bloodthirsty mob," said our host. "Where will all this end?"

The party broke up then. No one was in the mood for festivity. All of us must have been thinking of that frivolous girl who little more than twenty years before had come to France to make the brilliant marriage arranged for her, and we were all thinking: What now? To murder kings and queens makes a dangerous precedent.

As we left, our host looked earnestly at David.

He said: "Your father should be informed without delay."

David nodded.

He said: "We shall leave for Eversleigh tomorrow."

I was a little hurt that we should be leaving two days before we planned to go.

"It has happened. The Queen is dead," I complained to David. "What good can we do by going home so soon?"

"My father must know at once," he said.

I was exasperated. "But what can he do about it?"

"There is more to this than the execution of the Queen, Claudine."

"What more?"

We were in the carriage then, leaving London behind and riding through the open country.

"While the Queen lived there was a monarchy in France, even though a captive one. Now the monarchy is at an end."

"There is a Dauphin."

"A boy, poor child . . . in the hands of sadist torturers intent on making him suffer for being the son of a king. I tremble for him."

"It is France, David, and this is England."

"Everything that happens affects us all, particularly when it is happening so close to us. There are great fears in the country. Revolution is like a fire. Once it gets out of control, it spreads."

"You mean people are afraid we might have the same thing here?"

"Very few governments in Europe have enough support from their people to feel very safe. I think we in England may be more fortunate than most. Our King is no despot. He is a gentle creature. The people couldn't hate him. They might refer to him as Farmer George but there is an element of affection as well as contempt in the epithet. They could not hate such a mild man . . . a man of simple tastes who is determined to do his duty, even if he is not very clear how it should be done. We need reforms here, and rest assured we shall get them. But the last thing we need is revolution."

"Surely that is the last thing any country needs."

"I really believe that in their hearts our people do not want revolution. We have too close to us an example of what it can mean. The French are merely changing one set of masters for another, and I firmly believe that many sane people would prefer the first, however oppressive. The country may have been led by men who were selfish, effete, careless of the needs of the people, too eager to pander to their own—but even they were better than these bloodthirsty power-hungry murderers who are ruling them now."

"Then if our people know this, why should we have to hurry home?"

He was silent for a few moments, then he said: "There are agitators—men who did so much to stir up revolution in France. They aim to do the same all over Europe. They want to bring down the Church, the State and the Monarchy."

"Do you mean that these men, these agitators, are actually in our country?"

"I am sure of it. Their number will increase now and we have to be prepared."

"And what can your father do about it?"

David shrugged his shoulders, and I wondered how much he knew about Dickon's secret work.

There was nothing more to be said. The honeymoon was over.

David looked at me indulgently. "Don't forget," he said, "when things are better, we are going to take that trip to Italy."

I nestled close to him. "It will be wonderful. I do believe, David, that one of these days I shall know as much as you do."

"As long as you don't know more and despise me for my ignorance, I shall be happy with that."

I watched the passing countryside. Few of the leaves remained on the trees, but the colours of those which did were beautiful. In some of the orchards they were gathering the last of the fruit. Winter was almost upon us.

We had planned to arrive before darkness fell and at this time of year it grew dark early. But we made good progress and dusk was just beginning to fall when I saw the high wall of Eversleigh with the glimpse of the gates beyond, and my heart gave that little leap of pleasure as it always did when I saw it after being away.

As we passed through the gates and to the house the grooms came out of the stables—astonished to see us.

David helped me from the carriage and I turned to the house. I could scarcely wait to see my mother and tell her of the wonderful time we had had in London.

I went ahead of David running into the hall—the beloved hall with its high vaulted ceiling, its stone walls and the family tree over the fireplace.

The hall was deserted. Of course, they did not know we were coming that day.

I started up the stairs.

"Maman," I called. "It's Claudine . . . and David. We're home."

My voice seemed to echo back to me; and then suddenly at the top of the staircase, I saw a strange figure. It was grey and hooded. I thought it was a monk or a nun standing there and I felt myself grow cold with terror. In that moment I really believed I was face to face with the supernatural.

I stood very still and indeed if I had tried to move I believe I should not have been able to do so.

The figure moved slightly; a pair of burning dark eyes seemed to be boring through me.

Then a voice said: "It's Claudine . . . Oh, Claudine, you don't know me."

I cried out: "Aunt . . . Aunt Sophie."

Then I knew she was back. Jonathan, Charlot and Louis Charles had gone over to rescue her.

And Jonathan would always do what he set out to do.

What a homecoming that was!

Even as Sophie embraced me I heard my mother's voice. She appeared on the stairs and Dickon was with her.

"Claudine! David! We didn't expect you today." My mother hugged me. "My dearest, you look so well. It is wonderful to see you."

"There is important news," said David. "They have sent the Queen of France to the guillotine."

Dickon, who had come out, did not speak. He stood very still and I saw that he was frowning.

"We were at the Cranthornes'," went on David, "and the news came through to John Cranthorne. They wanted you to know at once."

Dickon nodded and my mother looked at him anxiously.

"We shall leave for London tomorrow," he said.

There was a brief silence and my mother said: "You see what has happened."

"Aunt Sophie . . ." I began.

"It is wonderful that she is here."

"And Charlot?"

My mother looked sad. "Charlot has not come back. Nor has Louis Charles. They have joined the army . . . the French army."

"Oh no!" I cried. "They'll be fighting against us."

"Fools," said Dickon.

My mother laid a hand on his arm.

"Charlot was always fretting to get back," she said. "At least he is alive and we have news of him at last."

There was one question I wanted to ask and I felt too emotional to say his name. But my mother answered it for me. "Jonathan brought Aunt Sophie back with Jeanne Fougère. You remember Jeanne Fougère?"

"Yes, yes, of course. So . . . Jonathan is safely home."

My mother looked at me intently. "Yes, Jonathan is back."

When David and I went down to dinner he was there. My heart leaped with excitement; he looked different—older and even more attractive than he had before he went away.

I looked at him quickly and then averted my gaze. I hoped no one noticed how the colour in my cheeks had risen.

Jonathan said: "I've been hearing about the wedding. So I have to congratulate you both."

"Thank you," I said faintly.

He came towards me and, placing his hands on my shoulders, kissed me lightly on the cheek.

"So," he said scoldingly, "you stole a march on me."

He gave a little laugh and I tried to smile. "How long have I been away? Eight months? And I come back to find you a wedded wife!"

He raised his eyes to the ceiling. He had spoken as though it were a joke and I felt relieved in a way because he took it all so lightly.

"When did you return?" I asked.

"Two days ago."

Two days, I thought. While I was riding in the Park, so contented, laughing, so happy, Jonathan had been coming home with Aunt Sophie. If I had known . . .

Sabrina, who had joined us, said: "Dickon is so relieved that Jonathan is home."

"Of course," I said.

"Poor darling, it has been an anxious time for him."

Aunt Sophie appeared then. That is the way to describe her movements. She glided rather than walked, and she was so quiet that one was almost unaware that she was there; and then suddenly one would lift one's head and see those burning intense eyes in the half-shrouded face.

I wondered what she looked like without her hood and how deeply scarred she was by those terrible burns she had received in the Place Louis XV at the time of the wedding of that Queen who was now a headless corpse.

She wore a gown of delicate mauve with a hood to match. I could see the dark hair at one side of her face—the hood hid the other side. There was about her an ambiance of tragedy, of which all must be aware.

"We are very very happy to have Sophie safe with us." My mother seemed almost pathetically anxious to make Sophie feel at home. She had always been like that with Sophie. I remembered that there were times when she almost seemed to hold herself responsible for Sophie's disfigurement, just because she had been present when the disaster had happened and my father, who had at that time been engaged to Sophie, had brought my mother safely out of danger while my Uncle Armand had rescued Sophie. It had happened long before I was born—about twenty-three years ago, so all that time Sophie had been living with her disfigurement. She must be nearly forty years old now.

"Jeanne Fougère has come too, I am happy to hear," I said.

"I wouldn't have left Jeanne behind," said Sophie.

"Of course not," put in my mother. "Jeanne has been a wonderful friend. I wanted her to join us at table but she would not. She is a stickler for formality. 'Jeanne,' I said to her, 'you are a dear friend. That is how we regard you.' 'I am Mademoiselle Sophie's maid, Madame,' she said. 'And that is what I wish to be.' I could not persuade her."

"If you have no objection I shall eat with her as I have always done," said Sophie. "It is a special occasion tonight and I wanted to be here to greet Claudine."

"Thank you, Aunt Sophie."

Her eyes were on me and I saw in them a hint of the warmth she showed for Jeanne Fougère, and I felt rather pleased that this strange woman should have a certain feeling for me. She always had had—and for Charlot too—but I think particularly for me. I remembered long ago in the Château d'Aubigné before that day—so far in the distant past now—when we had left for a holiday in England and never came back. It was the last time, before this, when I had seen Aunt Sophie.

"Do come to the table," said my mother. "They have brought in the soup and it will be getting cold."

We sat down to dinner and Jonathan said: "I claim the honour of sitting on the right hand of the bride." Whereupon he took the chair next to mine.

"No need to ask if the honeymoon was a success, is there, Dickon?" said my mother.

"Bliss and contentment shine from their eyes," replied Dickon.

"And to think," said Jonathan, "that while you were discovering the joys of matrimony, I was bartering for a boat in Ostend."

"So you came that way," said David.

"My dear brother, where else? How do you think an Englishman would fare in Calais or some more convenient port? An Englishman . . . bringing Frenchwomen across the Channel! Have you any idea what it is like out there?"

"A vague one," replied David. "I did not expect for one moment that you could come through France."

"Jonathan will tell you about it sometime," said my mother. She was flashing a look at me and glancing at Sophie. I understood what she meant and so did David. The subject was too painful to be talked of in front of Sophie. We should hear all later when she was not one of the company.

"Well, here you are now and that is wonderful," I said. "We have been so worried."

My hand was lying on the table and Jonathan pressed it briefly. It was outwardly a brotherly gesture, but the touch of his hand on mine made me shiver.

"I have given Aunt Sophie the nursery rooms," said my mother.

"Oh . . . they haven't been used for years."

"I liked them as soon as I saw them," said Sophie.

"They arrived in the early hours of the morning. What a day that was!" My mother went on talking quickly. "I was so delighted . . . and then I looked for Charlot."

Dickon said: "He is doing what he wanted to do. You can't stop people doing that, you know, Lottie. He's got to live his own life."

"What will become of him?"

"Charlot will do well," said Dickon. "He's that sort. He'll soon rise to be a general in that rabble, you'll see."

David said dryly: "It seems to be doing surprisingly well for a rabble army."

"Yes indeed," agreed Dickon. "A surprise for us all. They've got some fight in them, those rebels. The French have always been excellent soldiers. I will say that for them."

He was looking at Lottie tenderly. He would never feel the same for his sons as she did for hers. Dickon was too self-centred; he was not the man to form sentimental attachments. That was why his obsession with my mother was so remarkable; and all the more intense, I supposed, because his affections were not divided.

"Oh yes," he went on, "Charlot has found his niche in the world—and his shadow Louis Charles with him. When this stupid war is over, when these bloodthirsty citizens of the Republic settle down, when sanity returns to France, reality will come with it. Then, Lottie, my love, you and I will pay a visit to France. We shall be graciously received by Monsieur le Général, sporting all the medals he has won . . . and you'll be very proud of him."

"Dickon, you are absurd. But you're right. He does know how to take care of himself."

They had taken the soup away and we were now being served with the roast beef.

"The roast beef of old England!" said Jonathan. "Nothing like it.

How I have longed for it." He pressed a little closer to me. ". . . among other things."

"Nothing like an absence from the old country to increase one's appreciation of it," commented Dickon.

Aunt Sophie spoke little English and the conversation at the table was half English, half French. Jonathan's French was like his father's—extremely anglicised.

I said: "I wonder how you ever got along over there."

He put his fingers to his lips and my mother said laughingly: "Do you think Jonathan would be defeated by a mere language? He'd override such obstacles. He's like his father."

Jonathan and Dickon looked at each other and laughed. There was a rapport between them which was lacking between Dickon and David. I supposed this was because they were so much alike.

"I hope you'll be comfortable in the nursery suite," said David to Sophie. He understood French very well indeed and spoke it moderately well, but his accent and intonation did not make him readily understood. I imagined that now Aunt Sophie was with us he would want to put that right. I smiled indulgently. He would want to practise his French with me. That was typical of him. He always wanted to master any intellectual exercise. Jonathan was the same with those matters which interested him, so they were alike in some ways. Jonathan, however, would never concern himself with such matters as perfecting himself in a language.

Sophie said: "Yes, thank you. I am comfortable. Those rooms suit my needs."

Her mood was one of aloofness. I saw what she meant. The nursery was apart from the rest of the house just as her quarters in the Château d'Aubigné had been and her great desire had been to set herself apart from the rest of the family. I think that was why she always made me feel that there was something not quite normal about her.

"It is perhaps temporary," she went on.

"Temporary?" I cried. "Oh, Aunt Sophie, are you thinking of staying only a short time in England?"

"No. I must stay here. There is no place for me or for Jeanne in France. We accept that." She looked at Jonathan. "Oh, I am grateful . . . very grateful. We could not have gone on living like that for ever. It was necessary that we leave, and we could never have done so but for the daring of Messieurs Jonathan, your brother and Louis Charles."

Jonathan inclined his head.

"They were very clever . . . very resourceful. Jeanne and I are forever grateful. But we are not penniless. You looked surprised, Claudine. But we are far from penniless. Jeanne has been very clever. We have brought a fortune out of France."

"A fortune!" I cried.

All eyes were on Sophie. There was a faint flush in her cheeks. She said: "Jeanne is farsighted. She saw this coming. For a long time before the revolution came she had been collecting the jewels together . . . hiding them. She was good with her needle; she sewed them into our clothes . . . rings, brooches . . . pendants . . . all the priceless gems which I had inherited from my mother . . . jewels which had been in the family for generations. They are very valuable. We have them here safely. Monsieur Dickon has examined them. Monsieur Jonathan also. They assure me that I have enough to live on in comfort . . . affluence enough . . . for the rest of my life."

"That's wonderful!" I cried. "Clever, clever Jeanne."

"She is more than clever," said my mother, with tears in her eyes. "She is a good woman."

"Dear Step-mama," said Jonathan lightly, "you speak as though a good woman is something of a phenomenon."

"Anyone as good and selfless as Jeanne—man or woman—is a rare creature," said my mother.

"David, isn't that wonderful?" I said.

"It must have been very risky," replied David, "not only getting out of France, but bringing a fortune with you."

"I like risks," said Jonathan. "You know that, brother."

"But such a risk!"

Dickon was looking at his son with approval. He, too, loved risks; he too would have brought that fortune out of France.

"I shall find a house," said Sophie.

"That should not be difficult," I put in.

"Somewhere near perhaps. Neither Jeanne nor I speak the language well, and we should feel safer under the protection of Eversleigh."

"That's a wonderful idea!" I cried. "Then we can visit frequently. That's if you invite us."

She gave me a rather tender look. "I shall ask you to come to see me, Claudine," she said.

"There, my dear," said Jonathan again, touching my hand. "You are honoured."

"We shall all visit you," said my mother.

"Are there any houses near here?" said Sophie.

"The two nearest are Grasslands and Enderby. Grasslands is occupied, but Enderby is empty," I said.

"Enderby!" cried my mother. "Claudine, you're surely not suggesting Enderby!"

"I just said it was empty."

"It's a gruesome sort of house," said my mother.

"Only because of the shrubs which grow round it," pointed out David.

"It has an evil reputation," said my mother.

Dickon and Jonathan laughed. "You are fanciful, Lottie," said Dickon.

"No. I think this happens to houses."

"Is it for sale?" asked Sophie.

"I am sure it is," I said.

"Yes," said Dickon, "the key is at Grasslands. That's the nearest house."

"David and I went in there a little while ago," I said. "Didn't we, David?"

"Oh? Did you get the keys?" asked Dickon.

"No. A latch was broken on one of the windows and we climbed through into the hall."

"Such adventurous spirits!" said Dickon ironically.

"It's a grim old place, Aunt Sophie," I said.

"I tell you it is just a matter of cutting down the shrubs and letting in the light," explained David. "I am sure that would make a world of difference."

"I should like to look at it," said Sophie.

"At least," said my mother almost grudgingly, "it would be near us. And, as you said, you would not want to be too far away."

"Perhaps tomorrow I shall look. I shall take Jeanne with me. She will know."

"Oh dear," said my mother lightly, "are you so eager to leave us?"

"I do not wish to encroach . . ." replied Sophie.

"My dear Sophie, we are overjoyed to have you."

Sabrina, who had appeared to be dozing, suddenly said: "Enderby is a strange house. But when my mother was mistress of it, it was a very happy house. It was only after she died that it became morbid again."

"Well, you know the old house better than any of us," said my mother. She turned to Sophie. "Dickon's mother was born there. She lived her childhood there. So she can tell you what you want to know about it."

A glazed look came over Sabrina's eyes. "It is so long ago," she said. "Oh years and years and yet sometimes I remember those days more clearly than what happened yesterday."

"I look forward to seeing this house," said Sophie. "I will talk to Jeanne, and tomorrow, if that is possible, we will see it."

"We could send over to Grasslands for the key," said my mother.

"May I come with you?" I asked eagerly. "I should love to have a good look at the house."

"Won't it be rather tame going in through the front door after climbing through the window?" asked Jonathan.

"It is really something of an adventure setting foot in that house."

So it was arranged.

Dinner was over and my mother said: "Sabrina is very tired. I shall take her to her room. And I daresay Sophie would like to retire also, wouldn't you, my dear?"

Sophie said she would.

"Claudine will take you up."

"I can find my own way," said Sophie.

I went to her and laid my hand on her arm. "Please, I should love to see Jeanne again."

Sophie gave me that rather special smile which I noticed she rarely gave to anyone else, and we went up the stairs together.

Jeanne was waiting for her in the nursery rooms. "Jeanne," I said, "how good to see you!"

She grasped my hand and I studied her intently. There were grey strands in her dark hair. She had lived through much stress and strain.

"Mademoiselle Claudine," she said, "I am happy to be here and have Mademoiselle Sophie safe."

"Yes, your ordeal must have been terrible."

Jeanne nodded to me meaningfully. "You are tired," she said to Sophie.

"A little," admitted Sophie.

"Then I shall say good night," I said. "If there is anything you need . . ."

"Your mother has taken good care of us," Jeanne told me.

"I have heard of a house," said Sophie to Jeanne.

"I will leave you to talk about it," I said. "Don't get too hopeful. Enderby isn't everyone's home."

Then I said good night and left them.

On the way down I met my mother on her way from Sabrina's room. She put an arm round me and held me close to her.

"I am so glad you are back . . . and happy. Oh yes, I can see you are happy. It was wonderful in London, wasn't it? You with David . . ."

"It was perfect," I told her.

"What a pity you had to cut it short."

"I couldn't really see why."

"Dickon is deeply involved with . . . affairs. I worry sometimes. He has secrets . . . even from me. I think the death of the Queen will have some important effect on things over here. In any case, you and David can go back to London later."

"Of course."

"What do you think of Sophie?"

"She was always a little . . . strange."

"I thought she seemed more—friendly . . . more shall I say—normal. She must have suffered a great deal."

"I suppose all that would change anyone. Wasn't it wonderful about the jewels?"

"It was a terrible risk. However, you'll hear about it. We don't want to go through it all in front of Sophie. Jonathan will tell you all about it."

The men were in the punch room, where a fire was burning in the fireplace. They rose as we entered.

"Come and sit down," said Dickon. "Unless you are tired."

"I'd like to talk a little," I said. "There is so much to hear about."

Jonathan had come swiftly to my side; he laid a hand on my arm. "Come and sit down," he said; and I sat between him and David. My mother took the chair opposite Dickon.

"I didn't want to talk too much in front of Sophie," said my mother. "It must have been a nightmare she has been living through all this time. Just think of it. Day in, day out . . . never knowing when the mob would turn against them. Jonathan, do tell Claudine and David the story you have told us."

"I had better start at the beginning," he said. "We had already made arrangements for getting across when we left the house that day and made our way to the coast where the boat was ready waiting for us. It was a fishing boat and the owner was doing a very brisk business with émigrés. He was able to change our money into French currency, and there was a small rowing boat in which we were taken ashore at a very lonely spot on a dark moonless night.

"So we were there. Charlot was quite ingenious. He is a good actor. He transformed himself into a small trader with a cart—which we managed to acquire, with a horse, not very handsome in appearance but a strong creature of whom we all became very fond. Louis Charles and I were the servants. I was of a lower grade posing as dumb, as I was unable to speak the language proficiently. They were afraid for me to open my mouth, which they said would have given the whole show away.

"We made a slow journey to Aubigné, encountering difficulty after difficulty. I could not keep up the dumb act, so they thought my French might be mistaken for a patois. I was to be a native of the country in the south, right on the Spanish border, which was to be the reason why I spoke so badly. You'd be shocked if you could see the place, Stepmama. There are chickens running all over the lawns, the flowerbeds are overgrown and the pools full of stagnant water. I never saw it in its grandeur, but there was just enough of an outline left to show me how splendid it must have been."

"It was splendid," put in Dickon. "All that good land . . . gone to waste. The stupid vandals! They will ruin their country."

"Well," went on Jonathan, "our big disappointment came when we reached the *château,* for neither Sophie nor Jeanne was in residence. We dared not ask for them and we were in a quandary then. Charlot did not want to go too far away—and in any case we did not know where to go. But he was afraid he might be known and recognized if he went to an inn in the town, despite his disguise. Louis Charles also felt that. So I went to the wine shops there. I would sit about drinking and listening to the talk . . . not saying much and pretending to be a little foolish and not understanding what they were talking about. They were quite tolerant of me."

"It is always a good thing to act the fool," said David. "It makes others feel superior, and that is what they enjoy."

"Well, I did quite well really. There was a girl who served the wine. What was her name? Marie . . . that's it. She took pity on me and used to talk to me. I marked her down. I could discover a good deal from her, I believed. I could ask her what I dared not ask the others. I did rather well with Marie. I would creep out of the wine shop and join the others, who were sleeping in the cart. In time I got Marie to talk to me about the old days and the family at the *château.* What scandals I heard, dear Step-mama!"

"There are always scandals about people like my father."

"It seems he was quite good at making it. I heard about his romantic marriage with your mother and how she died. That was shocking. I plied Marie with the grape and finally I discovered that Armand had died and they had buried him at the *château.* His companion had left, so there were only three women at the *château* then.

"They were suspicious of them. How did they live? Mademoiselle Sophie was a kind of invalid but she was an aristocrat . . . and Jeanne and the old housekeeper were a smart pair. They must have held something back . . . and what were they doing anyway living with an aristocrat!

"Someone must have warned Jeanne that feelings were rising against them and she decided to move on, and one day it was discovered that there was no one at the *château.* How long they had been gone, no one was sure. Where had they gone? I wondered. Marie was a well-informed girl. She could guess there were two places to which they might have gone. The old housekeeper who was known as Tante Berthe had a family somewhere in the country. And Jeanne Fougère came from the Dordogne district. She was a secretive person but Marie remembered that one day someone had come from Périgord, and had seen Jeanne when she was shopping and had asked her name. When this person had been told that she was Jeanne Fougère who looked after a sick woman at the *château,* he said he thought he had recognized her for he knew the Fougère family who lived in Périgord.

"That was the best clue we could get, so we left for the south at once, driving the poor old horse over those rough roads, for we had to keep well away from the towns. Few showed any interest in us, so I suppose we looked like good old compatriots. Charlot sung the 'Marseillaise' with fervour and I learned to sing it with 'Ça Ira.' These are the great songs of the revolution and a knowledge of them is considered by the peasants necessary to a good patriot.

"I won't dwell on the details now, but I can tell you we had many a narrow escape. There were many occasions when we almost betrayed ourselves—and how near we came to disaster! It is very hard for an aristocrat—and Charlot is one if ever there was one—not to assume an air of superiority at times. I do believe I played my part with distinction —the half-witted loony from some vague spot in the south where they spoke a patois almost unrecognizable to good citizens of the République. It was easier for me than for Charlot.

"After many vicissitudes which I shall recall later—if any of you should be desirous of hearing them—we tracked down the good Jeanne's family. There was only a brother and sister left in the little farmhouse. They had taken in the wandering jewel-laden pair and tried to make a good little peasant out of Sophie—not with any great success, and there they were.

"The housekeeper had made her way back to her own family and Jeanne and Sophie were on their own. Well, they joined us in the cart . . . Sophie as Charlot's mother—a role which I think she rather enjoyed since she had to play a part—and Jeanne was the wife of Louis Charles. There was no one for me and I felt a little piqued at first—but of course it was due to necessity."

"It must have been doubly alarming travelling as you were with Sophie and Jeanne carrying the jewels," I said.

"Well, it was. But Jeanne is a clever woman. Sophie did as well as she could but Jeanne was wonderful. She went into the little towns to shop for us and of course she did not have to change her personality as we did ours."

"Did she go into the town with the gems sewn into her petticoats?" I asked.

"She must have done so. She did not tell us about the jewels until we were on the boat crossing the Channel."

"What would you have done had you known?"

Jonathan shrugged his shoulders. "What could we do? We shouldn't have left them behind. But I think our anxieties would have been increased. Jeanne knew that, so she decided not to place that extra burden on our shoulders. One of these days I'll tell you about some of the adventures we passed through, all the alarms and escapes. It will take weeks. And in any case I can't remember them all. When we finally got to Ostend Charlot decided he would go back to France and the army; and of course Louis Charles went with him. So they entrusted to me the task of bringing Sophie and Jeanne to England. I remember how we slipped away and they stood on the shore watching us." He turned to my mother. "Charlot hoped you would understand. He was very definite about that. He wanted you to know that he could not continue to live quietly in England while his country was in turmoil."

"I do understand," said my mother quietly.

She had been deeply moved when Jonathan was talking and Dickon watched her anxiously.

He rose and said: "Let us go up."

He and my mother said good night and left us—myself sitting between David and Jonathan.

We were silent for a while. I stared into the fire and saw pictures there. Jonathan in the wine shop with Marie . . . and I wondered what that had entailed. How strange that of all the adventures I should think of that. I pictured his trundling across France, playing his part. I was sure that he had enjoyed the danger of it . . . just as his father had. David would have hated it. He would have seen only the squalor, the pity, and the futility of it all.

A log had collapsed, sending out a spray of little sparks. Jonathan rose and filled his glass with the port wine he had been drinking.

"David?" he said, the decanter poised.

David said: "No thanks."

"Claudine?"

I too declined.

"Oh come, just a little toast to my safe return."

He poured the wine into our glasses. I lifted mine. "Welcome home."

His eyes met mine and I saw the blue flames which I remembered so well.

"You have been very lucky," said David. "So . . . welcome home."

"My dear brother, I am always lucky." He looked at me and frowned; then he added in a low voice: "Well, not always but almost always, and when I am not I know how to make the best of the situation."

"There must have been moments when you really thought the end had come," said David.

"I never felt that. You know me. I would always find a way out, however impossible the situation seemed."

"You certainly believe in yourself," I said.

"With good cause, dear Claudine. With very good cause, I assure you."

"No wonder Lottie was a little upset by all those revelations," said David. "That wine shop you were in with the girl . . . that must have been the one opposite the *mairie* where she was held on that awful night."

"Yes," I said. "I remember her telling how the mob ransacked the place and the wine ran out into the street all over the cobbles."

"Our father brought her home far more dramatically than I brought Sophie and Jeanne," said Jonathan.

"You brought them home. That was all that mattered," I told him fervently.

"And came safely through myself. Surely that is a matter of some importance to you."

"Of the utmost, of course."

He leaned over me very closely and said: "Thank you, sister-in-law. That's what you are now. You were step-sister before, weren't you? Now you are sister-in-law and step-sister both. *Mon Dieu,* as they say in that benighted country which I am so thankful to have left, what a complicated family we are!"

We were silent, sipping our port and gazing into the fire. I was very much aware of Jonathan and it seemed symbolic in some way that I was sitting there between the two brothers.

I felt very disturbed. All the peace I had known in London was gone; and something told me that I should never know it again.

I had to get away.

"I'm tired," I said. "I'm going to say good night."

David said: "I'll come up soon."

I went to my room. I hastily got into bed. It was not true that I was tired. I was, in fact, wide awake. I was trying to look into the future and I did so with some apprehension. There was that in Jonathan's attitude and one or two of his rather ambiguous remarks which had unsettled me.

I wished he had not come home. That was not true. I was wildly excited because he had come home. And I was looking into the future with trepidation because he would certainly be involved in it. I was fearful and yet awaiting what was to come with an intensity of feeling which I had never known before.

When David came up I pretended to be asleep.

He kissed me gently, tenderly, so as not—he thought—to wake me.

I resisted the impulse to put my arms about his neck and return his kiss. But I could not do that. I felt that if I did I might betray the inner excitement which possessed me and which he might guess had been engendered by Jonathan.

Voices in a Haunted Room

The next morning my mother sent one of the grooms over to Grasslands to ask for the key of Enderby, as a prospective buyer, who was staying at Eversleigh, wished to look over it during the afternoon.

The groom came back with a message from the manager to the effect that Mrs. Trent and her grand-daughters had gone into the town and would not be back until later that morning. As he did not know where the key was he could not send it, but if we would be at Enderby at three that afternoon he would make sure that someone came to us with the key.

That was very satisfactory, said my mother.

Enderby was no more than ten minutes' walk across country from Eversleigh, and Sophie said she would be quite happy to walk the distance; and she and Jeanne came along, with me to show them the way.

I said: "It is a big house and it will be dark soon after four, which leaves us about an hour to look round. But that will be enough for you to get an idea whether you want to think seriously about it. If you did, we could keep the key and you could browse there all through the next day. You might decide immediately that it is quite hopeless."

"Everyone seems determined that we shall think that," said Sophie. "But we shall make up our own minds, shan't we, Jeanne?"

Jeanne said that that was what Mademoiselle usually did.

"Well, I shall not say a word—for or against," I promised.

An early November afternoon was certainly not the best time to see Enderby. There was the faintest of mists in the air and little globules of moisture clung like crystal beads to the spiders' webs festooned in large numbers on the overgrown bushes.

The house rose before us, grey, grim and ghostly, I thought. I glanced sideways at Sophie.

She was staring at it, but as her hood hid the side of her face from me, I could not tell whether she was experiencing pleasure or revulsion.

Then Mrs. Trent emerged from among the bushes; she was smiling and holding the key.

"Oh there you are Miss er . . . Oh it's Mrs. now. Have to get used to that. No longer Mademoiselle de Tourville, but Mrs. Frenshaw."

"That's so. Thanks for bringing the key."

Her grand-daughters came from round the side of the house.

"Good afternoon," I said.

"Good afternoon, Mrs. Frenshaw," said the girls.

Dorothy—Dolly—was looking at Sophie as though fascinated, and I saw that Sophie had noticed her too. There would be a fellow feeling because of their disfigurement, I guessed.

"This is the lady who is interested in the house, Mrs. Trent," I said. "She does not speak much English. She is my mother's half sister."

"My word! Is she now! I'll open the door for you. When these keys are not used often, they get hard to turn. Ah, there we are!"

The door was opened and we were in the hall. Sophie looked at Jeanne and gave a little gasp.

I stepped in with them. I had expected the Trents to go but they came in with us.

"My goodness," said Mrs. Trent. "I'd forgotten how grand it was. Although I've got the key I never come in. That's the gallery where the musicians play. We've heard a lot about that gallery, haven't we?"

"Yes," I said, and added rather pointedly: "Thank you, Mrs. Trent, it was good of you to bring the key."

"Oh, that's nothing. I like to have a look round myself. The girls know quite a lot about it, don't you, girls? They've always been interested in this house."

"It's the sort of house you can be interested in," said Evie.

I noticed again how pretty she was with her fair curling hair and dark-lashed blue eyes. She was a real beauty—or perhaps one thought so in contrast to her sister. Poor little Dolly! Her sad face fitted the house.

"It's more exciting than Grasslands," went on Evie.

"Oh, is it, Miss? That's a nice way to talk about your home. I'll take Grasslands any day. At least we haven't got ghosts springing out round every corner."

I wondered what the owners would think of Mrs. Trent as a custodian of their property. She was certainly not going to encourage buyers with such talk.

I said with light reproof: "It is fortunate that Mademoiselle d'Aubigné cannot understand you or she would be deterred from considering the house."

Mrs. Trent clapped her hands over her mouth. "My big tongue! It always was a bit of a clacker."

Evie looked embarrassed and I noticed that Dolly watched her sister all the time as though she felt insecure without her.

"There is some furniture in the place," went on Mrs. Trent, by no means abashed. "Some of it's supposed to be quite good. It goes with the house. Mind you, a bit of renovation would be needed."

I walked away from her, following Jeanne and Sophie to the staircase.

"Do you want to see the rest?" I asked.

"But of course," replied Sophie.

"There's a loose board on the first floor," called out Mrs. Trent. "Evie . . . you know where. Go up and show them."

Evie followed Sophie and Jeanne up the staircase and Dolly went with her.

I was looking about the hall. I thought I would allow them to look round on their own and I hoped that Evie would go when she had shown them the loose board.

"The stairs are a bit much for me," explained Mrs. Trent. She came close to me. "What do you think of my Evie?"

"She's very attractive."

Mrs. Trent beamed. "She is. None could deny it. I'd like her to do well for herself." She spoke a little wistfully. "It's not easy. People have never taken to me in these parts. They never forget. Oh, I've been invited here and there now and again. But it's not the same. I want my Evie to do well. I'd like to see her mistress of some grand house . . . with looks like that."

I thought that perhaps in the right environment, which meant away from her grandmother, Evie might be very attractive.

"Well, there is time to go yet," I said.

"I wouldn't say that. She's sixteen, coming up to seventeen, much of a muchness with yourself. No hesitation about you. It was going to be one of them, wasn't it? And I don't suppose it mattered which one. They've both got a tidy bit coming to them."

She really was an impossible woman.

Evie appeared at the head of the stairs.

"Did you show them the loose board?"

"Yes, Grandmamma. And I told them where they must look for others."

"There's a lot wants doing to this house. Where's Dolly?"

"She was talking to the lady with the hood."

"Can they understand each other?"

"Not very well."

"I'll go and see how they are getting on," I said.

I went up the stairs, leaving Mrs. Trent and Evie in the hall. Why didn't the woman see that she was intruding? She was ignorant and ill-bred. I wanted to tell her that she would have little hope of catching a husband for her grand-daughter if she behaved with such crudity. I found Sophie with Jeanne on the first floor.

They were going through the bedrooms there.

"They are spacious," Jeanne was saying, "and could be made attractive."

Sophie replied: "Such a lot would have to be done."

"You would enjoy doing it," Jeanne told her.

They mounted the stairs with Dolly in their wake. I felt an urge to look at the rooms. I went into the main bedroom. There was a high four-poster bed there. I touched the curtains and they almost disintegrated in my hands, so old were they, but the wood of the bed was very solid and beautifully carved; and the court cupboard on the other side of the room would look very fine if polished. Yes, it was true, there was a great deal of good furniture in the place and going with the house.

But of course Sophie could not be seriously thinking of taking it. It was too large really . . . just for her and Jeanne. This was a house which needed people—lots of them—a jolly family, parties at Christmas and such times, dancing in the hall.

I went along to the smaller bedroom where I had once fancied I heard a voice. I stood in the centre of the room. There was a four-poster there, smaller than the other, more modern, and the curtains about it were quite good—heavy blue velvet; but they were very dusty and there were cobwebs in the room.

A ghostly room, I thought. But that was because I had fancied I heard a voice here.

Then I heard it again. The same hollow voice. It said: "You're being watched, Mrs. Frenshaw."

I stared up at the ceiling, at the walls; I stood, bewildered, looking about me.

"Who's there?" I cried sharply.

Silence, and then clearly I heard the quick intake of breath, the low laugh . . . horrible laughter. Someone was jeering at me.

I went to the door. There was no one in the corridor.

I was shaking. Why should I imagine I could hear voices in this room? There was no one here. I must have imagined it and yet I could have sworn . . .

Dolly was coming down the stairs.

"Is Mademoiselle still up there?" I asked.

"Yes. They like it."

"No," I replied. "They are just interested."

She shook her head. "They do like it. It suits the lady. It's what she wants."

"She won't make a hasty decision."

I had stepped back into the room and Dolly had followed me. I had a good opportunity of studying her. The drawn-down eye gave her an evil look at times—and yet the rest of her was so dainty, fragile even. Her good eye was large, blue and heavily lashed; her nose was delicate and well shaped. But for the deformity she would have been a beauty like her sister.

"Do you like this room, Mrs. Frenshaw?" she asked.

"No. I don't think I like any of the house."

"I like this house," she said almost rapturously. She stood in the middle of the room and looked up at the ceiling.

Then I heard it again, the quick intake of breath and the low, quiet, sneering laughter.

"Who is that?" I asked.

Dolly was staring blankly at me.

"Didn't you hear something, someone close . . . laughing?"

Dolly looked at me oddly. "I didn't hear anyone," she said.

"But—it was quite distinct."

She shook her head. "I didn't hear anything," she repeated. "There are echoes in old houses. Besides, who could there be? There's no one here."

I went to the door and looked out. I felt I did not want to stay in that haunted room with the strange girl.

I hurried up to the next floor. Sophie and Jeanne were in close conversation.

Jeanne was saying what could be done, how they would furnish it. How they would use the space.

It can't be true, I thought. Sophie is seriously considering Enderby.

On our walk back to Eversleigh Sophie was very quiet. Of course, I was telling myself, she is not really serious. There was something quite fascinating about looking at houses and considering them as potential homes; and I had to remember that Sophie had just come through a shattering experience. It must seem very exciting to her to be safe, to be in a position to consider making a home for herself in a new country.

My mother was waiting for us when we returned and Dickon was with her.

She said: "I was hoping you would come in before it was dark. How did you get on?"

"The Trents were there with the key—grandmother and two granddaughters."

"And what did you think of Enderby, Sophie?"

Sophie clasped her hands together and half closed her eyes. "I found it very . . . interesting."

"Oh, it's that all right. None would deny it, but . . . as a home . . ."

Sophie looked at Jeanne, who said: "Mademoiselle Sophie wants to see it again tomorrow."

"Oh," said my mother, "so you weren't completely put off."

Sophie shook her head emphatically.

"So you will go tomorrow," went on my mother. "Will you go with them, Claudine?"

"It is not necessary," said Sophie. "We know our way now and we have the key."

"I'd like to come . . . unless you want to go alone, Aunt Sophie."

She smiled at me. "Come with us then . . . but you mustn't try to dissuade me."

"I wouldn't dream of it. But you can't seriously . . ."

Sophie turned to Dickon. "I should like to talk to you about getting the money."

"I shall be going to London early tomorrow," said Dickon, "so perhaps you could talk to me right away."

"I'll come to your room."

He said: "I'll see you shortly, Lottie. Don't forget we are leaving at dawn tomorrow . . ."

My mother nodded and Dickon went off with Sophie, Jeanne following.

My mother looked at me in amazement. "She's surely not thinking of buying that house!"

"She seemed rather taken with it. It is a fascinating place. In a way she somehow seems to fit into it."

"Yes. I see what you mean. I hope she won't take it and live there like a hermit."

"Could she buy it?"

"Many times over, I imagine. Dickon has seen the jewellery they brought with them. It really is fantastic. The Count was a very rich man, one of the richest in France, and I imagine his first wife brought more wealth into the family. The jewels are priceless, so Dickon says, and there won't be any difficulty in disposing of them. Of course other émigrés are trying to sell what they have salvaged, but I should imagine few have such a collection as that which Sophie has brought with her. Jeanne had been hiding them for quite a long time. She is a farsighted woman; moreover her visits to the town and her chats with people must have given her a clearer view of what was coming than that of the people in the *château.* Sophie, most certainly, would be able to buy the house and live there independent of us all, as far as finances are concerned. She is delighted because although she is very welcome here, she wants to be on her own, and I understand that. She doesn't want to be dependent on Dickon's charity. Dickon says that Enderby is about one of the biggest bargains one could find anywhere in the country. It has stood empty for so long and it has that ghostly reputation. A great deal would have to be done, of course, but it is still a bargain. I believe certain furniture has been left there. Some of it is so big that it would be difficult to move it. It must have been made on the premises. Whether that's true, I don't know; but I believe some of it has been there almost as long as the house."

"Imagine Sophie and Jeanne alone in that house. They would have servants though . . . and perhaps guests to stay."

"What guests! Can you imagine Sophie entertaining? Oh, Claudine, I hope she doesn't take it. I've never liked the house. I hoped it would crumble away . . . that the roof and the walls would fall in and birds would rest there and the rats and mice take over the last stages of destruction."

"Oh, Maman, how can you condemn it to such a fate? It is a house, after all. I know it's haunted. I would never be happy living there, but to condemn it to destruction . . . it's like condemning a person."

"What on earth are you talking about?"

"I think we are both talking a lot of nonsense. . . . How long will you be in London?"

"As long as Dickon's work keeps him there."

"His work . . . in the bank?"

"I expect sometimes in the bank."

"What has that to do with the death of the Queen of France?"

"These things affect finance. There is a great deal involved."

"And Dickon is involved . . . and I suspect in many things."

"Dickon," she said with a little laugh, "has a finger in many pies."

"Secret pies . . . secret even from you, Maman?"

"If they were secret he couldn't tell even me, could he? And I could not ask him to."

"It is all so mysterious! I know that Dickon is a big landowner and banker and is mixed up with politics in a way about which we are not supposed to enquire. But when you think of the way in which he got you out of France . . . well, he must have many contacts there."

She smiled at me. "I should thank God for it, Claudine. If it had not been so, I should not be here at this moment."

I threw my arms about her. "I thank God for it too, dearest Maman. I can't bear to think of it. A world without you! Always be here!"

"Always here to do what I can for you, my love."

I drew away from her; her smile was tremulous.

She said: "Then, Claudine, let us be thankful for what is and not probe into matters which we are not meant to know. I must go now. I want to make sure they are packing the right things."

"Can I help you?"

She shook her head.

When she left me I went out into the gardens. Whenever I thought of how near my mother had come to death, I was so filled with emotion and terror that I had to be alone, to reassure myself that it was over. It's finished, I would tell myself. She is safe. We shall never let her risk her life again. Dickon would never allow it. I was thankful for Dickon—my powerful stepfather who loved her with an unswerving devotion; he would always take care of her, and because no one could get the better of him, she would be safe while he was there to protect her.

The damp November air cooled my cheeks. It was dark now. I should be glad when the nights began to draw out, which would not be until after Christmas. My thoughts went back to Enderby, that strange house, and the voices I had heard. What was the meaning of that? Some would say I was imagining I heard voices simply because Enderby was the sort of house where one would expect to. I knew about my grandmother Zipporah, who had loved the Count in this very house, and where it was almost certain my mother had been conceived. The house had played a big part in our family history, perhaps that was why it had such an effect on me. My grandmother had fallen in love, broken her marriage vows and taken her first steps towards a violent death in a square in a French town—and it had all begun at Enderby.

But the voices? I heard them on two occasions. Were they in my mind? That girl had said she heard nothing. But she seemed a little vacant, and the laughter had been low. I hoped Sophie would decide against the house and find somewhere else. Then I should never go near it again.

I must go in. It would soon be time to change for dinner. I wondered whether Sophie would join us. I expected she would as she would want to talk about the house. On the other hand she might prefer to talk about it alone with Jeanne. Perhaps she would change her mind in the morning. Would Enderby look any less sinister in the morning light? But the aspect of houses—as that of people—was not always seen in the same light by everyone. Beauty to some was not necessarily beauty to others; the same with evil; and what might arouse in some a desire to escape from it, might be irresistibly fascinating to others.

As I passed the shrubbery, a voice said: "Claudine!" and a hand seized me and pulled me into the shadow of the bushes.

"Jonathan!"

"I saw you leave the house," he said.

"Well, what do you want?"

"What do I want? That's an unnecessary question, isn't it? You know what I want. What have I always wanted? Why did you do it, Claudine? Why did you do it?"

He was holding me in a firm grip from which I could not escape. He drew me farther into the shrubbery.

"Let me go, Jonathan. I have to get back to the house."

"You'll talk to me first."

"What about?"

"About everything . . . this situation into which you have thrust me."

"I don't know what you are talking about."

His mouth was on mine. No, I thought. I must get away. I am afraid of him.

"You married my brother."

"Is that surprising? It was expected, and besides, I wanted to."

"You wanted me."

"No. You asked me, remember, and I refused."

"It was not meant to be a refusal."

"I am in the habit of saying what I mean."

"Not always," he contradicted. "Do you think I don't know? You are shaking now."

"Because you are behaving in a ridiculous manner. I don't like it and I want to go in."

"There speaks the virtuous matron."

"That is what I am and what I intend to remain."

"Do you really believe you will?"

"Jonathan, I am going in."

"Not yet. Why did you marry my brother? Why did you do this?"

"Because I love him and wanted him for my husband."

"You love him! What do you know of love?"

"A great deal more than you do, I imagine."

"There are many sides to love, Claudine. You need all of them. My brother knows more about the Greek philosophers than of love."

"I believe they professed to know a great deal about it."

He laughed suddenly. "Claudine," he said. "I don't give up, you know."

I shrugged my shoulders; he caught them in his hands and shook me.

"Do you think I'll let you go because of a mere marriage?"

"The adjective is most inappropriate. You are letting alliteration run away with common sense."

He laughed and said: "Claudine, it's good to be with you. What I wanted more than anything during those hideous months was to be with you. When I was lying in the grass at night with the stars overhead and the knowledge that the next day could be my last, I thought of you there with me, talking to me, making me laugh, and . . . making love together, Claudine."

"And with the girl in the wine shop?"

"Ah, you remember her! I saw your eyes glint when I was telling you about her. I knew what you were thinking. I was only able to tolerate her because in my thoughts I substituted you for her. That's how I feel about you. You are my Claudine. You always were since the day you came to Eversleigh . . . with your French clothes and your French manners and your amusing way with our language. I loved you even then. And now you are a respectable English matron, I love you even more. It grows every day and you cannot expect me to stand aside and say, 'It is over. She is now the wife of my brother. Adieu, sweet Claudine, you are not for me.' You *are* for me, Claudine. You are . . . and nobody is going to stop us."

"It takes two to come to such a decision."

"And when two are of the same mind it is inevitable."

"If they were, I suppose it would be. But in this case they most decidedly are not. I think you are despicable to make these suggestions to your brother's wife. How dare you talk about making love . . . if you call that diatribe love."

"It is not making love. It is the prelude to making love. If we can't make love within the sanctity of the church, we will do so outside it."

"What if I were to tell my mother what you have said to me tonight?"

"She would tell my father."

"He would be furious with you."

"On the other hand he would merely laugh. He would say, 'Let them work it out among themselves.' My father is very wise and experienced in these matters."

"And David . . . what if I were to tell him?"

"Ah, David, what would he say? There is bound to be a precedent for such an occurrence among the Greeks, the Romans, or the ancient Egyptians. He would consult his oracles and they would tell him what should be done."

"Jonathan, you must forget all this. Marry. Settle down. You are more often in London than here."

"I shall be where you are."

"You did not think that when you lightheartedly joined the expedition to France, and just left without telling us."

He drew me to him and held me against him. "I had to go, Claudine. It was very necessary that I go. And I had to go secretly."

"Without telling your father even! You just walked out."

"My father knew."

"But he was surprised."

"Things are not always what they seem," he said, shrugging his shoulders, and I thought: It is the secret matters in which they are involved . . . Jonathan with his father. They combine spying for their country with their business affairs. Jonathan is with his father in this. I am glad David is outside it.

"Tomorrow I leave for London," he said.

"So you are going with your father and my mother?"

He nodded.

"Secret business?" I asked.

He did not answer. "I shall be back soon," he said, "and then . . ."

"Nothing will have changed here."

"It doesn't need to. It will be as it is now."

"Then . . ."

"You want me as I want you, and I shall see that something is done about it."

For a few seconds he held me pressed against him; he kissed me fervently on my lips and throat. I allowed myself to stay with him . . . just for those few seconds. I knew he was right. I had never been aware of this ecstatic emotion with David.

Then I wrenched myself away and hurried into the house. He did not follow me, but I heard his low, triumphant laughter behind me.

As soon as it was light next morning, Dickon, my mother and Jonathan left for London.

Jeanne came to my room and said that she and Sophie were going to see the house again and she wondered whether I meant I should like to accompany them.

I said I should like to and within half an hour we were walking round by the road to Enderby. It was a little longer that way, but there had been a heavy downpour and it was too wet to go across the fields as we had on the previous day.

The house looked different again in the morning light. What a strange place it was! I had to admit that in spite of the fact that it appeared menacing, it attracted me, and I was as eager to open the door and go inside as the other two were.

Sophie said: "What I like about it is that it is apart. One would not feel overlooked here."

No, I thought, except by ghosts and spirits.

We were in the hall and the atmosphere closed round me. It was like tentacles drawing me in and holding me fast.

"This hall is really quite magnificent," I said. "Do you propose to hold dances here, Aunt Sophie? I can picture it with the minstrels playing in the gallery."

"No. I don't propose to entertain a great deal. But I like the hall, all the same. There is a sense of grandeur and yet it is simple in a way."

Simple? Yes, I supposed it was, compared with the *château* in which she had spent her childhood.

"Think of all the bedrooms," I said. "There are twenty of them. And then there are the servants' quarters at the top of the house."

"We shall need a few servants," said Sophie. "Your mother will help us engage them. It may be a little difficult for us . . . because of the language."

"I am sure she will be delighted to help. And if there is anything I can do, Aunt Sophie, you know I shall be only too happy."

"Thank you, Claudine. You're a good girl. Oh, there will be so much to do. I want to go upstairs. Come on, Jeanne. I can't wait."

I followed them up. I noticed the carved banisters and the elegantly moulded ceilings. Once it had been a beautiful house. Would it be so again with Sophie there? No, she was not what it needed. Again I thought this house is crying out for a big and joyous family to laugh and frolic and believe so fervently in the goodness of the world that they drive away all the morbid brooding ghosts.

Sophie would not do that.

I wondered what good, practical Jeanne thought of the project.

I had an opportunity to ask her while Sophie was in one of the bedrooms and I found myself in the corridor alone with her.

I said to her: "My aunt can't be serious about buying this house."

"But she is," said Jeanne.

"You must dissuade her. You must see how unsuitable it is."

"No," she said. "I think it is suitable. Have you seen how happy she is? There will be so much to do. It will take a very long time. I have always sought ways of bringing her alive to the world, of making her feel interested . . . excited even. Putting this house to rights will take a very long time. There will be work to be done, people to see, fabrics to be chosen. I plan to work on it room by room. It will take us several years. As soon as we came into the house I saw how it affected her and I knew it was what I had been looking for."

I was amazed, but I saw at once that Jeanne, with her usual practical outlook, was right. Sophie needed Enderby. Its very gloom appealed to her. She would not have wanted a house that was full of sunshine and ready for habitation. She liked its gloomy atmosphere, which matched her own, and the prospect of all the work which must be done made it very desirable in Jeanne's eyes.

"Jeanne!" Sophie was calling to her.

Jeanne smiled at me and immediately went to her mistress. They were in the main bedroom and Sophie was standing by the four-poster bed.

"Just look at this beautiful carving."

Jeanne said: "It is exquisite. And the furniture is included in the cost of the house."

"It is a bargain."

"It does show how eager the owner is to get rid of it," I reminded them.

"What colour curtains, Jeanne?" asked Sophie; and I had never before seen her so animated.

"We have to think of the rest of the room," said Jeanne cautiously. "We must decide nothing in a hurry. Let us wait and see what else we shall do."

I left them. I could not resist going into that smaller room along the corridor which I called the haunted room, the room of the voice.

I stood in the centre listening.

There was no sound at all but the light wind murmuring in the tall bushes.

Now that Jonathan had left the house it seemed a little more normal. David was very interested in Sophie's desire to buy Enderby. I told him what Jeanne had said and he thought she was right.

"The house could make all the difference to her," he said. "It will take her away from her own misfortunes. Give her an interest in life, something to be proud of."

He wanted to see it again and we went over it together. He had a way of making everything seem as it should be. It was hard to imagine I had ever heard—or imagined I had heard—voices, when I was standing in that room with David.

"Its aspect could be completely changed," he said. "I've always said that if those bushes were cut back and a little light let in, and the woodwork repaired, it would make all the difference."

"There's a great deal of work to be done."

"That's what Sophie has always needed . . . an interest."

"Fate has brought her here and led her to Enderby."

"Fate," he agreed, "in the shape of Jonathan."

The very mention of his name affected me. I could not forget that talk in the shrubbery. I shivered.

"Are you cold?" asked David.

"No . . . no."

"Just someone walking over your grave, as they say."

"I hate that expression."

"I do too. I shouldn't have said it. One shouldn't refer to one's grave when one is very much in the land of the living." He put an arm around me. "I believe you would like to live in this house."

"No, David, *no!*"

"I've often thought about these big family houses like Eversleigh with the whole family living in it. The sons marrying and bringing in their wives . . . and their children growing up there. It has occurred to me . . . in the last few days . . . that you might not like it and might prefer to get away."

"I hadn't thought of that." I was thinking of it now. Jonathan's living under the same roof. He had few scruples where his desires were concerned. He was like his father in that. I had heard tales of Dickon's wild youth. He had reformed not because he considered reformation desirable, but because he loved my mother exclusively. It was purely his own emotions—not a sense of honour—which kept him faithful. Eversleigh had become dangerous to me because it held Jonathan and me in close proximity. But how could I tell David that? And that the one I feared was not so much Jonathan as myself.

"There are houses on the estate," went on David. "For instance, the manager's."

"Occupied by a manager at the moment."

"Jack Dolland is a good fellow. I don't know what we'd do without him. It was just an idea. I don't think my father would like it . . . but I did wonder whether you did not care for living in the main house. Of course, your mother is there."

"I am sure she would be most upset if we talked of going anywhere else."

"Then we'll stay. In any case, I don't think it would be feasible just yet. It was just a thought."

"Why did you bring it up now? Oh . . . Enderby, I suppose. David, I love Eversleigh. I have since the moment I saw it. I should not want to leave it."

"Then that's settled," he said. "You know, this really is a bargain house."

"A great deal will have to be spent on renovations."

"Even so there is some good furniture in it."

"It will certainly save Sophie's buying a lot."

"I believe there is also furniture stored away in the attics at Eversleigh. I expect your mother will go through them and see what can be passed on."

"It is rather exciting, isn't it? I mean for us all, not only Sophie. It will be nice to have the place occupied."

He agreed, and arm in arm we went through the house. It was strange how different it felt with David.

They were pleasant days, though I could not quite recapture the honeymoon spirit. We rode round the estate together; David was welcomed everywhere. So was I.

Sophie and Jeanne spent hours talking about the house, and I told them that Molly Blackett would be able to make the curtains for them.

They discussed materials and colour schemes; and it really was extraordinary to see the change in Sophie.

Jonathan, my mother and Dickon were away for just over a week. The weather had changed and it was less mild than it had been. The damp and the mists had given way to an east wind—the one we knew very well in this south-eastern corner of England. It could be penetrating and fierce, and although we were sheltered a little, being a few miles inland, it was never very welcome.

It turned to the north and that could bring snow. I had been a little anxious for fear the snow would delay their journey, perhaps prevent their getting home, so when I heard the carriage turn in at the drive I ran down joyfully to meet them.

I embraced my mother and we clung together.

"Oh, I'm glad to be home," she said. "Just look at the sky. Ominous! Those are snow clouds up there."

"It's too early for snow," said Dickon. "It usually comes after Christmas. How have you been getting on without us, Claudine?"

He kissed me. And there was Jonathan, smiling at me, picking me up, swinging me high, holding me tightly and laughing up at me.

"Do you know," he said, "I forget she's a married woman now. I see her as little French Claudine."

My mother laughed and so did Dickon. They were so glad to be home.

Jonathan put me down and kissed me hard on the mouth.

"So you're pleased to have us home, eh?"

"Of course," I said, turning away and slipping my arm through that of my mother. "I think Aunt Sophie has really decided."

"I can't believe it," said my mother.

Of course, Jonathan's being home shattered my peace. He seemed to watch me all the time and I was constantly aware of him. I avoided him. Something warned me. It was that alarming discovery that I was not so much afraid of him as of myself. I was thinking of him all the time.

My mother—once she had recovered from her surprise and misgivings about Sophie's taking Enderby—threw herself wholeheartedly into the project. She brought in Molly Blackett and they discussed curtains and such things. She went through the furniture in the attics, and the main topic of conversation was Enderby.

Dickon said the sale would not take long to be completed. He had had no difficulty in disposing of a magnificent diamond ring which would be ample for the purchase of the house.

Sophie could not wait to get possession. Meanwhile we had the key of the house and she could spend as much time as she liked there. Molly Blackett had been summoned to take measurements; Sophie and Jeanne went into the town to make purchases. My mother said they should go to London where they would find a great variety of materials to choose from.

Sophie demurred but at last decided it was a good idea.

It was about three weeks before Christmas. The threatened snow had not come as the wind had changed abruptly and we were back to the warmish damp weather again—the kind which was usual at this time of the year in our part of the country.

My mother said she would accompany Sophie and Jeanne to London for they need stay only for a few days; and it was arranged that they should go. My mother had some Christmas shopping to do in any case. Right at the last minute—as I guessed he would—Dickon said he would go with them.

While they were away Molly Blackett was to do some more measuring and take down some of the old curtains to see if anything could be done with them; and also to note what fittings would be needed. I said I would go with Molly and explain what was wanted.

That was how it came about that I was in the house on that December day.

I had arranged with Molly to come at two o'clock, which would give us a good two hours before darkness fell. David would be busy all day on the estate.

I rode over and let myself in.

It was strange to be alone there. The house seemed different—my imagination again—as though it were watching and waiting . . . waiting to spring something on me.

I was early and Molly had not yet arrived. She had to come from the cottages on the Eversleigh estate, and I was sure she would be there in a few minutes, for she prided herself on her punctuality.

My impulse had been to wait outside for her; but chiding myself for cowardice, I had forced myself to go in.

My footsteps echoed on the stone floor of the hall; I looked up at the gallery and wondered what had induced Sophie to take such a place.

We were going to do the measurements upstairs, and I had a great desire to enter that room where I had heard the voice. I wanted to assure myself that I was not afraid, and that I was not so silly as to be frightened of an empty house.

I left the door open so that Molly could come straight in, and I ran up the stairs.

I went into the room and stood there.

All was silent; and almost immediately I heard the door shut and footsteps in the hall.

"I'm up here, Molly," I called.

I looked round the room. The blue curtains had already been taken down from the bed and lay in a heap on the floor. They were in good condition and could be beaten and brushed, Jeanne had said, and then they would be as good as new.

I went to the door and stared. It was not Molly who stood there, but Jonathan.

"What are you doing here?" I gasped.

"Looking for you."

"Molly Blackett will be here at any minute."

He shook his head. He came on slowly and shut the door, leaning against it.

"What do you mean . . . ?"

"Just that you will have to put up with me instead of Molly."

"What are you talking about? Molly is coming to do some measurements."

"She won't be coming."

"Nonsense. It has been arranged."

"It has now been *dis*arranged."

"What do you mean? Disarranged?"

"By me. I have had a message sent to Molly Blackett to say that you could not see her this afternoon and would make other arrangements. You will be engaged elsewhere this afternoon."

"You are . . ."

"Yes, I am, am I not! My methods are Machiavellian."

"You are most impertinent. How dare you interfere with my arrangements! How dare you send messages pretending they come from me!"

"I am daring by nature. I had to get you alone somehow. It isn't easy, is it? This seems a heaven-sent opportunity."

"I am leaving at once."

He shook his head.

"We are going to talk. We have to come to an understanding, Claudine, I love you. I've loved you ever since you came to England. I made up my mind then that you were for me, and I have never changed it."

"Look, Jonathan, I don't want to listen to this."

"You are not very truthful, you know. You should see yourself now. Your eyes flash. There is a flush in your cheeks. There is that in your voice which tells me you know as well as I do that you and I are meant for each other. It is fate, my dear Claudine. There is no going against it. You shouldn't have rushed into this absurd marriage . . . then it would have been so much easier. Now what are we faced with? Subterfuge . . . intrigue . . . secret meetings . . . stolen ecstasy."

"What on earth are you talking about? I'm going now."

He stood by the door watching me. I felt a terrible fear and an almost suffocating excitement. If I attempted to walk past him he would catch me and hold me captive. I dared not do that and yet . . . what else?

I hesitated and he went on: "You know very well what I'm talking about. Why do you pretend, Claudine? You betray yourself in a hundred ways. Do you think I don't know you want me as much as I want you?"

"You are quite . . . depraved."

He laughed. "No," he said. "I am just in love, and I am not the man to stand meekly by while others take what is rightly mine."

"Rightly yours! Have you forgotten that I happen to be married to your brother?"

"That makes no difference. You and I belong together. David is a good fellow . . . a very good fellow. He should have a pleasant quiet little wife. Not my fiery Claudine. She is not the wife for him. You are young and know nothing of love and passion and all the delights which I am waiting to show you. You would never learn them from David. He's worthy . . . oh yes . . . rather a noble fellow. He would never step aside from the path of respectability. But I am not like that. I defy conventions, Claudine, and so will you. They are made for people like David, not for us."

"I wish you would stop talking about David. He is my husband and I love him dearly. I am very contented with my life."

"When you talk so emphatically I know you are seeking to convince yourself. You are not satisfied. You thought you were. Look at you now. Your heart is fluttering and your eyes are alight with anticipation. Why are we wasting time in futile words?"

He approached me and when I attempted to elude him he caught me and held me firmly. He lifted me from the floor and held me in his arms as though I were a baby.

"You see, I am a great deal stronger than you are, Claudine."

"What do you think you are doing?"

"Showing you what has to be done."

"Jonathan, put me down. I want to talk to you seriously."

He lowered me and putting his arm about me led me to the bed. He sat down with me beside him; he had his arm tightly round me and he put his hand on my heart. "How it beats!" he said. "It beats for me."

"I want to go home at once," I said.

"I thought you wanted to talk seriously."

"I do. I want to say you must stop this, Jonathan. Don't you see how impossible life will be? You . . . living in the same house. Either we shall have to go away or you will. It would be easier for you. You could go to London. You are there a great deal with your banking and secret activities. Go and stay there. It will be better for us all."

He laughed. "I should not see you then. Would you condemn me to a life of frustration?"

"Please don't talk like this."

"What then should I talk of? The weather? Sophie's acquisition of this house? Is it going to snow before Christmas? Can you believe she has taken Enderby! No, my little Claudine. I have weightier matters on my mind. You, my lovely one. I am obsessed by you, Claudine. Claudine . . . my Claudine . . . who is different from all other women . . . who is a child and yet a woman . . . who has so much to learn, which I shall have to teach her. But she will be willing to learn. I detect that willingness. In fact, my dearest love, it is one of the qualities which I find so attractive."

"I wish you would talk sensibly. I must go back. I think it was very wrong of you—very inconsiderate to send that message to Molly Blackett. I remember that other occasion when she was making my dress . . ."

"Oh yes, and the silly creature came back too soon. History repeating itself, coming events casting their shadows before them. But this time she won't come, will she?"

"I must go."

I stood up and he was immediately beside me.

"I can't let you go, Claudine."

"I am going."

"How can you if I won't let you?"

"You mean you will hold me here . . . against my will?"

"I'd rather you stayed willingly."

"Willingly . . . What for? I am going now."

He had his arms round me. "Claudine, listen to me."

"There is nothing to listen to. There is no explanation. This is monstrous. I shall tell David . . . I shall tell my mother and your father."

"What a little teller of tales! You won't, you know."

"You seem to have made up your mind what I shall and shall not do."

"Claudine, I love you. You and I belong together. A few words said in a church can't alter that. What is between us is there for ever. It's like my father and your mother. You've seen them together. That is how it is with us. Preordained . . . Fate . . . Call it what you like. It is not often two people meet and know they are the only ones. That is us, Claudine, and it is no use trying to pretend."

"I daresay this is your set piece with all the married women you seek to seduce."

"I have never made that speech before. There is only one to whom it would apply. Claudine, don't go against what has to be. Face it. Accept it. And try to work out a solution from there."

"You seem to be of the opinion that I am as depraved as you are."

He bent back my head and kissed my throat. I wished that I did not feel so emotionally aroused. I ought to turn and run away. I knew I must, but he would not let me go; and if I were really truthful I had to admit that I did not want to.

"Jonathan," I said quietly. "Please, please let me go."

"No," he said firmly. "You belong to me. You have been foolish. You must have known all the time that you should never have married David."

"Stop!" I cried. "I love David. He is good and kind. He is everything I need."

"You say that because you do not know what you need."

"And you know, of course."

"Of course."

He slipped the bodice from my shoulders just as he had in the sewing room.

"No," I cried. "No."

But he had forced me back on the bed.

"You don't want to go, Claudine," he said. He took the pins from my hair and let it fall about my shoulders. I protested, weakly, I must admit, whispering—perhaps without conviction: "Let me go."

I heard him laugh and I felt his hands on me. It was as though I were sinking into mists of pleasure; and I knew that I had never experienced anything like this before, and that I could not go now . . . not even if he stood aside and allowed me to.

I forgot where I was . . . in this haunted room, this room of strange voices. I forgot everything but that I wanted to be with Jonathan, and that I had never known such ecstasy and that I wanted it to go on for ever. Perhaps somewhere in the recesses of my mind, I knew I must come out of this madness and face the wicked thing I was doing; but I could not at that moment. I was swallowed up in my desire and my overwhelming emotions.

I don't know how long I lived in that world of sensation when nothing outside it seemed of any importance. But the reckoning came . . . and soon.

I wrenched myself free. I tried to arrange my disordered dress, my loose hair. I stared about me. This room . . . this evil room! Were those voices a warning? Had I been told by some supernatural force that this room could be the scene of my shame?

I put my hands over my face and began to weep quietly.

Jonathan put an arm about me. "Don't, Claudine," he said. "Be happy. It was wonderful, wasn't it? Didn't you know it would be? You and I. It was perfect. Some people are meant for each other. We are like that."

"What have I done?"

He took my hands and kissed them. "Made me happy," he said. "Made yourself happy."

"David . . . What of David?"

"He will not know."

I stared at him in horror. "I must tell him. I must confess what I have done. I must do so . . . right away."

"My dear, dear one, you are not being reasonable."

"I have been so wicked."

"No, no. You have behaved naturally. You must not feel this guilt."

"Not feel guilty when I am guilty? Oh, how could you!"

"I did not force you, did I? You wanted to make love with me as much as I did with you."

"If you had not come here. If you—"

"If you were not you and I were not myself, yes, things would have been so different. Listen to me, Claudine. You are married to David. He is a good man. He would be bitterly hurt if he knew that you and I were in love with each other."

"I tell you, I love him."

"Yes . . . but differently, eh? You love us both. Well, we are twins, are we not? There must be a closeness between us. We started life together right from the beginning. We were together before we were born. There must be a bond between us. You love us both and because we are twins it is almost as though you love the same man."

"This doesn't help at all." I put my hands to my burning cheeks and started to pile up my hair. I was trembling, I could not bear to look into the future.

"Oh, why did you do this?" I cried. "Why did you send that message to Molly Blackett?"

"It had to be. I was seeking an opportunity. This seemed a good one."

"I don't think you have *any* scruples."

"Oh yes I have. But I accept the inevitable. This had to be."

"It must never happen again."

He stood beside me and kissed me gently. "It is our secret," he said. "No one need ever know."

"I must tell David."

"If you do you will ruin his happiness."

"What a pity you did not think of that before!"

"Before, I could think of only one thing. Listen to me, Claudine. This has happened. It had to happen at some time. Perhaps it ill happen again."

"Never," I cried vehemently. "It must never."

"Nobody knows we are here together. It can be our secret. Look at it like this: I had to do what I did. It obsessed me. It was such a desperate need that I had no feelings for anything else, and when you were there, close to me, Claudine, it was the same with you. It is a powerful attraction between us. You can do no good by confessions. Your secret guilt hurts only you."

"Perhaps you are right," I said slowly. "I want to get away from this house. I know it is an evil house. It does something to people. It makes them different from what they really are."

"Perhaps it shows them what they really are."

I wanted to get away. I wanted to think about this. I could not bear to stay there a moment longer.

I felt for the key of the house in the pocket of my dress. I was thankful it was still there for I feared it might have dropped out. There were certain cracks in the floorboards and it could have fallen down one of those. But there it was, safe, and the very feel of it brought me back to reality.

I ran down the stairs. Jonathan was right behind me.

Into the hall, across the stone floor, our footsteps echoing through the house, I turned to look at the minstrels' gallery and it seemed to me that there was a smug satisfaction about the house.

We came out and I locked the door.

I was dazed by my experience; and I felt as though I were still living in that world of wonderment to which he had introduced me. We walked across the fields to Eversleigh.

The house was quiet and I was glad I did not meet anyone on my way to my room. There I looked at myself in the mirror and it seemed that a stranger looked back at me.

This was not the same woman who had left that afternoon for the appointment with Molly Blackett. Of course it wasn't! I should never be the same again. I had broken one of the commandments: Thou Shalt Not Commit Adultery. And I had done this so easily . . . yet unintentionally—so carried away by the impulse of the moment. I had feared it, of course, but I had never truly thought it would happen. I had not realized that potent sexuality, that overwhelming power which silenced all qualms, which knew no conscience while one was in its thrall. I would never have believed this could happen to me.

I knew the story of my grandmother Zipporah, who had met a man in that very house and had behaved as I had today. She had been a quiet, virtuous woman, different from me, really, because I had always known that Jonathan could arouse desires in me which I must not give way to. What was that brooding evil at Enderby which had such an effect on the women of my family?

I was trying to shift the blame. I was trying to accuse the house of being responsible for my own misconduct.

How had it happened, so quickly, so easily? He had not forced me, he had said rather triumphantly. It was true. I had abandoned myself, willingly. I wished I could stop thinking of him. But I loved him, if loving was feeling more alive with some one person more than with anyone else, wanting to be with that person, to be close, to share intimacy, to be together every hour of the day and night.

Had I not felt that with David? David was interesting. He was kind and tender. It was a quiet relationship which had contented me until this afternoon. Love-making with David was quite pleasurable—as was everything else. But never had I experienced that wild excitement, that complete abandonment which I had known this afternoon.

Guilt weighed me down. If only I could go back to early afternoon. I should have waited outside the house. I should never have allowed it to wrap its tentacles around me. There I was, blaming the house again. There was no one to blame but myself . . . and Jonathan. And he had not forced me. I kept stressing that.

He was right. What good could confession do? If I were wise I should dismiss the incident from my mind. I should try to behave as though it had never happened. Perhaps in time I could forget it ever had. Forget it? That most shattering experience? Already I was thinking of being there, and seeing him there with me.

I must not tell David. It must be my secret . . . and Jonathan's. He was right. It must remain so.

Perhaps his conscience would trouble him, as mine did me. Perhaps he would to to London, stay there, visit Eversleigh only occasionally.

Perhaps the manager would decide to leave, and then David and I could have his house.

I knew what I was telling myself were possibilities were improbabilities. Jonathan would not stay in London; the manager would not go. Moreover, I wondered whether Jonathan would seek to trap me again. The very thought excited me. God help me, I wanted to be trapped. That was the frightening part of it. I revelled in my sin.

In the meantime I had to live through the next hours. I had to behave normally with my guilt clinging to me. Surely it was obvious.

I took down my hair which I had hastily pinned up. I undressed and got into bed. I would have a headache today. I could not go down to dine for I could not face anyone.

David was full of concern when he came in.

I said: "I have such a headache. I thought I'd go to bed. It's better when I'm lying down."

He bent over me and kissed me tenderly. Was there anything I needed? Should he have a tray sent up?

I told him no. I would rather sleep.

So I lay in my bed and when David came up I pretended to be asleep.

I almost burst into tears when he kissed me lightly because he feared to wake me.

I lay still, and I could not stop myself thinking of Jonathan, and of those magical moments in the haunted room.

My mother, with Dickon, Sophie and Jeanne, came home the next day. They were excited by their purchases. I had not seen Jonathan since our encounter and I needed all my cunning to act as though everything were normal.

Sophie was delighted with the materials she had bought and admitted it was a good idea to have gone to London.

"Did Molly get those measurements?" she asked.

I replied that she hadn't done so yet as I had been unable to meet her when I intended to.

"Well, there's no hurry," said my mother, "and Jeanne can supervise her."

At dinner that night everyone was there, even Sabrina, who appeared on special occasions, which was when anyone who had been away returned; and particularly if it happened to be Dickon.

Jonathan seemed exactly the same. I could not meet his eyes but I was aware of him all the time.

The sale of Enderby was now completed and Sophie could begin doing any repairs to the house and furniture she wanted to.

"I'll get Tom Ellin to come over and see you," said Dickon. "He's an excellent carpenter."

"We shall see wonders at Enderby," said my mother. "What an exciting project!"

"I think," put in Jonathan, looking at me, blue flames in his eyes, "that we are getting rather fond of that old house."

"David always said that cutting down some of the shrubs and trees would make all the difference," I commented deliberately, not meeting Jonathan's gaze.

"I shall not do too much cutting back," said Sophie. "What I like about Enderby is that feeling of seclusion."

Then my mother started to talk about Christmas.

"All this excitement has made me forget how close it is."

"I suppose it will be the usual entertaining?" I asked.

"It is the old tradition, isn't it, Mother?" said Dickon.

Sabrina smiled fondly at him, and he put his hand over hers and pressed it. He was always gentle and tender with her. I supposed such absolute adoration could not fail to bring a response.

"Carol singers and the punch bowl," went on my mother, "the wassailing, and of course the usual festivities of the day. I don't want too many this year. Just a few house guests. I think the Farringdons will have to stay a night or two. The Manor is not far off, but if the weather is bad . . ."

"It's a pity," I said, "that Christmas can't be in the summer when travelling would be so much easier."

"Oh, no, no," cried Jonathan. "The darkness adds to the joy. Those lovely log fires, coming in from the cold, hoping there'll be snow, picturesque on the trees—after everyone has safely arrived, and it must have thawed to allow them to depart at the appointed time. Why do people always want life to fit neatly into their plans?"

"I suppose you are right," I admitted. "Christmas wouldn't be the same at any other time."

He touched my hand lightly and said: "You will find that I often am right, little Claudine."

"No one can accuse Jonathan of an abundance of modesty," said my mother lightly. "What do you think of the Farringdons, all of you? They are quite a nice family and Harry would be an asset at any party."

"Oh yes, Harry is amusing and handsome," I said. "Quite an asset."

"I wonder they haven't married him off," mused Dickon. "He's quite a catch. He will be very comfortably placed when he inherits, as he will, as the only son."

"And of course the Pettigrews," went on my mother. "You'll like that, won't you, Jonathan?" She spoke with meaning. I think there had been an understanding between her and Lady Pettigrew that her daughter Millicent should make a match with either David or Jonathan, and now that David and I were married Jonathan was the free one.

"Very much, Step-mama," said Jonathan.

It was absurd, it was shameful, but I felt a pang of jealousy. I was trying to pretend that what had happened between us at Enderby would never happen again, and yet the thought of Jonathan with anyone else was excessively painful to me.

"And what about the locals," asked David. "The Dollands, of course."

"Of course," agreed my mother. "Emily Dolland is such a help with everything, and we all appreciate Jack, of course."

"He's a good man," commented Dickon. "David agrees, don't you?"

"Absolutely," said David.

"And I suppose," went on my mother, "we can't leave out the Grasslands people."

There was silence at the table and my mother went on: "Evalina Trent would be most put out. The girl, Evie, is getting very pretty. I saw her the other day. She looks very attractive in her habit and she rides well. I thought she was quite a beauty. The little one was with her."

"Poor Dolly," said Sabrina.

"We'll have to have them, I'm afraid," said my mother. "I must say I don't greatly care for Evalina Trent."

"She's a great pusher," Dickon put in. "Always has been since she was a young girl."

"She's been around for a long time, hasn't she, Dickon?" said Sabrina.

"Yes, she came to Grasslands when her mother was housekeeper here." He laughed suddenly, as though he was remembering something amusing.

"She seems to think a great deal of that pretty grand-daughter of hers," said my mother. "That's natural, but rather a responsibility for her since they have no parents. I suppose they'll have to come. Thank Heaven, they don't have to stay in the house. I wonder when Enderby will be ready. Well into the new year, I suppose."

"When do you hope to move?" asked Sabrina of Sophie.

"As soon as I can." Sophie gave a nervous little laugh. "Oh, that seems ungrateful. You have all been so helpful. But I want to be in my own house, you understand."

"Of course we understand," said my mother, "and we are only too pleased that it has all worked out so satisfactorily."

Satisfactorily? I thought. I wondered what she would say if she knew what had happened between Jonathan and me.

So the plans for Christmas went on.

I saw Jonathan alone in the gardens. He said to me: "I must see you again, Claudine . . . alone. I can't go on like this."

I begged: "Please don't. I'm beginning to forget . . ."

"You can never forget. It was too wonderful to be forgotten. Claudine, we must—"

"No, no," I said.

"Admit then that you love me."

"I don't know. I don't understand myself, you, or anything any more."

"But it was wonderful for you."

I was silent.

"You were tempted, weren't you? You could not resist. Do you think I didn't know! You're so marvelous. No one else will do for me, and it must be the same with you."

"It can't be. David is my husband."

"And I am your lover."

"It is an impossible situation."

"How can it be when it exists?"

"It must not exist. It is finished . . . Finished, I tell you."

"It will never finish, Claudine, while you are you and I am myself."

"Please, don't . . ."

"Admit it then. Admit that you love me. Admit that it was wonderful . . . more wonderful than you have ever believed anything could be."

I heard myself shouting: "All right. It was. It was. . . ."

Then I ran into the house.

Once I had made that admission, I knew there would be no holding back. He would seek every opportunity and when it came, snatch at it. And I knew that I should be there. I could not fight this. I was learning something of my own nature which I had not known until Jonathan aroused it. I was not the woman to be content with a quiet tender passion. I wanted to soar the heights, not just dally in the pleasant lowlands. He was right when he said I wanted both him and David. I did. I loved David. I found the way in which he seemed so delighted and almost surprised that I loved him, most endearing. I loved to read and discuss with him. I was interested in matters of the mind, but there was another side to my nature too. I was a voluptuous and sensuous woman. I had needs which demanded satisfaction; and as with such physical desires, when they presented themselves, they could subdue everything else.

Jonathan knew me better than I knew myself. He had probed that hidden part of me. It was that which appealed to him. He wanted the sort of woman I was. My position in the household had made me the most desirable wife he could have. It had never occurred to him that in such a short time after his disappearance, I could have married David.

His journey to France had not been one of those on-the-spur-of-the-moment decisions we had been led to believe it was. He was involved with his father's secret life, and Dickon, in the past, had made many journeys to France. Men doing such work contrived to have an obvious reason for their voyages, the better to help disguise the real one. Jonathan had gone to France not only to rescue Sophie but to gather certain information—of that I was sure now. He had seized the opportunity to go with Charlot and had intended to return when his mission was accomplished . . . and then he planned to marry me.

But I had ruined his plans by my hasty marriage to David. Looking back, I wondered why I had slipped into that so easily. It might have been because I was piqued by Jonathan's departure. Always it was Jonathan who was in my thoughts. Had I been older, wiser, I should have guessed; but because I was innocent, life seemed simple to me. I had imagined that when I married David that would be the end of all conflict and we should live happily ever after.

Now I was being revealed to myself and I saw a woman who would risk a great deal to be with her lover. My marriage vows, everything I had been brought up to believe was right, my guilty conscience . . . all could be pushed to one side when I was confronted by the overpowering need to make love with this one man.

I can make no excuses. I went into the next betrayal eagerly. We had the key of the house. We knew when no one would be there, and we went again to that room and made frenzied love, and it seemed to me more excruciatingly exciting the second time than the first.

Then my remorse returned. I was weighed down by my guilt. It was even heavier than before because I could not now tell myself that I had been trapped into the situation. I had gone willingly. I had clung to him; I had shared his impatience and his ecstasy. I had admitted that I loved him, that I had made a bitter mistake. I was a wicked and abandoned woman and, during the height of my passion, I revelled in my abandonment.

There *was* no excuse for me. I was wanton. I had deliberately deceived my husband.

Jonathan felt no such guilt, although he was betraying his own brother. He said fatalistically: "It had to happen. It was meant."

Afterwards I felt angry—mainly with myself. I was aghast at my own behaviour. I suffered anguish when I was with David, who was so kind always. I felt irritated with him merely because of his kindness, for his goodness only accentuated my depravity.

I wished that I could confide in my mother. I wanted to talk about it. I wanted to know why I—who previously had always had a sense of honour, a sense of duty—could behave so.

We must get away, I decided. Jonathan must go away. We could not continue to live like this under the same roof.

As we walked back to the house Jonathan said: "Tomorrow?"

"No," I cried. "It must never happen again."

But he only smiled at me, and I knew as well as he did that it would.

I was shocked, too, to find that I did not have such difficulty in behaving normally as I had done on the first occasion. I did not go to bed pleading a headache. I went down to dinner and we all sat round the table, talking, laughing, making Christmas plans—myself as merry as any of them outwardly, and it was only when I glanced across the table and caught Jonathan's blue eyes on me, and I looked sideways at David, that the terrible sense of remorse overcame me.

The Pettigrews arrived the day before Christmas Eve. Their carriage was very grand with the Pettigrew crest prominently engraved on it and Lady Pettigrew at least was eager that everyone should be aware of their importance. Lord Pettigrew was much quieter than his wife. No one would have believed that all her glory came through him. He held a post at Court which I imagined was so arduous that when he was in the heart of his family he was ready to agree to anything for the sake of peace.

The Honourable Millicent was a handsome young woman who looked as if she had a will of her own, and I imagined that she and her mother were a formidable pair who managed to get what they wanted.

It became obvious that what they wanted was Jonathan as a prospective husband for Millicent. I was acutely aware of anything connected with Jonathan and now suffered twinges of jealousy. Jonathan would be a match which would be highly approved of by Lady Pettigrew. Dickon was not only an extremely wealthy man but an influential one. Yes, I could see that Lady Pettigrew and Millicent had selected Jonathan for his role.

I mentioned it to my mother. She laughed and said: "Well, it wouldn't surprise me. I think Dickon would be quite pleased. He's very friendly with Lord Pettigrew. They have a great deal in common . . . in the City. Mind you, Lady Pettigrew is rather a forceful lady and I am not sure that Millicent doesn't take after her. But I think Jonathan would be able to handle that. Is anything wrong?"

"No. . . . What makes you think so?"

"I thought you looked a little depressed. Not tired are you?"

She was looking at me anxiously and the colour flooded my face. She thinks I might be pregnant! I told myself. Then suddenly the thought of what this could mean if I were swept over me.

"It's all right," I said firmly. "I'm perfectly normal."

She patted my arm lightly. "Well, Christmas comes but once a year, and sometimes I'm heartily glad of that."

Each day I was realizing more and more what a web I was being caught up in. My jealousy of Millicent, my sudden fear that I might have a child and should have to ask myself whose, brought home to me ever more strongly the seriousness of my predicament.

It must stop. I must never, never give way to my emotions again. I would get over this obsession. I would be a good wife to David and I would attempt to wipe this sordid incident right out of my mind.

The next day the Farringdons came. They were very charming people —Gwendoline, John and their son, Harry. Harry was in his mid-twenties, very good-looking. He helped his father run their estate, which I learned was the same size as Eversleigh.

In the early afternoon of Christmas Eve a party of the younger people went for a ride. There was David, Jonathan, Harry Farringdon, Millicent Pettigrew and myself. I rode between David and Harry while Jonathan with Millicent went ahead. I found myself watching them intently. You must stop this, I admonished myself. It only makes you wretched. You are risking everything that is worthwhile for the sake of a few sensational moments. I glanced at David. He looked contented and was talking of the estate with Harry—comparing Eversleigh with Farringdon.

We had the mist back again—it was damp and warm for the time of the year and clearly we should not have snow for Christmas. A wintry sun was trying to break through the clouds.

" 'If the sun shines through your apple trees on Christmas Day,' " quoted David. " 'When autumn comes they will a load of fruit display.' "

"Let's hope it shines through the apple trees then," I said.

"I like those old rhymes," commented Harry. "And they are very often right."

"They should be since they are culled from the wisdom of men who have watched weather for ages," replied David.

"I suppose you had them in France," Harry asked me.

"I suppose so, but I don't remember hearing any."

Jonathan had turned. "Why are you lagging behind?" he asked. His eyes met mine, dancing with mischief, and all my resolutions began to crumble away.

"We were talking about the weather and old rhymes," I told him.

" 'If New Year's night-wind blows south,' " said Harry, " 'It betokens warmth and growth.' "

"I can't wait for New Year's night," said Jonathan.

" 'If west, much milk and fish in sea,' " went on Harry, unperturbed. " 'If north, cold and storms will be. If north-east, flee it, man and brute.' "

"Very pretty," said Jonathan.

"And very probably true," added David.

"Truth and beauty—what a combination!" said Jonathan. "But why all this preoccupation with the weather?"

"If you worked on the land you would be preoccupied with it," David retorted.

"I bow to your superior wisdom. At least we are not having one of those romantic snowy Christmases. I can never understand why people set such store by them."

"It's rather exciting not knowing whether you are going to arrive or not," said Millicent.

"Travelling is always such fun," added Jonathan. "It is getting there that does not always live up to expectations."

"Well, I am determined that getting here is going to live up to *my* expectations," declared Millicent.

"Then rest assured that it will be a happy Christmas, for my Lady Millicent must always be obeyed," said Jonathan.

"It amuses you to laugh at me," said Millicent.

"There is little I like better than being amused."

"Come on," cried Millicent. "Which way?"

"Straight ahead," I said. "We'll pass my aunt Sophie's new house on the way."

"Oh, I should love to see it."

"We haven't the key," I said quickly.

"Well, from outside. Perhaps while we are staying at Eversleigh we could go and see it."

"I am sure you could," said Jonathan.

Millicent rode on and we all followed.

There it was. The house which had become so important to me, a kind of symbol of sin.

"It looks exciting, but a little grim," commented Millicent.

"I think it a very interesting house," Jonathan told her. He looked at me, smiling. "You like it, don't you, Claudine?"

"I admit it is a most unusual house."

"It looks as if it is in need of repairs," put in Harry, casting a businesslike look over it.

"You are right up to a point," said David. "But it is amazing what a solid old place it is. A little bit of rot here and there . . . just a sign or two of decay. It's amazing considering how long it has been empty."

"Strange that it should stand empty for so long," said Harry.

"Oh, it has a bit of a reputation."

"Ghosts?" cried Millicent. "Noises in the night? How very thrilling!"

I thought: And voices in a room on the first floor, a room which would be in my memory for ever.

"Well, there it is," said David. "We'll get the key before you leave, Millicent, and you shall have a real tour."

I was glad when we rode off.

As we were coming past Grasslands, Evie and her sister were riding in. We pulled up.

"Hello, Evie," I said. "This is Miss Evie Mather and her sister Dorothy. Evie and Dolly, you haven't met the Honourable Millicent Pettigrew and Mr. Harry Farringdon."

Both Harry and Millicent were, I think, a little taken aback by the sight of the sisters. I suppose it was the contrast they made, Dolly's deformity calling attention to Evie's good looks.

"Were you going for a ride?" I asked. "It's just the afternoon for it."

"We were just returning, as a matter of fact," said Evie.

"Well, it will be dark soon."

"Would you like to come in and have a glass of something?"

"It's getting late," I replied. "We want to be back before dark."

"And there are so many of us," added David.

Harry was looking at Evie. He said: "I'd like to. . . . We need not stay long."

"I have to get back," said Millicent.

"All right," put in Jonathan. "You three stay and I'll take Millie back."

Again that sick jealousy! I was annoyed. I hated the thought of leaving Millicent with Jonathan and going into Grasslands, but there seemed no way out.

"Au revoir!" called Jonathan gaily.

Millicent was smiling, well pleased. Glad to be rid of us, I was sure; and the rest of us dismounted and went into the house.

Evalina Trent came into the hall to greet us.

"Well, this is a nice surprise."

I introduced Harry and Mrs. Trent almost fawned upon him.

"Oh yes . . . what a *nice* surprise," she repeated. "Come along in. We'll all wish each other a merry Christmas."

So we sat in the little intimate parlour which led from the hall and we drank the wine while we chatted amiably about nothing. Harry had seated himself next to Evie and was talking animatedly to her. Mrs. Trent's eyes scarcely left them. She was very impressed by Harry.

"I know of Farringdon Hall," she said. "A fine old place. I said to myself when I rode by in the carriage . . . that was when my son Richard was alive . . . I said, 'Richard, that's a fine place, that is, and one of the best estates roundabouts.' "

Harry said he thought so too but perhaps he was prejudiced.

"Oh, you don't have to be. You've got it all. . . . You and your father before you, and his father before him have made the place what it is. We do our best here at Grasslands, but my husband died . . ." She sighed. "That was my second. . . . My first . . . Andrew . . . God bless him . . . passed away years ago."

I glanced at David, suggesting with my look that we curtail this visit as quickly as we could. I was faintly irritated with Harry for forcing it on us, and I was wondering all the time what Jonathan was saying to Millicent on their way back.

Harry was still talking attentively to Evie. I heard him say: "Shall you be at Eversleigh tomorrow?"

"Oh yes, we're invited."

"I'm glad," said Harry. "So glad."

At last we were able to escape. I gasped with relief as we came out to the road. Mrs. Trent, with a grand-daughter on either side of her, had waved us goodbye, or *au revoir* as she insisted on saying.

It was Harry who had excited her. His interest in Evie had been blatant.

When I was alone with David in our bedroom, I commented on it.

"I think Mrs. Trent is getting ideas. Of course Harry is a very good match. I am sure she is already making plans to bring Evie and him together."

"You can't blame her. She's got those two girls and I should imagine there is not a great deal she can do for them at Grasslands."

"I have an idea that Evalina Trent will always try to get the best of all that comes her way."

"Well, my love, isn't that what we all try to do?"

"David," I said, "you are a very nice man."

"Oh, have you just discovered it?"

"I've always known it, but sometimes it strikes me more forcibly than others. You always see the best in people. I don't believe you would see evil if it were right under your nose."

"I expect I'd smell it out," he said.

I threw myself at him and held him tightly. I was saying to myself: I must never hurt him. I must never again be alone with Jonathan . . . David must never know . . . It would hurt him too much.

I prayed then—a strange thing to do with all my sins upon me. I prayed for the strength I should need to live with this evil I had created.

When I returned to the house I found my mother busy in her private sanctum. She called to me.

"The carol singers will be round in the evening," she said. "We shall have to bring them in and give them hot punch and cakes. That will be enough for tonight and we'll hope to retire early in readiness for tomorrow. We shall eat in the hall tomorrow of course and while things are being cleared away for the dancing, I thought we'd have a treasure hunt. That always goes down well and the house lends itself to it so admirably. Another thing, there'll be a moon and therefore enough light for them to see where they are going when they prowl about the house. I never liked lighted candles all over the place."

I said: "That's a good idea, Maman. Do you want me to help you with the clues?"

"No, Dickon and I will do them. If you help you won't be able to join in."

I said: "We went to Grasslands."

"Oh, did you?"

"We couldn't get out of it. It was Harry Farringdon's fault. He wanted to go after he had seen Evie."

My mother laughed. "So he took a fancy to her."

"It was rather obvious. Mrs. Trent was very pleased."

"Oh dear, I hope she wasn't too obvious."

"She always is . . . rather."

"Poor old Evalina Trent! My mother disliked her intensely. I think something happened in the past. I have a feeling that she could be rather a dangerous woman."

"I feel that too. However, she does care for those grand-daughters."

"It's poor little Dolly I'm sorry for."

"Evie seems fond of her, and of course the poor girl dotes on Evie."

"It's sad to be born like that. Let's hope something comes of Harry's interest."

"What would John and Gwen Farringdon think of the Grasslands family? Dickon said Harry was a very good match."

"They'd look higher than Mrs. Trent's grand-daughter, but if Harry wanted it . . . Well, I reckon he's a young man who would have his way. But aren't we being a little premature?"

We laughed. "It's a good thing no one can hear us," I said. "Anyway, I hope things work out well for Evie."

"So do I," said my mother. "Dancing will be just right after the treasure hunt and that can take up the rest of the evening. I've arranged for the music. The musicians can have something to eat while the treasure hunt is in progress. That will keep them going through the evening."

I kissed her lightly and said: "You think of everything."

Evening came. We were in the dining room and were just finishing the meal when the carol singers arrived. It was very picturesque with their lanterns bobbing about outside the windows and after the first rendering Dickon and my mother opened the door and they all trooped into the hall. There they sang for us and we applauded and joined in with the carols. The big punch bowl was brought in and the drink was ladled into goblets which the ladies of the household handed round with the pies and cakes which had been baked for the occasion.

Then we went to the punch room and talked of Christmases of the past, and my mother described Christmas in France, which was celebrated more on Christmas Eve than on the day itself. There was midnight Mass, and slippers by the fire into which gifts were placed.

Christmas Day came. I awoke with that heavy sense of guilt which was almost always with me nowadays and as I lay in bed I thought of last Christmas Day when I had been an innocent, lighthearted girl.

"It must end," I said for the hundredth time.

We went to the little church in the village of Eversleigh for the morning service. With the unpredictability of our climate the weather had changed again and there was the faintest touch of frost in the air. After the service we walked home across the fields, and Jonathan suddenly started to sing a carol in which we all joined. He came and took my arm; on his other side was Millicent Pettigrew and her arm was slipped through his. He pressed mine against him and all my weakness returned. Momentarily I was happy because I was close to him.

I did not see him again that day until it was time to greet the arriving guests. My mother said that now I was a married woman I should take my stand with her to welcome them.

The Dollands arrived first, on foot of course, having come just from the manager's house. Emily wanted to know if there was anything she could do to help.

"You may be pressed into service later," said my mother, "but I think everything is under control just now."

My mother looked very beautiful in a peacock-blue velvet gown which accentuated the blue of her eyes. There was a radiance about her. I thought: She at least is happy. Yet, when I paused to think of it I realized that she had had to go through many trials before she reached that contentment. Perhaps that was the fate of everyone and I was just embarking on my troubles. Troubles are always harder to bear when they are of one's own making. It must be a comfort to have someone to blame . . . even if it was only Fate. That was denied me. I had not been forced into this situation. I had perhaps allowed myself to be led. But what effort had I made to escape it? Very little. I had gone willingly, and in my heart I knew I should do so again.

My dress was cherry-coloured. It was one of David's favourites and I had worn it for that reason. I had a passionate desire to please him all I could, because I was treating him so badly. . . .

The Trents arrived. Evie, in a gown of blue silk and lace, looked quite beautiful. Dolly was in blue also—painfully thin and gauche. I wondered if she might hide her deformity by wearing a patch over her eye.

Some patches could be quite ornamental. I remembered a picture I had seen of the Princess of Eboli who had lost an eye. She looked most decorative . . . mysterious and exciting with her patch.

Mrs. Trent was in purple velvet. It was a beautiful dress and she was really quite a handsome woman. Her manners betrayed her. If only she would be quieter!

"It's so nice of you to ask us," she was saying. "My word, this is a fine old place. Eversleigh! I remember it well, I know every nook and cranny. It takes me back to be here." Her eyes were darting about; searching for Harry Farringdon, I guessed.

He had found Evie. I believed he had been waiting for her. Now he was talking to her. I was glad that I had arranged with my mother that they should be seated together at the table.

I noticed Dolly, who kept beside her grandmother, although her eyes were wistfully on Evie all the time. It occurred to me briefly that she might resent anyone's taking Evie from her.

Sophie was with us for dinner. She and Sabrina would slip away immediately after we had eaten—Sabrina because she must retire early, and Sophie, I supposed, because she still felt ill-at-ease in company and would, in any case, wish to be with Jeanne.

The great table in the hall looked magnificent in the light from the candelabra. I wondered how many candles were burning in the hall that night. My mother sat at one end of the massive oak table, Dickon at the other. Jonathan was with Millicent, David was next to Mrs. Trent, and I had Jack Dolland on one side and Harry Farringdon on the other. I could hear him and Evie chatting together.

The meal lingered on. There were toasts to the guests and their returning ones to us; and everybody was very merry. A great deal of wine was drunk and food consumed; and at length the time came for the treasure hunt. My mother explained to the company that the hall would be cleared while the treasure hunt was taking place and then we should be ready for dancing.

"You will all work individually," she explained. "No collusion! The first lady and the first gentleman to bring me the six written clues will win the prizes. Now I shall give you all one clue and that should lead you to the next. When you have found it, pick up the clue—there is one for everybody—and go on to the next. The first to bring me six clues wins, and when everyone is assembled here . . . having completed the exercise or given up in despair, I shall make the presentation. We are grateful to the weather. Thank goodness it's a clear night. The moon will light your way."

People went off in different directions. There was much murmuring and suppressed laughter in the gloom.

I found the first clue easily. Perhaps I knew the way my mother's mind worked. Moreover, I knew the house well and could have found my way about blindfolded. I would tell my mother that members of the family had an advantage over visitors and should be handicapped.

I had mounted a staircase and was in a corridor when a hand came out and seized me. I was held tightly and kissed with fervour.

"Jonathan!" I whispered.

"I was waiting to catch you."

The door of one of the rooms was open. He drew me in and shut the door.

"It seems so long," he said.

I could see beyond him to where a shaft of moonlight fell on the court cupboard, which was close to the bed.

"Jonathan . . . please . . . we can't stay here."

"Tomorrow," he said.

"No . . . No . . . Never again."

He laughed softly.

"How many times have you said never and how many times have I proved you wrong?"

"It has to stop. I can't bear it."

"And I could not bear to stop."

"We've got to, Jonathan."

"Tomorrow afternoon," he said. "They will go riding in the afternoon. You stay behind and go to the house. I'll see you there. Dear old Enderby . . . in our room. You'll be there, Claudine."

"No . . . *no,"* I said.

"Yes, yes," he whispered. "Three o'clock. Oh, my darling, I do long for you."

I wrenched myself away. We could so easily betray ourselves. What if someone came into this room and found us here together? What of David . . . ? We must stop. We were running too many risks.

I ran down the stairs.

My mother was in the hall.

"Don't tell me you've found them already."

"No. But it has occurred to me that the family have an advantage and it is not fair to the others. We ought to be handicapped or disqualified if we win."

"I see your point," said my mother. "Stay here then. You look flushed and hot anyway."

So I stayed with her. I was afraid to wander through those darkened rooms and corridors in case I met Jonathan . . . in case we were seen together.

I realized to the full then how I should feel if David discovered my perfidy. He must never, never know. I must forget this infatuation. I must cut it right out of my life. It was so utterly foolish . . . so selfish to risk so much.

Evie was the first lady to finish and Harry the first man.

"I scent collusion," I whispered to my mother.

"It's understandable. Evie looks different. She looks really happy."

Evie received the ivory fan adorned with hand-painted roses and Harry the pewter tankard. There was loud applause and by that time the hall was cleared for dancing and the music began.

According to tradition my mother opened the dancing with Dickon, and David and I immediately joined them on the floor. Harry and Evie danced together and Jonathan with Millicent.

Rather mechanically I went through the minuet and the cotillion, and in spite of my fears and resolutions, when I danced with Jonathan I felt the excitement surging up in me.

"I can't wait until tomorrow afternoon," he said.

"I can't come."

"You will," he told me.

He was laughing, his blue eyes aflame; and I felt a rising resentment because he did not suffer remorse as I did. He was perfectly contented with what was taking place.

For the first time I began to wonder whether he enjoyed this situation because of the risks and that they added a fillip to his desire. Could he really *enjoy* deceiving his own brother, breaking the laws of honour and convention . . . and of religion? Was it then that my feelings underwent a change? I felt the same urgent desire; but rather naïvely I had imagined previously that he would feel the same as I did—carried away by passion, yes, but suffering remorse and a terrible regret that our emotions had forced us to behave in such a manner.

When the guests had all departed I was glad to retire to our bedroom.

David said: "You are very tired, Claudine."

I replied that it had been a long day.

"I think it went well," he continued. "Your mother certainly knows how to manage these affairs. It was very different here before she married my father." He lay down beside me and said: "Isn't it wonderful to see two people so much in accord as they are?"

"They spar a little."

"It is all part of that relationship, that inability-to-live-without-each-other-ness. I am so happy that they came through safely and that he brought her home and they married. Moreover it has given my grandmother absolute contentment in her old age."

He drew me to him.

"We shall be like that, Claudine, through the years."

I clung to him and thought: He must never know. I would rather die than he should know.

He made tender love to me and there were tears on my cheeks.

"Claudine," he asked, "what is it? Is something wrong?"

"Oh, David," I said, "I love you. I *do* love you."

He kissed me, and after he slept I lay awake staring into the darkness. Why had I let it happen? How could I deceive this good man?

Boxing Day, so called because those who had served us during the year called at the big house for what they called their "box," which was, in fact, a gift of money.

Dickon and my mother were seated in the hall while the ceremony was in progress, and a party of us went over to Enderby, as Millicent insisted that we had promised to show her the house.

There were myself, David, Millicent, Jonathan, Lord and Lady Pettigrew, and Gwen and John Farringdon with Harry. David had the key and when he opened the door and we went into the hall there were exclamations of amazement. It looked different by morning light. A little wintry sun shone through the windows and the place had lost something of that melancholy look; there was still an eerieness about it, though; that was something which could never completely disappear, I was sure.

Millicent said: "Is that the haunted gallery?"

"It is said to be so," replied David.

"Something awful happened there, I daresay. I'm glad I'm not alone here. Then I should feel positively scared."

"No need to," replied Jonathan, smiling at her. "There's a strong arm here ready to defend you from spectres with countless clanging chains and myriads of moaning ghosts."

"Stay close to me," commanded Millicent.

"No need to ask me that."

It was ridiculous to feel hurt by his light bantering with Millicent, but I did.

David was saying: "What a change! That carpenter is very good. He'll have the place in fair order within a few weeks, I'll swear."

"Aunt Sophie is very eager to move in," I said.

"Poor soul," murmured Gwen Farringdon. "Such an affliction! It has affected her deeply, hasn't it?"

Lady Pettigrew said briskly: "A great misfortune. But such trials must be faced and she is fortunate to have escaped from those dreadful French peasants. I hope she is suitably grateful to you." She beamed approval on Jonathan. "Now she can build a future for herself and it is a mercy this house is so near Eversleigh."

It had always amazed me how people like Lady Pettigrew made so little of the misfortunes of those about them, and I could not help wondering whether she would be quite so dismissive of her own.

We mounted the stairs and went into the minstrels' gallery. Now that the heavy red curtains had been taken down for cleaning and renovation it had lost much of that mysterious look.

Jonathan came up behind Millicent and said: "Boo!"

She jumped and turned round smiling at him. "You're determined to scare me."

"And I did," he said. "Admit it."

"Not with all these people about me."

"Ah, but if they hadn't been here . . ." He was laughing at her.

"You mean if I had been here alone with you! That's not likely, is it?"

"Alas!" he said, with mock resignation.

I thought: That is how he is. That is how he is with me . . . and with every woman.

We went along the corridors and he opened the door of that room in which we had made such passionate love.

"Much of the furniture was already here, I believe," said Gwen Farringdon.

"It went with the house," David told her.

"What a gift! It will not need such a great deal more."

"This is a nice room. I like this," said Millicent. She went to the bed and sat down on it; then she lifted her feet and lay full length on it.

"It's quite comfortable," she said.

"I feel sure of that," murmured Jonathan; he caught my eye and the corner of his mouth twitched a little.

I did not feel like sharing the joke. To me it was no joke. It was deadly serious.

We went over the house and found ourselves in the kitchens, which were vast and stone-floored.

There was one moment when Jonathan and I were alone; the others had gone through the screens and he and I stood a little way in the hall.

He caught my hand and said: "This afternoon."

I shook my head.

He came closer and kissed me. I wanted to protest but I did not. It appalled me that he still had the power to charm me.

I was glad when the tour of the house was over and we came out into the fresh air.

We walked back across the fields and everyone was talking about Enderby, what a fascinating house it was, and how fortunate Sophie had been to have such a bargain fall into her hands.

"It is a pity all French émigrés are not so fortunate," said Lady Pettigrew.

"She was so lucky to get away with her jewels," said Millicent.

"And her life," added Lord Pettigrew.

"She has Jonathan to thank for that," David reminded them.

"How wonderful!" said Millicent, smiling at Jonathan.

"Oh it was simple," he said lightly. "We went over and we came out with Mademoiselle Sophie and her maid and the clever creature had sewed the jewels in their garments and didn't tell me until we were crossing the Channel."

"It's no use your trying to pretend it wasn't marvellous," said Millicent sternly. "You are really very brave."

"I am a very perfect gentle knight," said Jonathan. "I deserve all your adulation, and most gratefully accept it . . . and shall probably beg for more. It is a commodity I have a great fancy for. You cannot give me too much of it."

Millicent slipped her arm through his. She was a little forward, I supposed, for the manners of our day, but her mother showed no sign of disapproving, which told me that the redoubtable Lady Pettigrew smiled on Jonathan as a future son-in-law.

I was restless and uncertain. I wanted to see Jonathan alone. I wanted to tell him that there must be no more love-making between us. I wanted to ask him what his feelings were for Millicent Pettigrew, and if that state of bantering flirtation which seemed to exist between them had any meaning behind it.

I had said I would not be at the rendezvous that afternoon but I was making excuses to myself. I wanted to *talk* to him, I kept assuring myself. I wanted to stress that our dangerous relationship must cease.

Or did I merely want to be with him? Did I know in my heart that once we were alone in that room, once he held me close to him, I would give way as I had before?

I watched them go off riding. I said I had certain things to do and could not join them. Jonathan waved to me as he rode off. His plan was to lose them as quickly as he could, return to the stables and leave his horse there, for it would be dangerous to tether it outside the house where it could be seen. It would not take him long to hurry across the fields.

In spite of having promised myself not to go, I set out.

I must talk to him, I must, I kept saying to myself.

That was my excuse.

I was a few minutes early. I hesitated at the door. My inclination was to wait outside, but that was foolish. What if someone passed by and saw me waiting there? Still, I hesitated. Was I afraid of an old house? To show myself that I was not, I took the key from my pocket, opened the door and went in, shutting it behind me. When he came, Jonathan would ring the bell. It was a little rusty, but it worked.

I advanced into the hall. Certainly it had changed and the minstrels' gallery without its curtains looked quite ordinary. I could not imagine any ghosts hiding there now. It was all a matter of shadows and darkness. How right David had been about those overgrown shrubs. They had not been dealt with yet and Sophie had indicated that they would only be trimmed, so she would still retain some of the old house's atmosphere.

I ran up the stairs to that room which I looked upon as ours.

I stood in it and thought of the first time. It had happened so swiftly that it had caught me unaware, and then once it had happened I was trapped; and it had been so easy, having made the first step, to go on.

How silent the house was!

Hurry, Jonathan, I thought.

Then I heard that voice . . . that whisper, preceded by a little laugh, and then: "Mrs. Frenshaw . . . remember the seventh commandment, Mrs. Frenshaw."

I stood there stunned. For some seconds I could not move. I was straining my ears listening. There was no sound . . . nothing but that frightening silence.

I ran out of the room and as I reached the stairs the door bell was clanging through the house. I ran down and opened the door.

Jonathan was there. He caught me in his arms. "What's wrong? What is it, Claudine?"

"I heard it again," I said. "The voice . . ."

"Voice? Where?"

"In the room. Our room."

"There's no one here . . ."

"I heard it. I heard it distinctly."

"Come on. We'll have a look," he said.

He put his arm round me and I clung to him. We ran up the stairs.

There was no one there.

He looked at me puzzled. "What was it like?"

"It was the way it was before . . . Echoing . . . Strangely muted."

"You mean as if someone were trying to disguise the voice?"

"I don't know. It laughed after it had said it. 'Remember the seventh commandment.' "

"What nonsense!"

"But it's apt, isn't it? The voice . . . it knows."

"My dear Claudine, I simply do no believe in disembodied voices."

"I tell you I heard it . . . distinctly. Just as I heard it before."

"Then there is someone here."

"But how could it be . . . in that room?"

"Is that the only place where you have heard this voice?"

I nodded.

"Come on," he said. "We're going to look."

We went into all the rooms, up to the next floor and the attics. Then we went down through the hall to the kitchens. It was as I guessed it would be—empty.

We were the only ones in the house.

"Where are you?" shouted Jonathan. "You of the idiot voice. Come out and show yourself."

His voice gave back a faint echo. Then the house was quiet. Not a sound. I looked up at the vaulted ceiling, at the stone walls, at the gallery.

"There's nobody here," said Jonathan.

"It's haunted," I insisted. "It's something horrible . . . something from the past."

"You don't believe that really. There must be some explanation, a logical one."

"What?"

"Someone is here . . . was here . . . someone playing a trick."

"Someone who knows—about us."

He admitted solemnly: "Yes, someone who knows about us. Or," he added, "you imagined you heard the voice."

"I heard it distinctly."

"You don't take this lightly, do you?"

"Take it lightly! No, I do not. But you do, Jonathan. That's what I am beginning to understand."

"Claudine, you are the most important thing in the world to me."

I shook my head.

"You are a very conventional lady," he said. "Brought up in that formal society, eh? It has always amused me, the rigorous formality of the French and the exploits they indulge in . . . in secret, of course. However, they brought you up that way, and now your conscience worries you. I am beginning to think that it was *that* which you heard."

"In other words, you believe I imagined I heard voices."

"Perhaps you did, Claudine."

"I did not."

"Then who? We've been round the house. No one is here but us. Who could have got in? You let yourself in with the key and shut the door. Is there any other key?"

I said suddenly: "The window. Of course. David and I looked round once. I told you about it. And we came through a window."

"Where?"

"It was somewhere in the hall." I crossed the stone floor with speed.

I said: "This is it. Look! The latch is broken. Anyone who knew could get in through it. It's simple."

He stood looking at me in dismay.

"So you think someone was in the house when you came in. But how could that person talk to you in that room? You would have heard whoever it was running down the stairs and out through the window wouldn't you?"

"I should think so."

"Claudine, you imagined it. That's the only answer. You imagined it."

"No. I know the difference between imagination and reality."

"Sometimes we all have fancies."

"I heard that voice," I said firmly. "Do you realize what it means? Someone knows . . . about us."

He shrugged his shoulders. "You're working yourself up, Claudine. Forget it. We're here, aren't we? I had the devil of a job to elude them."

"Millicent clung, I daresay."

"With a certain tenacity, I admit. But I was determined to be with you, so I escaped."

"Jonathan, I want to go."

"Go! Why, we've only just come."

"I came to tell you that it has to stop."

He raised his eyebrows and looked at me with that expression of mock exasperation.

"I can't go on deceiving David. I've got to stop it. I'm going to try to forget that it ever happened. You must too."

"Never," he said. "Forget the most wonderful experience of my life! You are asking too much. Come, my dearest. There is not much time, you know."

"No," I insisted. "I can't. I must go."

He drew me to him, but this time I felt stronger. I kept seeing David's face and remembering how much I loved him.

I said: "I'm going back to Eversleigh. I should never have come. Jonathan, I couldn't bear it if ever David discovered. I want everything to stay as it was between us."

"It's a little late for that now, isn't it?"

"I don't know. I can't think. I only know that more than anything at the moment I want to get away from this house."

"That silly old voice has unnerved you."

"It has frightened me, Jonathan, and it has made me fully realize what I have done . . . to myself, to David and to you. I have betrayed my husband. You have betrayed your brother."

"Darling Claudine, let's drop the histrionics, shall we? I love you. I want you. I want you more than anything. Isn't that good enough?"

"How can it be when I am your brother's wife?"

"There you go again! I want you. You want me. We've had some wonderful times together. You're a passionate woman, remember. You've wakened up. But you have this conscience that is bothering you. Everything is all right as long as we are careful."

I could detect the faint irritation in his attitude. He had come to indulge his sexual desires and I was baulking him. I saw him then more clearly than I ever had and a terrible desolation swept over me. I had destroyed my marriage for a brief sensational excitement.

I had mistaken the shadow for the substance.

Desperately I wanted to go back; but how can one ever do that?

I turned and ran out of the house.

He came after me calling my name.

We stood outside together and I locked the door with trembling hands. I felt that I had locked out that part of my life.

Then I ran back to Eversleigh and all the time I was thinking: That voice . . . Whose voice? The voice of someone who knows my guilty secret.

Amaryllis and Jessica

A new year had begun. I had not been alone with Jonathan since that visit to Enderby. I avoided him and I felt my determination growing stronger. My mother noticed that there was something wrong with me. She insisted that I retire early and I was only too glad to do so. I wanted to be alone to think of what I had done and whether I should ever escape from it.

Then the most appalling suspicion came to me that I might be going to have a child and this presented such a disastrous possibility that I refused at first to consider the idea. That was foolish, of course. If it were so, I must face it. I wanted a child. I always had. But if it should be happening now, how should I know who the father was?

I had thought that I could finish my relationship with Jonathan and grow away from it. But if what I feared was true, how could I ever do that? All through my life there would be a constant reminder of my guilt.

I had nightmares. I dreamed I was in that room and the voice was going on and on reminding me that I was a sinful woman, that I had offended against the laws of God and nature. I had acted with callous wantonness towards a husband who was the kindest man in the world.

I think my love for David had grown greater in those days which followed Christmas and it made me even more aware of the enormity of what I had done. I would have given anything to wipe out the last months, to go back to being the innocent young woman I once was, a woman of honour and integrity, a woman who appreciated that she was married to a good man.

How easy it is to repent when one sees the folly of one's ways! How easy to make excuses—youth, inexperience, excessive emotion, undreamed-of sensuality . . . all these might apply, but there was no excuse.

The guests had departed and Christmas was over.

Aunt Sophie was planning to move into Enderby in February and my mother was trying to dissuade her. But Sophie was eager to go.

"A big house like that needs warming up," my mother reminded her.

"We can manage. Jeanne and I will engage the servants, settle them in for a week and then we shall be ready."

I thought that in a way my mother would be relieved when she had gone. She told me that Sophie always made her feel guilty, and I, who knew great guilt, understood how it gnawed at one's peace of mind—although my mother had nothing to feel guilty about.

"I suppose," she said, "that people who are maimed like that sometimes have a way of making you feel in the wrong, particularly when . . . Oh but you know she was betrothed to your father before I married him."

"Yes, and she refused to marry him."

"It's true, and it was some time after when I married him."

"It's all so long ago. Do people ever forget?"

"They remember as long as they want to. They keep the memory alive. They get a certain satisfaction in keeping old wounds from healing."

I shivered.

"Claudine, you are not feeling quite yourself, are you?"

I started. "I'm perfectly all right," I said.

"I thought about getting Dr. Meadows to call in and have a look at you."

"Oh no, Maman, no." I spoke in panic.

She put her arm round me. "All right. Wait and see how you go."

Jonathan went to London at the beginning of the new year.

"There's a great deal of secret activity going on," said David to me in the quietness of our bedroom. "It's not only the war but the situation generally. What is happening in France has sent its reverberations all over Europe. There can't be one monarch who feels very comfortable when considering what has happened to the King and Queen of France. They must wonder if that sort of thing could spread to other countries."

"Do you think it could happen here?"

"It's what people fear, but I have a feeling we shall escape. We are not of the same temperament as the French and not nearly so likely to go in for that sort of revolution."

"We have had our riots. We even had a civil war last century."

"Yes, and perhaps it is too close in living memory for people to want anything like that again."

"And we did behead our King as they have Louis and Marie Antoinette."

"And restored a new monarch little more than ten years later. Moreover we have not the same reason here. Do you think the merchants of London want riots in the streets? They are too comfortably off. But agitators can do plenty of harm and there are criminals and vagrants who have nothing to lose. They could cause trouble."

"Do we still have these agitators here then?"

"I am sure of it. Jonathan and my father know a great deal, though they say little. Jonathan is taking over from my father, I think. They don't talk to me about it—which is quite right. Only those who are involved know what is going on."

"Your father does not tell even my mother of his secret work."

"He can tell no one, of course . . . not even Lottie. But I think he now does less of this work *because* of her."

I nodded and he put his arm about me and went on: "Are you sure nothing is wrong, Claudine?"

"Wrong?" I hoped my voice did not betray my fear.

"I thought you seemed preoccupied, as though . . . I don't quite know. Are you sure you are feeling quite well?"

I leaned against him and he put his arm about me. I was terrified that in a few moments I should confess. I must not. Jonathan was right about one thing. David must never know. Perhaps if it had been someone else he might have forgiven me. I was sure he would for he was of a forgiving nature. But his own brother! And how was I going to cope with Jonathan's actually living in the same house?

I forced myself to silence.

"Your mother thinks you should see the doctor," he said.

I shook my head. "I'm perfectly all right."

I assumed a gaiety I did not feel and I believed I managed to deceive him, as I had in that other matter.

Jonathan was in London for two weeks that January. I felt easier when he was out of the way, even though that which had occurred to me as a possibility had become a certainty.

I was pregnant after all.

I had told no one as yet. How could I tell David that I was to have a child which might not be his?

I kept my secret for two weeks. At times the prospect of a child overshadowed all else and for a brief spell my joy was boundless until I remembered that I did not know who the child's father was.

Jonathan came back from London. He was a little preoccupied; something of importance had evidently transpired there. As soon as he returned he was closeted with Dickon, and when they emerged Dickon looked very serious.

At dinner that evening Jonathan wanted to know how Enderby was progressing.

"It's full of workmen at the moment," I said pointedly.

"We shan't know the place," he replied.

"Sophie insists on going in in early February," said my mother. "I think she is unwise. She should wait till spring."

"What of the servants?"

"Jeanne is engaging them. I thank Heaven for Jeanne. She is doing most of the work. Were you busy in London?"

"Very." He smiled at her in a manner which said: No more questions please. He looked at his father and said: "You remember Jennings—Tom or was it Jack—he's been transported for publishing seditious literature."

"Transported! Surely not!" said Dickon.

"Yes, seven years to Botany Bay."

"Wasn't that rather harsh?"

"Not as things are. He was lauding Danton and stressing the wrongdoing of the monarchy in France and the rights of the people. Louis and the Queen were the bad ones and Danton and company the heroes."

"So there is real concern."

"You can call it that. It's right, of course. They have to be scented out. It was people like that who started the trouble in France."

"But transportation!" said Dickon. "That is a little harsh."

"I hope," said my mother, "that you are not thinking of making any more trips to London."

"Not just yet," Dickon assured her.

"And you, Jonathan?" asked my mother.

He lifted his shoulders, and his eyes rested on me. "I hope to spend a little time here among the joys of Eversleigh."

"How nice that you appreciate your home," said my mother lightly.

"Oh I do," he replied. "I do indeed."

When we were leaving the room I said to him: "I must talk to you."

"When?" he asked eagerly.

"Tomorrow. I shall ride in the morning, at ten o'clock."

The next morning I rode out alone and he was soon at my side.
"What of the house? Let's go there."
I replied quickly: "No. I don't intend to go to Enderby with you again. Moreover it would be impossible now even if—"
"Where shall we go then?"
"I just want to talk to you, Jonathan."
"I had to go away, you know. I hated leaving you. It was urgent business."
"It's nothing to do with that."
We turned off the road and into a field, where we pulled up.
"Jonathan," I said, "I'm going to have a child."
He looked at me in amazement.
"It's not so surprising, is it?" I went on.
"David's . . . ?"
"How could I be sure?"
He stared at me and I saw the corners of his mouth twitch.
"You find it amusing?" I asked angrily.
"Well, there is nothing to worry about, is there?"
"What do you mean? When I don't know whether it is yours or David's, you think that is nothing to worry about?"
"You're married. Married women are entitled to have babies. I find it rather intriguing."
I said: "You never took any of this seriously, did you? To you it was just a light affair. I daresay you have had many. This was a little different. Your own brother's wife. You found that rather piquant, didn't you?"
He was silent, still looking at me with that amused look on his face.
"What am I going to do?" I asked.
"Do? Do you mean shall you have it or not?"
"Are you suggesting . . . ? This is my child. Whoever its father is, it is still mine."
"Claudine, you are rather dramatic, my dear one. You are worried, but there is nothing to worry about."
"You don't think there is anything to worry about in passing off a child, who may be yours, as David's?"
"Well, if he doesn't know, what has he got to be upset about?"
How he revealed himself to me! What had I done? I had betrayed the best of men for the sake of a philanderer.
"Jonathan," I said, "it is clear that you do not take this situation seriously."

"I take you, Claudine, with the utmost seriousness. I am simply saying that there is nothing for us to worry about."

"This deceit! This betrayal! This bringing into the world of a child, letting David believe it is his when it might not be?"

"Very high-sounding," he said. "But, my dear Claudine, let us look at the facts. We have absolutely nothing to worry about. The child will have the best of everything. He'll inherit his share of Eversleigh. It's really very convenient, keeping it in the family as it were."

I turned away and he laid his hand on my arm.

"Claudine," he said pleadingly. "What a curse it is that all those people are working in Enderby. I've thought of you constantly all the time I've been away."

I had changed. That pleased me. I was no longer moved. I saw him too clearly, or was it because the child had already made me into a different woman?

I thought exultantly: It's over. He has no power over me now.

But it was too late.

I saw his expression of dismay change to resignation as I turned from him and galloped back to the house.

I was absolutely sure now, but I hesitated to tell David. That was going to be very hard. I knew that he would be delighted and I should feel this sick remorse because of the truth.

I went to my mother's room. She was resting, which was unusual for her. She was lying on her bed in a peacock-blue peignoir, looking rather languid and as beautiful as ever—no, more so because there was a special radiance about her.

"I've come to talk to you," I said. "No, don't get up. I'll sit here."

I sat on the bed and she looked intently at me. "I think I know what you are going to tell me, Claudine."

"Do you?"

She nodded. "I recognized the signs some time ago. My dearest, I'm so happy for you. It *is* a baby, isn't it?"

I nodded. She began to laugh suddenly.

"You find it amusing?" I asked.

"Very. Wait till you hear."

I looked at her in puzzlement and it was some seconds before she spoke. Then she said: "Me, too."

"What?"

"I'm so happy, Claudine. It was all I lacked and now, I'm going to have a child, too. Isn't that funny, gloriously funny. You and I, mother and daughter, in the same predicament."

She had sat up and caught me to her. We rocked to and fro for a moment laughing. Perhaps my laughter was a little hysterical, but in her joy she did not notice it.

I thought: If only I could tell her. A burden shared is a burden halved, someone had said. But then was it fair to make others carry your troubles? I had made them myself. They were my affair. I must not involve her. I must not put a cloud into all the happiness I saw in her face.

"Of course you think I'm old," she said. "But I'm not too old, Claudine. I can just about make it."

"You'll never be old. You're eternally youthful."

"There speaks my dutiful daughter, saying what she thinks Mother likes best to hear. You're right. I do. But truth is truth, is it not, and I am no longer in my first flush of youth."

"What does Dickon say?"

"Pure delight. Well, not exactly complete delight. Thrilled about the child, of course, but like you he remembers that I am not so young. I think he is going to fuss a bit. It will be odd to see him like that. He is already looking at me as though I might break at any minute."

"How lucky you are to love like that."

"Well, isn't it the same with you and David?"

I nodded because I could not speak.

"I'm glad it was David you cared for," she said. "Jonathan is very like his father . . . David is quite different."

"And you think Dickon is the perfect man."

"Oh, far from it. I soon discovered Dickon's weaknesses. Odd, that I should love them more than other people's virtues. Jonathan reminds me very much of what Dickon was at his age. I think he and Millicent will make a match of it. The Pettigrews want it. It joins up the banking interests, and Lord Pettigrew is very much involved with—that other work, I gather. But what about us? Two mothers, eh? What does David say?"

"I haven't told him yet."

"You haven't told him! You mean I am the first to know."

"You didn't tell me first," I said reproachfully.

"As a matter of fact I was a trifle embarrassed . . . at my time of life with a grown-up son and a married daughter. It seems indecent somehow."

"How absurd, Maman."

"Wait till Dickon hears your news. He'll be so delighted. He always wanted a grandson. I suppose you want a boy."

"I don't care what it is."

"No. And I feel the same. It's not so important for us. Dickon already has two sons. I think I should like a little girl." She looked tenderly at me and I put my arms round her. "Girls are closer in a way," she added.

I felt it would be a great luxury then to let myself weep, and to tell her everything that had happened.

She stroked my hair. "You mustn't be afraid, Claudine. I sensed that you have been a little, lately. Now I know why. There's nothing to be afraid of."

"No, no . . ." I said. "It's not that. It's just a little—overwhelming, isn't it?"

She agreed solemnly that it was.

I found it an ordeal telling David. How different it would have been if I had been sure the child was his, if I had never gone to Enderby and let myself be overpowered by my emotions, if I had never let that house spread its tentacles about me . . .

There I was, blaming the house again, blaming anything but my own weakness.

I had sinned and must pay for my sins.

David took my hands and kissed them.

"Oh, Claudine, I hoped and hoped . . . It is wonderful news. And you're happy, aren't you? You want this."

"Of course I want this . . . a baby of my own."

"Our own, Claudine."

I shivered a little. I wanted so much to tell, to rid myself of this burden of guilt. But I should have to carry it alone . . . all through my life.

I could not tell David any more than I could tell my mother.

What a celebration there was that night! The news was out.

Sophie was induced to join us at the table. It was a very special occasion, she was told. Sabrina came down too. She looked rather wan; she found the winters very trying and spent a great deal of time in bed now.

When we were all seated Dickon said: "I have an announcement to make. We have to drink the health of newcomers who will shortly be making their appearance at Eversleigh."

Sabrina and Sophie listened intently.

Dickon then waved his hand first to my mother and then to me.

"Lottie and I are going to have a child—and so are Claudine and David. It is a most auspicious occasion. One would have been a matter for rejoicing, but two—that means jubilation. We are going to drink the very best wine we have in the cellars to the health of our mothers. God bless them, and may all they desire be theirs."

Jonathan smiled at me as he lifted his glass.

Sabrina was shaking with emotion and I noticed that Sophie's lips were drawn down at the corners. Poor Sophie, once more she was thinking of all that she had missed.

The tears were running down Sabrina's cheeks.

"Come, come, Mother," said Dickon, "this is supposed to be a happy occasion."

"Tears of happiness, my darling boy," she said. "I know this is what you wanted to complete your happiness. A dear child . . . Lottie's . . . and another grandchild for me. I hope I live to see it."

"What nonsense!" said Dickon. "Of course you'll live to see it. I insist, and Lottie says you always do what I want."

They drank to the future; and in the kitchens the servants drank a toast to us.

There was a great deal of talk about babies at the table. My mother told of the births of my brother and myself and all the difficulties of pregnancies as though this was the most enjoyable experience known to womankind.

"I suppose," said Dickon, with feigned resignation, "this will be the burden of our conversation for months to come. I doubt we shall ever escape from nursery topics."

"It is a great deal more healthy than this continuous talk of revolution, and spies, and poor men transported merely for speaking their minds," retorted my mother.

"Wise men know when to keep silent," said Jonathan, "and that goes for women too."

He was looking straight at me and smiling.

I thought: Yes, he and Dickon are alike. Dickon must have been very like Jonathan when he was making his way to becoming one of the richest men in the country and not caring very much how he did it. Amoral, that was the word. Immoral too. But who was I to talk? I was realizing now how much I loved David; and yet I had played on him about the worst deception any woman can play upon a man.

There was no escaping my guilt. It was going to haunt me for the rest of my life.

A few weeks passed. We were in February now, and although it was cold there was the faintest hint of spring in the air. I felt very sick in the mornings and did not rise until midday; in the afternoons I felt quite well again. My mother did not seem to suffer from these signs of pregnancy.

Showing a certain resignation, Jonathan did not pursue me. I suppose I seemed a quite different woman to him now; and in any case I had lost all my desire to be with him.

I used to lie on my bed in abject misery, trying to look into the future and being unable to; and I used to think how easy it would have been to overcome this physical affliction if my mind were free from remorse. In the afternoons my mood changed, for the sickness passed and I felt surprisingly well.

I liked to ride then . . . alone. I should soon have to give up riding, and I wanted to make the most of it while I could still enjoy it.

Jonathan was very preoccupied; he and Dickon were a great deal together. Some days they rode over to Farringdon Manor and I believed Lord Pettigrew met them there. The position on the Continent was changing; and the war was not going as they had optimistically hoped. Who would have thought that a country in the throes of revolution would have been able to put an army in the field?

They were watchful; our whole country seemed to be, and that there were fears in certain quarters was certain. A great many people were being sent out to Australia for what was known as sedition.

However, I had my own problems, and on this February afternoon I decided to ride through the lanes and look for the signs of approaching spring. I had an idea that time would help me to come to terms with my problems. My baby was due in September, my mother's in August; and I looked forward to that date with an intense yearning. I had some notion that once I had my baby he—or she—would bring me such joy that it would overwhelm my melancholy.

I rode on, walking my horse. I would not gallop for fear of harming the baby—although, of course, it was too early a stage to be disturbed. However, I was cautious.

I found a certain pleasure in the sight of a few celandines peeping up among the grass. They were early—the first sign of spring; and there were crimson-tipped daisies making a brave show among the green. In the distance the river wound its way down to the sea. I rode towards it and passed over the wooden bridge which spanned it. I was startled by the sudden cry of a lapwing. They were mating down there; their cries sounded more melancholy than usual.

Soon the birds would be in full song. I used to love to listen to them. They were so joyous; *they* hadn't a care in the world.

I had a sudden desire to see the sea.

I remembered how Charlot used to look across to France with wistful longing eyes. Where was Charlot now? Charlot and Louis Charles—they were fighting with the French against the English. How would Charlot feel about that? What a complication we had made of our lives!

I could smell the sea now; the gulls were whirling round and round uttering their mournful cries, searching for food, I supposed. As I looked up and watched them I heard someone calling my name.

"Mrs. Frenshaw, Mrs. Frenshaw . . . can you come here?"

I turned my horse in the direction of the voice.

"Where are you?" I called.

"Down here." A figure emerged on the shaw and I recognized Evie Mather.

"I'm coming," I called, and rode towards her.

In a little cove, sheltered by protruded boulders, a man was lying stretched out. His face was pale, his eyes shut and his damp dark curling hair fell over his brow. He looked as though he had been washed up by the tide.

Dolly stood beside Evie, and their horses waited quietly.

"Who is he?"

Evie lifted her shoulders. "I've no idea. We've just found him. We heard someone and we came along to look. Then we saw him lying there."

I dismounted and knelt by the young man. I saw that he was young—under twenty, I should think.

I said: "He is breathing."

"He seemed to faint when we came along."

"We have to get him away from here," I said.

"That's what we thought, and we were trying to figure out how when we saw you."

"One of us could go back and send for help. Unless we can take him back with us. Do you think we could lift him and put him on my horse?"

"We could try," said Evie.

"The three of us might manage it," I replied. "It would be quicker. Could you take his feet and I'll have the other end. Dolly, hold my horse while we try."

It was not easy but we managed to get him up. He lay limply across my horse, his dangling hands almost touching the ground.

"It will be slow progress," I said.

"But quicker," repeated Evie, "than going all the way back and getting help."

"Let's go then."

I mounted my horse and we made our slow return to Eversleigh.

That was how we found Alberic Claremont.

As soon as we arrived at Eversleigh we got him to bed. He opened his eyes and looked at us vaguely.

"He's probably starving," said my mother. "We'll try him with a little soup. But first we'll send for the doctor."

When the doctor arrived he said the young man would soon recover. There was nothing wrong with him except that he was suffering from exposure and as we had thought, exhaustion. A few days' rest and some nourishing food, served in small quantities at first but frequently, and he should soon be quite fit.

The diagnosis proved to be correct. At the end of the first day the young man was able to open his eyes and speak to us.

He spoke in French so we guessed his story even before he told it to us. He had escaped from the Terror and was seeking refuge in England as so many of his fellow countrymen were doing at this time.

They had taken his father to the guillotine. He had done no wrong, but he had been a bailiff to one of the big estates in the south of France. His brother was in the army serving his country. He had been warned that he had been marked as an enemy of the revolution, so he had known there was only one thing for him to do—get away.

He had left his home and travelled through France disguised as a peasant. He had reached the coast. There were ways of getting across, provided money could change hands, and he embarked in a remote bay in France and landed at an equally isolated one in England.

"Were you alone?" asked my mother.

He shook his head. "There were two others. I do not know what became of them. I only know that they shared the boat with me and when I said I was so exhausted that I could not go on they left me."

"They might have looked after you," I put in.

"Madame, they were afraid. We have suffered much. I understood, and I implored them to leave me. They say there are too many émigrés arriving and that your government does not want them and may send them back." He shivered. "They were afraid that if there were three of us . . ."

"I wonder where they have gone," I said.

He lifted his shoulders and closed his eyes.

"He is very tired," said my mother. "Don't let us disturb him just now."

The next morning he was much refreshed. We kept him in bed and he seemed very pleased to stay there.

He spoke a little English but it was necessary for us to conduct our conversation in French.

He told us his name was Alberic Claremont. He said: "I can never go back to France. You wouldn't send me, would you? Would you?"

There was such terror in his eyes that my mother cried out fiercely: "Never."

Dickon, who had returned late in the evening, had listened to the story without any great surprise.

"They are flying from the Terror in hundreds," he said. "I wonder we don't get more of them. What sort of man is he?"

"He's young," replied my mother. "He seems educated. I think he has been through terrible dangers."

"That seems likely."

"I want to see him quite well before he leaves here."

"Where will he go to?"

"I don't know. Perhaps he has friends here. Perhaps he can find the friends he came with. I don't think much of them, leaving him like that on the shore."

I put in: "You know the spot, close by the old boat house. It's very lonely there. Evie and Dolly Mather just happened to find him."

"He might have stayed there for a long time if they hadn't," said my mother.

"He would never have survived at this time of the year."

"Well, let's see how he shapes up," said Dickon.

Sophie was very interested to hear how we had rescued the young man. She came to see him and sat by his bed talking to him in their native tongue, and I could see that she had taken a fancy to Alberic Claremont.

Next morning Evie called with Dolly to enquire about the young man they had rescued.

I took them up to his bedroom. He was lying in his bed looking quite different from the young man they had found on the beach.

"So you are the young ladies who found me," he said in French.

His eyes were on Evie and she flushed a little as she replied in English: "My sister and I were riding. We often go down to the sea. How glad I am that we went yesterday."

He could not understand very well and I said: "Monsieur Claremont speaks very little English, Evie. Have you any French?"

She flushed again and stammered that she had a little but not much. "Grandmamma insisted that our governess teach Dolly and me French. But we aren't very good at it, are we, Dolly?"

"*You* are, Evie," said Dolly.

"Not very, I'm afraid."

"Try," I said.

And she did. She had just enough to make herself understood in simple sentences, and Alberic Claremont seemed to be very pleased to assist her. He tried to speak English and they laughed together while Dolly sat silent, watching her sister's face all the time.

When she left, Evie asked if she might call again.

I said but of course she must.

My mother commented: "Evie is delighted with him because she has probably saved his life. There is nothing more endearing than someone who owes you a great deal, and what could be more than a life?"

"You sound more like Dickon every day."

"I suppose one grows a little like someone with whom one is in constant contact."

"Don't grow too much like him, dear Maman. Stay yourself."

"I promise," she said.

Within a few days Alberic was quite well.

We had family discussions about him. What could we do for him? There he was, a young man restored to health; he had brought French currency with him, but what good was that in England? Where could he go? What could he do? Could he work somewhere? The French were not very popular in England at this time.

It was Sophie who came up with the solution.

She needed servants. She was looking for them now. What if she offered Alberic a post in her household? What could he be? A butler? Could he work in the gardens? It was not so important how he worked as that he did. She would talk to him and discover for what he was best suited.

"In any case," she said, "he can come to Enderby and stay there until he decides what he must do. When this terrible revolution is over, perhaps there will be changes in France. In which case those French who are sheltering here might want to go back."

It was a solution, and when it was put to Alberic that for the time being he should go to Enderby and work there for Aunt Sophie in whatever capacity they found most suitable, he accepted with alacrity.

At the end of February Sophie moved into Enderby. Alberic delighted her and Jeanne approved of him. He was an indefatigable worker, and he was so grateful to Sophie for providing a home for him that he declared he would die for her.

Dickon said cynically: "It might be a different story if the noble young gentleman were called upon to carry out his promise. All the same, French melodrama apart, he is reasonably grateful, and as Sophie was looking for people to serve her, she has found one, who because of his position and the fact that he shared her nationality, could prove satisfactory."

At the beginning of March Jonathan went to London. I was always relieved when he was not in the house, and I was beginning to sink into a sense of security. I was completely absorbed by the baby as it grew within me, and other matters just slipped through my consciousness without my taking much notice of them.

My mother and I were together a great deal. As we both needed rest, we would often lie side by side on her bed and she would talk to me of her life, of her marriage to my father, of his death, and the knowledge that it had always been Dickon whom she had loved.

"My mother came to great happiness late in life, and so did I," she said. "I think perhaps this is the best time for happiness to come. Then you appreciate it more; and it is not so easy to strive for it in one's mature years, as it is when one is young. When you are young you believe in miracles. You think you just have to catch them and they are yours. When you are older, you know they are rare, and if one comes your way, how you cherish it, how you appreciate it!"

I was able to draw on her contentment, and it said a great deal for my powers of deception that I was able to convince her that I was as happy as she was.

We discussed the nursery. "It will be as though the babies are twins," she said. "What if one of us did have twins? There are twins in the family. Twins for you and twins for me. Four of them, Claudine. Just think of that."

I could laugh with her.

During that month Sabrina caught a cold which persisted. She lay in bed looking very small and wan.

Dickon spent a great deal of time with her, and that gave her immense pleasure.

We were all aware that she was dying and for several years we had watched her carefully through the winters. She liked to have my mother or me with her when Dickon could not be there. She would hold my hand and talk to me of the past, and again and again she stressed the great joy which had been hers when Dickon came home with my mother.

"He loved her as a child," she said. "But your grandmother did not want the marriage. Oh, she did what she thought was right, and the result was that your mother—dear Lottie—was taken away from us. Dickon married and so did she, but now it is as it should be and they are together. It is wonderful that their marriage is to be fruitful. If I could have one wish it would be to see their child. But, my dear Claudine, I do not think I shall manage that."

"You will," I said. "Dickon says you must, and you know you always have pleased him."

"He has brought the greatest joy into my life. When his father was killed in that dreadful battle at Culloden, I thought it was the end of everything for me, and then Dickon came and I started to live again."

"I know," I said. "And Dickon has made you happy."

"He is the most wonderful of men, Claudine. And so are his boys. And now he is to have another child . . . and so are you. The family goes on. That is the important thing, Claudine. We come and we go; we live our lives; we make our marks. And I suppose every one of us has a part to play. Then we pass on. But the family remains. It will go on through the generations."

I said she must not tire herself with too much talking; but she replied that it did her good to talk.

"Be happy, Claudine," she said. "There is too much unhappiness in the world. I remember the guilt I felt as a child. It should never have been. It was only when I married Dickon's father that I started to live. Then I lost him and would have mourned him all my life, but Dickon was born and then I was happy."

I sat listening to her; and I saw clearly what I must do. Not only for my sake but for that of everyone else. There was no way of telling whether David or Jonathan was the father of my child, but I was going to believe that David was. I was going to try to put the past behind me and be happy.

March was gone and April had come in milder and with a touch of spring in the air.

It seemed that Sabrina had lived through another winter after all. But that was not to be. One morning in early April, her maid went into her bedroom as usual to take in her morning hot chocolate and could not wake her. Sabrina lay quietly, serenely, at peace.

Death in the house. It had come quietly and was not unexpected, but that did not make it any easier to bear. Sabrina had lived quietly, in the background; there had been days when we had not seen her; but she was part of the household and now she was gone.

Dickon was very distressed. She had adored him so unreservedly, and all his life she had been there to applaud his virtues and excuse his faults, and to assure him that he was the perfect man. My mother comforted him, but she, too, missed Sabrina.

Jonathan was away at the time and Dickon said that they must send for him to come home for the burial. I had thought that he was in London, but the messenger was sent to the Pettigrews', and Jonathan came, accompanied by Lord and Lady Pettigrew and Millicent.

Sabrina was to be buried in the family mausoleum and there was to be a service for her in our own chapel. The priest who had married David and me read the service and we all followed the solemn procession to the mausoleum.

I was surprised to see that Harry Farringdon had arrived with several of those people who lived near enough to join the company.

Evalina Trent was there with her two grand-daughters. Afterwards they all returned to the house, where wine and food were served.

Everyone was talking about Sabrina, stressing her many virtues as people do at funerals, and we were all saying how much she would be missed.

"At least she died easily and happily," was the verdict. "She was so delighted at the prospect of the new babies."

I saw that Harry Farringdon was talking to Evie and that there was a slight flush in her cheeks. I thought: I hope something comes of that. It would be such a good match for Evie, and she is a nice girl, different from that dreadful grandmother of hers. Poor girl, she could not help her relations.

I sat down because I was beginning to feel tired, and in view of my condition I felt everyone would understand.

I was not long alone. To my dismay it was Evalina Trent who came and sat down beside me.

"Nice to get your feet off the ground," she said cosily. "I expect you're beginning to feel the weight. What'll it be now, four months eh?"

"Yes," I said.

"Then there'll be rejoicing up at Eversleigh . . . and your mother too! That's really a bit of fun, don't you think?"

"It is very agreeable for us both."

She looked at me slyly.

"Oh, you're a lucky young lady. Such a good husband—and a little one on the way so soon! You're one of the favoured of the gods, as they say."

"Thank you."

"I wish I could do more for my girls. I worry a lot, Mrs. Frenshaw."

"Do you?"

"Well, look at my Evie now. Pretty as a picture. She's old enough now to be out and about in society. And what can I do for her?"

"She seems very happy."

"She's a good girl. But I'd like her to have her chance."

"In what way?"

"In the only way! I'd like to see her make a good marriage, be settled like."

"I daresay she will marry."

"Yes . . . but what sort of marriage, eh? I'd like someone of some position." She was watching Harry Farringdon intently. "Such a pleasant young man. He's very rich, I believe."

"You mean Harry Farringdon? Well, I don't exactly know the state of his family's fortune."

"Ha! You think I'm speaking above myself, don't you? Perhaps I am. It's Evie that bothers me. I've brought her up as a lady. The best of education . . . It's not been easy. Grasslands is not Eversleigh, you know. My Richard . . . he's gone now, God rest his soul . . . but he was a bit of a gambler. He lost a lot of what my first husband Andrew left to me. Not that it was anything like Eversleigh even then. But I've had a struggle to make ends meet, you know, and I was determined to give Evie the best."

"I think you did very well."

"She should be gracing some rich man's table."

"Is that what she thinks?"

"Her? She's romantic. Young girls dream about love, not security. Mrs. Frenshaw, that Mr. Farringdon is taken with her, wouldn't you say?"

"Yes, Mrs. Trent, I suppose I would."

"You see I can't give balls and banquets at Grasslands. Not the sort they'd expect. But I'd like her to have her chance."

"I understand," I said.

She put out a hand and took mine; hers was cold and bony; for some reason it made me shiver.

"Would you help me, Mrs. Frenshaw?"

"Help you?"

"With Evie."

"I certainly would if I could, but I don't see how . . ."

"Well, there are ways. You could—er—bring them together. You know what I mean. Pair them off and all that. You get my meaning?"

"But . . ."

She gave me a little nudge. "You will if you can, I know. Oh, there's ways. You could invite him . . . and then have my Evie there. You know what I mean."

"Well, we shan't be entertaining for a while at such a time."

"Oh, it needn't be a grand entertainment. He just comes . . . and my Evie's there. You could find a way . . . if you would."

"I don't think they'll need my matchmaking."

"A little helping along never did any harm." She was looking at me steadily. "There's reasons why you should help me, Mrs. Frenshaw."

"Reasons?"

She nodded, smiling slyly, and my heart started to beat uneasily. What was she hinting?

"Oh," she went on, "there's a lot of secrets in life. Things happen . . . and you wouldn't believe it unless you knew they were true."

"What things?" I said sharply.

She leaned towards me. "One of these days I'll explain. Then I think you would want to do all you could for my Evie."

My mother was calling me and I said: "You'll have to excuse me, Mrs. Trent."

"Of course I will. Don't forget what I said though, will you? Do all you can for my Evie. I think you'll be rather glad that you did."

I escaped.

"I could see that awful woman was bothering you," said my mother. "I thought I'd rescue you."

"Thanks," I said. "I'm glad you did."

I could not get her out of my mind; and that night she seemed to haunt my dreams.

The Farringdons left on the day of the funeral, but the Pettigrews stayed with us for a few days.

It could only have been two days after we had buried Sabrina that the news broke about the execution of Georges Jacques Danton, one of the prime movers in the revolution.

Dickon was grimly amused. "Ironical," he said, "that the very Revolutionary Tribunal which he set up should be the one to condemn him."

"It is clear," commented Lord Pettigrew, "that the revolution is coming to an end."

"There is still Robespierre."

"Wouldn't you say his days are numbered?"

"It would be wonderful," said my mother sadly, "if they all stopped making this trouble and life returned to normal in France."

"Life in France will never again be what it was," said Jonathan.

Everyone agreed with that.

"Heads are falling fast," was David's comment. "Just imagine Danton's living only six months after the execution of the Queen. It shows that this is a struggle for power. I daresay some of them started out with ideals. Perhaps they did want to fight for the rights of the people. Then they grasped power . . . and they struggled for more and when they had destroyed those they thought of as the enemy, they began to fight among themselves. This is the struggle of the giants. Danton could not have believed it possible that this could happen to him."

"Robespierre has rid himself of Danton, but his turn will come," prophesied Dickon. "And when that happens the revolution will be at an end."

"Their successes with the army are just amazing," said Lord Pettigrew. "There is talk of a young soldier . . . Napoleon Bonaparte, I think he is called . . . He seems to be making a name for himself in the army."

"I've heard of him," said Dickon. "He's hand in glove with Robespierre. If Robespierre falls, that could be the end of this enterprising young soldier."

"Events are moving fast," put in Lord Pettigrew. "I think we are going to see changes."

"Which will be very pleasant for us all," said my mother. "The talk at this table is of nothing else but the French revolution."

"I thought it was apt to centre on these blessed infants who are shortly to join the family circle," said Jonathan.

"A much happier subject," admitted Dickon.

"I think it is perfectly wonderful," added Lady Pettigrew.

My mother and I used to rest immediately after the midday meal for an hour or so and then we would feel refreshed until the evening. We often spent the time together. We would lie on the big bed chatting, and we both looked forward to those sessions. Sometimes one of us dozed and the other would lie quietly. Even though we did not always talk we liked to be together.

On this afternoon, she said to me: "So it has come at last. They were going to announce it, but it did not seem an appropriate time because of the funeral."

"Who and what?" I asked.

She laughed. "Oh . . . Jonathan and Millicent."

"Yes?"

"Well, we always knew it would happen. I am so glad. It will take Dickon's mind off his mother's death. He feels that so deeply, far more so than you'd think. He always wanted a link with the Pettigrews."

I said faintly: "Banking interests?"

"They were in a sense rivals. Together they'll be supreme, the most influential in the country, I imagine. It is what they both want, the Pettigrews as much as Dickon."

"I see."

"You took David . . . and that left Jonathan."

"Dear Maman," I said, "how wordly you have become! You talk as though marriage were just shifting counters on a board. This one is taken so the other will bring in the banking interest."

"It's not like that at all. You can see Jonathan and Millicent like each other. I assure you neither of them had to be persuaded."

"I suppose Jonathan would always be aware of the advantages. Millicent too. They seem to be ideally matched."

She laughed. "You and David were so much in love and I'm glad of it. That can't happen so idyllically to everyone. But that doesn't mean that things can't be worked out very satisfactorily."

"Will they live here when they are married?"

"I suppose so. It's the ancestral home, after all. It's usual for sons to bring their wives to the house which will one day be theirs. I see what you are thinking. In a way there'll be three mistresses of the house. Two have worked out very satisfactorily, haven't they?"

"You are my mother. That's different."

She was thoughtful. "Millicent is rather a forceful young lady," she mused. "It's a strange situation. Twin brothers . . . and Eversleigh belongs to them both. There isn't an elder son really, though Jonathan was born a little while before David. Dickon doesn't say much about it. I believe he thinks there will be plenty for both of them when the time comes, which pray God will not be for a very long time. And Eversleigh will always be the family home. Claudine, don't worry about this marriage. It'll be all right. I shall be here. And I think they will spend a great deal of time at the London house. That's where Jonathan's interest lies. He is rarely here for very long stretches at a time. He was . . . just before Christmas. I have never known him to stay so long before."

My heart was beating uncertainly, and again I had one of those impulses to confess all to her.

Fortunately it passed.

"They'll be announcing their engagement soon," went on my mother. "They will have to put off the wedding for a while, however, because of Sabrina's death. But there could be a quiet wedding at Pettigrew's place, of course."

I closed my eyes.

"You're tired, aren't you? It was rather a strenuous morning. And all that Danton talk at the table! I'm so tired of it . . . and it always upsets me. It brings back memories."

"Dear Maman, don't think of it now." I smiled at her wryly and said as she so often said to me: "It's bad for the child."

I saw the smile on her lovely face. She pressed my hand and we both closed our eyes. I guessed that in spite of everything, she was thinking of that terrible time when she was in the hands of the mob and Dickon had come, like a shining knight, to rescue her. My thoughts were of Jonathan married to Millicent, living here in Eversleigh; and at the back of my mind loomed up the sly eyes of Mrs. Trent, telling me that she was sure I should want to do all I could for Evie if she explained . . . What had she meant?

The oppressive weight of my guilt had descended on me once more.

The afternoon was warm. I had walked across the lawn and sat down on the seat near the pond about which the yellow daffodils were waving in the slight breeze.

I looked at the beautiful flowers, and I thought then, as I had a thousand times before, how happy I could have been if I had been a faithful and virtuous wife to David.

Jonathan came quietly across the grass and stood behind me. As he laid a hand on my shoulder I turned and got to my feet.

"No," he said. "Sit down. I have to talk to you."

He drew me down and sat beside me.

"Don't be so agitated," he said. "What is wrong with this? Brother and sister-in-law sitting side by side on a seat in the garden exchanging pleasantries. There's nothing wrong with that."

"I was going in," I said.

"And now you will stay and chat for a while. I want to tell you something."

"I know. You are engaged to Millicent Pettigrew."

"So you knew."

"My mother told me. There would have been an announcement but because of the funeral it has been held back."

"You mustn't think this makes any difference."

"What *do* you mean? I should have thought there would have been a great difference between being married and unmarried."

"I meant to us, of course. I'm still in love with you."

"Jonathan," I said, "I don't think you have ever been in love with anyone except yourself."

"*I* think that most of us, if we're honest, have to admit to a lifelong passion for ourselves."

"Some people care for others too."

"That's what I'm telling you. I have always loved you. I always shall and nothing is going to make any difference."

"Haven't you understood that all that is over? I thought I had made it rather clear."

"You've been different, of course, aloof. But that is natural. It's all this baby business."

"You haven't understood at all. I deeply regret what happened. I have been weak and foolish and everything that is despicable."

"You were adorable. You are a passionate woman, Claudine. You have desires like the rest of us and it is only natural that you should gratify them."

"I am very satisfied with what I have. I wish to God I had never done what I did."

"You have forgotten that joy we had together."

"It meant little."

"Oh come now, Claudine. You have the maternal spirit with you now. It will be different when the child is born. You'll come back to me then."

"I wonder what Millicent would say if she could hear her prospective bridegroom trying to make assignations with someone else's wife even before the engagement to her is officially announced."

"You don't propose to tell her."

"No, I don't. And I don't propose to see you alone again ever."

"You are most dramatic. That's the French blood. You'll feel differently later on."

"You are quite—cynical."

"I'm realistic."

"If this blatant conduct is realism . . ."

"I know you prefer to live in your fantasy world. You are a strange girl, Claudine. Perhaps that is why I love you. You can be practical and yet so fanciful. Remember the voices you heard."

"I often remember them."

"That was when the trouble started. You got an attack of conscience."

"A disease from which you are never likely to suffer."

"It's strange," he said. "Our relationship has always been like this . . . sparring. Until those moments at Enderby in that room when you stopped pretending and admitted the truth. Remember?"

"I'm doing my best to forget, Jonathan. There is one thing I ask of you. Please, let me forget."

He looked at me intently. I saw the light in his eyes; it was not that intense blue which I likened to flames. It was calculating, speculating. I saw that he did not desire me sufficiently now with my bulky body and what he called my maternal spirit; but he was thinking of the past and I guessed that with his natural arrogance he believed he could rekindle those fires in me which had been temporarily dampened down by my condition.

He said: "You are young in the ways of the world."

"If you are an example of an adult, I never want to grow up."

"You're broody, maternal. I wouldn't recognize you as that eager young girl."

"You will never see her again."

"I will find her. Rest assured of that."

"There is one thing I rest assured of, and that is that you never will, for she has gone forever."

"That would be a calamity too great to be endured. Trust me. I will find her. I will bring her out of her hiding place."

"I wonder what your future wife would think," I said. "Oh look. Here she comes. Shall we discuss it with her?"

It was true. Millicent was coming across the grass towards us.

"Oh there you are," she said. "I've been looking for you. What a pleasant afternoon!"

She sat down on the other side of Jonathan and put a proprietorial arm through his.

Sophie had settled into Enderby. The house suited her sombre mood. She did not seem to notice its ghostly ambiance and if she did it did not disturb her.

Alberic Claremont had proved a great asset and she was clearly delighted with him. He was of a very merry nature with a gift for making friends—quite different from Sophie herself—and it surprised us all that she was so pleased with him. He had quickly taken the role of major domo, working in conjunction with Jeanne who, fortunately, did not resent this, but encouraged it. Jeanne would do anything to make Sophie's life happier and she must have realized that her interest in this young man helped her to forget her own troubles.

There was another frequent visitor to the house. This was Dolly Mather. I could understand that well. Dolly was disfigured, as Sophie herself was, and lame ducks were special protégés of Sophie. It was natural, for they helped her to minimize her own misfortunes, whereas someone like my mother—beautiful and beloved, the mother of children—brought home most forcibly to Sophie that life had treated her unkindly.

She had a certain feeling for me and she was interested in the coming baby. I was made more welcome than most, and once, in a very unusual communicative mood, she told me that she often thought of me as her daughter. "If," she said, "that tragic firework disaster had never taken place in the square that night, I should not have been like this. My marriage would have gone ahead. I should have been your father's wife and you and Charlot would have been my children."

I did not point out that my mother had also had a share in making me, and I believed I should have been a very different person if I had been Sophie's daughter.

She talked of Leon Blanchard, whom she had loved much later. I remembered him. He had come to the *château* to be tutor to Charlot and Louis Charles and we had all liked him very much. Then he had left. I remembered that he and Sophie had had some romantic attachment. He had turned out to be no real tutor but an agitator who had wormed his way into the *château* to spy and he was urging the people to revolt.

Poor Sophie. Life had been cruel to her.

And now here she was with her own household in Enderby, making a life for herself with her lame ducks; poor Alberic, who had escaped from France, and Dolly, who was a sad little creature.

It was July. I was getting very heavy now, but I still liked to walk when I could, and the distance to Enderby was just about as much as I wanted, particularly as I could rest there before making my way back.

As I arrived I saw Evie and Dolly at the entrance to the house. I immediately thought of Mrs. Trent's words at the funeral, and wondered whether Evie had had any communications with Harry Farringdon. It must be rather unsatisfactory to be living so far away and the Trents and Farringdons not being the kind of families who would be on visiting terms. It seemed to be a somewhat slight romance. No wonder Mrs. Trent wanted to speed it up.

Evie said: "Oh, hello, Mrs. Frenshaw. Dolly's going to see Mademoiselle d'Aubigné. She's invited."

"And you?" I asked.

"No . . . not me. Only Dolly."

I supposed that a lovely girl like Evie would remind Sophie of her affliction. How sad that life had to be seen that way by some! Poor Sophie! But who was I to criticize her for human failings?

"I am calling on her, too," I said.

Alberic came out of the house then. He bowed to us. His eyes went to Dolly.

"Mademoiselle d'Aubigné will be delighted to see Madame Frenshaw and you, Mademoiselle."

"I hope so," I said.

"She awaits you," he told Dolly.

Dolly took her horse to the stable and I went into the house, after Evie had said goodbye and ridden off.

Sophie was seated in a small room which led from the hall and where she received her visitors. She was dressed in that pale mauve which suited her dark colouring and her hood matched her dress.

She said: "It's good of you to come, Claudine."

"I wanted to know how you are. I shan't be able to come much longer—until after the baby is born."

"Sit down at once, dear child. You must be tired."

I said that the little journey was just about as much as I could manage.

Jeanne came in and greeted me.

I said: "What wonders you have worked on the house, Jeanne!"

"It has been such a pleasure."

"It must be nearly finished now."

"We are always discovering new things."

Dolly came in then, rather shyly, and Sophie held out a hand to her.

"Come and sit down, Dolly. We'll have some lemonade. Alberic, will you bring it?"

"Lemonade!" I cried. "I should love some. I knew French people love it. I remember how people used to sell it in the streets of Paris before . . ."

"Before everything went wrong."

Jeanne said: "I have some little cakes. English cakes to go with the French lemonade."

She left us then and I said: "Well, Aunt Sophie, you've worked a miracle with this house."

"I am so glad I found it. It has made such a difference. I have my independence now. Jeanne and I appreciate that."

"I understand."

"And I have my friends." She touched Dolly's arm and the girl smiled shyly. "We are teaching Dolly French and Alberic English. It is amusing."

That Aunt Sophie should find anything amusing was in itself miraculous, and I had a notion that Dolly and Alberic were doing as much good for her as she was for them.

Alberic came in with the lemonade.

"As we have a visitor today," said Sophie, "there will be no lesson."

"It is very pleasant for Mademoiselle to have a visitor," said Alberic in halting English.

"Very good," said Aunt Sophie. She spoke in French telling him to pour out the lemonade. "Dolly, hand round the cakes."

Dolly rose with alacrity, a smile of pleasure on her face.

"They are very good today," said Sophie as she bit into one of them. "They must have known we were going to have the honour of a visit from Eversleigh."

I told her that I should be delighted to come whenever she asked me.

She nodded and enquired after my mother's health.

"She is very well, thanks, and getting very near her time."

"August, is it? Poor Lottie, she is a little old."

"She doesn't consider herself 'poor,' " I said quickly.

"No, of course not. She always had . . . everything. I suppose there is a great fuss going on."

"About the baby, you mean. The midwife is already there. It's a little soon, but Dickon insisted. He is really quite nervous. I have never seen him like that before."

Perhaps I should not have stressed his devotion to my mother; it was one of those aspects which Sophie found it hard to accept. I sometimes believed that she would like some misfortune to come to my mother. The thought so horrified me that I disliked Aunt Sophie in that moment. Why could she not accept her misfortune? Why did she allow her resentment to make her so bitter?

But who was I to criticize others? I was sure I was going through my life with the knowledge that my own sin was far greater than those I was condemning in others.

"An August baby," said Aunt Sophie. "And yours is to be September. Imagine two babies in a nursery which must have been empty for so long."

"That is how it is with nurseries," I said.

"It makes it easier to have the two so close together," remarked Jeanne practically. "They will be companions for each other."

"That's what I think," I said, smiling at Jeanne.

Alberic came over to bring me more lemonade, which was cool and delicious, and after a little while I said I would be leaving as I seemed to want a great deal of rest nowadays.

"It's wise to do as your body bids you," commented Jeanne. "If you feel tired, that means you need rest."

I smiled appreciatively at Jeanne. She was so reasonable and seemed to bring a breath of sanity into any situation.

"Before you go, would you like to look round the house?" she asked. "We have made alterations. Or do you feel too tired?"

"I'd like to see them. I've always been fascinated by this house."

"I will show Madame Frenshaw round," said Jeanne; and I kissed Aunt Sophie and said goodbye to her, Dolly and Alberic.

As we went out I heard Aunt Sophie say: "Now, my dears, we can proceed with our lesson. You begin, Dolly. You must talk more in company. There's no need to be shy, you know."

Jeanne smiled at me as she shut the door.

"It gives her great pleasure," she said. "They are a pleasant pair. Little Dolly is a mouse. Alberic, he can roar like a lion. They amuse her, and they are coming along with their talking. Dolly is quite good but there is a shyness she must overcome. Alberic . . . he is not so afflicted."

"It's wonderful that she has found this interest."

"That and the house. She needs to be interested. It is what I have always wanted for her."

"You have been wonderful, Jeanne. You know how we appreciate you."

"We owe so much to Monsieur Jonathan. He brought us out of France. We could not have long survived. We shall never forget."

"It is the sort of adventure which he does very well," I said shortly.

"He is like his father, who has been the good husband to Madame Lottie."

"Yes," I said. "Oh, I see you have the curtains up in the gallery."

"It was so bare without them. They were such good curtains. Mademoiselle d'Aubigné would have had new ones but I saw that a good cleaning and a little stitch here and there, and they would be as good as new."

"Always practical," I said. "And they certainly look magnificent. They've restored that look to the gallery. That mystery. To think that it all comes from curtains!"

"Shall we start at the top and work down?"

"Excellent," I replied.

We climbed the stairs.

"You do not find them too much?" she asked.

"Not if I pause here and there. I'm really very well . . . just weighty."

"I understand. And what joy for you when this little one comes."

"Oh yes, I long for it."

We were passing the room. The door was shut. I would steel myself to look at it later.

We went up the stairs to the next floor.

"You will see that we have done much," said Jeanne. "But there is still much to do."

"It is miraculous."

"I do not wish to finish too soon."

"You like to keep the interest going for Mademoiselle d'Aubigné."

Jeanne nodded. "There are many discussions and we discover what can be done about this and that. It adds a great excitement."

"Of course."

"You see we have new curtains in some places . . . but in many we have used those which were already here. And much of the furniture too. We have done rather well—with what your mother has given us from Eversleigh."

"Indeed you have."

We were down to the first floor. She showed me the big bedroom with the four-poster bed in it, which Sophie had taken for hers when they had first come to the house.

"She no longer sleeps in this room. She has moved and I have the room next to her. If she wants me in the night she has only to knock on the wall. I have given her a brass poker. It rests by her bed."

"Does she need you in the night? She's not ill, is she?"

"Oh no, no. It is just in case. She is nervous since the trouble started. While we were in France we never knew from one night to the next whether someone would be coming for us. I always had my bed in her room then, so I was within call. She is nervous if I am not at hand, so I thought of the poker."

"Dear Jeanne, you think of everything. She has taken one of the other rooms then."

"I will show you. Come."

She led me along the corridor. I felt a little faint, for she had opened the door to that room which was so well known to me. I saw the bed with the blue velvet curtains—now cleaned and seeming a brighter shade of blue. I looked at the court cupboard, now polished and shining.

"So," I said faintly, "this is now her bedroom."

Jeanne nodded. "And mine is next to it. We made a discovery here . . . such an interesting one."

"Oh?"

"Come. Look here . . . by the door. It is very cleverly done. You can hardly see it."

"What is it?"

"A hole in the floor . . . right against the wall. Do you see it?"

"Oh . . . yes."

"It's the end of a tube. A kind of speaking tube."

My heart began to beat wildly.

"Are you all right, Madame?" asked Jeanne.

I put my hand to my stomach. "It was—just a flutter."

"Sit down on the bed. You are overtired, I think. You must go back in the carriage."

"Oh, no. I'm perfectly all right. Tell me about this speaking tube."

"It is cleverly constructed. When I first noticed it I had a vague notion that I had seen something like it before. I put my hand to the hole and shouted down it. I could not hear my voice, but I knew that it was coming out in another part of the house. We were immediately over the kitchens, so it seemed likely that the other end of the tube was in the kitchens. Someone must have had it put in when the house was built . . . perhaps someone who wanted to send messages from the bedroom down to the kitchens."

"It's ingenious," I stammered.

"Are you sure you feel all right?"

"Quite sure. Do go on about the tube."

"Dolly was here at the time. I made her shout through the tube and I went down to the kitchens. I heard her voice and discovered exactly where it was coming from. I was soon about to find what I sought. A cupboard has been built round it. But there it was. What an amazing discovery! When I told Mademoiselle about it she wanted to move into this room. She said that if I was in the kitchens she could talk to me from the bedroom. I can see you think I have exaggerated, Madame. Allow me to go to the kitchens. I will speak to you through the tube."

I sat there on the bed and in due course the voice came up to me.

"Mrs. Frenshaw. You can hear me, I believe."

It was all coming back: the memory of my abandonment on this very bed, the voice through the tube. It did not sound like Jeanne's voice exactly; it was muted, hollow, in the way that other voice had been.

I stared at the door.

There had been someone in the house then . . . someone in the kitchens, someone who knew that I had been here with Jonathan.

That other voice echoed in my mind. "Mrs. Frenshaw, remember the seventh commandment."

Jeanne came back triumphant.

"You heard?"

I nodded.

"You could have answered me through the tube. What a discovery! This house is full of surprises. I am so glad we came here."

I walked home slowly across the fields. Jeanne wanted to accompany me but I wouldn't hear of it.

There was one thought which whirled round and round in my mind. Someone was there. Someone saw us go into the house. Someone knew.

All through the sultry days of July we awaited the birth of my mother's child. We were all a little anxious . . . except her. She had no qualms. I had never before seen Dickon in such a state of nerves. He had always been so calmly sure of himself and his ability to get what he wanted; now he was in a state bordering on terror.

Even the news of Robespierre's execution did not arouse great interest in him, although he had been predicting it during the previous months and was sure that his removal would mean the end of the revolution.

He had no thought for anything but my mother.

On the fourth of August my little half sister was born and the moment she put in an appearance our anxiety evaporated. It was a quick birth; my mother came through with rare ease; and the child was perfect. We were all sitting tense, waiting; and I shall never forget the sound of that baby's crying.

I ran to Dickon and embraced him, and as he looked at me I was sure there were tears in his eyes. But his first thought was, of course, for my mother, and later when I went in to see the child, he was there, holding her hand, sitting by her bed; and I was overcome with emotion just looking at them.

They were delighted with a baby—quite sure, both of them, that there had never been such a perfect child. They marvelled over her possession of ten toes and the requisite number of thumbs and fingers—all fitted with nails. They gazed at her red wrinkled face as though it were the very pinnacle of beauty; she was everything they wanted to complete their happiness.

There was a great deal of discussion about a name; and finally my mother said she was to be Jessica. She did not know why, but the name seemed just right.

So Jessica she became.

I had another month to wait and the days passed quickly.

I was not going out now, apart from an amble round the garden. My mother had quickly recovered and liked to have me with her. We talked about babies mostly, and that meant for my mother the perfections of Jessica.

The midwife stayed on to be ready for me, and my mother had engaged a nurse—Grace Soper—who would look after the two babies when mine arrived.

Everything was in readiness, waiting.

Often enough during those last weeks I had forgotten my fears. I lived in a world of serenity. I had recovered from the shock of discovering that it had been no ghostly voice that I had heard, and that a living person had actually been in the house while I had been there with Jonathan; and that person shared our secret.

It had been a devastating discovery and one which filled me with dread, yet I could forget it. I could think of nothing but the coming of my child.

At last the day arrived.

My delivery was not as swift and easy as my mother's. I suffered long and intensely and now and then the thought would come into my mind that I was being punished for my sins.

But at last it was over and my child was born. There came that moment of sheer bliss when I heard my baby's voice for the first time.

"Another little girl!" That was the midwife.

A little girl! I was exultant. In that moment I did not care what had brought her to me. All that mattered was that she had come.

They put her in my arms. She seemed prettier than Jessica. But perhaps that was just a mother's prejudice. She had fine fair hair whereas Jessica's hair was dark brown. Her face was smoother. I thought her beautiful. She reminded me of a lily.

They were at my bed—David and my mother. David was marvelling at the child which he believed to be his. My mother's eyes were on me, proud, full of tenderness.

She is David's child, I thought. She is. She must be. But how could I be sure?

My mother said we had the two most beautiful babies in the world. And what was I going to call mine?

The name came suddenly into my head and after that it seemed the only one possible. Rather fanciful, yet fitting her perfectly: Amaryllis.

During the next few weeks nothing was of any importance to me but my child. I thought of her every moment of the day. David shared in my enthusiasm—and I was happy.

My mother arranged that the two babies should be christened at the same time, and she thought we might choose a day at the end of October.

I agreed that was an excellent idea, and she went ahead making plans.

"We don't want a grand affair," she said. "We couldn't, since Sabrina has been so recently dead. So I decided just the family and a few special friends. What do you think?"

I said that would be ideal.

"Well, we'll fix the date."

So we did.

The Pettigrews were invited and we could scarcely not include the Farringdons. But my mother thought they should be the only ones outside the family. "Of course," she added, "the Pettigrews *are* family or soon will be, but I could not leave out the Farringdons. It will be very quiet. I expect the Pettigrews had better stay. And shall we ask the Farringdons to stay for a night, too? The nights will be drawing in and it is rather a long ride."

The babies flourished and there was some question as to which of them should wear the family christening robes.

I said that Jessica should, as she was the elder.

"Are you sure you don't mind?" said my mother.

"Not in the least. I don't think it's important."

"I'll call in Molly Blackett. She shall make the most beautiful robes for Amaryllis."

So it was arranged.

It was about two weeks before the christening when I went over to Enderby to call on Sophie. She told me that Alberic had gone to London for a few days. Jeanne had wanted some special material and had sent him up to get it. "He has been up on several occasions and has done well. It is something of an upheaval for us to go, and he is there and back so quickly."

I sat talking to her for some little time, telling her about the christening; and as I was on my way back, quite near Grasslands, I met Mrs. Trent.

Her face lit up when she saw me.

"Well, if it isn't Mrs. Frenshaw. How are you? You look well, my dear. Having babies suits you."

"Thank you," I said.

"And how is the little angel?"

"Very well, thank you."

I was about to pass on when she laid a hand on my arm.

"Why don't you pop in for a little chat and a glass of something."

"Not now, thank you. I have been visiting Enderby and should go back."

"Just a little refreshment," she said. "I did want to have a talk with you."

My heart missed a beat and I began to form excuses.

"Come on," she said. "It is rather important. I am sure you will think so when I have told you."

My legs were trembling and I felt a flush rising to my cheeks.

"Haven't been overdoing it, have you? Have to take care, you know. Having a baby's no picnic, I can tell you."

"I'm perfectly all right, thank you. Only just now—"

"Come along in. I must talk to you. I'm sure when you've heard what I have to tell you . . ."

She was leering almost. I thought: She knows. What now?

I had to discover the worst. If I did not find out what she was hinting at I could imagine something perhaps even worse . . . disastrous.

I allowed myself to be led towards Grasslands.

"Come on in. We'll be nice and cosy. My girls have just gone out. I reckon they've gone up to Enderby. Mademoiselle Sophie has been so kind to my Dolly. She seems to have a feeling for her. Dolly's very fond of her."

"Yes . . . I have seen her there."

"Nice for her and nice for Mademoiselle. You can't have too many friends in this world, I always say. What will you have to drink?"

"Nothing, thank you. I did have something with Mademoiselle d'Aubigné."

"All right then." She had taken me into a small parlour near the hall.

She shut the door and when I was seated, she looked at me steadily and said: "It's about my Evie."

"Yes?"

"I'm worried about her. She's such a lovely girl. You see, that Mr. Farringdon was quite fond of her. But nothing comes of it, and for why? Because he never sees her, that's why. I reckon that there could be a match there before long. He's a nice sort of young man. Perhaps a bit slow, but sometimes they're the best sort. But he needs a bit of a push. Will he be coming to this christening party?"

"Oh, it's not a party, Mrs. Trent. The babies will be christened and then it's just the family."

"I reckon those Pettigrews will be there . . . seeing as Mr. Jonathan's engaged to the young lady."

I thought: She knows everything about us!

"In a way they are family," I said.

"And the Farringdons?"

"They are rather special friends of Mr. Frenshaw Senior, and perhaps they will look in."

"They'll come for sure . . . and their son with them. I wish he could see more of my Evie. I reckon if he did he'd ask her to marry him."

"I really don't know about that, Mrs. Trent."

"I do. If ever I saw a young man ready to fall in love, that man is Harry Farringdon. But what happens? He sees her for an hour or two and then he is whisked away. He's fond of her all right. She's such a lovely girl. I reckon if she was only in the right society . . . You get what I mean?"

"I do, of course, and I really will have to be going if . . . er . . ."

"Mrs. Frenshaw, ask my Evie to the christening party. Let that nice young man see her again. Oh, I worry about those girls, Mrs. Frenshaw. You've no idea. I have done everything I could to bring them up well—and you must admit I've made a good job with Evie. You see, I'm not well off . . . not like your family. It's all very different for me. I've had to skimp and scrape. It was my son, Richard, you see. He was rather a wild one. Goes off and gets married. Then she dies when Dolly was born. And he's left with two girls and he brings them to me. And then before Evie's ten years old he's gone. And Evie's a girl to be proud of. I want to see her do well. I want to see her settled."

"I do understand."

"Then ask her to this christening party and whenever that young man is coming to you, make sure she's there too. That's all I want."

I said: "My mother arranges that sort of thing."

"She would listen to you."

"I would see that Evie was asked if it were a more formal occasion. This is really just for the family and a few—"

"You mean the Farringdons, and if they are in it, why shouldn't my Evie be? I know you'll do this for me. You will when I tell you something, something you ought to know."

I felt sick and faint. Now it was coming. This was blackmail. She knew. She was the one who had been in the house and spoken through the tube. She was going to say: If you don't do what I want, I shall tell.

I heard myself say in a voice which sounded a long way away: "What is it . . . that you want to tell me?"

"Oh, well, we all have our secrets, don't we? And human nature being what it is, there's things we don't always bring into the light of day, nor should they be. But if a wrong's been done . . . right-minded people . . . well, they want to be able to right it, don't they?"

I heard myself give a false laugh. "I don't really understand you, Mrs. Trent."

"Well, you've got to make excuses for people when they're young. The blood runs hot then. They do things they're sorry for after, but it's too late then. We should think of these things . . . things like consequences . . . when we indulge in our little bits of wickedness."

"Please, Mrs. Trent . . ."

"All right, my dear, I'm coming to it. What I am saying is that my Evie has as much right to a good life as anyone. If she had had her due she'd be up there at all those dances and parties. She'd have a real launching into society, which would help her find someone who'd give her a good home and look after her in the future."

She seemed to have strayed from the point and I wondered when she would return to it, threatening me to do as she wanted as the price of her silence.

"I'm telling you this, Mrs. Frenshaw, because I know you're a sensible young woman. You've got kindness in you, too. You wouldn't judge anyone too harshly, would you? I've got a feeling you'll understand."

"Do tell me what it is I have to understand."

"It goes back a long way."

"Please tell me, Mrs. Trent."

"It was before you were thought of, Mrs. Frenshaw. It was when your grandmother was here at Eversleigh."

I began to breathe a little more freely. It did not seem to be what I had feared, unless of course she was coming to that later.

"I was here with my mother, the housekeeper at Eversleigh, looking after the old gentleman. Your grandmother came and stirred things up. Then he came down . . . that Mr. Frenshaw . . . Dickon, the master of Eversleigh. Oh, he wasn't that then. He had some place miles away . . . not much consequence but he got Eversleigh and a wife to bring him a great fortune. He became a very important gentleman . . . but I knew him when he was nothing much more than a boy. I was only a bit of a girl myself. We had been up to games . . . if you know what I mean . . . that was before I married my Andrew. Then I came to Grasslands and Andrew got fond of me. I was fond of him too . . . and he married me. You can imagine what they all had to say in the neighbourhood about that."

"Yes, Mrs. Trent," I said. I felt that I was coming alive again. This could not possibly be anything to do with me.

"People are not always kind, are they? They never forget, and in places like this it is passed down through the family. I know my mother left Eversleigh under a cloud. They said she was lucky to get away. But it all came back to me, didn't it? I was still here. My Andrew was marvellous. He was a good man; and when Richard was on the way he couldn't have been prouder. I don't know whether he really believed Richard was his. He was so proud. I couldn't tell him, could I? There's a time to keep silent about these things. It would have broken his heart . . . so I let him believe and we were all happy. You see what I mean?"

"Yes," I said faintly.

"What I'm telling you is that my Richard's father was your mother's husband."

"Oh no!"

"Oh yes. That's the case."

"Does he know . . . ?"

"I reckon he knows all right. It was possible with him whereas it wasn't with my Andrew, and there wasn't anyone else it could have been. But it was good for me to say it was Andrew's child, good for Andrew and good for Mr. Frenshaw."

"Who knows about this?"

"I know and nothing will convince me that Mr. Frenshaw didn't know. And now you know."

"And you let me into this secret which you have kept for years."

"Only because I want to do what is right and proper. It's Evie's right, don't you see?"

"Yes," I said.

"Of course, now it wouldn't matter so much people's knowing, would it? My poor Andrew went to the grave thinking he'd got a son . . . but that's years and years ago. These things settle in time. It's just that it's right . . . and I want it for my Evie. You understand me, don't you?"

"Yes, I do understand."

"Then you'll help my Evie, won't you?"

I was so relieved that I felt drawn towards her. After all, she was only concerned with the welfare of her grand-daughter, which was very natural.

I said: "I'll do what I can, Mrs. Trent."

"I knew you would. You'd be understanding. You know how it is with people. To tell you the truth, if I could see my Evie married into that Farringdon family, I'd die happy, because I know my Evie would look after Dolly—and that's the two of them taken care of."

I said I would have to go, and this time, having made her point, she did not attempt to detain me.

It was easier than I had imagined it would be. I said casually to my mother: "I think it is a shame that Evie Mather can't see Harry Farringdon more often."

"The romance does seem to be wilting. It wouldn't have been very suitable. I don't think John and Gwen would greatly care to be allied with Mrs. Trent."

"I know she is a rather dreadful woman, but I think she is genuinely fond of Evie, and Evie is quite a nice girl. I do think we ought to help a bit. Harry will be at the christening. Couldn't we ask just Evie?"

My mother grimaced. "I wouldn't mind but there's her grandmother and her sister, who always seems to stand about in brooding silence."

"Still, I should like to ask Evie. I wonder if we could ask her alone? I know what I'll do. I'll say it is just a family affair, but if Evie cared to come . . . just as a representative of Grasslands . . . or something like that."

"Oh, I've got no objection to Evie," said my mother.

I said I would ask her.

Then I fell to wondering what Mrs. Trent would have done if I had ignored her request. Would she have raked up that long-ago scandal, and what would my mother think of her husband's youthful misdemeanours? She would surely not be very grieved. It was so long ago and these things settle down in time. I had to thank Mrs. Trent for that comforting thought.

I rode over to Grasslands the next day and saw Mrs. Trent.

"It is just family, Mrs. Trent," I said, "so could Evie come alone . . . just to represent Grasslands, as it were."

Her face broke into smiles, and I felt very pleased.

"I knew you'd help, Mrs. Frenshaw," she said.

I was glad to have done this service. She was quite right. If her story were true, Evie certainly deserved some little help—and even if it were not, Evie still deserved it.

The priest who had married David and me presided at the christening, which took place in our own little chapel at Eversleigh. It was a moving ceremony. Jessica looked magnificent in the christening robes, which had been worn by Eversleigh babies for the last hundred years; and Molly Blackett had done her best to make Amaryllis no less splendid.

Amaryllis bchaved impeccably, but Jessica indulged in a screaming fit at the font and refused to stop until she firmly grasped the priest's rather predominant nose which he recklessly allowed to come within reach of her hands.

Apart from that all went well; the babies were taken back to their nurseries, divested of their ceremonial garments and put to sleep in their cots.

After everyone had had a peep at them and expressed admiration, we went back to the hall, where wine was served with sandwiches and my mother and I between us cut the christening cake.

Aunt Sophie had come over with Jeanne. They had been driven by Alberic, for she had acquired a small carriage, more like a trap which held her and Jeanne comfortably, and there was room for the driver up front. Alberic drove this round and he took great pride in it, I believed.

I insisted that Jeanne join us, which she did, rather against her will. Alberic went to the kitchens. He was very friendly with one of the servants—young Billy Grafter, for whom he had actually found a job in our kitchens.

Engaging staff was usually left to the housekeeper or butler. I knew they had been looking for a replacement for old Jem Barker, who had died a few months before, and when Billy Grafter appeared, the butler asked permission to engage him, which was immediately given for he was bright and young and supplied references which assured us that he was a willing worker. It appeared that on one of his visits to London, Alberic had met Billy when he was working at an inn. Billy was a country boy who did not like town life and he jumped at the chance to come to us.

I knew that he and Alberic were often in each other's company. Alberic had to exercise Sophie's two horses and as there were several in our stables, the young men often went off together in their spare time.

Sophie was pleased about this. She said Alberic's English was improving and she was glad he had a friend at Eversleigh.

My attention that day was on Evie and Harry Farringdon. They seemed so happy together. I wondered why Harry did not make some effort to see her. He could always make some excuse to visit us and go to Grasslands.

Mrs. Trent was a very wily woman. She knew she could not invite the Farringdons to Grasslands, for she was not the kind they would welcome into their family. No, Evie had to fascinate the young man to such an extent that he would suggest marriage even without the enthusiasm of his family.

That was probably where the affair was flagging. If Evie had come from a suitable family, they might have been engaged by now.

I would do my best for Evie. I liked her. She was different from her grandmother and sister. She was a pleasant, pretty, ordinary young girl.

Jonathan had come home for the christening. Outwardly he seemed devoted to Millicent. Only I knew what a farce that was, for he conveyed to me by his looks and the occasional whispered word that he had not given up hope yet and he was sure I was not going to abandon him.

To tell the truth, he filled me with misgiving. There was some potent sexuality in him of which I could not help being aware and I was horrified to realize that I was still unsure of myself.

I must tread warily, I knew.

I spent as much time with David as I possibly could. I believe he had never been so happy in the whole of his life. He adored Amaryllis and was so delighted when he fancied she knew him. It soothed me a great deal to watch him with her, and I could not help thinking of that old man, Andrew Mather, who had been so happy with the child who was not his. But Amaryllis *was* David's. I was sure of it—or perhaps I was trying to convince myself that this was so.

After the christening Aunt Sophie had been driven home by Alberic, for she had merely come for the ceremony. My mother said it was amazing how she had changed. "At one time, when we were in the *château,* she would not emerge for anything."

"Enderby has done a great deal for her," I said.

"Enderby, Jeanne, of course, and I think she has a great interest in that boy Alberic."

"Thank Heaven she found something to be interested in!"

"I hope she will become more and more reconciled," said my mother.

She had asked Evie to stay for a rather informal supper and Evie accepted with alacrity. It was a pleasant meal; we were very merry; we heard at length about Millicent's christening, and Gwen Farringdon talked about that of Harry. There was no mention of the state of affairs on the other side of the Channel and that was pleasant.

We all sat in the punch room afterwards conversing until everyone began to droop a little and my mother suggested we retire. Evie should be escorted home. Harry immediately offered to take her and my mother thought that either David or Jonathan should accompany them, discreetly implying that it would not be quite acceptable for the pair to go alone. David offered to go and my mother and Dickon said good night.

I went along to the library to get a book which I had left there and was coming out when Jonathan came in. He shut the door and leaned against it, smiling at me.

"I thought you had retired," I said.

"No. I saw you come down here, so I followed."

"For what purpose?"

"Unnecessary question. To do that which you are making increasingly difficult. To talk to you."

"What about?"

"Us."

"There is nothing more to be said."

"After all we have been to each other! You can't dismiss it like that."

"It was madness . . . momentary madness."

"Oh come, Claudine. It wasn't momentary, was it? Didn't we meet by arrangement?"

"I admit I did a terrible thing. Please, Jonathan, forget it, and let me forget it."

"You are never going to forget that, Claudine. Nor am I. Besides, we have our little angel upstairs to remind us."

"No, no," I said. "Amaryllis is David's."

He smiled at me maliciously. "It's a wise father who knows his own child. How wise is David? How wise am I?"

"It pleases you to be flippant. Jonathan, let me alone. It's over . . . done with. We have sinned terribly against David. I shall try to do everything I can to make him happy. Won't you help me?"

"I certainly will. You don't think I'm going to tell him: 'Your wife is a very passionate little lady, which I discovered to my delight.' What do you take me for?"

I looked at him steadily and wondered: What? He frightened me. Why, oh why, when he stood before me with his blue eyes alight, should I feel that desire to be close to him, to forget for a while everything but that overwhelming sexual satisfaction which he alone could provide?

I was trembling a little. I was sure he was aware of it. He was a man who had had a great deal of experience in what he called love. I am not sure that I called it that.

What was it I felt for him? Love? No. It had a less pleasant name. It was lust. But where did lust end and love begin? I loved David. I wanted to be with David. I wanted never to hurt him and yet this man had made me break my marriage vows and hurt David in a manner which could be more wounding than anything else I could do; and still, although I was trying not to admit it, I was drawn to him.

I was ignorant, inexperienced. I could not understand myself and I was afraid.

I tried to speak firmly. "It's all over, Jonathan. I'm deeply regretful that it ever happened. I don't know what possessed me."

He came closer and laid a hand on my shoulder. "I do, Claudine," he said softly. "I do."

I stepped backwards.

"You can't do without me," he said, "any more than I can do without you. We were meant for each other. What a pity you galloped into marriage!"

"And now you are about to do the same."

"Not a gallop. A graceful, well-planned canter."

"I'm sorry for Millicent."

"You shouldn't be. She is perfectly contented."

"When she discovers she is married to a philanderer, what will she think? A man who is contemplating marriage with her and at the same time is trying to seduce another woman."

"She is delighted with the amalgamation of the two families. You don't realize what that is going to mean. She does—and so do her papa and mama. Millicent is too worldly not to realize that there are certain concessions to be made even in the best of bargains."

"You are so calculating."

"All part of my success."

"And I am tired. Good night."

He caught my hand.

"Are you going to tell me that you don't love me any more?"

"I never loved you. It was something different. I know that now."

"Well, whatever it was, it was rather fierce, wasn't it?"

"I was foolish. I can only say ignorant. Please, Jonathan, I want to forget it. When you are married you will be mainly in London. Don't think we can ever start again."

"Is that what you want?"

"With all my heart."

"For the sort of man I am it is a challenge. That which is out of reach is always more desirable than that which falls into one's hands. You're challenging me, Claudine."

"I am telling you to let me alone. Good night."

I went to the door. He laughed and I heard him say: "I never give up."

I ran into the hall. David was just coming in with Harry.

"Safely delivered to her home," said David, referring to Evie. He put an arm round me and I smiled at him.

"You're tired," he said.

"It's been a long day."

"The christening went off perfectly," said Harry. "The babies were very good . . . on the whole."

"Particularly Amaryllis," said David proudly. "She is a beautiful child."

Harry smiled at me. "Fond parent," he said.

"I think Evie enjoyed it," I put in.

"Oh yes," agreed David. "She was rather reluctant to go home, I believe. Grandma Trent was waiting up for her. There was a candle in one of the windows. She was obviously watchful. She dashed down and wanted us to come in for some sloe gin or elderberry or dandelion or something. We pleaded the lateness of the hour."

"She is devoted to her grand-daughters," I said.

"No doubt about that," added Harry.

We had come to the room which Harry was using so we said good night and left him there.

David and I went on to ours.

"Such a happy day it's been! Shall we just peep into the nursery to look at her?"

So we went there and stood on either side of the sleeping child.

David looked down at her with wonder. Nothing . . . nothing must disturb his happiness.

Meeting in a Coffee House

Christmas came and went. There were the usual feasting and games. Our neighbours came in as they had done the previous year and that included Mrs. Trent with her grand-daughters. The Farringdons were our guests and of course the Pettigrews. Lady Pettigrew said that we should have spent Christmas with them this year, but the babies made travelling difficult and so it was easier to celebrate the festive season at Eversleigh.

The marriage of Jonathan and Millicent was to take place in June and we must travel there then, said my mother, for the babies would be older, and that would simplify matters.

It was hard to believe that it was a year ago that I had been in the midst of my affaire with Jonathan. It was last Boxing Day when I had ended it abruptly and almost immediately afterwards discovered that I was going to have a child.

Harry Farringdon had still not declared himself; and I asked my mother if she thought he ever would.

"The courtship—if courtship it is—does seem to drag on. I would say that Evie is in love. One can tell that sometimes."

"And Harry?"

"Well, he does seem to delight in her company."

"Do you think the delay is due to his parents?"

"Or her grandmother."

"A man does not marry his wife's relations surely."

"No. But they might give him cause for thought. I imagine Harry is a cautious young man."

"Well, I think he should make up his mind soon."

"You give them every opportunity, I must say. You've become a matchmaker, Claudine. At least where those two are concerned."

I did not tell her why. I was not sure whether it would have disturbed her or not. But I had a strong conviction that I should help Evie all I could, and there was no doubt that marriage into the Farringdon family would be very desirable for her.

Jonathan went back to London. There was great consternation over the war, which seemed to be resulting in successes for the French throughout Europe. Dickon was in London with Jonathan and now that my mother had a baby she did not accompany him as frequently as she had once.

There had been more causes for alarm in January when Utrecht, Rotterdam and Dort fell into the hands of the French, and the Stadtholder and his family made their escape to England, arriving in an open boat. It was a wonder they survived, for the weather had turned bitterly cold and everything was frozen up.

Throughout the house great fires burned but even so the wind seemed to whistle through the windows and there were draughts everywhere.

The men seemed greatly concerned about the French victories which, according to Jonathan, were due to the genius of one man—a Corsican adventurer by the name of Napoleon Bonaparte. It had been hoped that with the fall of Robespierre there would be an end to these successes, for Bonaparte was a well-known supporter of the tyrant; but by some clever manoeuvring he managed to extricate himself from the slaughter when so many suffered the same fate as their friend and master. So Napoleon Bonaparte continued with the army.

"Even the bloodthirsty mob have the sense to realize what he is doing for his country," commented Jonathan.

We talked often of Charlot and Louis Charles, who might well be involved in these successful campaigns. But we had no news of them.

My mother used to say: "Charlot is well. Something tells me that. If only he could get a message to us! But how could he with his country at war with the whole of Europe."

When Dickon and Jonathan were with us the talk was all of war and political matters. Prussia was asking for a loan and endlessly they discussed the rights and wrongs of this.

And all the time we shivered, until February came bringing with it the melting snows, and then it rained so heavily that there was the problem of flooding in many parts of the country.

Then Tuscany made peace with France.

Dickon said: "I can see others doing the same."

David's point was that the revolution was over now and the Republic had to be accepted. He said: "At least we shall settle down to peace.

The French have chosen the government they want. There is nothing to be done but leave them to it."

Dickon replied: "They have gone to a great deal of trouble, much blood has been shed, and now they are learning that it need never have happened. They have exchanged one set of rulers for another every bit as harsh."

"The Monarchy would never have abdicated," said Jonathan. "The people wanted to be rid of them and they saw that the only way of doing so was through the guillotine."

When the Swedes acknowledged the French it seemed obvious the way things were going.

"If this continues," said Dickon, "we shall be left alone fighting the French."

He and Jonathan went up to London, and this was one of the occasions when my mother did not go with him.

It was a cool March day. There were still signs of the heavy flooding and some of the fields were under water. I had been out with David during the morning and we had ridden round the estate. I enjoyed these morning rides, meeting the tenants, chatting with them, stopping to taste their wine.

David never hesitated to discuss their ideas with them, which made an ideal relationship between landowner and the people who lived on his estate. Jonathan would never have had the same patience, the good will, the unselfishness, the ability to see a matter from someone else's point of view. They had chosen their careers wisely—or perhaps their father had selected them for them—for Jonathan was suited to the worldly life of London society and all those secret matters of which even my mother could not guess.

On that afternoon I was in the sewing room with my mother and Molly Blackett going through materials and discussing clothes for the babies when one of the servants came in and said: "There is a lady and gentleman downstairs, Madam. Friends of the master, they say. I've taken them to the hall and they are waiting there."

"I'll come down," said my mother.

I went with her. Standing in the hall was a rather tall fair-haired man of about forty, and the lady with him appeared to be a few years younger.

When he saw my mother the man came towards her, holding out his hands.

"My dear Mrs. Frenshaw. I would have known you from Dickon's description. How are you? I am James Cardew and this is my wife, Emma. I wonder if he has ever mentioned me to you."

"No," said my mother, "I don't think he has."

"I come from the North. Dickon has always said I must call and see him at Eversleigh if ever I was in the neighbourhood, and he would be most offended if I did not. I wonder if he is at home?"

"No, I'm afraid not. He is in London."

The man raised his eyebrows in exasperation. "What bad luck! Of all the times he has insisted I call. And now I find that he is away."

"He may be back tomorrow," said my mother. "But let me introduce you to my daughter."

He had taken my hand and was looking at me intently. "This is another Mrs. Frenshaw. Claudine, is it?"

I laughed. "You seem to know a good deal about us."

"Dickon has talked of you. This is my wife, Emma."

She was attractive, with dark lively eyes.

My mother said: "Well, it is a great pity that my husband is not at home. You will need some refreshment. Do come into our little winter parlour and I will have something brought to us. Have you eaten yet?"

"We had a meal some miles back," said James Cardew. "A little wine would be welcome . . . to slake the thirst."

"Come along then. Claudine, will you ask them to send something to the winter parlour," said my mother.

I went away to do her bidding and then returned to the visitors. They were sitting down and saying what a wonderful old house Eversleigh was. They felt they knew it well, Dickon had talked so much about it.

"Have you seen him recently?" asked my mother.

"Well, it must have been a year ago. I happened to be in London for a brief spell."

"I expect I was with him," said my mother. "I usually am, but not so much now since my baby was born."

"Unfortunately we didn't meet then. Tell me, is Dickon well?"

"Very well, thank you."

"Have you ever known Dickon otherwise?"

"He does enjoy good health."

"He is the most vital man I have ever known," said James Cardew.

My mother looked pleased, and as the wine arrived then, she poured it out for our guests.

"Delicious," said Emma Cardew. "I must admit to being thirsty. It is thirsty travelling."

"Did you say Dickon will be back tomorrow?" asked her husband.
"We can never be certain," said my mother. "But I do expect him. Something may turn up to keep him though."
"Yes, yes. We live in strange times. You are well aware of that if anyone is, Mrs. Frenshaw."
"I see Dickon has been talking freely about us."
"He is a very brave man, Mrs. Frenshaw."
"Amen to that," said my mother fervently.
"I was delighted to hear about the babies," put in Emma.
"Oh, you are very up-to-date with our news."
"As a matter of fact," explained Emma, "I was talking to someone at the inn. It is amazing how much people know about their neighbours. And don't they love to pass on information! We mentioned we were looking for Eversleigh, and the babies were mentioned. Two of them in fact. That seemed something to talk about. Oh dear, I do hope we are not going to miss Dickon."
"Are you staying at the inn?"
"As a matter of fact we did ask, but they hadn't a room for us."
"Had they not? At this time of the year!"
"Well, they had something to offer. Emma declined it."
"I'm a bit particular," explained Emma. "It was more or less a cupboard that they offered us."
"I know the accommodation is not very good," said my mother, "but there is not very much about here."
"Never mind. We'll go on to the next town. Our horses are in your stables. Your grooms dashed out and took them. I daresay they'll feed and water them. Poor things, they have travelled fairly far."
"You must stay for dinner," said my mother.
"Oh, no, no. Not if Dickon isn't here."
"He would want you to."
"I think," said Emma slowly, "we ought to be making our way. We have to find somewhere to sleep for the night."
My mother said warmly: "Of course we can give you a bed."
Emma and James spoke simultaneously. "Oh, what a relief!" said Emma.
"We couldn't possibly encroach on your hospitality," said James.
"Nonsense," replied my mother. "We have plenty of room. There is no one staying here at the moment. Dickon would be put out if we let you go. Besides, he will probably be back tomorrow. You can catch him if you don't leave too early."

They were beaming their satisfaction.

"Will you go and see about it right away, Claudine?" asked my mother.

I said I would and went to the servants' hall, where I told them that we had visitors and that a room was to be prepared.

"The bed is made up in the red room, Mrs. Frenshaw," said one of the maids. "I'll light a fire and put the warming pan in the bed. That's all that will be needed."

I went to the nursery to look at the babies. They were fast asleep in their cots, which stood side by side. I had a word with the nurse, who told me that Jessica had had a little tantrum earlier, but that Amaryllis had been as good as gold.

"Such a contented baby, Mrs. Frenshaw. Madam Jessica is of a fiery nature."

"Can you tell so soon?" I asked.

"Oh yes, indeed you can. They start to show their natures almost as soon as they are born."

I stooped and kissed the little faces—Amaryllis pink and white, Jessica dark-haired. Her eyes were fast shut but they were deep blue like my mother's.

I felt contented as I always did when all was well in the nursery, and I told the servants in the kitchen to lay two more places for dinner.

They were entertaining company, James and Emma Cardew. They talked knowledgeably about affairs, the state of the country and what was happening across the water. But my mother soon changed the subject—of which we had far too much when Dickon and Jonathan were home—and turned the talk to more domestic matters. Emma told us about her children; she had two, a boy and a girl, and their ages were fourteen and sixteen. The son would take care of their estate in Yorkshire when he was old enough; at the moment they had an excellent manager. James and Emma paid visits to London occasionally when they made arrangements for the sale of their wool.

David was interested and asked a good many questions and so the evening passed pleasantly.

"Meeting new people is always stimulating," said my mother when we had taken our guests to the red room, which looked cosy with its red velvet curtains drawn to shut out the weather, and a fire blazing in the grate.

In our bedroom David and I talked about the guests.

"I gather their money comes mostly from sheep," he said. "They would be big farmers, I imagine."

"They seemed to know a great deal about us," I commented. "I wonder if they keep a dossier of all their friends."

"They seemed the kind who would be interested in people."

"I'm surprised that your father talked so much about us all. It is the last thing I would have expected him to do."

"Oh, he has changed a lot since he married your mother. But I do agree, it would be unlike him to talk a lot about the family. I hope he gets back tomorrow."

"They'll be disappointed if he doesn't."

David was thoughtful for a moment; then he said: "I hear that the war is going to be over soon."

"Do you think the French are going to beat the allies?"

"What with Tuscany making peace and Sweden acknowledging the Republic, I hope we are not going to be left fighting on our own. I think it must end soon, and when it does, Claudine, you and I will have that promised honeymoon. Italy! I long to see Herculaneum." He put his arm about me. "In the meantime, my dearest, you will have to put up with an extended honeymoon, here in Eversleigh."

"Honeymoons are to start married life with. We are no longer beginners."

"I love you more than I ever did."

He held me close to him and it was all I could do to stop myself crying out: "I don't deserve it." I felt I should never rid myself of this burden of guilt as long as I lived.

And later, when there should have been perfect intimacy between us, I kept thinking of a gondolier singing Italian love songs, and as we floated down the canal my company was not David but Jonathan.

In the morning, as I passed through the hall, I noticed that the silver punch bowl, which always stood in the centre of the big table, was not there.

David and I went to the dining room. My mother was already seated. She said: "Oh hello, my dears. Our guests are not up. They must have been tired out. Travelling can be so exhausting!"

"They didn't seem exhausted last night," commented David.

"What's happened to the punch bowl?" I asked.

"Oh, you noticed too. I expect they've taken it to the kitchen to clean it."

While we were eating one of the servants came in.

"Something awful's happened, M'am," she said. "I think we've been broken into."

"What?" cried my mother.

"Cook has noticed there's things missing from the hall. Silver and things . . ."

"The punch bowl!" I cried.

We went into the hall. Several of the servants were there.

"It must have been vagrants," said my mother. "How could they have got in? Who locked up?"

"The doors were all locked last night," said the butler quickly. "I always see to that myself. And this morning the doors were shut but unbolted. I couldn't understand it."

"Extraordinary!" said my mother. "What could have happened? Did anyone hear anything in the night?"

Nobody had.

"We'd better look round quickly and see what has been taken."

On the floor leading from the hall were one or two rooms including the winter parlour and Dickon's study. The winter parlour seemed to have been untouched. This was not the case with Dickon's study. The door of the cupboard had been forced open and papers were scattered on the floor. One of the drawers of his desk had been broken open.

"This is terrible," said my mother.

At that moment a maid appeared. She said: "Madam, I took hot water up to the red room. There was no answer so I knocked again and when there was still no answer I went in. There was no one there and the bed hasn't been slept in."

We were all aghast and hurried up to the red room. The maid was right. The bed was untouched. It was instantly clear that the people whom we had entertained last night were not Dickon's friends, but had come here expressly to rob us.

My mother was filled with trepidation. She had welcomed them and had entertained them; and all the time she had been harbouring thieves.

We went round the house to try to discover what had been taken. Dickon's study seemed to have been the main object of their interest. That was what was so alarming, for there was not much of value there. It was true they had taken silver, but why overturn Dickon's office?

The people calling themselves James and Emma Cardew were clearly no ordinary thieves.

It was no use trying to send someone after them. They would be well away by now, and who could say what direction they had taken?

We were helpless and stupidly gullible to have been so deceived.

"But they seemed so genuine," my mother kept saying. "They knew so much about us. They must have known Dickon was not home. To think of them prowling about down here while we were all in our beds! It makes your flesh creep. And what were they looking for in Dickon's study? Did they find it? Oh, I wish he'd come home."

He returned in the early afternoon.

When he heard what had happened he turned white with anger. He immediately went to his study. Jonathan was with him. In a short time we knew that something very important had been taken. Dickon said little but there was a flush in his face and a glint in his eyes which told me that he was very disturbed.

"What were they like?" demanded Jonathan.

We described them as best we could.

"It didn't occur to us . . ." cried my mother. "We didn't realize that they could be criminals. They knew so much about the family. I naturally thought that they were friends."

"They had their informants," said Jonathan. "And they knew that we should be away."

"They couldn't have pulled it off otherwise," added Dickon. "My God, how far has this gone? They knew what was in my study. I'll have to go back to London at once. We have to follow this up. Lottie, you will have to come with me. It may be that someone will know who they could be."

"I'll get ready at once," said my mother. "Oh, Dickon, I'm sorry, but we have all been taken in."

"Of course you would be. They would be clever enough and well informed enough to deceive anyone."

"They took some silver too."

"Oh, that was to make it seem like an ordinary robbery. It was what was in my study that they came to get. It is better that the servants should think that was the case. We don't want them to talk."

My mother nodded.

"I shall want to leave in an hour," said Dickon.

He with Jonathan and my mother left for London. The servants could talk of nothing for days but the effrontery of the people who had called themselves Cardew.

To us who knew that there was some ulterior motive for the robbery, the incident seemed very sinister. I wondered more than ever about Dickon's and Jonathan's affairs. It had been clear to me for a long time that they were not merely bankers; they were engaged in some secret diplomatic work and of course in such times as ours such work must become increasingly important.

They did live dangerously. Both Dickon and Jonathan were men who knew how to take care of themselves, but I guessed that the work they did made them ruthless, and of course, those who worked against them would be equally so.

I hoped Dickon would not run into danger. I trembled to think of what my mother would do if anything happened to him.

And Jonathan? I tried not to think of him; but he did intrude often into my thoughts.

For a few weeks no subject was discussed in the servants' quarters but the audacious burglary at Eversleigh, and it was talked of with equal interest in the neighbourhood I was sure.

Dickon, back at Eversleigh, had decreed that there should be no mention of important papers having been taken and that the impression should be given that it was only valuable silver which had been stolen.

"I believe there is an old proverb which says that it is too late to shut the stable door after the horse has been stolen," I said.

"Quite right," answered my mother. "But I intend that no more horses shall be stolen."

"Is Dickon still very upset?"

"Yes, indeed he is. I do wish he were not so *involved.* These people are dangerous, capable of anything. It worries me . . . but this is Dickon's life. He always has taken risks, and I suppose he always will. Jonathan is the same. I am so glad you chose David. I married two adventurers."

"And you were happy."

"My first husband went to America to fight and died there. I worry a lot about Dickon. But it was worth it. I wouldn't have him otherwise."

But in due course the burglary became a nine-days' wonder and the excitement shifted to Jonathan's and Millicent's wedding.

Another wedding was to take place in April—that of the Prince of Wales to the Princess Caroline of Brunswick.

"I thought he was married to Maria Fitzherbert," I said.

"So he was," replied David, "but the marriage was not considered legal."

"Do you remember we saw them once at the theatre? I thought they looked so handsome and so fond of each other."

"Times change, Claudine."

"And they are no longer in love."

"They say he greatly resents having to marry Princess Caroline, and would not if he could avoid it."

"Poor kings, poor princes."

"How lucky we are!" said David. "We should always remember that, Claudine. We should never let anything spoil what we have."

"We must not . . . ever," I said fervently.

There were to be celebrations for the royal wedding and my mother suggested that we go to London to join in them.

"We could do our shopping during the visit. We shall both need new gowns for Jonathan's wedding."

I said that would be wonderful and we could feel quite safe leaving the babies in the charge of Grace Soper, who was proving herself to be an excellent nurse.

"Fashions have changed so much in the last years," went on my mother. "Everything seems to be so much simpler. I suppose it is something to do with France, as the fashions have always started there. This new simplicity has grown out of the revolution. I'm glad we're rid of those hooped petticoats. They were so restricting. I rather like those high-waisted gowns, don't you?"

I said yes, but did she think Molly Blackett could do them justice?

"Molly's a good dressmaker. She'll try. I don't think she likes the new simplicity though. It makes much less work for her, I suppose, and it is not so easy to hide the little flaws. I thought if we got the material now there would be plenty of time for her to make them up before the wedding. We shall need some lace for fichus and perhaps shawls. The low-cut shoulders can be a little chilly. So you see, we shall have plenty of shopping to do. . . ."

"I'll look forward to it," I said.

"We'll go in good time. The royal wedding is on the eighth. If we arrived on the fifth we could get the shopping done first. I doubt the shops will be open on that day. Shall we try that?"

I said it would be excellent and as Jonathan and Dickon agreed to the dates, the four of us set out in the carriage. David said he would take the opportunity of going over to the Clavering estate—another of Dickon's properties—as it was some time since he had been and another visit was due.

I always enjoyed London. I felt excitement grip me as I drove through those crowded streets. There were people everywhere bent on their own business, dashing around as though they were in a mighty hurry. I watched them all with pleasure—the hawkers, the ballad singers, the lavender women, the apple women, the watercress sellers—they were all there. I used to listen to their cries and was delighted to discover new ones like that of the lady with her paper of pins who stood on a corner singing in a high cracked voice:

Three rows a penny pins,
Short whites and middlings.

There was the Flying Pieman who ran from Covent Garden to Fleet Street between noon and four o'clock crying:

Who's for a mutton or a Christmas pie
Buy, buy, buy
A piece for a penny,

while people stopped him for a piece of his meat pies or baked plum pudding.

Won't you buy my sweet blooming lavender,
Sixteen branches one penny,

sang the lavender woman.

"Fine fritters, hot fine fritters," cried out the woman who was frying batter on a tripod over a fire set on bricks.

I loved to hear the bell of the muffin man as he wandered through the streets, performing an admirable balancing feat as he carried his basket on his head.

Every time I came to London I tried to discover a new trader and I invariably did.

I enjoyed watching the carriages trundling through the streets—hackney coaches and private carriages, the phaetons, barouches, calashes—and of course the highly polished mail coaches the colour of claret, drawn by four splendid-looking horses driven by the coachman in his box coat fastened by enormous buttons of mother-of-pearl, in his big-brimmed hat looking very powerful and able to deal with any hazard of the road.

And the shops! How I revelled in the shops! We were treated with such respect, and chairs were found for us that we might rest while we studied the bales of material which were brought for our inspection.

Then there were the theatres. The opera houses in the Haymarket and Drury Lane and Covent Garden as well as the pleasure gardens, which were all a delight.

We saw little of Dickon and Jonathan. They were always on business somewhere. I wondered a great deal about Jonathan's life here for it was true that he spent more time in London than anywhere—as I believe Dickon had done before his marriage. What a different life it would have been for me if I had married him, I thought a little wistfully.

But I should never have been sure of him. Jonathan could never be faithful to one woman. I doubted Dickon could in his youth; but Dickon and my mother were now truly lovers, as the Comte, my grandfather, had been with my grandmother. It needed real love to change men like that. Dickon had, strangely enough, found that love, as my grandfather had, and as I knew many people had marvelled in the change in the Comte, so they now did in Dickon. I guessed it must be something very rare. And I thought sadly that Jonathan had not yet reached that stage.

I was ungrateful to wish for anything different from what we had. I had the best of husbands, an adorable child. What more could one ask for?

It was the excitement of the big city and all the pleasures that were to be found in it that made me thoughtful. But were the pleasures important compared with peace and contentment and the knowledge that one could trust completely in a husband's love?

One would not want to visit the theatre every night, to wander through the pleasure gardens, to visit the shops every day. These things were exciting because they were rare. Familiarity bred contempt. That could be true. I must learn to accept what I had, to realize its worth and be grateful for it.

My mother and I spent a great deal of time choosing our materials. Silk was very expensive since it had become scarce, for much of it had come from France in the past and of course that industry had halted when the people began murdering each other. The same applied to lace. No other people seemed to make these materials with the elegance of the French, so it took us a little longer to find what we wanted.

We went to the theatre in the Haymarket and heard Handel's *Acis and Galatea,* which was an uplifting experience; and then for contrast next day we went to Mrs. Salmon's Waxworks, close by the Temple. We were very amused by the effigies outside the door of an old match seller on crutches, carrying a basket of matches, and beside her a beefeater in the most splendid costume. They were so lifelike that people came up to peer at them and make sure that they were not real. How we laughed and marvelled at the figures! There were the King and Queen Charlotte with the Prince of Wales, side by side with Dr. Johnson and John Wilkes and other notable figures—all startlingly lifelike. I loved the next room, which was a pastoral scene with shepherds courting shepherdesses. In another room was a model of a ship in a sea of glass. So we felt we had good value for our sixpence entrance fee and bought some marbles and Punch-and-Judy figures from the shop which was part of the establishment.

"The children will love them in a few years' time," said my mother.

She and Dickon were to attend the royal wedding, for Dickon was influential in high places and of course my mother must accompany him. I was looking forward to hearing an account of the wedding first hand. We had already seen the wedding cake going into Buckingham House, and it was so enormous that it had to be carried in a coach. The people had cheered it as it went along its route.

The Queen was to hold what was called "a drawing room" and Dickon and my mother would attend this after witnessing the ceremony in the Chapel Royal at St. James's.

I had told my mother that I was a little envious.

"Oh, these ceremonies!" she replied. "Everybody wants to have been asked to them but nobody really wants to go. While I am standing there making sure that my behaviour is exactly as it should be in the royal presence I'll think of you and Jonathan relaxing at peace and enjoying the day."

It was my mother who had suggested that Jonathan should look after me while she and Dickon were at the palace. "You'll want to see something of what's going on, I daresay," she said. "And I wouldn't want you on the streets alone."

"I'll take good care of her, Step-mama," said Jonathan.

"All the rogues and vagabonds will be out today," added Dickon. "I'll swear the beggars and pickpockets come in from fifty miles away. They're looking for good pickings. You'll have to take care."

"Trust me," said Jonathan.

I told myself that I was thrust into this situation. It was no fault of mine that I was to spend the day with Jonathan. How could I possibly have refused to be with him? It was no use pretending that I was not exhilarated by the prospect and I warned myself that I should have to be careful.

I took pleasure in watching my mother while she dressed in her court clothes. She had always been outstandingly beautiful and in all her splendour she was very lovely indeed. No one would have guessed that she was the mother of a son old enough to be a soldier—and fighting with the French at that.

I watched them leave in the carriage.

Her last words to me were: "When you go out, keep close to Jonathan. You'll be safe with him."

If only she knew!

Jonathan gleefully told me that he had plans for the day and that he intended to make up to me for not being included in the royal invitation.

"*You* must be disappointed," I said. "I was under the impression that you would be honoured."

"Places are limited, and one for father and son would be asking too much. It is an omission which, in the circumstances, gives me untold pleasure. I intend to enjoy every moment of this glorious day. We shall start on our horses."

"Jonathan," I began earnestly, "I want you to understand I will not have . . ."

He interrupted me. "I assure you I shall behave impeccably. I can on occasion, you know. I have decided to dedicate today to proving to you that I am not such a bad fellow after all. I shall respect your wishes in every way. There! Does that satisfy you?"

"If I could believe you . . ."

"You can. On my honour."

"I was not aware that you were overburdened with such a quality."

"Then that is something else I have to prove to you. Let us go soon. The streets will be impossible as the day wears on. Get into your riding habit at once and we'll leave."

"Jonathan," I began uncertainly.

"I swear to you nothing shall be done against your wishes."

"I did not seek this."

"It was thrust upon you. There. I understand everything. Go on . . . change. This is going to be a day to remember."

As we rode out into the streets the bells were ringing and the guns were booming from the park and the Tower. Carriages were making their way to St. James's and people were shouting loyal slogans.

"Nothing like a royal wedding to bring out the patriotism," said Jonathan.

"Who would believe now that people in this country—serious politicians—such a short time ago feared we should follow the example of the French."

"They still fear," said Jonathan. "Don't be deceived by the flagwaving and the loyal shouts."

We turned into Hyde Park and rode along by the Serpentine.

"Is it true," I asked, "that the Prince is going into this marriage reluctantly?"

"I'm sorry for him. She appears to be rather an unattractive creature."

"I feel sorry for her."

"You support your own sex, of course."

"Naturally when the man is said to flaunt his mistress before his bride, and, by the way, has already gone through a form of marriage with a good and virtuous lady."

"Life can be cruel," sighed Jonathan. "I thought we'd get out of London. Let's get down to the river. I know of an inn where we can get a good meal, and as many people will be coming into the city for the wedding, it will not be too crowded."

We rode down to the river and beside it for some distance.

It was true that the farther we rode, the more peaceful it became.

"Where are you taking me?" I asked.

"To the Dog and Whistle. It's an old inn I know. They serve the most excellent roast beef."

"I shall not want to be too late in returning."

"Have I not told you that you may trust me to deliver you safely and in perfect order to your dear mama? Don't forget, I am proving myself . . . winning my spurs, I think they call it. I expect to emerge from this day with a shining halo. You are going to say: I misjudged him. He is not the villain I thought him."

"I think I shall wait until the end of the day before passing judgment."

I thought how handsome he was with his fair hair and those deep blue eyes. I was glad that wigs were out of fashion. One scarcely ever saw them now. They had gone with powder—another fashion eliminated by the revolution. My mother said that men were becoming careless of their dress, led by people like Charles James Fox. Dickon explained that they did it to show their sympathy for the revolution, while Pitt and the Tories refused to comply with the new ways and wore splendid scarlet waistcoats to show their loyalty to the monarchy.

It was a beautifully warm April—one of the loveliest months of the year with the birds in full song and the trees in bud, and I could not help feeling happy on that morning. For one day I was going to forget my past sins; I was going to take my mind off my guilt; I was going to be completely happy . . . just for today.

"April showers bring forth May flowers," I quoted irrelevantly.

"Pray that the showers will keep off until we reach the Dog and Whistle."

It came into view, standing apart from the few houses which formed the hamlet. The sign swayed gently in the light breeze. The dog was brown and the whistle a bright red.

"Follow me," said Jonathan. "We'll take our horses round to the stables. They'll look after them while we eat."

We went into the inn parlour. It was a charming room, oak-panelled, and brasses gleamed on the walls while a fire burned in the grate.

The host came out rubbing his hands together.

"Well, sir, this is a nice surprise . . . to see you here today of all days."

"Shall we say, Thomas, we are escaping. This is my brother's wife."

"Good day, my lady. Welcome to the Dog and Whistle."

"Thank you," I replied. "I am told it is a most excellent hostelry."

He bowed in acknowledgement of the compliment and turning to Jonathan said: "And your noble father is, of course, with the royal party?"

Jonathan said this was so. "I trust your good lady is well," he added.

"Oh, Matty will be here in a trice when she hears what company we've got. She's got nothing cooking till tonight, sir. There's only the cold lamb and roast beef."

"Put Matty out of her misery at once, Thomas. It's the cold roast beef we've come for."

"That's a mighty relief. I'll just call her." He went to the door and shouted: "Matty! Matty! Guess who's here."

There was a patter of feet and a plump woman arrived, a mobcap on her thick dark hair and a white apron over her blue cotton dress.

Jonathan went to her and picking her up swung her round.

"Oh sir," she said, dimpling, "you will have your ways, won't you?

And you here with a young lady . . . and no warning so that I can cook something special for you!"

"Then I shall send you to the Tower and insist that you are hanged, drawn and quartered."

"Oh sir, don't say such things even in a jest."

"All right, Matty. I'll be good, as it is a special day. We want some of your famous roast beef, of which Thomas assures me there is a goodly supply."

"Give me fifteen minutes, sir, and you'll be surprised."

"Fifteen minutes, it shall be."

"And what shall it be for now . . . some ale . . . or would you like wine?"

"I've got something very special in the cellars," said Thomas with a wink.

Jonathan returned the wink. "We'll trust you, Thomas, and if it doesn't come up to expectations you shall go along with Matty to your judgement. Oh, I forgot . . . I'm on my best behaviour today."

He put Matty down. She was flushed and looking at him with something like adoration. Was this always the effect he had on women? I thought of Millicent and myself.

Matty curtsied and said she would be off. She'd so much to do and she had to do what was right for such a lady and gentleman.

Thomas brought in the wine and poured it into goblets with such reverence that it might have been the nectar of the gods.

Jonathan sipped it and raised his eyes ecstatically to the ceiling while Thomas beamed.

They seemed really fond of him, those two. Or perhaps this was the way they welcomed all their visitors to the Dog and Whistle, I thought cynically; but I did not really believe that.

"There'll be crowds in the City, I reckon," said Thomas, gazing at the wine and then back at us, and it was hard to detect which he admired most.

"All are celebrating the wedding with glee—except the bridegroom, it appears," said Jonathan.

"They say he compares his bride with Mrs. Fitzherbert."

"And," added Jonathan, "the comparison is not very favourable to the Princess."

"But there's that Lady Jersey, sir, his latest. If you ask me, His Royal Highness doesn't know what he wants."

Jonathan smiled at me. "He's like a great many more of us, I fear," he said.

"There you are, sir. I'll just go to the kitchen to give Matty a hand. She'll be ready as soon as she can."

"Tell her not to hurry. We're happy here."

The door shut on us.

"What luck to have the room to ourselves. Usually it's crowded. See how wise I was to come here."

"They seem very pleasant . . . the host and hostess."

"They're a good hardworking couple."

"And you come here often?"

"Frequently. They know me well. But I must assure you that I am on excellent terms with many keepers of inns and taverns."

"Ah," I said. "It is this secret work . . ."

"You are very interested to know more about that, are you not, little Claudine?"

"I am interested in everyone."

"Well, you are right. People frequent taverns. They are inclined to drink too much. They talk. Do you understand?"

"I see. You are a very mysterious man."

"That's what makes me so attractive."

"To people like Matty, for whom you know how to mingle the right brand of condescension and flirtation."

"Oh, did you like the mixture?"

"I saw the point of it, of course."

"Matty liked it."

"I'm sure she did. The grand gentleman . . . the one who spends money in her husband's inn. Of course she liked it."

"You have to admit it was a slightly different approach."

"Absolutely. But you did promise to forget all that, to behave in a manner which would be acceptable in any company."

"I don't remember the exact words, but I have promised to show you a new Jonathan, the man of honour."

"I think you are going to find it rather hard to convince me."

"Nevertheless, before this day is out you are going to change your opinion of me. I know you are very fond of me . . . in a special way. It is just that I offend certain codes which you have been brought up to observe. Believe me, it is merely a matter of how one interprets the rules."

"Surely there must be only one interpretation of right and wrong."

"That is the superficial view, dear Claudine. There are shades of right and shades of wrong, and it depends entirely on the angle from which you study these matters."

"You have a talent for talking round a subject, trying to hypnotise your listeners so that after a while they begin to wonder whether black is really black and white white."

"Is that so? Then it is yet another of my talents. Isn't this fun . . . you and I here together, talking, actually talking! For so long you would scarcely speak to me."

"We said we would not refer to that time."

"It is you who insist on veering towards it."

"Tell me then, how often do you come out here . . . in the course of your duty?"

He considered. "Once a month, shall we say?"

"And the obliging Matty and Thomas keep a check on their customers. They listen to their conversations and report what they think might be of interest."

"Now we are getting into deep waters."

"Secret matters. I wish I knew what you were involved in."

"Do you worry about me?"

"I try not to think of you."

"That is rather unkind."

"It's very wise really."

He looked at me steadily, his eyes a burning blue. "I understand. In your view it would be unwise to think of me."

"I want to forget," I said. "And why are we talking like this?"

"You have brought us back to it again. It must be very much in your mind."

I stood up and walked round the room, examining the brasses.

"Thomas has some very fine stables," he said. "This is a typical coaching inn. I'll show you round after we've eaten."

There were some old hunting prints on the walls; he walked round explaining what they represented and while he was doing this Matty came in with the soup.

"There," she said, "that will warm you before you get down to the cold. I've always got a cauldron of soup. People ask for it again and again."

The pease soup was delicious and so was the roast beef, garnished with herbs, served with hot crusty bread and a fruit pie to follow.

I sat back, drowsily content. Jonathan watched me closely.

"You agree that I have brought you to a worthy inn?"

"It was a very good meal."

"Imagine what Matty would have done if she had known we were coming!"

"It could not have been better."

"Oh, you don't know Matty."

We complimented her while she cleared away and Jonathan said we would rest awhile before resuming our journey.

I felt very happy. I knew I shouldn't be, but Jonathan had that certain effect on me. It was a kind of bewitchment. There were warning voices in my mind, reminding me what could easily happen again. It must not be.

I kept telling myself that my being here was not of my contriving. Excuses come glibly when one has need of them.

I just knew that I wanted this to go on. I had never felt the same with anyone else. Never with anyone had I felt the desire to catch at time and hold it, making moments last for ever.

He talked about London, how he would be there more and more, for his father was gradually relinquishing the London business to him.

"It was a good thing," he said, "that there were two of us . . . and so different. David the countryman; myself the townsman."

"I think your father arranged it."

"Would even he be clever enough for that?"

"He always seemed to get what he wanted."

"A trait I sincerely hope he has passed on to his son."

"I think there is no doubt that you have inherited a little of that spirit."

"A little? I was hoping it was a great deal."

"Well, you are young yet. I don't suppose that when he was your age everything fell quite so neatly into Dickon's hands. For one thing, he wanted my mother and he didn't get her, did he, until later."

"But in the end he did."

"Only after years . . ."

"And thank Heaven it worked out that way or where should you and I be today, somewhere in the region of the unborn . . . if there is such a place." He stood up. "Let's go. We'll ride along by the river. There are some pretty spots. That is what is so delightful about London. It is teeming with life . . . yet in a short time you can be out in the heart of the country."

What a perfect afternoon that was! We said our goodbyes to Matty and Thomas, complimenting them on the excellent meal, inspected the stables, mounted our refreshed horses and set out.

About a mile from the inn we came to a grassy bank and Jonathan suggested that we tether the horses to a nearby bush and sit down to watch the river. A few craft passed . . . one or two returning home after having been in the city for the celebrations.

Contentment . . . forgetting all evil . . . sitting on the grass idly watching the ripples in the water . . . looking up as the occasional vessel floated by.

Suddenly Jonathan said: "We should have married, Claudine, you and I."

I was silent and he went on: "It would have been ideal. You know it, don't you? You and I . . . loving . . . really loving."

"I would want a faithful husband, and you would never be that."

"I might. Who knows?"

"No," I said. "It is not in your nature."

"Look at my father. He had adventures far and wide. Now there is not a more faithful husband in the country."

"He has matured and grown wise. You are young yet."

"My dear Claudine, are you wishing that we were old?"

"I wish—"

"Come tell me what you wish. You wish that you had not hastily married my brother. You know that I am the one for you. You long for the kind of life you could have shared with me . . . exciting, adventurous."

"Your wife would not be very happy."

"Oh, she would. There would be the reunions after my absences. It would be like starting all over again . . . the honeymoon, the perpetual honeymoon."

"No," I said firmly. "I am happier as I am."

"You merely accept life, Claudine."

"You seem to have forgotten that you will soon be a husband yourself."

"It has not escaped my memory."

"Oh, Jonathan, do you feel no shame at all! You would deceive Millicent, and what we did, you and I . . . you don't regret that . . ."

"How could I regret the most exciting experience of my life?"

"Save such talk for your gullible victims."

"On this occasion I speak the truth. I love you, Claudine. I did, right from the first moment I saw you. You remember . . . a little girl who spoke such quaint English. I thought, She's mine. From the moment I saw you I thought that."

"We did a terrible thing, Jonathan."

"Is it so terrible to love?"

"In the circumstances, yes. I deceived my husband. You deceived your brother. Surely you see how despicable that is. I cannot understand why you do not feel shame. You don't, do you?"

"No," he replied coolly.

"You think we did no wrong?"

"We shall only have done wrong if we are discovered." He laughed at me. "You are shocked. Listen, Claudine, this is the way I see it." He picked up a stone and threw it in the river. "Sin . . . wickedness is hurting others. If others are not hurt by what one has done, then one has done no wrong."

"But *we* know that we did."

"We do indeed . . . and I shall never forget. Constantly I long to be with you . . . as we were in that room. I shall never forget it. I can't regret . . . As long as David does not know, what harm have we done?"

"You are amoral . . . as well as immoral."

"Perhaps you are right. We were happy, you and I, and happiness is a rare and wonderful gift. Could it be a sin not to take it when it is offered to you?"

"When it is a sin against one's marriage vows and duty towards one's brother?"

"I repeat that if no one is hurt there is no need to regret. The trouble with you, Claudine, is that you have been brought up to observe a set of conventions. You believe they are unalterable. They are the Right and the Wrong, and to offend against them is to incur the wrath of God . . . or at least the wrath of your relations. That is too simple. It is not as easy as that. The rules are flexible. Take my simple one: Do not hurt anyone. Keep people happy. That is as good a doctrine as any."

"But don't you see how bitterly you and I have sinned against David?"

"Only if David discovers. Then we shall have hurt him. If he does not know, what harm is there? I can tell you I have rarely seen David as happy as he is now."

"It is impossible to make you see reason."

"Your reason, Claudine. I am trying to make you see mine."

"Yours is trimmed to suit yourself."

"Perhaps yours is too."

"And," I said, "there is something else I have to say to you. Someone knows about us."

"What? Who?"

"I don't know. You laughed at my voices. They were not fantasy. Jeanne discovered some sort of speaking tube, which extends from that room to the kitchens. So . . . someone was in the Enderby kitchens when we were there. It was that person's voice I heard."

"Is that really so?"

"It is. It surprises you, doesn't it? You see, if someone knows, we could find your theories thrust aside. If that someone told David, what then?"

"Who can it be?" he said.

"I don't know. I suspect Mrs. Trent."

"That wicked old woman!"

"She has not said anything to me, but she did try to blackmail me . . . well, that's hardly the word . . . *persuade* me to help Evie along with Harry Farringdon. She said that her son Richard was Dickon's son."

"I know there was a suspicion of that. My father has helped her quite a bit. Grasslands was doing very badly and he put money into it. Richard Mather was a gambler and he drank too much. He almost ruined the family. My father has helped them out of various difficulties."

"So you think she is right about Richard's being your father's son."

"I daresay. There were always women with him, and what happened between them must have been when he was very young. It would give her a feeling that she had certain rights, I suppose . . . or at least Richard's daughter had."

"Yes, that was what she implied. She didn't threaten or anything like that, but during the conversation there were one or two innuendos which might have suggested she knew something about me."

"We'll have no nonsense from her."

"I did what I could for Evie . . . but that was because I was sorry for her and I did not know how my mother would feel about old scandals being raked over."

He leaned towards me and took my hand.

"If she attempts to make any trouble, don't try to handle it yourself. Let me know. I'll soon settle her."

I felt a relief sweeping over me. I had been more anxious than I cared to admit since Jeanne had shown me the speaking tube at Enderby.

"Thank you," I said.

"After all," he went on, smiling at me, "it's our secret matter, isn't it . . . yours and mine?"

"I shall never take your view of that sort of thing."

"You might . . . in time. It's the wise view."

"I shall never forget. Every time I look at Amaryllis . . ."

"She's mine, isn't she?"

"I don't know. I never shall."

"I shall think of her always as mine and David will think of her as his."

"David adores her," I said. "I believe you hardly ever give her a thought."

"You know so little about me, Claudine. It could take a lifetime to learn all the intricacies of my nature and to explore its hidden places."

"I shall have to leave it to Millicent to make that voyage of discovery."

"She will not make the attempt. Millicent accepts in the same way as you do. Our marriage will be an ideal one from her family's point of view and from my family's too. Important families are obsessed by what they think of as linking up. They've been doing it for centuries. It is the rock on which many of our noble houses have been founded. Little families become larger families, larger families become big ones. They grow in wealth and importance. Their watchword is Wealth and Power through Union."

"It is all so cynical."

"And all very wise."

"And what of the people who are used to make these great edifices? Are they of no importance?"

"Of the utmost importance. They are the bricks and stones which one by one build up the tower of strength. It is their united cooperation which makes us what we are."

"My mother brought nothing. It is true she would have been extremely wealthy . . ."

"And that would have delighted Dickon. However, he is so much in love with her that he took her penniless . . . as I should have taken you."

"But your father had done his duty once in marrying your mother. I gather she contributed in great measure to the Eversleigh fortunes."

"Ah yes, indeed. She brought in much of the London side. The banking . . . and all the interests that entailed. My father did his duty to the family admirably and therefore he earned the right to marry for love."

"You are the most cynical man I ever met."

"Because I look facts straight in the face, because I do not pander to sentimentality?"

"You don't love Millicent."

"I like Millicent. She amuses me. There will be battles between us, for Millicent is a very strong lady who likes to command. So is her mother, who has had a fair success with old Pettigrew. Look at Lady Pettigrew and there you see Millicent thirty years hence."

"And the thought does not terrify you?"

"Indeed no. I admire Lady Pettigrew. I would not care for a mild simpering wife. Battle will be more stimulating than cloying reproaches."

"Perhaps there will be reproaches."

"Undoubtedly."

"You do not present yourself in a very favourable light."

"Yet I have a notion that you have some regard for me, Claudine. Have you?"

"I suppose you are what is called a rather fascinating man."

"I am flattered."

"I have seen you with people, with Millicent—the way the women servants look at you—and Matty today. It's a sort of challenge to sex, I suppose."

He laughed. "I like women. They are so pleasant to look at, and when they are clever, so interesting to talk to. I like battles . . . battles of words."

"You like the sparring kind of flirtation at which you excel."

"You do, too, Claudine."

"I can't think why you should imagine that."

"Because you do it so well. People always like what they do well."

He turned to look at me and I saw the blazing blue of his eyes and I thought: No, no. Not again. It must never happen again.

"Claudine," he said seriously, "I love you. It will always be you, you know."

He had drawn me to him and for a blissful moment I allowed myself to lie against him. I wanted to be with him; I wanted to be in that little room again. He had caught me in his spell and something told me he would never let me go.

I said: "I think we should go back."

"It's early yet. There'll be crowds in the streets. All the Court ceremonies won't be over for a while yet. The servants and apprentices will be out in their thousands. You couldn't keep them in on a day like this. We could go somewhere . . . be quite alone . . . together."

For a moment I actually considered it. Then I was filled with shame.

"No," I said firmly. "Never again. Sometimes I wake in the night. I have been dreaming . . ."

"Of me . . . of us," he said.

"Of you and myself, and I awake hating myself. Your standards are not mine. You are soon to be married. We are actually preparing for your wedding. And I am married to David, your own brother. He is such a good man."

"Yes, David is a good man."

"He is at Clavering now, working hard as he always does, thinking perhaps that we shall soon be together. You have tried to explain yourself to me . . . your philosophy of life. It is so cynical, Jonathan. You think so little of matters which are of the utmost seriousness to me."

"We won't hurt David. He shall never know."

"How can you be sure? I'd rather die than that he should know."

"He won't suspect. He would never doubt you. He is completely straight himself and he thinks others are the same, particularly you. He has lived his life along lines laid down for him. I know him well. We were in the nursery together; we shared tutors. I was the devious one. I made adventure. I used to spy for my old nurse when she became quite mad, and was so upset by my mother's death that she watched my father, hoping to catch him in some villainy. Every woman who interested him she wanted to know about. I actually enjoyed that. Once I followed him and your mother into Enderby. That old house, how it crops up! It seems to be a place for secret assignations. David is simple . . . I don't mean mentally. He is very clever, intellectually, far more than I ever was, but he is ignorant of life . . . my sort of life. He lives conventionally, thinks conventionally, and he is inclined to bestow on everyone else the same qualities which he possesses. Therefore he would never suspect."

"If this terrible wrong I have done him . . ."

"I have told you it is only a wrong if it is found out."

"I don't accept your cynical deductions. But if this terrible wrong I have done him can be kept from him, I shall never, never do anything that can hurt him again."

"It is unwise to make such vows, Claudine."

I stood up and he was beside me.

"What a beautiful day," he said. "The river, the quiet of the countryside . . . and you alone here with me."

"Let us go back," I said.

We rode back and when we reached the City the crowds were still in the streets.

There were one or two servants in the house. They told us that they were having time free in the evening when the others returned.

It was about five o'clock.

Jonathan said: "As you have no desire to remain in the house, I suggest we go out again. In an hour, eh? We'll get a boat and I'll row you down the river . . . or up if you prefer. You shall decide."

I was so happy and the day was not yet over. I wanted so much to be with him. I believed I enjoyed the battle within myself and I was gratified because I was sure of my ability to win.

"Change into something, not too elaborate," he said. "We don't want to attract the attention of rogues and pickpockets. We'll look like a merchant and his wife out to enjoy all the fun."

It must have been about six o'clock when we left the house. The river was even more crowded and the taverns overflowing. Jonathan put his arm through mine protectively and held me close against him as we made our way down to the river's edge, where he hired a boat.

There were a lot of craft on the river and Jonathan said we must get away from the crowds. It was not easy but Jonathan was determined, and as most people did not want to stray too far from the centre of the town where all the fun was, in due course we found ourselves passing through Kew on the way to Richmond.

There was magic in the evening, or perhaps I felt that because Jonathan was beside me. He managed the boat with easy skill. I trailed my hand in the water and thought: I'm happy. I want this to go on and on. There was no harm in being happy, was there?

"This is pleasant isn't it?" he asked.

"It's lovely."

"You look contented. I like to see you thus. This has been a wonderful day for me, Claudine."

"I have enjoyed it very much."

"And do you feel you know me a little better now?"

"Yes. I think perhaps I do."

"And do I improve on closer acquaintance?"

I was silent.

"Do I?" he insisted.

"I could never think as you do, Jonathan. I could not take such a view of life."

"So you would suffer agonies of remorse when there is no need to."

"Oh, Jonathan, as I see it, there is every need to."

"One of these days I will make you see from my point of view."

"It is too late," I told him. "I married David and you are going to marry Millicent. Let your consolation—if consolation you need—be that her father's financial interests will make very sturdy bricks in that great family edifice which it is so important to build. If you had married me, I should have brought you nothing. Think what you would have missed!"

"David would have had Millicent then."

"David . . . Millicent. Oh no!"

"I agree he would have been no match for her. Accept life, Claudine. He takes you. I take Millicent. But you and I are caught in love, and if in life one cannot have everything one wants, at least one can take what one can get."

"I had never before considered how magnanimous it was of your father to agree to the marriage of one of his sons to a penniless girl."

"The circumstances were unusual. There was your mother's influence and you were no ordinary penniless girl. As long as one of us took Millicent, the other could have you."

"I cannot believe it was worked out like that."

"Not so plainly. These matters are arranged by gentle suggestions. But they are nonetheless firm for all that. But why waste this evening on such sordid matters? Do you like it here, Claudine? The stars will be coming out soon. I know of a very pleasant inn near the Richmond towpath."

"How knowledgeable you are about the inns of the country!"

"It is quite an art to know where to eat well."

"More friends of yours?"

"All innkeepers are friends of mine. Yes, I am right. There is the first star. Venus, I think. See how bright she is. The star of love."

"It could well be Mars," I told him.

"Oh Claudine, why did you do this? What fun we could have had, you and I together. Your miserable conscience could have gone slumbering on."

"You promised not to talk of it," I said.

"So I did . . . and I think the inn is just along here. There. You can see the lights. I'll pull in at the privy steps and tie up the boat."

He lifted me out and held me for a few seconds, smiling up at me. Then he took my hand and we went into the riverside inn. There were several people there and ale was being served which the people were drinking while they ate the whitebait, which was a speciality of the inn.

I was amazed to see how easily Jonathan fitted in with this kind of company. We sat at one of the tables, drank mild ale, and ate the fish which was brought to us.

"There," he said. "You have never done this before."

"Never," I agreed.

"Enjoying it?"

"Very much."

"Is it the venue or the company? Come, Claudine, you can be honest."

I said: "I think perhaps it is both."

He speared a whitebait on the prong of his fork.

"Delicious," he said. "Small but none the worse for that, eh? No wonder whitebait is becoming more and more popular."

Someone started to sing. The singer had a good tenor voice but his song was one which could be called controversial on a day such as this. I knew it well, as most people did. It had been written by a Yorkshire man, William Upton, about his lady love; but it fitted another couple so well that this was the very reason why it had become so popular.

The Richmond Hill in the song might be that Richmond in Yorkshire, but there was also a Richmond near London and Mrs. Fitzherbert had lived at Marble Hill close by; moreover there was a rumour that she and the Prince had met on the towpath at Richmond. So that song had become popular throughout the country—made so by the Prince's romance, without which Mr. Upton's song would have gone unnoticed.

On Richmond Hill there lives a lass
More bright than May day morn,
Whose charms all other maids' surpass
A rose without a thorn.
This lass so neat, with smiles so sweet
Has won my right good will.
I'd crowns resign to call thee mine
Sweet lass of Richmond Hill.

The last lines were particularly apt because there had been a time when the Prince of Wales had considered, some said, resigning his crown for the sake of Maria Fitzherbert. However, all that was past now; he had repudiated Maria, and if his new wife was Caroline of Brunswick, his mistress was Lady Jersey.

Some joined in the chorus, but there were some who refrained from doing so and showed more than a little repugnance.

Then one man rose, and taking the singer by the lapel of his coat with one hand, shouted: "It is an insult to the monarchy." At which he threw the wine from his half-filled tankard into the face of the singer.

There was a scuffle and it seemed that the company was taking sides.

Jonathan seized my arm and hustled me through the crowd.

When we were outside he said: "We'll leave the royalists and the republicans to settle their score."

"Do you think it was really serious?" I asked. "I should like to have stayed to see what happened."

"They've drunk too much."

"The singer had a pleasant voice and I am sure he meant no harm."

"He chose the wrong song at a time like this. People are looking for trouble. They are seizing opportunities to declaim against the monarchy. To sing of the Prince's amours on his wedding day was lesemajesty in the eyes of some . . . or it may be that the gentleman made his graceful gesture of aiming his drink into the other's face merely to start trouble. I'm sorry for the innkeeper; he's a good man and keeps a respectable house."

We could hear the shouts coming through the night air.

"Here's the boat," said Jonathan.

"You got out very quickly."

"I recognized the signs and I have a precious charge. I assured your mother that I would look after you, and I would not let you run the slightest risk."

He had taken the oars and we slid away from the bank. I looked back at the inn. Some of the people had come outside and were shouting at each other.

"I was enjoying the whitebait," I said.

"I was enjoying the company . . . and as long as I still have that, little fishes do not concern me. There will be many a little contretemps before the night is out, you can be sure."

It was dark now. I looked up at the stars and then at the bushes on the bank. I was happy.

Jonathan started to sing. He had a strong tenor voice which was attractive, and the song he sang was full of a haunting beauty.

Drink to me only with thine eyes,
And I will pledge with mine;
Or leave a kiss but in the cup
And I'll not look for wine.
The thirst that from the soul doth rise
Doth ask a drink divine:
But might I of Jove's nectar sip
I would not change for thine.

And as I sat back in that boat and looked at his face in the starlight and listened to the rise and fall of his voice and the beautiful words which Ben Jonson had written to a certain Celia, I knew that I loved him and that nothing . . . my marriage . . . his marriage . . . could alter that.

I think he knew it too, and that, in his way, he loved me. We were both silent until we came to Westminster Stairs and we left the boat and walked home through the streets.

There was still revelry; people were singing and some danced and many were drunk. Jonathan showed a tender concern for me and I felt very safe, secure and happy.

When we reached the house, my mother and Dickon had returned. They were seated in the small sitting room before a fire.

"Oh, I'm glad you've come," said my mother. "We were getting quite concerned, weren't we, Dickon?"

Dickon answered: "You were. I knew Jonathan would take good care of Claudine."

"What a day!" said my mother. "Are you tired? Are you hungry?"

"Not tired. We've been on the river and we came away when a brawl started."

"Wise," commented Dickon. "There'll be plenty of brawls tonight, I can tell you."

"Why does a day of rejoicing always have to end up in fighting?" I asked my mother.

"Put it down to strong drink and human nature," said Dickon.

He poured out wine and gave it to us.

"Our whitebait supper was interrupted," I said.

"That was very unfortunate," said my mother. "Well, you both look as if you have enjoyed the day."

"We did," I told her.

"We rode to the Dog and Whistle at Greenwich and then afterwards went by boat to Richmond."

"You kept away from all the fuss."

"That was the idea," said Jonathan.

"But you are the ones who have been right in the centre," I added. "Do tell us what happened."

"It was rather sad," said my mother. "I was so sorry for the Princess. She is so gauche and so plain, and you know the Prince's taste for things exquisite."

"It must be awful to be forced into marriage," I said.

"The penalty of royalty," commented Dickon. "The Prince likes all that goes with his royal state. All right. That's fine. But he has to pay for it."

"Everything has to be paid for in this world," said my mother.

Jonathan disagreed. "Sometimes it can be avoided," he said. "After all, some kings have had brides whom they have loved deeply. They had the right woman and the royalty too."

"Life is not always very fair," I added.

"As for the Prince," went on Jonathan, "it's only a momentary discomfort. This marriage is not going to make much difference to his way of life. He just has the inconvenience of spending a few nights with his bride, and once she becomes pregnant he can be off."

"He did seem very put out though, didn't he, Dickon?" said my mother. "I am sure the two dukes who walked beside him were holding him up because he had been drinking so much that he was unsteady."

"There was a moment when I thought he was going to refuse to go ahead with it," said Dickon.

"Oh yes," continued my mother. "The King must have felt sure of it because at one point he stood up and whispered something to the Prince. It was quite conspicuous, for the pair were kneeling before the Archbishop at the time and the Prince had actually got to his feet."

"He must have been very drunk," said Dickon.

"I believe he was. But at one point I really did wonder what was going to happen. I was quite relieved when it was over. The music was lovely, the choir sang:

For blessed are they that fear the Lord.
Oh well is thee! Oh well is thee!
How happy shalt thou be.

But it was rather unfortunate to talk about happiness, for both the bride and groom showed clearly that that was the last thing they were feeling. And then the chorus of 'Happy, happy shalt thou be' sounded a little hollow."

"Well, you have had the satisfaction of being present at a historic occasion," I reminded her.

"I shall never forget it. I particularly noticed Lady Jersey. She seemed more contented than anyone."

"She was afraid the Prince might have a beautiful bride with whom he would fall in love," said Dickon.

"Temporarily, of course," added Jonathan. "His amours are generally transient. But a lady of uncertain age like Madam Jersey cannot afford even little interruptions."

"It is a great pity he left Maria," said my mother. "She was so good for him and I think he truly loved her."

"He couldn't have done or he wouldn't have repudiated her," I put in sharply.

"Imagine the pressure," said my mother. "I don't think he has ever been happy since they parted."

"Don't waste your sentiment on HRH," said Dickon. "I think he is quite capable of taking care of himself."

"Well, he didn't seem so today," said my mother. "Tell us about the Dog and Whistle."

We sat there talking desultorily and sleepily but none of us wanted the day to end. The candles guttered and some of them went out but no one thought of replacing them. It was very pleasant, very intimate. There were long silences which no one seemed to notice. I suppose we were all busy with our own thoughts and they seemed to be pleasant ones.

I kept going over the incidents of the day. I could smell the river; I could taste Matty's roast beef; I could see the shining brasses in the inn parlour; I could hear the soft lapping of water against a bank.

It had been a happy day.

The spell was broken as the fire collapsed into the grate.

"It will soon be out," said Dickon.

"And it's getting chilly," added my mother.

She yawned and rose. She and I went upstairs together, her arm through mine. She kissed me at my door and I went in and lighted the candles on my dressing table.

I looked at my reflection. I seemed almost beautiful by candlelight. Candlelight can flatter, I told myself; but there was something more than that. There was a softness, a radiance, about me. It had been a day I should never forget.

I brushed my hair dreamily and thought of "Drink to me only with thine eyes."

Suddenly I rose and locked my door.

Surely he would not attempt to come to me, not here in this house with my mother close at hand. But would he not dare anything?

That was why I must lock my door, for if he did come, how could I trust myself on a night like this?

In spite of the late night we were all up early the next morning, and my mother was already at breakfast when I went down.

"Oh, there you are!" she said. "Did you sleep well after all the excitement?"

"Not at first, but I feel surprisingly refreshed."

"What a day! I shall never forget it. I'm glad it's over though. I'm longing to see Jessica. I do hate leaving her so long. And you must feel the same about Amaryllis."

I admitted I did.

"I thought we'd go back the day after tomorrow."

"Yes, why not?"

"If Dickon can make it," she added.

"Has he said so?"

"He's not quite sure. But in case he does I want to go to the mercer's this morning. I must get some more of that lace. He said he would have it in today. Will you come with me this morning? I might want your opinion."

"I'll like that."

"All right then. Ten o'clock? We can walk there. It's not more than ten minutes away."

"I'll be ready."

We went to the mercer's shop and were some time choosing the lace. My mother also bought some pale mauve and pink ribbons which she thought would be useful for the babies' clothes.

As we came out of the shop she said: "I know what we'll do. We'll have some coffee or chocolate. I do think the coffee houses are interesting."

I agreed with her that they had become a part of London life and they were more than just a place to stop and take a drink of coffee or chocolate. One could eat there, read the papers which were available for clients, could write letters and most of all listen to the conversations of the great. Certain coffee houses were frequented by people in various walks of life; there were the political coffee houses, literary coffee houses, musical coffee houses, and there people could congregate and join in discussions on their favourite topics. Sometimes well-known men of wit and erudition frequented them. In his day Samuel Johnson had held court at the Turk's Head or the Bedford or Cheshire Cheese; and Walpole and Addison had rivalled Congreve and Vanbrugh at the Kit Cat.

The coffee house we chose was only a few steps from the mercer's. It was Benbow's—named, I heard, after its founder, who had made a fortune at the gaming tables. At this hour of the day there were no wits present and I imagined the house was probably used by people like us who merely wished to stay for as long as it took to drink our coffee or chocolate.

When we went in we were effusively greeted by the owner. He knew who my mother was and she told me afterwards that she had been in the place with Dickon on their last visit to London.

He ushered us to our seats. "Here in this little alcove you will view the company in comfort," he added with a little wink.

"This is my daughter," said my mother.

"I am delighted to make your acquaintance, my lady," he said.

He bowed with great dignity and I said: "And I to meet you."

We were drinking the excellent chocolate when my mother said suddenly: "Oh dear, I've left the ribbons at the mercer's."

"We must go back and get them when we leave here."

"I'll run back now. It won't take long. You stay here."

She rose and Mr. Benbow came forward.

My mother said, "I am going to the mercer's just along the street. I have left a parcel there. My daughter will wait for me here."

"I will take the utmost care of her in your absence, my lady."

I laughed. "Oh dear. Is it so dangerous?"

He lifted his shoulders. "Not exactly dangerous, but with a beautiful lady, gallants can be tiresome. I will guard her with my life."

"I hope that won't be necessary," said my mother with a smile.

I looked about the room as I finished my chocolate. A man came in and sat down. As soon as he did so I had a strange sensation. I fancied I had seen him before, but for a few moments I was at a loss. It must have been a long time ago. It would have been in France. But who? Where? My mind went back to the *château*. That was it.

I had it. It was the tutor who had come long ago to teach Charlot and Louis Charles. Or if it was not, it was someone very like him.

I had been young at the time but this man had created quite a stir. I remembered he had left suddenly to go and look after his aged mother. And much later, when my mother had gone back to France and was in such acute danger, she had discovered that he had been a spy in the *château*, and it was due to him that the Comte's son, Armand, had been taken to the Bastille.

I must have been staring at him for he was looking at me now. Clearly he did not recognize me. I had been a small child when he was at the *château*. It was coming back vividly to me now. There could be no doubt. He was the spy-tutor and his name was . . . I racked my brains. Then it came to me in a flash. Léon Blanchard.

I felt very uneasy. He had been a revolutionary. An agitator. Then what could he possibly be doing in Benbow's Coffee House?

My heart gave a lurch, for someone else had come in. I almost cried out. It was Alberic.

He went straight to the table at which Léon Blanchard was sitting. He sat down and said something. For a few seconds they talked and then Alberic looked up and saw me.

I called: "Alberic . . ."

He rose. "Miss—Claudine—" he stammered. He was obviously shaken. "I—I—am doing a commission here for Mademoiselle d'Aubigné. Are—are you alone?"

"No, my mother is here. She will come in a few minutes."

Léon Blanchard had risen. He moved towards the door.

"I must go," said Alberic. "Good day, Miss Claudine."

He followed Léon Blanchard out of the coffee house.

They had not been gone more than a minute or so and I was still sitting there in a state of bewilderment when my mother came in clutching the ribbons.

"I have just seen something rather strange," I blurted out. "Alberic came in here. He was meeting a man. I thought I recognized him. I'm almost sure. It was Léon Blanchard, the tutor. Alberic left in a great hurry. They both did."

My mother turned pale.

"God help us," she murmured under her breath. Then she said: "Léon Blanchard . . . and Alberic. That can mean only one thing. I think we should go back without delay. Dickon must know of this at once."

By great good fortune, Dickon and Jonathan were in the house, though just about to go out.

Breathlessly my mother explained what had happened.

Dickon was dumbfounded.

Jonathan looked at me incredulously. "Are you sure . . . ?"

"Sure it was Alberic, of course," I replied. "He spoke to me. The other one . . . Well, I was puzzling over him and then it suddenly came to me."

"It makes sense," said Dickon. "And there isn't a moment to lose. Now . . . how best to act." He looked at Jonathan and went on: "They'll both go into hiding. Alberic must have had a shock to see Claudine, and Blanchard will be afraid that she has recognized him. He was obviously scared of being seen by Lottie. Then there would have been no doubt. It may be that Alberic will try to get to France."

"Taking information with him, no doubt. He must be stopped."

"And what of Billy Grafter in our own household . . . recommended by Alberic. We've had them both under our roof. That explains the visit by the Cardews. We know what they got away with. God, how careless we've been."

"No use going over that now," said Jonathan. "How best to act is the point."

"You should leave for Eversleigh right away. Alberic may have certain things to clear up there. He may even have left something in Enderby. He'll have to warn Grafter. There's a possibility that he'll have to go back to do that. On the other hand he may stay in hiding here in London." He was thoughtful for a second. "Yes, Jonathan, you go back to Eversleigh. I shall have to stay here for a while. We've got to find him. If we can, it might lead a trail to the rest of them. I'd like to get Blanchard. But there is a possibility that Alberic will try for France. He is thoroughly identified now. What fools we were to be deluded by that old émigré story. How soon can you leave?"

"In half an hour."

"And er—take Claudine with you."

"But why?" I asked.

"I don't know how long I shall be here. Lottie naturally will stay with me. It would arouse comment if you stayed on with us after David is back at Eversleigh. No, this is the best. There's no time for discussion. We have to act quickly. I'll take care of these things, and if he's not here we'll scent him out. He's got to be stopped getting back to France."

Jonathan said crisply: "I'll see that the horses are made ready. Claudine, be ready in half an hour."

I was bewildered. My mother came to my room to help me prepare.

"It seems so . . . dramatic," I said.

"It is. I accept it. I was caught up in France, remember. That man Blanchard went round the country inciting the French to revolution. He and his kind were responsible for my mother's death. I narrowly escaped through Dickon's courage and resourcefulness. What happened in France must not happen in England, and that is what men like Blanchard and Alberic are trying to bring about. We have to help. We have to do all we can, and if we don't always understand at the time, we have to wait for explanations later."

I could not believe that only yesterday I had been sitting on a riverbank watching the water flow by, philosophically talking to Jonathan.

The horses were waiting for us. "You should get a good way by tonight," said Dickon. "Then go to an inn and rest for a few hours, but be off with the dawn, and you might with luck reach Eversleigh by early afternoon. He can't get there much before you."

We went through the city, past the Tower—grey, gloomy and menacing; then we were away. Jonathan looked different, very determined. It was fortunate that I was a good rider. The bantering mood of yesterday was gone and in its place was one of intense seriousness. He was going to get Alberic . . . if that young man had decided to return to Enderby.

All through the afternoon we rode, stopping only to slake our thirst and eat a little cold lamb and bread. Then we were off again.

It was about ten o'clock that night when we pulled up at an inn. Our horses were flagging and I wondered if Jonathan was as tired as I was.

They had only one room. At any other time I should have protested, but we had to eat and sleep if we were going to make the long journey next day.

We ate in the inn parlour. As it was late, there was only cold food—mutton pie—and ale to drink. It was enough, and I was almost asleep over it.

There was only one bed in the room. I took off my boots and fully dressed lay down on it and was immediately fast asleep.

I was awakened by a light kiss on my forehead. Jonathan was standing over me.

"Wake up," he said. "Time to be off."

Then I remembered where I was and sprang up.

"We won't stop for food," he said, "We'll try to snatch something on the way."

We went out to the stables; our horses had been fed and watered and were rested. They were as frisky as ever.

As we rode out, Jonathan laughed heartily. I asked what was so amusing.

"It has just occurred to me. I have often thought of spending a night with you . . . to find you lying there beside me when I awoke. I've imagined that often enough, and when it does happen, all we did was sleep. It's funny, you must admit. Come on. With luck we'll make it by early afternoon."

The journey was long and arduous. Twice we stopped for light refreshment but mainly to rest the horses. It must have been two o'clock in the afternoon when we reached Eversleigh.

"First," said Jonathan, "we'll go to the stables and get fresh horses. These have done enough. Then we'll go to Enderby. I want you to find out whether Alberic is back. It will come better from you. Don't let them know we want to see him urgently. There may be others of his friends in the neighbourhood. We don't want them warned."

"Don't you think he would have got away by now?"

"He might. But he hasn't had much time. He couldn't have beaten us here by much, even if he left immediately after seeing you in the coffee house. Come on."

We went through the gate and into the stables.

One of the grooms came out to greet us.

"We want fresh horses, Jacob," said Jonathan. "Quickly, these are tired. We have to go out immediately."

"Yes, sir. You've come back and, master . . ."

"Never mind now. Get the horses and see to these two. . . . They've had a pretty long ride."

"Shall I tell the household you've returned?"

"Do that. Is Billy Grafter about?"

"I'll see, sir."

"If he's there, make sure he doesn't go away. I want to talk to him seriously . . . but not now."

"Right, sir."

"Make sure you have him ready for me. Lock him in one of the rooms so that he doesn't stray."

All the servants at Eversleigh had learned to obey Dickon without question, and I could see the same applied to Jonathan.

Twenty minutes later I rang the bell at Enderby and one of the servants opened the door.

"Oh, Mabel," I said. "I'm not calling to see my aunt. I just wanted a word with Alberic."

"You've just missed him, Mrs. Frenshaw."

"Missed him! He's back from London then?"

"Only just a little while ago. He's been in and out again."

"Where did he go?"

"That I don't know, Madam."

"All right. Thank you very much."

I hurried back to Jonathan. As I mounted my horse I said: "He's been . . . and he's gone."

"That could mean he is trying to get to France. You stay behind. Make sure you hold Grafter till I return."

"I'm coming with you," I said.

He was off and I was beside him.

I shouted: "How will you find him? He could be anywhere along the coast."

"We'll go where you found him."

"It's a lonely spot."

"Isn't there a dilapidated boathouse somewhere?"

"Yes."

"It is possible that he has anticipated an urgent flight. I wonder what was in that boathouse?"

"Nobody ever goes there. It will be washed out to sea one of these days. It only needs a gale to break it up."

"But it would serve to keep a boat in readiness."

"Do you really believe that?"

"Dear Claudine, my way of life leads me to believe everything is possible."

"If he is not there . . . what then?"

"I shall go along the coast. He's got to be stopped getting away. They will all be alerted. Unless my theory is correct and he has a boat in readiness, he is not going to find it very easy to get out of England."

"There are many coves and bays along the coast which are isolated."

"He'll need a boat and that will be difficult."

We were off again and it was only when we were forced to slow down that we could talk.

I could smell the sea now, hear the melancholy cry of the gulls. We had galloped down to the bay. This was the spot where Evie and Dolly had called me to their aid when they found Alberic.

We went down to the sandy beach.

I stared. A little boat was a short distance out at sea bobbing on the waves.

"Alberic," I shouted.

He was battling with the oars, desperately trying to fight the sea. He could not possibly hope to cross the Channel in such a boat, could he? Perhaps it was just possible and he was a desperate man.

Jonathan stood there watching. He was looking helplessly about him. There was no one in sight, no vessel which could take us after the fugitive.

We had come so far; we were in sight of our prey and the wind was helping to carry him out of our reach.

Alberic had now shipped his oars and was letting the wind act for him. For a few seconds we stood there staring at the little craft bobbing about on the waves, every second being carried farther away from the English coast.

I was close to Jonathan and the explosion nearly knocked me off my feet.

I was looking out to sea. As far as I could discern, Alberic was slumped over the side of the boat. It turned over suddenly and Alberic was in the sea.

Jonathan lifted his gun and fired again. I saw the reddish tint on the water all round the boat.

Jonathan stood still watching. It seemed a very long time that we stood there. The waves were tossing the boat about as though it were light as air. It was being carried out to sea. I watched it go farther and farther away.

There was no sign of Alberic.

I turned to Jonathan. I had a great impulse to run away, to be alone, to overcome this terrible emotion which beset me. I had never seen a man kill another before.

Alberic is dead, I kept thinking. Jonathan killed him. Death is awesome; even the deaths of those one does not know affect one. And this is someone with whom I have laughed and joked . . . someone merry, and happy and good-natured. It had shattered my peace to see him killed by a man with whom I had shared the utmost intimacy.

Jonathan breathed with satisfaction.

I said: "You killed him. You killed Alberic."

"That was lucky. Half an hour later and I should have been too late."

"But we knew him. Aunt Sophie was fond of him . . . and now he is dead."

He took me by the shoulders and shook me. "Stop it," he said. "You're getting hysterical. He's dead, yes, and rightly so. How many people do you think might die if he were allowed to continue with his work? Your own grandmother was murdered by his kind. Thank God we found out what he really was."

"You . . . you're quite callous . . ."

"When it comes to his sort, yes. I have no more compunction in killing him than I would a snake."

I put my hands to my face and felt the tears there.

"Come on," he said. "Don't be a fool, Claudine. We were out to catch him . . . and we've caught him."

I looked at him in horror and I said: "But it was because of *me* . . . don't you see? It was I who saw him. It was I who told . . . and because of that he's dead. I killed him, in a way."

"Congratulate yourself. One more little spy eliminated. You did good work, Claudine."

"I . . . killed him. I have committed adultery and now . . . murder."

He burst out laughing. It did not occur to me that he, too, was overwrought. He had just killed a man, a man whom we had all known, and he had ridden full speed from London in pursuit of that man. I had glimpsed the ruthlessness of him, which I had always known was there, but I had never seen it put to such practice as I had in the last half hour.

"Sometimes I think I hate you," I said. "You are so—uncaring. Even if he had to be killed . . . even if he is responsible for the deaths of others . . . you seemed to enjoy killing him."

He said coolly: "I enjoy seeing a mission satisfactorily concluded."

I looked out to sea. "I can see the red tinge still there."

"He's dead, all right. I want to wait awhile. I wouldn't want him to be washed ashore and nursed back to health by well-meaning little girls."

I turned away but he caught me and held me to him for a few moments.

"You're learning about life and the times we live in, Claudine," he said. "Not very pleasant sometimes, I have to admit. We have to keep this country prosperous. We have to serve our country's needs and when the snakes appear we scent them out and kill them. That's how it is, Claudine. It was the greatest good luck that you happened to be in Benbow's. You were sharp to recognize Blanchard. That has been a great help to us, to know that he is in London. But when Alberic came in, that was sheer good fortune."

"For you," I said. "For him . . . death."

"Oh dear, you are determined to be melodramatic and sentimental with it. Alberic was playing with death. He knew that and he wouldn't be so very surprised that it has caught up with him. There." He kissed me gently. "We've got Alberic. Now we have to be careful. The fishes will finish him off."

"Oh, please don't talk like that about a human being."

"Poor little Claudine, you keep rough company, I'm afraid. Never mind. You were one of us for a day or so. You did very well on the journey. I was proud of you. Now let us think what shall be done. We shall go back to the house. I doubt Grafter will be there. I imagine Alberic warned him. I wonder what papers he was taking with him. They are at the bottom of the ocean by now. This is to be a secret matter, Claudine. You don't know what happened to Alberic, remember. He'll be missing and maybe presumed drowned. As for Billy Grafter, if we've missed him and he's disappeared, it will be thought he was with Alberic. But let's hope he was not warned and is still at the house. There must be no shouting the truth from the housetops. The less that is known, the better."

"I'll say nothing," I said.

"That's right. I shall have to go back to London."

"At once?"

"Yes, the fact that Blanchard is known to be in London will cause a flutter. He is one of the founders of the French revolution. You can guess what he is trying to do here."

But the revolution is over now. The Republic is being accepted by some states."

"The French would still like to see us behave as madly as they did.

We're enemies, remember. We're actually at war with them. I shall leave for London early tomorrow morning. They'll still be searching for Alberic. Claudine, you must pull yourself together. You must not betray anything. Do you understand?"

"Yes, I understand."

"You have to put aside all those sentimental notions of yours. Alberic might have been a very pretty boy but he was a spy working against this country and he got his deserts. Remember that. He would have done the same to me if he had had the chance. It's all the luck of the game."

"I understand," I repeated.

"Good. I'm now sure he's dead. We can safely leave him. I can't see any sign of the boat now. Oh . . . is that broken spar right out there . . . part of it? Yes, I think it is. Now, Claudine, are you calm? Are you ready? We shall go back to Eversleigh and I shall leave tomorrow. You will resume life as though nothing extraordinary has happened. You can tell everyone about the excitement of the royal wedding and how the Prince had to be held up at the ceremony because he was drunk. That'll make them laugh. And you'll not betray you know where Alberic is . . . because he is going to be thought missing . . . possibly drowned. That's the best way for us all."

I mounted my horse and he was beside me.

"Now, are you ready? Back to Eversleigh."

I explained to the servants that my mother was staying on with Dickon and that Mr. Jonathan would be returning to London the next day.

They accepted this as normal, for the comings and goings of both Dickon and Jonathan had always been erratic.

We were disturbed—but not entirely surprised—to find that Billy Grafter was not in the house. "Clearly he was warned," said Jonathan. "But we'll get him."

I was glad that David was still at Clavering. It would have been difficult to behave normally with him.

I slept heavily that night and when I arose Jonathan had already left for London.

During the morning one of the servants from Enderby came over with a message from Aunt Sophie. She had heard that I was back and would like to see me.

I went over to Enderby in the afternoon. Jeanne greeted me. "Mademoiselle d'Aubigné is in bed. She has had a bad night. She is rather worried about Alberic. He returned from London yesterday and went straight out. He hasn't been back all night."

I heard myself say in a distant voice: "Oh . . . what has happened to him then?" And I despised myself for my falseness.

"That's what Mademoiselle d'Aubigné is worrying about. He didn't see her when he returned, which was rather strange. Do come up."

Aunt Sophie was lying in that room with the blue velvet curtains. My eyes went immediately to that spot where I knew the speaking tube to be.

"Madame Claudine is here," said Jeanne.

Aunt Sophie looked as melancholy as I remembered her from long ago, and I realized how much she had changed since she came to Enderby. Dolly Mather was seated by the bed, a book in her hand; she had obviously been reading to Aunt Sophie.

"Stay with us, Jeanne," said my aunt.

Jeanne nodded, placed a chair by the bed for me and took one herself some little distance away.

"Did you enjoy your trip?" asked Aunt Sophie.

"Yes, it was very interesting."

"I'm worried about Alberic," she said.

"Oh?" I answered faintly.

"Yes, he went to London on some business for me. You know he is good at that."

"I know he goes up quite often for you."

"Well, he returned yesterday. Apparently he looked in briefly and then went out again. He hasn't been back since."

"Then you have no idea . . ."

"He might have left something in London and gone back for it."

"Without telling you?" put in Jeanne.

Sophie smiled fondly. "He took such a pride in those London missions of his. He always wanted to do something for me and if he had forgotten something I asked him to get, he would not want me to know it. He would have gone straight back to get it. That's the only thing I can think of. I thought you might help, Claudine."

"I?"

"Well, you came to see him yesterday, didn't you, as soon as you arrived back. Why?"

I was caught. I had not expected this.

"You did come yesterday, didn't you?" insisted Aunt Sophie.

They were all watching me—Sophie and Jeanne questioningly and Dolly with an unfathomable expression on her face.

"Oh . . . I remember now. It was something about my horse. She seems to have a little colic. I had heard Alberic say something about a cure they have in France. I was so worried that I came to him without delay."

"You should have gone to the stables," said Jeanne. "They might have known."

"No . . . It was a French remedy. However, the mare is better now."

"When you came, you didn't see him, did you?"

"No. They told me he had gone out."

"I heard Billy Grafter is missing too," said Jeanne. "He must be with Alberic."

How quickly news travelled in the servants' world. They already knew that Billy Grafter had disappeared—and it was only natural that they should connect it with that of Alberic.

"I thought you might have seen him," said Aunt Sophie.

"No, he had already gone."

"It's not like him," said Aunt Sophie.

"He'll be back," Jeanne assured her. "He has too good a post here to want to leave Enderby."

"I shall scold him, when he comes," said Sophie. "He should have let me know he was going back."

I kissed her cheek and said that I would come again soon to see her.

"Yes, do," she said.

Jeanne walked down the stairs with me.

"She misses him," she said. "He could always cheer her up. He has that merry nature and she loves talking to him. Fortunately Dolly is here. She teaches her French, you know. The girl does quite well. She surprises me. She's quite intelligent although it is not always apparent. I just hope Alberic comes back soon. I shall give him a piece of my mind. He has no right to stay away like this."

"It is strange," I said, "that she should be so taken by a young servant. He hasn't been here so very long."

"She always took fancies. I was so glad that there was someone at last in whom she could take an interest. He responded to her, being of our nationality. He seemed to know just how to behave towards her. She took to him from the start."

I said goodbye to Jeanne and came away very sad. I seemed to have caught Aunt Sophie's melancholy. Poor Aunt Sophie! She would never see Alberic again.

The Suicide's Grave

The next day David came home from Clavering.

He was delighted to see me and I was filled with great tenderness towards him. I felt that having been so happy on the day of the royal wedding, I had been unfaithful to him. I wanted to make up to him because I was so fascinated by Jonathan.

It seemed to me that there was another barrier between us: the secret of Alberic's death, which I could not stop myself thinking of as Alberic's murder.

It was not as difficult to keep my secrets as I had imagined it would be. I seemed to have become adept at deception. But perhaps David was not as perceptive as his brother. I was sure I should never have been able to hide so much of myself from Jonathan.

I told him about the wedding and what my mother had told me about the ceremony. He said that the current rumour was that the Prince had been so intoxicated that he had spent the greater part of his wedding night lying in the fireplace of the bedchamber, whither he had fallen in a drunken stupor—and his bride had been content for him to stay there.

"It grows worse and worse," I said. "We heard that he was about to refuse to go on with the ceremony and that he had to be persuaded to by his father."

"How much truth is there in these stories?" he asked.

"My mother and your father seemed to have the impression that there was something in them."

"And you? Were you disappointed to have no royal invitation?"

"Oh no. Jonathan and I went out riding. My mother insisted that he accompany me. They didn't want me to go out alone on such a day."

"I should think not. There would be rogues everywhere."

"Yes. And we went to an inn called the Dog and Whistle near Greenwich, and there the host served us with the most excellent roast beef."

"So it was a pleasant visit was it?"

"Oh yes."

"And Jonathan immediately returned to London."

"Yes. My mother does not know how long she will be there, and they wanted to bring me back so that I should be here when you returned."

"Thoughtful of them." He kissed me tenderly. "I've missed you so much . . . you and Amaryllis."

I loved him, tenderly, dearly, steadfastly. So it is possible, I told myself, to love two people at the same time in different ways. To be with David was like taking a draught of crystal-clear water when one was thirsty. By the same analogy Jonathan was a sparkling intoxicating wine.

Was there something strange about me? If I looked right into my mind I had to admit that I wanted them both.

They were brothers . . . twin brothers. Could there be some explanation there? It was hard to imagine them as one person. They were so entirely different. And yet . . . I wanted them both.

"Well, we shall be having the wedding soon," said David. "I daresay there's a great deal of activity at the Pettigrews' place."

We talked about Amaryllis.

I spent a great deal of time in the nursery with her. The little girls were growing fast; they looked different every day. In the nursery I could have forgotten Jonathan if every time I looked at Amaryllis I did not have to think of him.

The day after David's return a storm blew up. The wind howled at gale force and the rain beat horizontally on the windows. Nobody went out that day because it was almost impossible to stand up in the wind.

The next morning when we awoke it was quite calm. The birds were singing with joy and those flowers which had not been battened down looked fresh and beautiful; damp dripped from the trees, but when the sun rose they would be dried out.

It was a beautiful morning.

I said I would ride round the estate with David and he was delighted that I should join him. There was so much to catch up with, he said, after his being away at Clavering.

Just as we were about to leave, a messenger came from Jeanne. Would we please come over at once?

"Oh dear," I said to David. "It's going to spoil the morning. I wonder what it is now? Ride over with me. We need not stay long."

I was trembling because I feared it might have something to do with Alberic, and if it were I should need David's support.

We were met by a white-faced Jeanne. She came running out of the house and must have been watching for us.

"Oh Mrs. Frenshaw, Mr. Frenshaw, I am so glad you have come. A terrible thing has happened."

"What?" I cried.

"It's Alberic. They've found him."

"Found him!" cried David. "Where has he been all this time?"

"He's dead, Mr. Frenshaw. His body was washed up by the sea."

"Drowned!"

Jeanne dropped her head and was silent for a few moments. I was trembling, wondering what was coming next.

"All this time," murmured Jeanne, "and we were wondering where he was."

"Drowned?" repeated David.

"Murdered," Jeanne corrected him. "They said he's been shot through the lungs. I don't know what will happen now."

"But who . . ." began David. "Just a minute. This is such a shock. I think my wife does not feel very well."

He lifted me from my horse and kept his arm about me.

"It's such a shock," he said.

"Come into the house," said Jeanne.

"Yes, I think we'd better, darling," said David.

I sat in the cool hall and the faintness passed. So they would know now. What would they do? What would be the verdict as to what had happened to Alberic?

There was no talk of anything but Alberic's death. It was impossible to escape from it. Rumour was rife. Who had killed Alberic? Poor innocent Alberic, who had done nothing wrong but to take out a boat for a little pleasure trip.

His friend Billy Grafter must have been with him, they said, since Billy had disappeared at the time Alberic came back from London.

There was an inquest. There was no doubt that Alberic had been shot at, although he had died by drowning. The verdict was murder against some person or persons unknown.

It was terrible to have to live with such a secret. I had nightmares and would awake crying in the night. David would hold me close to him soothingly and I wanted to be beside him, thankful for his presence.

In the morning I would try to reason with myself. Jonathan was right. The times were dangerous. I must remember what had happened to my mother and my grandmother, Zipporah. I could picture the latter going into the little town to shop in her splendid carriage with the d'Aubigné crest emblazoned on it, and coming out to the mob. Alberic's death was a judicial killing. One should not look on it in a different light. It was logical. It was the law of survival.

During the day I could believe that. It was at night when the hideous dreams came.

Jonathan had come back to Eversleigh for the inquest.

I did not attend, but immediately it was over he sought an opportunity to be alone with me.

I said: "They will search for the one who killed him. Jonathan, what if—?"

He shook his head and smiled at me rather sardonically.

"They will talk of an enquiry. They will make a show of having one. But I can assure you that nothing will be revealed. That has been taken care of. It is for the country's security, and that is understood in certain quarters."

"It is all so . . . subversive."

He laughed. "What did you expect? It is the very nature of the matter. How are you feeling now? You've not told anybody?"

I shook my head firmly.

"Not even David? He'd understand, of course. He's always logical. But there is no point in people's knowing when it is not necessary. I'm only sorry you had to see it."

"What of Billy Grafter?" I asked.

"He got away. Never mind. We know what he looks like. He might provide a useful lead. And we know Léon Blanchard is—or has been—in London. I shall shortly be going to London again and when I come back I daresay Dickon and your mother will come with me."

I put my hand to my head and said wearily: "I wish it would all end."

"Poor Claudine! Life is very complicated, is it not?"

"I want mine to be simple . . . peaceful."

"Oh come, you are too young for peace." Then he kissed me briefly. "*Au revoir,* my love," he said.

I was glad when he went. He added to my disturbed state of mind.

I went to see Aunt Sophie.

Jeanne greeted me. "She is in bed. She's been poorly. This has upset her more than I would have believed possible."

She certainly looked wan lying in her bed with the blue curtains drawn back.

"Oh, Claudine . . ." she said.

"Dear Aunt Sophie, you have been unwell, Jeanne tells me."

"This is a house of mourning, Claudine," she answered. Her fingers picked restlessly at the sheets. "Why is life always like this to me? Why is it that when I have a fondness for someone something like this happens?"

"There is always tragedy around us, Aunt Sophie."

"For me, certainly," she said.

"I'm sorry . . ."

"That poor boy, that poor innocent boy . . ."

Ah, Aunt Sophie, I thought, not so innocent. It is amazing how little we know of those with whom we live closely.

"What did he do? He only took out a boat . . . for a pleasure trip . . . and some wicked villain shot him. Can you understand it?" she demanded. "It doesn't make sense," she went on piteously.

"It is difficult to understand, Aunt Sophie. Why was he in the boat, do you think? Hadn't he just returned from London? You thought he had gone back because he had forgotten something. But why should he have taken that moment to go out in the boat?"

"A whim," she said. "People do have whims. His horse, Prince—how he loved to ride Prince!—found his way back to the stables. He must have ridden down on Prince to get to the sea."

"Did you know he had a boat?"

"No. He never said. He and Billy Grafter must have acquired it between them. Poor boys . . . poor innocent boys."

I said: "It seems rather odd that they should both have decided to go out then."

But Aunt Sophie was not interested in why they had gone. All she cared about was her grief. I should not talk either. I should not set people speculating. Let it be thought that the young man, having been in London, was so eager for a breath of fresh air that he could not wait to take his boat out.

Aunt Sophie said: "Murdered! Cut off in the prime of his youth. He was a beautiful boy, bright and merry. It made me happy just to have him here."

"I'm so sorry, Aunt Sophie."

"You, my child, what do you know of loneliness? You have your husband, your dear child . . . You are fortunate, whereas I . . ."

"But, Aunt Sophie, we're here. We're your family. My mother . . ."

"Your mother was always lucky. Fortune smiled on her. She had Charles de Tourville . . . and now this husband of hers who thinks such a lot of her. Oh, I know she's beautiful and she has the sort of nature that people seem to like, but it's so unfair, Claudine, so unfair. And just because this young man is pleasant and makes me laugh and I have enjoyed having him in my house, someone has to murder him."

I looked helplessly at Jeanne, who lifted her shoulders. I supposed she had to endure a great deal of Aunt Sophie's self-pity.

Sophie was looking straight at me. "I shan't rest until I know who killed him. And when I do, I'd kill him . . . I would."

"Oh, Aunt Sophie . . ."

"Please don't try to soothe me. I will not be soothed. I lie here, Claudine, and the only thing I have left to me is my hatred . . . my desire for revenge. When I know who killed Alberic, I will find a way of getting even with him."

I could not suppress a shiver. She looked hardly sane with the fanatical light in her eyes, and her hood had fallen back. I could just catch a glimpse of the wrinkled scorched skin which she took such pains to hide. The unusual colour in her face accentuated it.

I felt an overwhelming pity and terrible fear, because somewhere in my mind was the terrible conviction that if she knew what had happened she would call me his murderer. True I had not fired the shot, yet but for me it would not have been fired. No one would have known of Alberic's secret life but for me, and he would now be charming Aunt Sophie and working for his country against ours.

I said I would have to go. I kissed Aunt Sophie and she gripped my hands.

"If ever you should discover anything," she said, "let me know. I am determined to find Alberic's murderer."

Jeanne walked downstairs with me.

"That is how she is, most of the time," she said. "Sometimes I think it is a good thing to let her go on about it. While she is thinking of revenge she is not brooding on his death."

I shook my head, and Jeanne went on: "She will grow calmer. She will accept his loss, for perforce she must."

I went slowly back to Eversleigh.

By the end of May the death of Alberic had become a nine-days' wonder. At first people had expected startling revelations. There were rumours of Alberic's having enemies in the neighbourhood; there were even suspects, though it was hard to imagine who would have wanted to kill such an amiable young man. The weeks passed and nothing happened. People watched out for Billy Grafter's body to be washed up and there was even a wild story in circulation that he had been found on the beach riddled with bullets. This persisted for two weeks and then died down. I think people gradually began to accept that Alberic's murder would never be solved and that Billy Grafter had been with him and they had drowned together.

My mother came to my room on her first night back from London.

"You must not let this upset you," she said. "It had to be. He was a spy. We cannot afford to let them go . . . however pleasant they may appear to be. Believe me, Claudine, I've been in the thick of it. I've seen Armand come back scarcely alive after his sojourn in the Bastille . . . put there by spies. You can say that killed him. Then there was my mother. I never forget that, and what they would have done to me but for Dickon. Living through that does something to you. It makes you understand that enemies of the state have to be eliminated, and if it can be quick—as it was with Alberic—that is the best way. I am only sorry that you were there when it happened."

"It was my fault. Jonathan asked me to stay behind but I went."

"And you saw it, and it upset you. You don't blame Jonathan, I hope. He was doing what had to be done."

"I see all that," I said. "I just wish it hadn't had to happen."

"My dear girl, that's what we all wish. We've got to forget this. David says you have nightmares. It's that, isn't it?"

I nodded.

"Such a pity. But you've got to grow away from it. It was like that with me . . . after that night in the *mairie* with the mob screaming for my blood outside. It comes back even now. Sometimes I dream. One can't come through these experiences unscathed. There is only one thing to do . . . grow away from them . . . that is, accept them as a necessary part of the world we live in."

"You are right, of course. Dear Maman, I will try. I will think of what they tried to do to you. I will think of my grandmother . . . and then I will see that it has to be."

She smiled. "And now," she said, "there is the wedding. I've such a lot to talk to you about concerning that. For one thing, I don't think we should take the babies."

"No. I was thinking of that."

"Grace Soper is quite capable of taking charge."

"She does in any case."

"She adores them both and they love her too. They would miss their nursery. I don't fancy the journey with them. Then of course they would be in a strange place . . . and after all we shall only be away for a few days."

I agreed with her.

Then we talked about clothes and all the time I was thinking about Jonathan and Millicent taking their vows—which he would never keep. I wondered if she would.

The wedding was to take place on the first of June. A few days before, our party set out for Pettigrew Hall, which was on the way to London—in fact it was about midway between the City and Eversleigh.

My mother and I rode in the carriage with Mary Lee, my mother's lady's maid, who would look after us both, and with us were the trunks containing our clothes and anything we should need. David and Dickon went on horseback and we were easily able to make the journey in a day, having set out very early and arriving at Pettigrew Hall at six in the evening.

We were warmly welcomed by Lord and Lady Pettigrew. Jonathan was already there.

Pettigrew Hall was more modern than Eversleigh. It had been erected just over a hundred years before when the great hall was no longer the centre of the house, and was a squarish solid stone edifice built round a court; and the kitchens, buttery and pantry were all underground. A magnificent staircase, which went to the top of the house, wound round a well as it went, so that from the very top landing one could look right down into the hall.

The drawing room was on the ground floor and it had glass doors through which the very beautiful gardens could be seen. The dining room, which was also downstairs, had similar views; and there were many bedrooms. The servants' quarters were in the attic at the top of the house. It was richly furnished and there were several specimens of the Gobelin tapestry which had begun to be manufactured in France about a hundred years before and soon found its way into English country houses.

Lady Pettigrew's taste seemed to me a little flamboyant; she had scattered pieces of marquetry all over the house; the hangings of the beds and the curtains were in the richest colours; and some of the ceilings had been painted with allegorical scenes. It was as though she wished to proclaim her importance to the world in everything she did—so naturally it would be obvious in her home.

The room I was to share with David was next to that assigned to my mother and Dickon. They were large and lighter than our Elizabethan ones and I thought them charming with their tall windows and marble fireplaces.

There would be several people staying at the Hall for the wedding. The Farringdons were of course there, being great friends of the Pettigrews; and Lady Pettigrew told us as she came up with us to show us our rooms—a very gracious gesture from such a grand lady and one which showed us how delighted she was to have us—that she was eager for us to meet the Brownings. They were such charming people and she was sure we were going to enjoy the company of Sir George and his wife Christine and their truly charming daughter Fiona.

David said when we were alone: "She is indeed an overpowering lady, and I fancy her daughter takes after her. But I don't think she will be able to subdue Jonathan as Lady Pettigrew does his lordship."

"I am sure," I replied, "that Jonathan will know how to look after himself."

"Oh yes. You can trust Jonathan for that."

It was to be a grand wedding. Lord Pettigrew was very influential in banking and, I suspect, political circles; and that meant that the marriage of his daughter was an event of more than usual importance. And as Dickon held great sway in the same society there would be many people who would want to attend the wedding.

The ceremony was to take place in the village church in the morning, after which all the guests would return to Pettigrew Hall for the reception. Many would come down from London as well as from the surrounding country. Ourselves and the Farringdons and Brownings were the only house guests—though perhaps one or two might stay for one night, as Lady Pettigrew did not want them to leave too early after the reception.

When we went down to dinner that night we were greeted by the Farringdons—Gwen, John and Harry—and George and Christine Browning and their daughter Fiona, who was very pretty and about eighteen I should imagine.

"Are we all assembled?" said Lady Pettigrew, bearing down on us.

"Let us go in to dinner. I daresay you are all ready for it. Travelling is so exhausting. I am glad you are staying with us and not popping in and out as I fear so many of the guests will be doing. How could it be otherwise? So many people want to see my daughter married."

John Farringdon murmured that it was indeed a happy occasion.

"And none the less so because we have had to wait a long time for it," added Gwen.

"Oh circumstances . . . circumstances . . ." cried Lady Pettigrew, waving her hand as though to dismiss these tiresome eventualities. She was of course referring to the death of Sabrina on account of which the wedding had been delayed. "Now let's go in. George, will you take Gwen, and John, Christine. Now, Jonathan, I am going to make you very cross. You are not to take Millicent. David shall take her and you can take Claudine."

I felt that ridiculous emotion as I slipped my arm through his. He gave me a one-sided grin and in some way I felt that we were conspirators.

I whispered: "I'm sorry to be the reason for making you cross."

He laid his hand over mine and squeezed it gently. "Just a brief contact such as this sends me into paradise," he said.

I laughed softly. "Ridiculous as ever . . . even on the eve of your wedding."

I was seated next to him. Millicent was opposite next to David. Lady Pettigrew at one end of the table surveyed us all as a general might his officers while she also kept her eyes on other ranks serving from the kitchens. I noticed Lord Pettigrew, from the other end of the table, watching her with a mixture of exasperation and tenderness. I thought: He is very different from Jonathan; and it occurred to me that if Millicent became more and more like her mother as the years passed, Jonathan's marriage might be a stormy affair.

There was a buzz of conversation as neighbours whispered together, but Lady Pettigrew was the sort of woman who could not bear her command to slip even for a moment and she liked to know everything that was being discussed, and such was her forceful personality, that the conversation soon became general.

It was not long before the subject of the war in Europe cropped up and in particular the successes which Napoleon Bonaparte was achieving all over Europe.

I noticed that Harry Farringdon, who was seated next to Fiona

Browning, appeared to be rather taken with her, and I felt a little qualm of uneasiness as I remembered Evie Mather.

I had not seen Evie for some time. She had been at Aunt Sophie's once or twice with her sister, and I wondered now about her. Mrs. Trent had been so anxious that something should come of her friendship with Harry Farringdon, and Mrs. Trent was, in her way, as forceful a woman as Lady Pettigrew, and the manner in which Harry was paying attention to Fiona Browning indicated that Evie's might be a lost cause.

"The Reverend Pollick is determined that there shall be no hitch," Lady Pettigrew was booming from the head of the table. "He is a man who takes his duties very seriously and for that we applaud him, do we not, Henry?" Lord Pettigrew murmured agreement. "He insists on a rehearsal. So tomorrow it is going to take place. It won't be necessary for everyone to attend . . . only the principals of course. But if any of you would like to step into the church, I think you might find it interesting."

Everyone at the table declared they would not miss it for anything.

"Such a fussy little man, the Reverend gentleman. Mind you, he always remembers that he owes his living to us, and I suppose, understandably, he'll look upon this wedding as his personal triumph."

There was talk then about previous weddings and Lady Pettigrew went on: "Your turn next, Harry." At which everyone all lifted their glass to Harry Farringdon and I noticed that Fiona Browning had turned quite pink.

We left the men with their port while Lady Pettigrew led her battalion to the drawing room, where she held forth on the blessings of marriage, and how happy she was to see Millicent joined in matrimony to a man of her parents' choice.

"They have been lovers from childhood," she said indulgently. "Isn't that so, Millicent?"

"We have known each other since we were children."

"That's what I'm saying. And this, of course, has been in our minds since they were tots."

I asked Fiona where she lived and I wondered why I had not met her before.

"We have only been in the south of England for two years," she told me. "We come from the north."

"That is why we have never met."

"My father has estates in Yorkshire and he now has an interest in breeding sheep in Kent. He has bought a place on the Essex borders. He always went to London a good deal, but it was a long journey. It is so much easier for him to get up there now."

"You like it here?"

"Oh yes."

Gwen Farringdon leaned forward. "We have taken them under our wing," she said with a smile. "We have become great friends."

So, I thought, the Farringdons approve of Fiona as a future daughter-in-law. Another nail in the coffin of Evie's aspirations.

Millicent said that she and Jonathan were going to London immediately after the wedding. They planned to spend the honeymoon near Maidenhead. "The Grenfells . . . You know Sir Michael and Lady Grenfell . . . they have offered us their place for the honeymoon, but Jonathan wants to be in London. Of course, I should have liked to go abroad. We've talked of Italy . . . Venice . . ."

I felt myself go cold and heard myself say: "Floating down the canals while a gondolier sings Italian love songs."

Millicent gave her rather shrill laugh.

"That's exactly it," she said.

"Never mind," said Lady Pettigrew. "We'll soon defeat those wretched foreigners."

"It looks as though the French are being successful all over Europe as they were saying earlier," I said.

"Oh, it is this miserable Bonaparte or whatever his name is. What they should do is get him. That would soon stop them. It's absurd . . . Those wretched revolutionaries allowed to overrun Europe. I can't think what they are doing."

I said, not without irony: "They should make you generalissima, Lady Pettigrew."

Everyone applauded and Lady Pettigrew seemed modestly to agree that it would be an excellent idea.

The men joined us. David came over and sat beside me. Jonathan was engaged in conversation with Lord Pettigrew and Dickon. I saw Fiona smile rather tremulously at Harry.

I whispered to David: "We shall soon be able to retire. I'm tired."

"Yes. Journeys are so exhausting."

My mother joined us. "You look a little tired, Claudine," she said anxiously.

I guessed that I must have looked strained. I found the situation an uneasy one. Jonathan's cynical marriage to Millicent, and in the background of my mind was the thought of Evie Mather's melancholy.

"I think I will suggest to Lady Pettigrew that we go to bed," said my mother.

She did and it seemed that the others had the same idea, for after good nights were said the company broke up.

I sat brushing my hair at the mirror and from the bed David watched me.

He said: "What do you think of it . . . Jonathan and Millicent?"

"Oh, it's the perfect marriage, isn't it—uniting the family interests?"

"But that is not really what marriage is about, is it?"

"I should imagine that it is exactly what quite a number of them are about."

"Millicent seems contented enough, and so for that matter does Jonathan."

"David, did you notice Harry Farringdon?"

"You mean with that girl, Fiona Browning?"

"Yes."

"H'm," said David. "He seems to have taken a fancy to her."

"Do you remember how he was with Evie Mather?"

"I remember . . . yes."

"I thought something might come of that."

"Marriage, you mean?"

"Well, I am sure that was what Mrs. Trent hoped for."

"I've no doubt she did. Evie won't have much coming to her and the Farringdons are rich."

"I'm sorry. Poor Evie. She's a nice girl. And now it looks as though Fiona Browning . . ."

"Oh, I wouldn't count on that. Harry never seems to be able to make up his mind. There have been many girls like that in his life. I've seen it happen before. It's serious . . . while it lasts . . . but it doesn't last and some other charmer comes along. Harry will need a big push into matrimony. He's that sort." He yawned. "Come on. I'm getting sleepy."

I blew out the candle and got in beside him.

David did not go to the rehearsal; nor did Dickon. I sat with Gwen Farringdon at the back. Fiona came in late and sat with Harry close by.

Lady Pettigrew was in command and it was amusing to see her hawklike eyes on the Reverend Mark Pollick, who had a will of his own and was very definite as to how matters should be conducted in his own church.

Lord Pettigrew walked in with Millicent on his arm. I saw Jonathan rise and they stood before the Reverend Mark with Lady Pettigrew audibly commanding Millicent to stand up straight and speak up.

It was really rather funny and as my mother said, unnecessary.

The music, chosen by Lady Pettigrew, was very stirring. The choir had been assembled to sing the anthem, and as the music filled the little church, I saw Harry Farringdon take Fiona's hand and they turned their faces towards each other and smiled.

I thought: It is all over for you, Evie.

And I wondered how deeply she had felt for him. Evie was not a girl who betrayed her feelings. There was something secretive about her—just as there was about her sister.

Evie might have been more realistic than her grandmother and could have known that the Farringdons would not willingly have agreed to a match between her and Harry; and yet on the other hand, if Harry had been sufficiently in love, I was sure John and Gwen could have been persuaded to give way to his wishes. Now he was behaving with Fiona as, not long ago, he had with Evie.

We went back to the house, all talking about the wedding rehearsal and saying how beautiful the music was. Lady Pettigrew exuded satisfaction, so I presumed she was sure everything was as it should be.

When we were at dinner that evening Lady Pettigrew said she had something to tell us, and she thought this was the moment to make the announcement.

"A little bird has whispered to me," she began in a somewhat coy manner quite alien to her usual forceful utterances, "that we have a matter to celebrate."

There were exclamations of surprise at the table.

"Fiona and Harry . . . My dears. God bless you both. You have guessed. Fiona and Harry have become engaged to be married. Is that not charming? I know John and Gwen are absolutely delighted and so are Fiona's parents, because they have all told me so. Dear Fiona, your happiness . . . and yours too, Harry, but that goes without saying . . . for what is Fiona's will now be yours . . . and yours hers."

All raised their glass and Harry and Fiona sat close together, their hands clasped, looking faintly embarrassed but undoubtedly happy.

"It seems that weddings are infectious," said Dickon.

"It must have been that lovely ceremony in the church which made them feel they wanted it to happen to them," said my mother.

Then once more everyone drank the health of Fiona and Harry.

Afterwards when I was in the drawing room with the ladies while the men were drinking their port at the table, I found myself next to Gwen Farringdon, who was looking very pleased.

She whispered to me: "I'm so glad. Fiona is such a charming girl. And we like the family. There was one time when I was very much afraid . . ."

"Afraid?"

She came a little closer. "Oh, you remember, there was that girl he rather liked. She was most unsuitable. She had that dreadful grandmother."

"You mean Evie Mather."

"That's right. John and I were afraid . . . but then Harry's not the sort to rush into anything, you know."

"Yes, I know."

"Well, that was all a long time ago, but we did have some qualms, I can tell you. However, all's well that ends well."

Millicent joined us. "What are you two whispering about?"

"We were talking of weddings," I said.

"Seeing how happy you and Jonathan are has had its effect on Harry," said Gwen.

"Sent him flying into an engagement, I see," said Millicent. "It's very satisfactory. The Brownings are the right sort."

"Absolutely. John and I are delighted . . . just like your parents."

"And now all we have to do is live happily ever after," commented Millicent.

I could not sleep that night. Tomorrow was the wedding day. I kept thinking of Jonathan and wondering whether anything would happen at the last minute to stop his marriage to Millicent.

What nonsense! As if it would! He wanted this marriage as much as the Pettigrews did. Dickon wanted it. It was the way they managed their affairs.

That night I said to David: "I'm surprised your father allowed you to marry me."

"What?" cried David.

"I brought you nothing. Everything we had was lost in France. How strange that he should raise no objections to our marriage."

David laughed. "If he had, it would have happened just the same."

"What if you had been cut off with a shilling!"

"I'd rather have you and a shilling than Eversleigh."

"That's a pleasant note to retire on," I said.

But I kept thinking about Jonathan, who would be Millicent's husband tomorrow—and I could not entirely forget Evie Mather.

Jonathan and Millicent were married on the following day. The ceremony passed without a hitch. Millicent looked beautiful in her white satin gown with the Pettigrew pearls about her neck and Jonathan was a very handsome bridegroom.

We went back for the reception and during it Lord Pettigrew made a speech in which he formally announced the engagement of Harry Farringdon to Fiona Browning.

Toasts were drunk, more speeches made, and Jonathan and Millicent left for London. The guests who had come for the day began to leave and only those staying in the house remained.

It had been a wonderful wedding, everyone proclaimed; and now that the bride and groom had disappeared, there seemed little reason to continue the rejoicing.

My mother said we should go the next day. She hated to leave Jessica long, and I certainly felt the same about Amaryllis.

When I went to my room I found Mary Lee putting things together; she told me my mother had sent her to do what she could for me.

"There's very little, Mary," I said. "I can manage."

She went on folding my things.

"I shall be glad to get back," I said.

"Yes, Madam. To see the little babies."

"They'll soon be old enough to travel with us."

"The wedding was beautiful, wasn't it, Madam?"

I nodded. I could not bring myself to speak of it. Beautiful! Jonathan so cynical . . . realistic, he would say; and Millicent, was she the same? I think there was a little more to it for Millicent. In spite of her rather worldly approach and an attitude which might have indicated indifference, I had caught a gleam in her eyes as they rested on Jonathan. He was an extremely attractive man. Was it possible that he had found a way to Millicent's heart which I had thought must be a replica of her mother's, only to be softened by conquest and material advantage?

"And what a surprise about Mr. Harry and Miss Fiona."

"Yes, it was."

"They talk downstairs," she said. "They say Mr. Harry was one for shilly-shallying. He never seemed to be able to make up his mind."

"Well, he has now, Mary."

"Madam, I was wondering . . ."

"Yes?"

"Well, it's about Miss Mather at Grasslands. At one time we thought . . . well, we all thought something was coming of that."

"Well, we were wrong, Mary."

"I wonder . . . what Miss Mather will think . . . ."

It was what I had been wondering about. However, I changed the subject and said that I could well manage the rest, which was dismissal, and Mary was too well trained a maid not to realize that.

We returned to Eversleigh the day after the wedding.

My mother and I went straight to the nursery, where we were delighted to find that all was well in the good hands of Grace Soper.

We played with the babies and marvelled at the manner in which they had grown, and delighted in their intelligence, which we were sure was more than that of normal children.

Yes, it was good to be home, and I wished, as I had so many times, that my life was less complicated—as it would have been if Jonathan had never intruded into it.

Try as I might I could not forget him and he was often in my thoughts. I wondered about Millicent and wondered whether she was going to be bitterly hurt. I had always felt that she was a young woman who could take good care of herself; but when I thought of that potent charm of Jonathan's—so like that which had brought his father so many conquests and what he wanted in life—I did wonder.

I tried to interest myself more in David's ways. We read together and talked for hours on our favourite subjects; he taught me a little archaeology and again we still discussed the possibility of going to Italy when the war was over.

I made a habit of riding round the estate with him. I wanted to know all that was happening; I wanted to share his life and atone for my infidelity. That was not possible, but I could try.

I went to see Aunt Sophie to tell her about Jonathan's wedding. She scarcely ever left her room, Jeanne told me. "Alberic's death is a terrible setback for her."

"Is she still brooding on it?"

"She mentions it every day. She gets quite angry about wanton murderers being allowed to escape justice."

"Shall I go and see her?"

"Yes, do go up. She likes to see you—although she doesn't always seem welcoming. Dolly Mather is with her now."

"Is she here often?"

"Oh yes. She's always been about. You know Mademoiselle d'Aubigné has taken a great liking to her. She is so sorry for her."

"I understand that."

"And I'm glad. The girl cheers her a good deal."

"Jeanne," I asked, "have you seen anything of her sister, Evie?"

"No, I have not. She used to come here sometimes with Dolly, but Mademoiselle never cared for her in the same way. No, I can't say I have seen Evie lately."

"I'll go up."

Aunt Sophie was seated in a chair which had been placed by the bed; she wore a long mauve dressing gown with a hood of the same colour to hide the damaged side of her face.

I went to her and kissed her. I smiled at Dolly. "How are you?"

"I am well, thank you," said Dolly quietly.

"That's good. I've come to tell you about the wedding, Aunt Sophie."

"Get a chair for Mrs. Frenshaw, Dolly," said Aunt Sophie, and Dolly immediately obeyed.

I described the rehearsal and the wedding reception. Dolly listened intently, her eyes never leaving my face. I always felt a little uncomfortable under her scrutiny, and I often avoided looking at her, for I found my eyes unconsciously resting on that strangely drawn-down eye.

"A great deal of excitement, I am sure," said Aunt Sophie. "You didn't hear anything while you were away, I suppose?"

"Hear anything? You mean about the war? They talk about little else."

"I meant about Alberic."

"Why, Aunt Sophie . . ."

"I mean about finding his murderer. It is a sorry state of affairs when innocent people are shot at and drowned and nothing is done about it."

"I think they tried . . ."

"Tried! They don't care. They thought he was just a poor émigré. But one day I am going to find out who murdered him . . . and when I do . . ."

She paused and I wanted to say: Yes, Aunt Sophie, what will you do? What would you do if you knew the truth?

She said: "I would kill the one who murdered that poor innocent boy. Yes, I would . . . with my own hands."

She looked down at her hands as she spoke, long, tapering fingers, very pale, the hands of one who has never in the slightest way laboured physically.

Poor Aunt Sophie, she looked so defenceless . . . tired and old, except for the shine in her eyes and the determination in her voice.

"Oh yes," she went on, "nothing would deter me. And I shan't rest until those who did this wicked thing are brought to justice." Her voice sank to a whisper. "It is someone here . . . someone close to us . . . Think of it! We have a murderer in our midst . . . and I shall not rest until I have found that murderer."

"Aunt Sophie, you must not upset yourself. It is bad for you."

"Bad for me! What is good for me? To lose the people I am fond of? To have them taken from me . . . wickedly done to death?"

"There is much that we do not know," I said.

"This I know," she said: "Wicked murder has been done . . . and if no one else will bring that murderer to justice, I will."

"But Aunt Sophie . . ."

"You think I'm talking nonsense, don't you? But I know something of what goes on here. I have my friends."

Jeanne had come into the room.

"Mademoiselle Sophie," she said, "you must not excite yourself."

"Oh Jeanne . . ." For a moment Sophie leaned against Jeanne. "It is such a wicked world, and I have only to love someone and that is disaster for me . . . for them."

"No, no," said Jeanne. "That is not so. There is much that is good."

Jeanne nodded to me over Sophie's head, indicating that I should leave.

I rose and said: "Well, Aunt Sophie, I must go. I'll come in again and see you later."

Jeanne came after me.

She said: "It's this obsession. She was like that when . . . You remember that tutor, when he went away: She thought fate was against her then and she never believed the things they said about him. She thought it was a conspiracy to take him from her. She was so much better—and then this has to happen with Alberic. She works herself into it. I don't like it. It's going right back and I thought she was much better when we came to Enderby."

"We are so thankful that you are here to look after her."

"I always shall be until God takes one of us away to another world. I wish they could solve that mystery. I think that would help a lot. If they could find the man who shot him . . . and if he were brought to justice, I really feel she would begin to grow away from it.

I rode sadly back to Eversleigh.

July had come in rather sultry. I had not seen Jonathan since his wedding. He had remained in London and he and Millicent might have spent a week or so at the Grenfells' house in Maidenhead.

One morning I decided to go with David, who was proposing to look at some cottages which were in need of repair.

It was a dull morning—a trifle misty but it would be hot when the mist cleared. The woods were looking beautiful now. I glimpsed foxgloves in the glades between the trees and the poppies made a dash of scarlet against the gold of the corn.

When Jonathan was away I could forget the past for hours at a time—and then I think I was really happy.

David was talking now about the possibility of several of the cottages needing repairs to the roofs.

"It was the same at Clavering," he was saying. "I set all that in motion there. It looks as though there'll be a similar problem at Eversleigh. You ought to have come to Clavering with me. When Amaryllis gets a little older we'll all go. Gerrand's an excellent manager, but I do think we should put in an appearance more often."

"Dickon never goes now," I said.

"Well, no, but he keeps an eye on things though. He always goes through accounts and that sort of thing himself . . . as he does here. But I have always felt his main interest was in London."

"Secret matters?"

"I'm glad not to be involved in that."

"I am glad too. It is better so . . ."

"Much more suited to Jonathan. In fact we both fitted into our different niches very satisfactorily . . . don't you think?"

"Yes, I do, and I'm glad you got this particular niche."

"The best thing I ever got was you, Claudine."

Was it? I wondered. If you knew everything, would you really think that? And the weight of my sin enveloped me and spoilt the beauty of the morning.

"I want to go and have a look at Lammings Bridge," said David. "I thought it was a little shaky yesterday. It may need propping up a little."

"It would be disastrous if it collapsed while someone was riding over it."

"Yes, the river is fairly deep at that point. It could be dangerous. We'll just call at the cottage first and tell them I'm sending a thatcher along to look at the roofs. There might be other things that need attention."

I knew it was David's policy to talk to tenants and explain what was going on, and that made it easy for them to bring their troubles to him. I realized afresh that morning what an ideal relationship he had established with the tenants. It could never have been the same when Eversleigh was Dickon's main concern. I think they must all have been afraid of him.

I was proud of David and my spirits rose again.

Yes, I was happy. I thought, as I had a thousand times before: I must never make him unhappy. I owe that to him, and the only way I can make sure of that is by keeping my secret.

"We mustn't forget the bridge," said David.

"Come on then."

There it was—Lammings Bridge, named, so I believed, after the man who had built it more than a hundred years ago. It was small wonder that it was in need of repair since it had stood the stress of weather and traffic all that time.

We dismounted and tethered our horses to some bushes on the bank. David prodded the wood.

"Yes," he said, "it's a little broken here. Can easily be patched up though, I think. Oh, not a great deal to be done . . . if taken in hand quickly."

I leaned on the parapet and surveyed the scene. It was very peaceful with weeping willows trailing into the water and loosestrife giving a touch of purple to the banks. Then I saw something in the water. I stared. It looked like a woman.

"David," I called shrilly.

He was at my side immediately.

"Look!" I cried. "What's that? Over there?"

"Oh God . . ." he murmured under his breath. Then we ran across the bridge and down to the riverbank.

I shall never forget that moment. She lay there, white and still; she appeared to be smiling . . . peacefully. She was beautiful. Oh poor, unhappy Evie!

David brought her out of the water and laid her on the bank.

He said: "She's been dead for hours. Poor . . . poor child. What could have made her?"

We looked at each other in horror, and though we did not speak, we were thinking of Harry Farringdon.

"There's nothing we can do for her," said David. "We'll have to get the doctor and some conveyance."

"Oh what a terrible tragedy," I said. "Poor Evie . . . and poor Mrs. Trent . . . and Dolly."

Soberly we rode back.

What followed was terrible. We were all shattered. She had been such a gentle, pleasant girl, so pretty too. It was tragic to realize that she was dead. I kept thinking of her smiling in her quiet way with Harry Farringdon.

She must really have cared for him. The news of his engagement would have been brought to her. Mary Lee would have talked to the servants of Eversleigh and they would have carried the news to those of Grasslands.

What a cruel fate! She must have thought he was serious in his affections for her; she had clearly loved him, and when he became engaged to someone else, found life unbearable.

I wondered what was happening at Grasslands. I wondered whether to go over and see, but was unsure. Evie had met Harry Farringdon under our roof. It was no fault of ours, but Mrs. Trent would be distracted. She would blame us perhaps.

There were startling revelations to come.

Evie Mather was pregnant and had been so for the last three months.

This was worse than ever. Poor girl! Why had she not talked to someone? My mother would have done anything to help her and so would I. David certainly would . . . even Dickon. He was always lenient with that sort of predicament.

But she had kept it to herself. I could imagine the devastating effect this was going to have on that household.

People spoke of it in hushed whispers. In the servants' hall I was sure they spoke of nothing else.

I felt I must go and see Mrs. Trent because there was a special sort of relationship between us since she had told me that Evie was connected with our family, as Richard Mather had been truly Dickon's son.

It was with great trepidation that I called.

I had not told David or my mother that I was going, for I felt sure they would try to dissuade me. Indeed I should have needed little dissuasion, for I was very unsure whether I should be welcome.

The curtains were all drawn across the windows. The door was opened by a servant who took me into a little room which led from the hall. She said she would tell Mrs. Trent that I had come.

After a while Dolly came in. Her face was distorted by grief and her eyes seemed more awry than ever.

"Oh, Dolly," I said, "I'm so terribly sorry. This is heartbreaking."

Her lips quivered. "She's gone. Our Evie . . . gone forever. I shall never see her again."

"Oh Dolly." I was crying with her.

"There wasn't any need," said Dolly. "She would have been all right."

"We would have taken care of her," I said.

"*I* would have taken care of her . . . and the little baby as well."

I nodded. "How is your grandmother taking it?"

"She doesn't eat. She doesn't sleep. She thought the world of Evie."

"I know. I would have come. My mother would have come, but we were not sure whether she would wish to see us . . . just yet."

"Yes, she wants to see you."

"I would like to comfort her. I wish I knew how."

"There's no comfort," said Dolly, "or not much. But she wants to see you."

"Is she in bed?"

"She's up there. She doesn't seem to know where she is."

"Shall I go up?"

"Yes. I'll take you."

Mrs. Trent came out of her bedroom and we went into a small dressing room. There were two chairs in it and we sat down. Dolly stood by the door. Mrs. Trent was wearing a grey dressing gown which she must have slipped over her nightdress. Her face was blotched with weeping and her eyes swollen. She did not look like the perky Mrs. Trent we had known.

I took both her hands in mine and on impulse kissed her cheek.

"Oh, Mrs. Trent, I am so sorry. We are all so distressed."

She nodded, too emotional to speak.

"If only we could have known . . . we could have done something," I said.

"I'd like to murder him," she muttered, coming to life. "I'd take him to that river and I'd hold his head down and not let him go until he was dead . . . as she is."

"I understand how you feel."

"She couldn't face it, you see. She couldn't face *me*. I shouldn't have made her feel like that. She ought to have been able to come to me in trouble."

"You mustn't say that, Mrs. Trent. I know you would always have done anything for her."

"I would and all . . . but she knew how I'd set my heart on her doing well. I've gone wrong somewhere."

"You always did your best, Mrs. Trent. None could say other than that. You must not blame yourself."

"I blame him," she said fiercely. "The dirty swine! He deceived her, he did . . . promised he'd marry her and when this happens it's goodbye and he goes off to marry a real lady. *She* was a real lady, my Evie was."

"Yes, of course, Mrs. Trent."

She clenched her hands together and I knew she was imagining them round the throat of Harry Farringdon.

"And now there's this Reverend gentleman . . . the vicar. He won't take my Evie. He says the likes of her can't be buried among decent folks."

"No, Mrs. Trent!"

"Yes. He says suicides can't be buried in consecrated ground. They will put her at the crossroads. They'll give her the suicide's grave. I just can't bear that . . . not for my little Evie."

"Something will have to be done about that."

She looked at me with hope in her eyes.

"I'll go and see the Reverend Manning. Or my husband will. Don't worry about that, Mrs. Trent. Evie is going to be buried properly. There must be no doubt about that."

"It's kind of you . . . and it's her due. You know who she is. It's different I suppose with the gentry. No one would think of putting them anywhere but in a proper grave."

I was glad that there was something I could do, something which would relieve her, even though nothing could ever bring Evie back. I said: "I will go along to the vicarage now and see him. Don't worry, Mrs. Trent. I am sure it will be all right."

"Thank you," she said; and there was that glint of determination in her eyes which I had noticed before her grief had descended upon her and made her a pathetic shadow of what she had been. "It's her due," she said with a certain firmness.

Dolly conducted me to the door.

"Goodbye," I said. "I will do everything I can."

I went straight to the vicarage. It was not as easy as I had thought it would be.

The Reverend Richard Manning was the kind of man I disliked on sight. He was pompous, self-righteous, and I was sure completely lacking in compassion and imagination.

We saw little of him for the living did not belong to Eversleigh. The family had always had its own chapel and although nowadays we did not have a priest living in the house, there was one who had a small place on the estate and whose duty it was to officiate when needed. He came every morning to conduct prayers for the household.

Therefore the family had no jurisdiction over the Reverend Richard Manning.

I told him that I was concerned about the burial of Evie Mather.

"The suicide," he said, and I immediately felt a sense of outrage at the cold and precise tone of his voice, and to hear Evie spoken of in that way.

"Her grandmother is very distressed because you are denying her normal burial."

"I have said that according to the laws of the Church she cannot be buried in consecrated ground."

"Why not?"

He looked surprised. "Because she has offended against the laws of God. She has committed the sin of inflicting death on a human being."

"Herself," I said.

"It is a sin in the eyes of the Church."

"So everyone who is buried in your churchyard is quite beyond reproach?"

"There are no suicides buried there."

"There must be greater sins than finding one's life so intolerable that one takes it."

"It is a sin against God's laws," he said complacently.

"I do want you to understand that this is a terrible blow to her family. Could you not waive the laws for once and give her the burial they want for her? It means such a lot to them."

"You cannot ask me to break the holy laws of God."

"Is this a holy law? Is it God's will to inflict greater pain on people who have already suffered infinitely?"

"You miss the point, Mrs. Frenshaw."

"On the contrary, I think you do that. But please, will you do this for the sake of humanity . . . for pity's sake . . ."

"You cannot be asking me to go against the rule of the Church?"

"If these are the laws of the Church, then I will say they are cruel . . . unkind . . . uncaring . . . and yes, wicked. And I want nothing to do with them."

"You are coming near to blasphemy, Mrs. Frenshaw."

"I will speak to my father-in-law."

"I am not responsible to Eversleigh," he said. "This living never has been. This is a matter between me and my conscience."

"Then your conscience, if it has any humanity in it, should give you a very uneasy time."

"Mrs. Frenshaw, you must leave now. I have nothing more to say."

"But I shall have a great deal to say."

I rode home in a fury. My mother was astonished to see me in such a state.

I told her what had happened.

"Oh no!" she cried. "Not this as well."

"Poor Mrs. Trent . . . she cares so much about this."

"I understand that," said my mother.

"What can we do? The man is adamant."

"Unfortunately we have no power over him."

"I know. He made that clear. But something has to be done. I am determined on that."

I chose a moment when I knew that Dickon would be alone. My stepfather had always maintained a mild friendship with me; I fancied that in his heart he harboured a certain resentment because he was not my father, and he had loved my mother even when she was married to my father.

"Claudine," he said now. "This is an unexpected honour."

"I want you to do something," I said.

"Well, if it is in my power to serve a beautiful young lady, rest assured that it shall be done. What do you want?"

"I want Evie Mather to be buried in the normal way."

"Is that old idiot Manning making a fuss?"

"Exactly."

"He would. I'm sorry, Claudine, there's nothing I can do. I can't threaten him with the loss of his living because the living isn't mine to bestow."

"Nevertheless you could do something."

He shook his head. "No. If he says no . . . then it has to be so. It's in his power to decide."

"The poor woman is distraught."

"It's a terrible business. What a foolish girl! Girls have had babies before."

"Harry Farringdon has behaved badly."

Dickon shrugged his shoulders. "These things happen. She ought to have known that he was unlikely to marry her."

"I expect he promised."

"She should have made sure."

"You're very unsympathetic."

"No . . . I understand. I just think she was a fool, that's all. I daresay if she had come to your mother, she would have helped her . . . and you certainly would."

"Don't you understand how a girl would feel? And there's that grandmother . . . you knew her well . . . so you must realize how much she wanted good things for her grand-daughter . . . all that she herself had missed."

He nodded.

"We've got to help her," I said.

"It's no use with old Manning."

"I know. But there are other ways."

"Such as?"

"You do own land in the cemetery . . . Eversleigh land. I mean where the family is buried."

"Yes."

"Well, I want Evie to be buried there."

"Among our people!"

"Dickon," I said, "isn't Evie one of us?"

He showed no sign of embarrassment. "You must be referring to that little entanglement between me and Grandmother Evalina in the distant past."

"Yes. I am."

"H'm. Well, it took place."

"Then Evie *could* be your grand-daughter."

"It's a possibility. Evalina was a shrewd little piece."

"If Richard Mather was your son . . . then Evie has a right to a plot of your ground."

I saw the smile break out on his face. "I love you, Claudine," he said. "You're like your mother."

"Dickon, will you?"

"You know how hard it has always been for me to refuse a beautiful young lady anything she asks."

"Dickon . . . thank you. Thank you so much."

I was in tears. He looked at me in a benign, amused kind of way.

My mother came in.

"What are you doing in here, you two?" she asked.

"Your daughter has just made a request which I have granted."

"A request . . . and she's crying. What are you crying for, Claudine? It's so unlike you."

I went to her and kissed her. "Dickon has just made me so happy."

"Oh?" she said, looking in puzzlement from one to the other of us.

"It's that old hypocrite Manning," said Dickon. "Wants Evie Mather in a suicide's grave. Retribution from his God. The sanctimonious old devil."

"And . . ." began my mother.

"Dickon has promised me that she shall be buried in our ground . . . among the Eversleighs. Oh, it has made me so happy. I'm going to tell Mrs. Trent right away."

My mother was smiling. "Oh Dickon," she said. "Thank you. You're so wonderful."

I lost no time in getting over to Grasslands.

I was taken at once to Mrs. Trent, who was still in her grey sombre robe.

I said: "Don't worry, Mrs. Trent. It's going to be all right."

"You've seen him . . . that vicar?"

"We don't have to worry about him. I have spoken to my father-in-law. Evie shall be buried in Eversleigh ground."

"Consecrated Eversleigh ground," she cried, wonderment dawning on her ravaged face.

"Yes," I told her. "He has promised me that it shall be so."

"Oh thank you, Mrs. Frenshaw. Though it's no more than her due."

"I know. I know. But that little trial is over."

She nodded. "Thank you, thank you," she said. She was silent for a few moments, then she went on: "I worry . . . I worry so much about Dolly."

"Dolly will be all right," I assured her.

"If I went, where would she be? I used to think when Evie married she would go with her and be looked after. That's all changed now."

"I'd see that she was all right, Mrs. Trent. Don't worry about Dolly. We'd see that she was all right."

"It's like the family . . . in a way," she said.

I felt almost happy. It had been so wonderful to bring her that little bit of cheer.

It was the day of Evie's funeral. It was hot and humid. There was a stillness in the air—a hushed silence everywhere. People talked in whispers in the house; and there was no breeze to make the slightest rustle in the trees.

Dickon had promised to go to the church and David and I would go with my mother. I was sure that would please Mrs. Trent.

In the morning there was a visitor to the house. I was in the garden picking some roses which I was going to lay on Evie's grave. I saw him coming and my heart missed a beat. I ran to him and said: "You shouldn't have come." It was a strange way to greet a visitor.

He looked pale and distraught.

"I heard," he said. "I was so shocked."

"I'm not surprised."

I hated Harry Farringdon as he stood there, although he was all contrition. I could not help thinking that but for him Evie would be alive today.

"I had to come," he said.

"It would have been better if you had stayed away."

"But I was fond of her."

"That was unfortunate for her."

"You don't believe that I . . ."

"Harry," I said, "don't go into the house. I think it would be better if you were not seen. Go right away . . . now. I don't know what would happen if Evie's grandmother saw you. I believe she would try to do you some harm."

"I have behaved badly."

"Indeed you have."

"But is it true . . . what I heard about a child?"

"Yes," I told him. "It's true. Evie was three months pregnant, and it seems that was the reason she could no longer face the world."

"You don't believe that I . . . was the cause of her condition?"

I looked at him angrily.

"Oh, no, no! It's not true, Claudine. I swear to you. It could not be. There was never anything like that between us . . . never any intimacy."

"Do you expect anybody to believe that?"

"Yes, because it's true."

"We all knew that you were interested in her."

"I was. I was very fond of her."

"So fond of her that you deserted her?"

"It was just that we did not meet very often."

"You liked her in a mild sort of way. You led her to believe your feelings went deeper . . . and this happened."

"It is months since I've seen her. It couldn't possibly have been my child, Claudine."

"She was such a quiet, gentle girl. Please don't try to blacken her character, Harry."

"I would have done anything I could for her."

"A not very taxing exercise since she no longer needs your assistance."

"Oh, Claudine. You doubt me."

Of course I doubted him! We had never heard of her having another lover. And we should surely have known if there had been anyone else. Who could there be? I had imagined Harry coming surreptitiously to Grasslands, their meeting in secret, his persuading her to become his mistress . . . no doubt with a promise of marriage. It was an old story.

I said: "Harry, for Heaven's sake, don't show yourself. Go away. The mischief is done now. Nothing can bring her back to life."

"But I was fond of her . . ." he began.

I looked at him in exasperation. "Harry, go away. You must not be seen. You would be torn to pieces by a lot of angry people. We don't want a scene at the funeral. That would be the last straw."

"I wish that you would believe me," he said. "I swear to you, Claudine, on everything that I hold sacred, that the child was not mine."

"All right, Harry, but go away. Don't let anyone see you here. I'm glad you didn't come to the house."

"Are those roses for her?" he asked.

I nodded.

"Oh, Claudine, I wish I could have helped her."

"It's too late now, Harry. Please go away."

He turned away and as I watched his retreating figure my hands were shaking.

I had always felt there was something weak about him. He had never been able to make up his mind. Whatever he said, I should still believe that Evie's child was his. He was so full of remorse now. Well, so he should be.

How fortunate that I had seen him. If he had appeared at the graveside anything might have happened.

There was a simple service in our chapel and Evie's body was taken in the Eversleigh carriage to the churchyard and there we laid her to rest.

We stood silently round her grave, listening to the fall of the earth as it struck the coffin. As I threw down the roses I had gathered that morning, I saw Mrs. Trent reach for Dolly's hand and hold it tightly.

When we were leaving the grave I saw the figure of a man partly hidden by some bushes.

I recognized Harry Farringdon.

So he had not been able to keep away.

The Fifth of November

August had come. It was several weeks since Evie's funeral. I often went to her grave and took flowers with me. I noticed that a rose had been planted there and I wondered by whom.

I thought a great deal about her. I could well understand her succumbing to temptation. Who better than I? And often I thought how harsh life was with some people and lenient with others. I had sinned more deeply than she had, for I had betrayed my husband; yet she had suffered and I had gone free—not exactly free, but to be troubled only by my conscience.

Life is so unfair, I thought. If only she had confided in me and I had been able to help her! I could have found comfort in that for myself. What agony of mind a person must endure to come to the conclusion that there was no other way than to end it all!

Mrs. Trent kept largely to her house and I rarely saw her. I had called once or twice, but I think seeing me recalled Evie to her more vividly and it seemed that it was better to leave her alone.

Aunt Sophie was horrified by what had happened. She could always have pity for others' misfortunes; in fact she was apt to brood on them as she did on her own; and Jeanne said that she talked incessantly about Evie's death and the wickedness of men who betrayed women.

Young Dolly was with her a great deal.

"Poor child!" said Jeanne. "It is a terrible blow to her. She adored her sister. She has become more withdrawn than ever; but she and Mademoiselle seem to bring some comfort to each other."

"Time will help," I said. "It always does."

Jeanne agreed with me. "Time," she repeated, "even with Mademoiselle and the little Dolly . . . it will help."

There was a change in the air. Events were moving fast and it was clear that what was happening on the Continent must affect our lives. England was indeed deeply involved in the conflict.

In June the little Dauphin had died in the Temple. He had been twelve years old. Now there was no king of France. I often thought of that little boy. What a sad life he had had! And how he must have suffered, parted from his mother, forced to make cruel and even obscene allegations against her. And then . . . to die. How had he died? We should never be sure of that.

Oh, what a cruel world this had become.

There were riots in some parts of the country due to the high price of food. I wondered if Léon Blanchard had helped to rouse the mobs. Jonathan was right. Agitators must be eliminated—even young men like Alberic.

There was some consternation when Spain made peace with France; and it seemed that all our allies were deserting us because they realized that France, led by this adventuring Corsican Napoleon Bonaparte, war-torn though it was by revolution, was a power to be reckoned with.

It was afternoon. I had been in the garden and as I came in I saw Grace Soper on the lawn with the babies. Jessica was now a year old, Amaryllis a little younger. They were both crawling all over the place and could now take a few staggering steps. Soon they would be running about.

"That's the time we shall have to watch them," said Grace Soper. "My word, that Miss Jessica, she's a little madam, she is. She wants this, she wants that and I'll tell you this, Mrs. Frenshaw, she won't be happy till she gets what takes her fancy. Miss Amaryllis is such a good little girl."

My mother took as much pride in Jessica's waywardness as I did in Amaryllis's docility; they were both perfect in our eyes.

I looked into the little carriage in which they slept side by side. Jessica with her dark hair and long sweeping lashes, cheeks faintly tinted, was beautiful in a striking way; I thought she might be like my mother except that her eyes were dark and my mother's a brilliant blue. "She must get them from some of her fiery French ancestors," my mother said.

"The Eversleighs can be somewhat fiery too on occasions," I replied.

She admitted it. "Amaryllis looks like a little angel," she said; and so she did with her fair hair and blue eyes and a certain air of fragility which alarmed me sometimes but which Grace Soper said was due to small bones, and that my Amaryllis was in as perfect health as her robust nursery companion Jessica.

I left them slumbering side by side under the shadow of a sycamore tree on that peaceful August afternoon and went into the house.

It must have been about half an hour later when I heard shrieks coming from the garden. I hastily ran downstairs. Grace Soper was there with my mother and they were both distracted. All my mother could say was: "It can't be . . . How can it be? What does it mean?"

Grace was shaking so much that she could scarcely speak.

"The babies . . ."

My mother cried: "Jessica . . . she's not there . . ."

I looked into the baby carriage. Floods of relief swept over me, for Amaryllis was lying there fast asleep. But then the horror of what had happened dawned on me. Jessica was missing.

"How . . . what has happened?" I cried.

"They were asleep," stammered Grace. "I went into the house. I was only gone five minutes . . . When I came out . . ."

"She can't be far," said my mother.

"Could she have got out of the carriage?"

Grace shook her head. "They were both strapped in. I always see to that."

"Oh, God help us," I prayed. "Someone has taken Jessica."

Fortunately Dickon was at home and he took charge in that calm efficient way of his.

"The strap could have been loose," he said. "She might have undone it."

"It wouldn't have been easy for her to get out even then," said my mother. "Someone's taken her. Oh . . . Dickon . . . who? Who? We must find her."

"We'll find her," said Dickon. "Now first of all we must have a thorough search of the garden and all around. It is possible that she could have got out. She could have crawled into the bushes somewhere. That's where she'll be. We'll waste no more time."

The servants had come running out of the house. Everyone was deeply shocked. The search began; but although the gardens were thoroughly checked there was no sign of Jessica.

I took Amaryllis from the carriage. I couldn't bear to let her out of my sight. Poor Grace Soper was in a state of collapse, blaming herself, which we assured her she should not do. She was an excellent nurse and had been assiduous in her care for the babies. She had left them for only five minutes asleep in their carriage.

The straps were examined. There was nothing wrong with them and that brought us to the only conclusion.

Jessica had been kidnapped.

Dickon said that there would almost certainly be a demand for ransom.

"I hope so," said my mother. "I hope so . . . soon . . . anything, just anything, to get my baby back."

Dickon himself led a party and searched and questioned everyone on the estate.

The news spread.

I don't know how we lived through the rest of that day. My mother was distracted. I think we all were. It was so unexpected.

Dickon immediately had posters set up in the town offering a reward for any news of his daughter. He sent messengers out to all the neighbouring towns and to the ports.

By the end of the day we were all exhausted with anxiety. Night had fallen and there was still no sign of the child. There was nothing further we could do. We all knew it. We sat in the punch room—silent and desperate.

Grace Soper was upstairs in the nursery. She would not go to bed, but kept her vigil beside Amaryllis's bed. Dickon said: "You can rest assured we shall hear something in the morning. They are giving us time to work ourselves into a frenzy. I know these people. We shall hear, you see."

We sat through the night. My mother stared before her, huddled close to Dickon. Every now and then he would murmur something reassuring. "You see, we'll hear something in the morning. I know the way these people work."

"But what will they do to her . . . my little baby. She'll be hungry . . ."

"No, no. They'll look after her. You'll see. In the morning . . ."

Should we hear in the morning? I wondered.

David put his arm round me. He knew I was fearful for Amaryllis.

All through the next day we waited. There was no news. The usual rumours began to circulate, for the whole neighbourhood knew that Jessica was missing. Someone had seen a stranger carrying a baby hurrying through the main streets of the town. Dickon and David hastened off to make enquiries and when the woman was tracked down she proved to have been visiting her relations in the town—so naturally she was a stranger to some people.

I shall never forget the look of hopelessness in my mother's eyes when they returned.

I suppose the most difficult thing to endure in such circumstances is the frustration, the utter helplessness of not knowing which way to turn.

"How can anyone be so cruel as to do this?" I cried for the twentieth time. "Do they not think of mothers . . . ."

David soothed me.

"Dickon's right. It's money they want. It'll be a ransom."

"We'll pay and they'll give her back. You really think that?"

"They know my father is a rich man. It can't be anything but that. What point could there possibly be in harming Jessica?"

I shook my head. "There are so many things I don't understand. Why do people want to inflict torture on others . . . without a reason?"

"There's always a reason. In this case it is money. You'll see. Dickon will pay. He'd give anything for the family . . . and particularly your mother."

I knew it was true. But the waiting . . . the anxiety . . . the terrible fear of the unknown . . . they were hard to endure.

My mother looked like a ghost. All her vitality seemed to have been drained away. I tried to persuade her to rest and I did induce her to lie down for a while. I sat by her bed but I could think of nothing to say which would comfort her; she just lay staring ahead of her and then she rose saying that she could lie idle no longer, although there was nothing we could do.

I went to the nursery and played with Amaryllis. I felt so grateful that she was safe—and yet the very sight of her brought back more acutely the terrible loss of Jessica.

Poor Grace Soper continued to blame herself. She needed comforting. She said that someone must watch over Amaryllis day and night, and she would see to it that no one got at that precious little mite.

The long, long morning ended and the long weary afternoon began.

No news. Let something happen soon, I prayed. We can't go on like this.

Dickon and David had been out all the afternoon. They were searching everywhere they could think she might possibly be; they were seeing everyone who they thought might help. They came back and even Dickon was dispirited. His prophecy that a ransom would be demanded had not happened.

That night we made a pretence of going to our bedrooms to sleep; but none of us could rest.

David and I sat through the night talking desultorily. Now Jessica had been away two nights and we were really getting very frightened.

There was one horrible thought which had occurred to me. I would not have mentioned it to my mother but I did to David, as I wanted him to reassure me that it could not be.

I said: "David, your father must have many enemies."

David was thoughtful.

I went on: "A man in his position surely would have. He is rich and the rich are envied—and envy is a powerful force. This could be a form of revenge."

David's words horrified me. "I had thought of that," he said. "He has many contacts . . . not only in this country but abroad. There must be many who would wish to do him some injury."

"I know there are these secret matters and that he and Jonathan are involved in them."

"It is so. You remember those people who came to stay for a night. It was something in his study they were after. Some secret document. And they found it. If you live dangerously you must expect your enemies to strike you in unexpected ways."

"So it could be possible that someone has taken Jessica out of revenge . . . against Dickon?"

David was silent for a few moments. I knew he wanted to comfort me; but that inherent honesty made it difficult for him to dissemble. At last he said: "It is possible. But I don't think we should allow ourselves to think the worst. The most likely answer is ransom, and perhaps we can deal with that."

"But why don't the kidnappers ask for it? Why do they delay?"

"Because they want to keep us in suspense."

"Do you think they are looking after Jessica?"

"Yes, they usually do in these circumstances. A live child is of more value to them than a dead one."

So we talked, and at length from sheer exhaustion I dozed, only to be startled into wakefulness by a nightmare—confused and horrible, in which I was clutching Amaryllis to me while someone was trying to drag her away.

"It's all right," I heard David saying. "It's all right."

I opened my eyes.

"I think it is better to stay awake," I said.

We watched the dawn come. Another day! Another weary vigil! What would it bring forth? I asked myself and trembled as I tried to dismiss the thoughts which crowded into my mind.

I felt a sudden urge to get out of the house, to walk through the gardens, to make yet another search.

"I can't stay in," I cried. "Let's go into the garden."

"All right," said David.

He put a cloak round my shoulders. "It will be a bit chilly," he said, "and the grass will be damp."

We opened the door and stepped into the porch.

Something was lying there. I stared. I thought I was dreaming. Then floods of joy swept over me. Lying there wrapped in a blanket was Jessica.

I picked her up. David was staring at her. She opened sleepy eyes, looked at me, gave a big yawn and closed them again.

"It is!" I cried. "It is!"

I went into the hall shouting: "She's here. Jessica is here."

My mother came first. She ran to me and snatched the sleeping Jessica from me. There was Dickon . . . Grace Soper . . . all the servants.

"She's back! She's back!" cried my mother; and I thought she would collapse from very joy.

Dickon took Jessica. "She's in fine shape," he said.

My mother snatched her. "She's well," she murmured. "She's not harmed . . . Oh, my little baby."

Jessica opened her eyes; she gave a crooked smile and when she saw her mother started to wail.

After the joy of having Jessica back we fell into a state of great uneasiness, asking ourselves: Who could have done this? And for what purpose?

It was clear that during her absence the child had been well cared for and she seemed to accept her return to her family without any great show of delight—although she did smile with a rather special contentment when her mother held her fast in her arms.

Who had submitted us to this suffering, seemingly without purpose? We could not forget it and the memory hung over us like a pall clouding our days. The babies were never left alone for a moment. First thing in the morning my mother and I would hurry to the nursery to assure ourselves that they were safe. Grace had her bed moved into the night nursery and she said she slept with one eye and one ear open.

Her niece, a pleasant girl of about fourteen, came as nursery maid and her room led out of the night nursery, so she was on the alert too.

But we should never feel entirely safe again.

In September Jonathan and Millicent came to Eversleigh; they were only staying for a few days and then going on to Pettigrew Hall for a short visit before returning to London.

I was suffering from a return of that apprehension which I always felt when Jonathan was under the same roof. I tried to discover surreptitiously what difference marriage had made to him. I could see none; Millicent had changed, though; she seemed softer, more pleased with life; I supposed that meant she was finding her marriage satisfactory.

She would certainly find Jonathan a charming husband, I thought, until she discovered his true nature.

He had not changed at all. He was daring, completely without restraint, defying conventions as he had always done when he contrived to be alone with me.

The babies were sleeping in the garden in their carriage just as they had been on the day Jessica had disappeared. Grace Soper and her niece were sitting near the carriage and my mother was there talking to them.

I was gathering some of the autumn flowers. I had some purple asters and Michaelmas daisies in my basket and as I was cutting them Jonathan came and stood beside me.

"What joy to see you again, Claudine," he said. "I have missed you."

"Is that so?" I asked, lightly snipping at a Michaelmas daisy.

"Indeed it is. Should I say so if it were not so?"

"You might," I replied.

"Are you pleased to see me here?"

"My mother likes to have the entire family gathered together under one roof."

"What a way you have for parrying the question. You should be in Parliament . . . or in the diplomatic service. Claudine, you do miss me sometimes. Come on. Tell the truth."

"Not often," I lied.

"Do you tell falsehoods to yourself as well as to me?"

I said sharply: "Enough of this. You are a married man. I am a married woman—and we are not married to each other."

He burst out laughing and my mother looked up and smiled in our direction.

"I am me and you are you," he said. "Nothing can alter that, my love."

I replied almost pleadingly: "Jonathan, it is wrong of you to talk like this—and you so newly married. What if Millicent heard you? I thought she looked so happy."

"She is happy. Is she not married to me? I tell you, Claudine, I am the very model of a husband."

"On the surface," I said. "You do not seem to fit the description at this moment."

"And who is to blame for that?"

"You are to blame."

"Not entirely. I share the blame with you."

I was angry. I had tried so hard to forget what had happened and he only had to look at me to remind me. I despised my weakness in the past, and it was particularly shameful because I could so easily fall into temptation again. I vigorously snapped a stem.

"Don't blame the daisies for fate, Claudine," he said. "Poor little starry creatures. It is not their fault that you and I were meant for each other and that you discovered it too late. But you should be grateful. You would never have known how perfect a relationship can be . . . but for the time you spent with me."

"I have never known real peace since."

"Poor Claudine. You would have gone on living in ignorance, contented perhaps in a mild cosy way . . . never really living. Safe in your little paradise, never venturing into the real world . . . the world of passion and adventure and the excitement which comes from living life to the full. Into your self-made paradise, walled in with the security of cosy unawareness, came the serpent one day and tempted you to eat of the tree of knowledge . . . and this you did. You tasted the true joy of living . . . and ever since you have been afraid . . . afraid to live . . . afraid to love . . . You know this and you long to escape to me . . . You won't admit it. But I know it and so do you . . . in your secret thoughts."

"I must go in," I said.

"Retreat is a symbol of defeat."

I turned to face him. "I am trying to forget that ever happened."

"You never will."

"Jonathan, I am going to try."

"Face the truth," he said. "What I have said is right. You will never forget. You have tasted the fruit of the tree of knowledge. Rejoice, my darling. Life was meant to be lived joyously."

"I want to live mine . . . honourably," I said.

And I turned and walked across the lawn.

"Isn't it a beautiful afternoon?" said my mother. "There won't be many more this year. Come and sit down for a while."

I thought she might notice the colour in my cheeks, that sparkle of battle in my eyes which came when I had these encounters with Jonathan, so I said: "I think I should put the flowers in water first. They wilt so quickly. Then I'll join you."

Jonathan threw himself down beside my mother.

I heard him say as I hurried across the lawn: "How beautiful you are, dear Step-mama!"

Later I had a talk with Millicent, and that again made me uneasy.

She wanted to borrow one of my brooches which she needed for a dress she was wearing; she explained that she had left most of her jewellery in London. She knew my garnet-and-diamond brooch well . . . and if I could spare it . . .

"Of course," I said. "I'll bring it along when we go upstairs."

When I went to her room she was seated at the dressing table wearing a peignoir of magenta colour which suited her. Her dark hair was loose and she looked so much prettier than she used to.

"That's what I wanted," she said. "Thank you, Claudine."

I hesitated. This was the room which they shared legitimately. I thought of that other room . . . dusty blue curtains and the mysterious voice which had come to me through the speaking tube.

I did not want to think about Millicent and Jonathan together. I could imagine so much so vividly. I felt a frustrated anger as I looked at her. I had to admit that I was jealous. What was the use of pretending that I did not care for him, that I wanted to forget? No. I wanted to remember. I wanted to dream about those days when I had forgotten my marriage vows, when I had behaved so wantonly and been so happy.

It was no use deceiving myself. Whatever he was, I wanted him. Did I love him? Who could truly define love? I loved David. I would have done a great deal not to hurt him. There were times when I hated myself for what I had done. But if feeling wildly excited, that the world was a delightful place and that I had so much to learn of many things which I wanted him to teach me . . . if that was love . . . then I loved Jonathan.

She had picked up the garnet brooch and held it against her peignoir. "It's very pretty," she said. "So kind of you, Claudine."

"It's nothing. I'm glad you like it."

"One can't take all one's things when travelling."

"Of course not."

"And we left in rather a hurry. That's how it always seems with Jonathan." She smiled indulgently.

"Yes, I supposed so. You look . . . very happy."

"Oh, I am. I never dreamed . . ." She was smiling, looking back, I imagined . . . thinking of their being together.

"Well, that is how it should be," I said, trying to speak in a cool matter-of-fact way.

"Some people think it was a marriage of convenience."

"You mean . . . you and Jonathan?"

She nodded. "Well, the parents were rather pleased."

"Yes, it was what they hoped for on both sides."

"You would have thought . . . in the circumstances . . . But it was not at all like that."

"It is good that you have found such happiness."

"In a way," she said, "it is a sort of challenge."

"You mean marriage. I suppose it often is."

"Not in the same way. You and David . . . Well, David is quite different from Jonathan, isn't he? And twins are supposed to be so much alike. But they are opposites. No one could be less like Jonathan than David. What I mean is . . . you always know what David is going to do."

I said rather formally: "One always knows that David will do what he considers to be right."

"People have different ideas. Right to one might be wrong to another."

"Oh come . . . there are certain standards."

"I know what you mean. But David is predictable and I think that Jonathan must be the least predictable person on earth."

"And you prefer unpredictability?"

She lifted a hairbrush and began brushing her hair, smiling secretly at her reflection in the mirror.

"Of course. It makes life an adventure . . . a challenge. You will be sure of David. I shall never be sure of Jonathan."

"And you want . . . to be unsure?"

"I have no help for it. That is Jonathan's way. David will always be the faithful husband."

I could not resist saying: "And you think Jonathan will not be . . . and you find that challenging . . . adventurous?"

She turned to me and nodded slowly; her eyes glittered in the candlelight.

"He will have his little *affaires de coeur.* He always has and marriage will not stop him. I understand that. They will make him all the more ready to come back to me."

I was astounded and I showed it. "I should have thought you were the last one to . . . er . . ."

"To be accommodating, to turn a blind eye to a husband's misdemeanours?"

"Your mother . . ."

"Everyone compares me with my mother. I know I'm like her in a way. I am sure she never had to deal with the situation we are discussing. My father is a very moral gentleman."

"Perhaps your mother would never allow him to be otherwise."

I knew I ought to take my leave for I had a feeling that there was something dangerous about this conversation.

"My father and Jonathan are poles apart."

"I am sure they are."

"And my methods will be quite different from hers. No man of spirit would be so completely subdued as poor dear Papa is. I think he is fond of her in a way. He is a very gallant gentleman and I love him dearly."

"It is always pleasant to hear of filial affection."

"You are quite amusing, Claudine . . . sometimes so formal. I suppose that is the French in you. Oh yes, I shall know how to manage my life."

"I am sure you will be very good at it."

"So . . . I shall accept what has to be accepted. I shall countenance the little love affairs. It would only be if there was something greater—"

I felt my heart beginning to beat very fast. For a moment I wondered whether Jonathan had told her of his relationship with me. Surely he could not have done so. But who could say with Jonathan? Hadn't she herself described him as unpredictable?

"If I thought I had a really serious rival, I could . . ." She hesitated and one of the candles spluttered and went out.

There was a brief silence which seemed eerie. I felt uncertain and had a great desire to escape from the room with its elaborate curtained bed, a desire to escape from the visions which kept coming into my mind.

"These candles!" she said. "They are always doing that. I shall complain that they do not make them properly now. Never mind. There is enough light." She put her face close to the mirror and the reflection looked back at me. "What was I saying?" she went on. "If there was someone who was not a light o' love . . .. someone important to him, do you know, Claudine, I think I should hate her so much . . . that I would be tempted to kill her."

I shivered.

She said: "It's a little chilly in here. I'll ring for the maid and ask her to build up the fire. Well, we are into autumn now."

"I must go and get dressed."

"Thank you for the brooch."

I hurried out, thinking: Is it possible that she knows? Is she warning me? She had said: "I would be tempted to kill her."

In that moment her reflection had looked wicked, ruthless.

Yes, I said to myself. I believe she would.

I was relieved when they left, although the days seemed empty and colourless.

I went over to see Aunt Sophie, who still mourned Alberic and talked of little else. She had been deeply shocked by Jessica's disappearance and talked a good deal about that. Any disaster attracted her; sometimes I felt that, when there was a happy ending, as in the case of Jessica, she lost interest. Although, of course, there was the question of who and why; and this could involve a great deal of unpleasant speculation.

Dolly Mather was with her as much as possible. I had been to Grasslands to call on Mrs. Trent once or twice. The first time I had been shocked by her appearance. She felt the death of Evie very much and she could not stop herself raging against the cruelty of fate and the wickedness of the one she spoke of as "the man." I think if Harry Farringdon had put in an appearance she might well have tried to do him an injury, which was all very understandable, of course.

Then later when I called, Dolly told me that she was lying down. She was not well and felt too ill to receive visitors. She hardly ever went out. The servants at Grasslands reported to ours that she was getting "a little strange."

There was gloom all round us and it all stemmed from Alberic's death.

David announced that he had to go to London to procure some stores for use on the estate; he also had to see our agents about the sale of farm produce. Some of our farmers had been introducing extra sheep to their land, and the wool products were requiring more and more marketing.

My mother said to me: "Why don't you go with David? You haven't been in London together since your honeymoon. It would make all the difference to him if you went. Instead of regarding it as rather a bore he'd look forward to it. You have the house to yourselves because Jonathan and Millicent will be at Pettigrew Hall."

I hesitated and she went on: "I know you are thinking of Amaryllis. I understand just how you feel." She winced. The memory was still more than she could bear. "She would be perfectly safe with us here. We'd guard her as we do Jessica. You know Grace can't bear the children out of her sight. I still have to impress on her twenty times a day that what happened was not her fault. Jessica would miss her if she went. They are getting such little people now. They notice everything. Do stop fretting about what's happening here. We can manage without you for a week or so, you know."

"Oh Maman," I said, "I should like to go, but . . ."

"No buts. Why, if you stayed at home because you were afraid to leave Amaryllis, I should take that as an insult to me. Amaryllis will be under surveillance night and day."

So I decided to go.

We went by post chaise, which was perhaps the most pleasant way of taking to the road, for the posting houses were the very best of the inns, and although those who travelled this way paid highly for it, it was well worthwhile to enjoy the extra comfort.

We travelled leisurely with two stops on the way. It seemed, now that I was accompanying him, more like a holiday than a business trip, said David.

I found it thrilling driving into the City, to see in the distance the bastions of the Tower and to drive along by the river and suddenly to find myself caught up in that vitality.

The servants were prepared for us at the house, for my mother had sent a message on ahead of us to tell them to expect us. I remembered how we had come here just after the wedding—in the days of my innocence, I thought; and I was glad that Jonathan was at Pettigrew Hall. I should not have come if he had not been.

David, too, was remembering, and we had a pleasant candlelit meal in the dining room while the servants flitted silently in and out attending to our needs. David was blissfully happy but it was at times like this that my conscience troubled me most.

Then we retired to our bedroom—that pleasant gracious room, so different from Eversleigh—with its long windows to let in the light and the delicate curtains and Queen Anne furniture.

David said: "You have made me very happy, Claudine . . . happier than I ever thought to be." Then he kissed me and noticed that there were tears on my cheeks.

"Happy tears?" he asked, and I nodded, for how could I tell him that they were tears of contrition and that while I loved him for his goodness, his gentleness, his selflessness, I could not stop thinking of someone else who was as different from him as a man could be, someone who was ruthless, without sentiment, dangerous . . . and yet who had taken possession of my mind as well as my body and whom—although I deplored my bondage to him and my deceit towards the finest of husbands—I could not stop loving. Was that the word? Perhaps not. Obsession was more apt.

I tried to shake off my melancholy, to refuse to admit to my regrets that it was not Jonathan who was with me now. I tried not to think of him when David made love to me.

But the truth was that I was obsessed, and here in London, which was so much more his home than anywhere else because he spent so much time here, it was stronger than ever.

I felt better the next day. I accompanied David on his various journeys and I was glad that I was quite knowledgeable about the matters which were discussed. He was delighted in my interest.

I thought: We are so suited. We understand each other. We are a perfect match. The other . . . is madness. It is like a disease. I must cure myself and I can when I do not see him.

The following day David said: "There will be little business done today. There will be the crowds in the streets for the opening of Parliament. It might be fun to go out and mingle."

"I hope we shall see the King," I said. "I wonder what he looks like now."

David shook his head rather sadly: "Very different from that bright and earnest young man who came to the throne thirty-five years ago."

"Well, people must change in thirty-five years—even kings."

"He has had his trials. His family, for one thing. The Prince of Wales has caused him great anxiety."

"Yes, of course. The morganatic marriage with Mrs. Fitzherbert, and now his strained relations with Princess Caroline."

"And not only that. He has never got over the loss of the American Colonies, for which he blames himself."

"And rightly so."

"Well, that makes it all the more a burden on his mind."

Indeed it did, I thought, and wondered why I turned everything back to my own case.

"He says over and over again, 'I shall never lay on my last pillow in quiet as long as I remember my American Colonies.' He does repeat himself. It's a feature of that mental illness he had about seven years ago. I am sorry for him. He tried so hard to be a good king."

"He's recovered now though."

"They say so, but I think he is a little strange at times."

"Poor King. It is all very sad."

"And more so because he is a good man . . . a family man . . . a man who has tried to do his duty."

"Well, I shall look forward to seeing him. What do you propose we do?"

"Go out. Take little money, wear no jewellery of value and join the sightseers."

"It sounds interesting."

"We'll get out early then."

When we did go out the people were already lining the streets, but there was something about certain elements in the crowd which was rather disturbing.

One or two seemed to be talking in raised voices. I caught their words as we passed along. High taxes . . . low wages . . . unemployment . . . the price of bread.

I called David's attention to this and he said: "There are always people like that in the crowds. They find it a little dull and are trying to bring about what they think of as excitement."

We went into a coffee house and drank hot chocolate while we listened to the talk. It was mainly about the relationship of the Prince of Wales and his wife. He was reputed to have said: "Praise be to Heaven, I do not have to sleep with that disgusting woman any more."

They were all laughing and speculating as to the sex of the child and whether it would resemble its father or mother. The Prince of Wales was not exactly popular but there was no doubt that the people were deeply interested in his affairs.

When the King's carriage was due to arrive we were out in the streets. The crowd along the roadside was deep and David drew me a little apart from it. We were standing there when the King rode by, too far to see him clearly, and as I was straining to get a glimpse of him in his splendid robes, suddenly a shot rang out. There was half a second of deep silence. The bullet had struck the window of the King's carriage. Pandemonium broke out then. People were shouting. They were pointing at the window of an empty house. We were all gazing at a window from which the shot must have been fired.

The King's coachmen whipped up the horses and the carriage trundled on. Some men were running into the empty house. David put an arm round me. Neither of us spoke.

There was noise everywhere. People seemed to be shouting at each other.

"The King . . . do you think they shot him?" I stammered.

"I don't know. Come on. Let's go in here."

It was the coffee house which we had previously visited. People were crowding in, talking all the time.

"Did you see? Is this the end of George? Is the Prince now the King?"

"What happened? What happened?"

The trouble was that nobody was sure, and being unsure, they provided their own stories. Rumour was wild. We were in revolt. It was Paris all over again. The revolution had started.

"Not here," said someone. "Not here. We've seen enough of revolution from the other side of the water."

"He's not dead. He went straight on to Parliament."

"He's got courage, I will say that for him. He may be bumbling old Farmer George, but he's got courage."

"Who was it?"

"One of those anarchists, they say. They didn't get him. He fired from an empty house and got away."

"We shall hear the truth in due course," said David.

When we left the coffee house the King was returning from opening Parliament. I saw him in his carriage and felt a great relief that he was unharmed. The mob seemed a little downcast—disappointed perhaps that he had survived. Why do people always relish disaster? I wondered.

He sat there, old and resolute. I felt sorry for him, for I knew it was true that he had tried hard to do his duty. It was not his fault that he had been thrust into a position for which his mental capabilities and his state of mind made him unfit.

I hated to see the cruel faces in the mob. It was distressing to see how they threw stones at the carriage. One hit the King on his cheek. He caught it in his hands and sat there impassive, as though he was quite indifferent to the abuse.

The carriage passed on and David said to me: "Would you like to go home?"

I said I would, and we walked back to Albemarle Street in silence.

The next day we heard that the King had returned safely to his palace and that when the bullet had struck his carriage he had been less agitated than his companions. He was reputed to have said: "My lords, there is One who disposes of all things, and in Him I trust."

He kept the stone which had hit him—as a memento, he said, of the civilities he had received that day.

"David," I asked, "what does this mean? Is what happened in France going to happen here?"

David shook his head. "No. I feel sure it won't. There are not the same reasons. But we have to find these agitators. We have to stop them. I'd be ready to swear that many of these people who were throwing stones at the King's carriage had become caught up in the excitement of the moment and ordinarily would have been the King's docile subjects. They are egged on by the agitators. Mob frenzy is a madness, and the agitators know this. They start haranguing the people, telling them of their wrongs, and before long there is a riot . . . as we saw today."

"Is it known who these agitators are?"

"They would not exist for long if it were. They are clever. The ringleaders get others to do the task for them, and I'd be ready to swear that they are moving about the country so that they don't become too well known in one place."

I was sure he was right and the following day a proclamation was issued offering a reward of a thousand pounds for information about those who had attempted to assassinate the King.

"Do you think there will be a response?" I asked.

"It's a great deal of money," mused David, "but I doubt it. These people are well organized. They are professional revolutionaries. It must have been well planned; the assassin was in his place at the precise moment the carriage passed along."

"Many would know it was due to pass this way."

"That is more than likely."

Later we heard that Lord Grenville was introducing a bill into the Lords "for the safety of His Majesty's person," and more important, Mr. Pitt in the Commons was making his plans for the prevention of seditious meetings.

Later that day Jonathan and Millicent came to London and the peaceful domesticity was shattered.

Because of the disturbances David said it was necessary for us to stay in London rather longer than we had originally intended, for in view of the attempt on the King's life, people were less inclined to discuss business. The attempt had been made on the twenty-ninth of October and we were still in London on the fifth of November.

I knew that Jonathan had hastily come to London because of what had happened. I guessed that more disturbances were expected and there was a secret state of emergency.

Jonathan looked alert, keen-eyed, as he did when he was in the throes of an adventure. Clearly he had come to London because he had work to do.

Millicent was serene. I believed that she did not care whether she was in London or the country as long as she was with Jonathan.

She told me that she believed she was to have a child. It was early days yet but she was sure . . . or almost. It was clear that the possibility made her very happy indeed.

It was the fifth of November, a very significant date in English history, because it was the anniversary of that day when Guy Fawkes had tried to blow up the Houses of Parliament and had been discovered just in time. It was a date which had been celebrated ever since, and even though it had happened long ago, in the year 1605 to be precise, people were still as zealous in their determination to remember the day as they ever had been.

Jonathan and David had gone out. I was not sure whether they had gone together, but I knew David had some business deals to conclude and I had decided not to accompany him. Millicent was in her room; she had declared that she was feeling a little delicate and would stay in bed for a while.

I was alone . . . thinking of the difference which had come over the house since Jonathan had come and telling myself that perhaps it was just as well that David and I would soon be setting out for Eversleigh.

I heard someone come in.

I thought it was David and went to see, but it was Jonathan who stood smiling at me.

"At last," he said. "Alone."

I laughed at him and said uneasily: "You are ridiculous."

"I am sure of it. But is it not exciting to be by ourselves at last? David is like a watchdog; Millicent is like a shadow; but shadow and watchdog are no longer beside us."

"The shadow could well appear at any moment."

"Where are you going?"

"I'm getting ready to leave. I think we shall probably start out tomorrow."

"Just as I have come!"

"That seems as good a reason to go as any."

"Still afraid of me?"

I turned away.

"I am going out," he said. "Come with me."

"I have so much to do here."

"Nonsense. One of the servants can do it. Do you remember that lovely day we had in London? The time of the royal wedding?"

"It is not very long ago."

"And they say our Princess is fruitful. I am glad for the Prince's sake. Poor fellow. It was hard on him to have to do his duty."

"I think he is able to take care of himself."

"Like the rest of us he needs the solace of congenial feminine company. Listen to me, Claudine, I want to go out . . . just to mingle with the crowd and watch. Come with me."

"Is it people like Léon Blanchard and Alberic you are looking for?"

He came closer to me and looked at me intently. "You're caught up in this, Claudine," he said. "I'd rather you weren't, but you are. From the moment you saw Alberic and recognized the man he was meeting, you became involved."

"Yes, I see that."

"It will be easier for me if I am escorting a lady. I want to look like an ordinary sightseer—looking at the guys which are being paraded through the streets. I want to see what is going on. You can help me, Claudine."

An excitement was gripping me. I told myself it was because of the nature of the exercise rather than because I should be with him.

"Oh come on," he said. "You are not doing anything important, are you? No business with your husband. A little jaunt can do no harm and I'll be perfectly harmless on the streets, won't I? What tricks could I get up to there?"

"I'll come," I said.

"Brave lady!" he said ironically. "Go and get your cloak. I'll be here. I shall just slip up and tell Millicent that I have to go out."

"Tell her that I shall be with you," I said.

He smiled at me slyly and said nothing.

There was excitement in the streets of London—and not only because I was with Jonathan.

"The best time is at night," he said, "when the bonfires are lighted. We must come out tonight."

"Do you think the others would want to?"

"David . . . perhaps . . . Millicent . . . perhaps too. It would be more fun if you and I were alone."

I said: "Look at that extraordinary guy. What is it supposed to be?"

"I could not begin to guess. Perhaps just Master Fawkes himself."

Six ragged little boys carried the straw-packed figure, singing as they went:

Guy, guy, guy, stick him up in high,
Hang him on the lamp post and there let him die.

Jonathan slipped a coin into their proffered hands which set them grinning with delight.

"Who is your guy?" he asked.

"It's the Pope, mister," said the tallest of the urchins.

"How stupid of me not to recognize him," replied Jonathan lightly. "The likeness is remarkable."

The boys gaped at him and we passed on, laughing.

"Most of them don't know what it's about," said Jonathan. "Something to do with Catholics, that's all. Let's hope they don't start insulting people of that faith. It can happen when they get rowdy later on."

We saw many guys—grotesque figures made of straw and old rags which would burn well on the bonfires which would be lighted that evening.

The words were chanted through the streets and I found myself singing with them.

Remember, remember, the fifth of November,
Gunpowder treason and plot.

We see no reason, the gunpowder treason
Should ever be forgot.

Jonathan took me where I might see the parade of the butchers who came from all the markets to join in the procession, clapping marrow bones together.

A stick and a stake for King George's sake
A stick and a stump for Guy Fawkes' rump
Holler boys, holler boys, make the bells ring.
Holler boys, holler boys, God save the King.

I watched with amusement and I said: "How different from the mob at the opening of Parliament."

"The mob is here already," he answered seriously. "It's ready to emerge at the appropriate moment. On occasions like this it is lurking."

"And you are watchful."

He said: "We should all be watchful. The King was very lucky the other day. Shall we go to a coffee house? Would you like coffee or chocolate? We'll hear some amusing talk, I daresay. We might learn something. I know of a good one close to the river. Jimmy Borrows' Riverside Inn. You can watch the boats from the windows while you drink."

"I should like that," I told him.

He took my arm and I could not help it if I was happy, as I had been on that other occasion when we were out together.

It was a short step to the river. Jimmy Borrows evidently knew Jonathan.

He gave him a wink and nod as we entered and after I was seated Jonathan went over to him to have a word. They were in earnest conversation for some moments.

I knew enough now to understand that the tavern men were supplying information to Jonathan. I was beginning to learn a little about this secret business. Men like Jonathan and his father had contacts everywhere. It was for this reason that Dickon had been able to find the help he needed when he brought my mother safely out of France against such tremendous odds.

Jonathan returned to me, and hot chocolate was brought to us.

"Now, is this not pleasant?" he asked. "Here we are, you and I together, which is how it should be . . . often."

"Don't spoil it, Jonathan, please."

"As if I would ever spoil anything for you!"

"I think we have spoiled a great deal, you and I between us."

"I thought I had put that right. I thought you were beginning to understand."

"Oh, you are referring to your philosophy. One is only guilty if one is found out."

"It's a good one. Look at these people strolling along by the river. How contented they look! Out to enjoy themselves! What dark secrets do you think they are hiding?"

"How could I know?"

"I asked you to guess. Look at that pretty little woman smiling up at her husband. But is he her husband? I suspect he is her lover. And if he *is* her husband, then she is far too pretty to be consistently faithful to him."

"You are determined to bring everyone down to your level," I said. "I believe there are virtuous people in the world."

"The chaste and the pure! Show them to me and I'll find sins of which they are guilty. They probably suffer from self-righteousness, pride in their virtue, condemnation of the weaker vessel. Now I would say that is a sin . . . far more than a little pleasant dalliance which has brought the greatest pleasure to two deserving people."

I was staring out of the window. Alighting from one of the boats was a party of men. They carried a guy with them and there was no doubt who this one was meant to represent. It wore a farmer's coat and there was a straw in its mouth. It had been very well done and on the head was a crown.

I said: "It's the King."

Jonathan was not facing the window and he said: "What . . . where? Coming down the river . . . surely not."

"It's a guy . . . made to look like the King," I said. "And they are going to burn it."

"That's mischief." Jonathan was up, but before he reached the window, I cried: "Jonathan, look. Billy Grafter is with them."

Jonathan was beside me. The men were on the bank now . . . the guy in the arms of one of them.

"By God," said Jonathan, "I'll get him now."

He ran out of the inn; I was immediately behind him.

Just at that moment Billy Grafter saw him and if ever I recognized panic in a man's face I did then. Grafter turned and jumped into the boat and within a matter of seconds was pulling away from the bank.

Jonathan looked round him. There were several boats moored at the spot. He did not hesitate. He took my hand and almost threw me into one of them; then he was there beside me.

I could see Billy Grafter rowing as fast as he could. The tide was with him and he was making progress. But then so were we.

"I'll bring him in," growled Jonathan. "I'll get him this time."

The distance between us remained the same. Billy Grafter looked as though he was rowing for his life, which he probably was.

I clutched the side of the boat. I thought I was going to be thrown into the river at any moment. Jonathan was gaining when another boat drew level with us.

"Get out of my way," shouted Jonathan.

The man in the boat said: "You insolent knave. Why should I? Do you own the river?"

"You're obstructing me," yelled Jonathan.

I could see Billy Grafter rowing furiously a little way ahead of us. Jonathan spurted forward. We were almost on a level with him now. Then the man who had come up beside us turned sharply, barring our way. Jonathan shot forward and within a matter of seconds we were in the water and Billy Grafter was getting farther and farther away.

Jonathan grabbed me and brought me back to the bank. I had never seen him look so furious.

"Are you all right?" he asked.

I nodded, gasping and shivering. I felt as though my lungs were full of water and my muddied stained dress clung coldly to my shaking body.

Jonathan was equally bedraggled.

A little crowd had gathered to watch us; some seemed amused. I supposed it was not such an unusual occurrence for a boat to be overturned.

Someone brought in the boat and one of the watermen said: "Best get back to Borrows' Inn, sir. He'll dry you and the young lady off there."

Jonathan said: "Yes . . . yes. That's best."

"Get in, sir and I'll row you back."

The crowd began to disperse. The little entertainment was over.

"I saw what happened," said the boatman. "Looked like deliberate to me, it did."

"It was," said Jonathan shortly.

"There's some as likes a bit of mischief. Well, you'll get into something dry and you'll be none the worse."

We had come to the inn. Jimmy Borrows came out rubbing his hands in consternation.

"We had a spill," said Jonathan. "Can you help us dry our clothes?"

"Of a surety. Come in . . . come in. There's a fire in the parlour. But first the clothes. You'll catch your deaths if you stay in those."

He took me to a bedroom and Jonathan to another. I was given a dressing robe which was far too big for me and slippers which would fit a man. Never mind. I was glad to get out of my wet clothes and rub myself down with a rough towel. The odour from the river was none too sweet. My hair hung limply about me, but there was colour in my cheeks and my eyes were bright and sparkling.

Jimmy's wife, Meg, gathered up my clothes which she said she would put on a horse before the fire. I could go into the parlour, where the gentleman already was, and warm myself up. Jimmy had taken him mulled wine, which was just what was needed at such a time.

I went down to the parlour. Jonathan was already there. He wore a robe not unlike mine only his was too small. He laughed at me; he had recovered from his anger.

"Well, who can say this is not cosy! Borrows thinks you should have some of this mulled wine. It is very good and Mrs. B. has supplied some fritters which she says go with it."

I sipped the wine. It was warming. I shook out my damp hair.

He said seriously: "I lost him, Claudine."

"Yes."

"It was the man in the boat . . . a fellow conspirator obviously."

"I am sure that must be so. It was bad luck."

"Bad strategy. I should have thought of that. I ought to have been quicker. Then I would have had him." He looked at me steadily. "You know how I love to be with you, but I wish you had not been with me today."

"Why?"

"Because this involves you even more than you were already. You know what happened there. You know that people . . . innocent people . . . like your mother and grandmother can be caught up in this holocaust. How much more danger is there for those who have special information."

"You mean that I know for sure that Billy Grafter is a spy."

He nodded. "You see, I have brought you into this."

"No. I brought myself into it when I recognized Alberic in the coffee house. That was none of your doing."

"You'll have to be careful, Claudine. I think they'll move Billy Grafter out of London. They know now that we are aware that he is here. He runs the risk of coming face to face with me or my father. He will be transferred to do his evil work elsewhere."

"Which is inciting the people to riot."

Jonathan nodded. "The same method which was used so successfully in France."

"They shot at the King . . ."

"One of their fraternity most surely. If that had succeeded it would have been a start. I worry about you."

"Oh, Jonathan, I shall be all right. I can look after myself. I don't know much of all these things—but at least I now know a little."

He came to me and took my hands in his.

"You are very precious to me," he said.

"Oh, please, Jonathan . . . don't," I said tremulously.

He was silent for a while—more serious than I had ever known him to be. He had been greatly shaken, not only by the incident and its failure for him; and I knew in that moment that he really was deeply concerned for me.

The wine was warming me. I gazed into the blue flames which spurted out of the logs. I could see all sorts of pictures in the fire—castles, fiery red faces . . . figures, and I thought: I wish this could go on.

But that was how I always felt when I was with him.

It must have been about an hour that we sat there before Meg Borrows came in to say that our things were dry enough to put on now and would we like some more mulled wine?

I said: "We must be going. They'll be missing us."

"I'll have your things taken up to the rooms," said the obliging Meg, "and you can go up when you like."

Jonathan looked at me. "Let us have a little more of your excellent wine," he said.

Meg looked delighted and went off to get it.

"We should go back," I said.

"Just a little longer."

"We ought . . ."

"My dear Claudine, as usual you are concerned with what you ought instead of what you want."

"They'll be wondering what has become of us."

"They can wonder for a little longer surely."

Meg brought in the wine, poured it out and carried it to us.

Jonathan watched me as he drank.

"In the years to come," he said, "I shall remember this moment. You and I in our ill-fitting robes, damp from the river, alone, drinking in paradise. This stuff tastes like nectar to me and I feel like Jove."

"I do believe your tastes run in similar directions."

"You find me godlike?"

"I believe he was constantly chasing women."

"In various shapes when doing so . . . swans . . . bulls . . . what a gift!"

"Presumably he felt he was not attractive enough to be as he really was."

"I can see I do not need such a gift. I believe I am irresistible just as I am."

"Are you?"

"Almost," he replied. "I have no rivals except dull Duty, who is a formidable one, I agree, where a certain would-be virtuous lady is concerned."

"I wish you would be serious."

"I have to be . . . most of the time. Let me dally for a while. At this moment I should be on my way back to the house. I should be changing into presentable garments. I am sure those we are wearing are ruined. I have work to do. You don't realize, Claudine, how desperately I long to be with you, for when I am, I forget that I should be hot on the trail of our enemies. You are the seductress."

"No," I said, "it is you who are the seducer."

"Claudine, listen to me. Just one thing before we go. Here we are in our natural state, you might say. Will you answer me one question truthfully?"

I nodded.

"Do you love me?"

I hesitated before I said: "I don't know."

"You like to be with me?"

"You know I do."

"It is more exciting than anything else?"

I was silent.

He said as though to himself: "Construe silence as an affirmative."

Then he went on: "Do you ever think of those hours we spent together?"

"I try to forget."

"Knowing in your heart that wrong as you might have thought them, you would not have missed them."

"I've had enough of this catechism."

"You have answered all my questions. Claudine, what are we going to do? Are we going on like this all our lives . . . seeing each other fairly frequently, finding that this love between us is growing, that it is never going to fade? Do you really believe that all our lives we are going on denying ourselves . . ."

I stood up. "I shall go and put on my dry things now. We must go back."

I ran out of the parlour and up to the room. I was trembling as I put on my clothes. They were stained with mud and smelt none too savoury, but at least they were dry. My hair was still damp about my shoulders.

I went downstairs. Jonathan was dressed and waiting for me. Jimmy Borrows had offered his gig to take us back to Albemarle Street. We should look rather odd arriving at the house in that, but it was quicker than trying to find some other conveyance.

As we came into the house, Millicent appeared. She stared at us.

"Hello, my love," said Jonathan. "You are astounded by the spectacle, are you not?"

"Whatever happened?"

"A spill on the river."

"Did you go on a boat then?"

"We were not walking on the water."

"What on earth were you doing?"

"Rowing . . . and some idiot ran into us."

"I thought you were going out on business."

"It was business, and we took a boat. Well, here we are and I want to get into some clean clothes. I have to go out immediately."

I went up to my room and changed everything. I was sitting at my dressing table combing my hair when there was a knock on my door and Millicent came in. Her eyes were wide and suspicious, I thought.

She said: "It must have been quite a shock."

"It was."

"You might have been drowned."

"Oh, I don't think so. There were lots of boats on the river."

"I did not know that you had gone out with Jonathan."

"It was decided right at the last minute. I was here and he thought I might like to go out . . . and as David wasn't here and you were resting . . ."

She nodded. "Your clothes will be ruined," she said.

"I daresay."

She shrugged her shoulders and went out.

I felt very uneasy. She is aware of something, I thought, and she is suspicious.

Jonathan went out and was away all that day. When David came back I told him of our adventure.

"I thought you weren't going out today, as you had so much to do in the house," he said.

"I meant to get ready for our departure, but as it was a special sort of day . . . Guy Fawkes and all that . . . I thought it would be silly not to see something of the fun, and as Jonathan was going out he said he would take me along with him."

"Did you enjoy it?"

"The guys and everything, yes. The ducking, well, that was less pleasant."

"I should have thought Jonathan could have managed a boat better than that."

"Oh, it was an idiot in another boat. He went straight into us."

"Well, you are none the worse, I hope."

"No. Fortunately, the inn was close by and we were able to dry off there. The host and hostess were very helpful. We are going home tomorrow, aren't we?"

"I think we could. You're missing Amaryllis."

I admitted that I was.

"I too," he said.

I thought how much easier he was to deceive than Millicent.

I was very much aware of her. She seemed to be watching me. Night came and from the windows I looked out on the night sky which was red from the light of the bonfires which were burning all over London.

"It looks," I said to David, "as though London is on fire."

The Last Farewell

The next day we went back to Eversleigh—all except Jonathan, who said he had business to keep him in London. Millicent came with us. Jonathan would be away for the greater part of the days and she did not wish to be alone; and in any case, Jonathan said he would be back at Eversleigh in less than a week, so it was a good idea that Millicent should travel with us.

All was well at home. My mother was delighted by our return, particularly as Dickon was on one of his rare visits to Clavering. She had not gone with him because she did not want to leave Jessica, who had a slight cold. Amaryllis was more beautiful than ever and as she was now very much aware of what was going on and expressed a certain delight in seeing me, I was very happy.

The days passed in pleasant domesticity; on the third day I accompanied David on the rounds of the estate. As usual we were taken into the kitchens when we visited the farms, and the farmers' wives always insisted on our tasting their homemade wines.

We were at the Penns' farm that day with Jenny Penn, a big buxom woman, who took a great delight in her kitchen and all that she produced in it. But there was one thing she liked better than her food and that was a gossip.

David used to say that we could catch up on what was happening on the estate from Jenny for she knew everything that was going on, not only on the land her husband farmed but all the others too.

"Now what do you think of this brew, sir?" she said to David. "And you, Mrs. Frenshaw. I've got a feeling that it is better than the last. A bit too sweet that. I always say to my Len, 'Wine wants a bit of a tang to it!' That's what I say. Too much sweetness can kill a wine."

We both agreed that it was a perfect vintage, which pleased her; and it was just as we were about to leave that she said: "And what do you think of our ghost? If you was to ask me I'd say it was a lot of fancy." She put her hands on her substantial hips and added: "I was never much of a one for ghosts myself."

"Ghosts?" I asked. "We haven't heard anything about ghosts."

"Well, it's that young man . . . the one that drowned, you know. He was shot at and that was the end of him. Someone said he'd been seen on the shore like . . . coming out of the sea."

"But he's dead and buried."

"I know. But this was his ghost, you know, sir. Ghosts don't take heed of coffins. And the other one was with him."

"What other one?" I asked.

"Oh, that young man he was friendly with. Him as was working up at the big house. What was his name?"

"Billy Grafter?" I said.

"Yes, that's him. He was drowned when the boat was upset. Well, he's been seen . . . according to some. Or his ghost has."

"He's been seen . . . here?" I asked faintly.

"Why, you look all shook up, Mrs. Frenshaw. There's nothing to be afraid of in ghosts."

"Who saw this?" I asked.

"Oh, it was one or two of them. Patty Grey's girl, Ada, said she was down on the beach with her brother collecting wood that had been thrown up by the tide . . . and she said he was there. He appeared . . . and then he was gone."

"It was inevitable that someone should start imagining these things," said David. "It made quite a stir at the time."

We put down our glasses.

"That was enjoyable, Mrs. Penn," went on David. "I am sure you are right about the tang."

She ushered us out.

"Very good farmers, the Penns," said David, as we rode away. "Everything in order. I wish there were more like them."

But I could only think: Someone has seen Billy Grafter. Was it imagination or does that mean that he is here . . . in the neighbourhood?

We were rather worried about Aunt Sophie for she was not very well. My mother said one of us should call every day.

"She hasn't been the same since Alberic died," Jeanne told us. "And now there is all this talk about ghosts, she fancies Alberic can come back and talk to her . . . tell her who his murderer was . . ."

"Is there a lot of talk about ghosts?"

"Among the servants, yes. Two of them have said they have actually seen Alberic's friend who was drowned with him, and now she has the idea that Alberic is trying to reach her. She talks about it all the time. Dolly Mather is there with her a good deal. Poor Dolly, she doesn't have much of a life. Mrs. Trent has changed so much since that suicide. You know how she always wanted to be included in everything . . . now she hardly ever goes out. Dolly is here a lot. I think she must find it a relief to get away from Grasslands. And Mademoiselle likes to have her. They talk constantly of Alberic."

"I heard the rumour that Billy Grafter had been seen," I said.

"Yes. He's supposed to look as though he has walked out of the sea . . . dripping water and ghastly white."

"It's a lot of nonsense."

"She takes comfort in thinking that Alberic could come back."

"Was she really so fond of him when he was here?"

Jeanne looked at me shrewdly. "She took an interest in him. She liked to have him around. You know he was very useful. There weren't many she would have trusted to go up to London and do little commissions for her. She let him ride the horses. I think it was his being of our own nationality and being upset by everything that was happening in France . . . It was a common tragedy."

"And the fact that he is dead would endear him to her."

Jeanne said nothing and I went on: "Oh, you know as well as I do that Aunt Sophie revels in misfortune. If only she would try to see the bright things of life. She shuts herself away . . . lives like a recluse . . ."

"That is Mademoiselle d'Aubigné," said Jeanne soberly. "And we must accept this and do all we can to make life tolerable for her."

"You are right, Jeanne, as always. Does she really want us to visit her?"

"Oh, yes, she looks forward to seeing you. She likes to rest and meditate in the early afternoon but as you come at three and go at five . . . that's as she likes it. She was always one for regularity. She likes life to go to a pattern."

"Well, I shall come every afternoon as long as she wants me, and if I don't, I expect my mother will."

"Oh, I think she would rather it was you. She still broods on the past and often talks about your father. She was very much in love with him, you know, and I think she has never quite forgiven your mother for marrying him. And she thinks of you as the daughter she has never had."

"Then I'll come."

And I did. Each afternoon I rode over and I made sure that I left precisely at five.

Aunt Sophie talked often of Alberic.

She did believe that people sometimes—as she said—"came back" and "got into touch" with those of whom they had been very fond; and if they had died a violent death they sometimes came back to haunt their murderers.

Dolly Mather was usually with her when I arrived and sometimes she stayed awhile. I think she offered a great deal of comfort to Sophie, who would see them as kindred spirits, both maimed in a way, both treated unfairly by fate, both having suffered the loss of a loved one.

They talked of Alberic and of Evie, and Sophie constantly said that she believed one day they would "come through" to her.

"And when they do," she said, "Alberic will tell me the name of his murderer, and then I shall do my best to see that the wicked ones . . . for perhaps it was more than one . . . are brought to justice."

I wondered what she would say if I told her that Alberic had been a spy, that it was men such as he who had helped to bring about the revolution which had resulted in so much misery for her own country.

She would never have believed me.

It was always dark when I left Enderby. The candles in Sophie's room had to be lighted at four o'clock at this time of the year. I always thought the room took on a special quality in candlelight. It had always been a room of haunting memories for me; and on these occasions when Jeanne called up through the speaking tube—as she did now and then—my heart used to race uncomfortably for I reminded myself that someone knew I had been here with Jonathan . . . I had been lulled into a sense of security about that because no one had ever hinted to me that he . . . or she . . . was in the secret. There was only that muffled voice coming over the tube, not recognizable as any one of my acquaintances. Even Jeanne's voice with its distinctive accent sounded different through the tube.

Aunt Sophie was in one of her brooding moods.

She said that Dolly had been with her in the early part of the afternoon and she had felt very close to Alberic, and Dolly to her sister Evie.

"They'll break through one of these days," said Aunt Sophie. "I am so sorry for Dolly. She cared so much for her sister, and that grandmother of hers is very strange. She comes to me, poor child, and tells me her troubles."

I said that it was comforting for them to be able to talk together.

"Life is unfair to some of us, and to others . . . everything comes. Take your mother, for instance."

Poor Aunt Sophie! She was obsessed by my mother's good fortune throughout life and compared it frequently with her own ill luck.

I was always rather relieved to get away.

As I came down to the hall, Jeanne appeared.

"I am glad I caught you," she said. "I wanted you to look at some materials I have. They are really rather lovely. Mademoiselle does love a pretty gown and I want to keep her interested in them. It's a great help to her."

"I'd like to see them," I told her.

"I've got them down here. I won't keep you long. I know you like to get away sharp."

"Oh, I've plenty of time."

The materials were pale pink and Aunt Sophie's favourite lilac; and there were a deeper purple and red.

I said I thought the paler colours suited Aunt Sophie better than the deep ones.

"I fully agree," she said. "And this softer material lends itself better to the hoods. I want you to see some ribbons."

I duly admired these and it must have been about fifteen minutes later when I left Jeanne.

I mounted my horse and started for home. I always took the same route, which meant going through a short bridle path where thick bushes grew on either side. This path was rarely used and as it was straight and narrow I always cantered through it.

Suddenly my horse drew up sharply and I almost fell out of the saddle.

"What is it, Queenie?" I asked.

I peered into the darkness. At first I could see nothing, but the mare refused to move.

I dismounted. The bushes were tall and the path shaded; there was no moon and thick clouds obscured the stars.

Then I saw that a man was lying across the path.

I stared. Someone had tied a thin rope across the path about a foot from the ground. It had been attached to the bushes and had obviously been put there as a trap.

I was dumbfounded. I heard a movement and then I saw the horse which was standing nearby.

It was clear what had happened. The unsuspecting horse had tripped over the rope and thrown the rider.

What a wicked thing to do! I went to the man lying there. His eyes were shut but he was still breathing.

I must get help at once, and in the quickest possible way.

My heart leaped with horror, for the man lying on the ground was Billy Grafter.

I stood looking down at him for what seemed a long time, but it could only have been a matter of seconds.

So he was here! It was true that people had seen him. They had believed it was his ghost but it was in fact Billy Grafter in the flesh. What was he doing here? He must have friends here. Who?

He looked very pale and there was a trickle of blood on his forehead. I must get help at once.

As I looked at him the thought struck me that he could not have been there very long. Five minutes perhaps. I had been late in leaving Enderby. If I had not been, should I have been the one who tripped over the rope?

The suspicion came to me. It had been meant for me.

I was shaken. Someone had wanted to kill me. Someone had planned an accident . . . for me . . . and Billy Grafter had come along and been the one who was caught.

What should I do?

I was midway between Eversleigh and Enderby. The best plan would be to go to Eversleigh. There were plenty of grooms. I would get Billy Grafter to Eversleigh and then send for Jonathan.

I rode as fast as I could. There was no one in the stables, but when I shouted several of them came running.

"There's been an accident," I cried. "It's that man Billy Grafter who people thought was drowned. He's on the bridle path midway between here and Enderby. Someone tied a rope about the bushes so that it was across the path and riders would trip in the dark. He'll have to be brought here. You'll need a stretcher."

They gaped at me for a few seconds and then set about doing my bidding.

I went into the house. My mother was in the hall. She began: "What on earth has happened? You look as if you have seen a ghost."

I said: "There's been an accident. It's Billy Grafter. There was a rope tied across the path. His horse must have tripped and thrown him."

"My dear Claudine, what are you saying? Here. Sit down. You don't look too well yourself. Tell me exactly what happened."

I told her that I had been visiting Aunt Sophie and when I came back through the bridle path I had found Billy Grafter lying there because his horse had thrown him.

"Mischievous children," said my mother.

I shook my head. "I've sent them to bring him in. They shouldn't be long. We'll have to look after him."

I had not told her that I had seen Billy Grafter in London when I was with Jonathan. I knew that I had to be careful. I had become involved in those secrets which were part of the life of my stepfather and his son; and I knew that even my mother was excluded from some of them.

I wondered if I had been wise to mention Billy Grafter, but as I had already told myself, they would know him when he was brought in.

I was waiting with my mother when the men came back.

Billy Grafter was not with them.

They looked very strange, I thought, and they avoided my eyes.

I cried out: "What . . . Where?"

"Mrs. Frenshaw, Madam, we went there. We went to the path. We looked everywhere. There was nobody there."

"Nobody! But I saw . . ."

"No, Mrs. Frenshaw, Madam . . . there was no one."

"But his horse?"

"Nor horse. Nor man."

"There was a rope round the bushes . . . across the path."

They shook their heads. "We looked for a rope. There was nothing there."

"But it's impossible. He was lying there . . . unconscious. I saw him. The horse was there too. I left him because I wanted to get help as soon as possible."

They shook their heads.

I knew they thought that I had been the victim of an hallucination. I had seen the ghost of Billy Grafter, for when they had gone to the spot there was no sign of him, no man, no horse, no rope. Nothing.

It was to be expected that such an event would be wildly commented on. It went through the servants' hall and from there to every dwelling in the neighbourhood.

What Mrs. Frenshaw had seen was the ghost, it was said. He had come back to avenge his murderer . . . and the murderer of his friend, Alberic.

I knew there was one thing I had to do and that was get a message to Jonathan. He wanted Billy Grafter, and I, who had clearly seen him lying there, and who knew that he had not died with Alberic as people here believed, and that he was engaged in spying for those who wished harm to our country, was fully aware that Billy Grafter was close at hand. He must have friends who helped him. He could not have recovered in time to take himself and his horse away and at the same time remove the rope from the bushes. He had an accomplice and that accomplice could well be someone whom we knew.

I should have liked to set out for London but that was impossible. If only Dickon were at Eversleigh I could have left this to him. It was unfortunate that he had chosen this time to go to Clavering.

I wrote a letter to Jonathan telling him what had happened. I chose one of the grooms who had been with us since he was a boy. His grandfather had served the Eversleighs and I felt he could be trusted. He had to leave without anyone's knowing, I told him. I would speak to his father and let him know that it was most urgent and secret business.

He was young enough for a secret mission to appeal to him, but I imagined he would think my motive in sending a letter to Jonathan might be a romantic one. But there was no time to worry about that now. I had to act promptly.

I said: "Leave immediately. Make the journey as quickly as you can. Mr. Jonathan will understand when he reads my letter, and make sure you give it to no one else."

As I left the stables I ran into Millicent. I felt myself flush deeply. I was, after all, sending a letter in secret to her husband.

She said: "I saw that groom . . . what's his name . . . Jake Somebody . . . dashing off somewhere . . . looking very important." The manner in which she kept her eyes on me embarrassed me. She was suspicious. "I stopped him and asked why he was in such a hurry. He muttered something about having to do something for you."

"Oh yes, of course," I said, trying to speak lightly and wondering if she had overheard anything.

She went on: "That was a strange business about the ghost of the man Grafter."

"Yes," I answered cautiously, "very strange."

"You seem to me the very last person to come face to face with a ghost. And you were so sure . . ."

"Yes, it was very strange."

"I suppose you're a believer now. You were rather sceptical before, weren't you?"

"I would always be sceptical until I had the evidence of my own experience."

She kept her eyes on my face and I thought: Was it you, Millicent, who tied the rope across the path? How much do you know about me and Jonathan? My memory flashed back to a scene in the bedroom. Had she not said: "I think I would kill anyone he was too fond of . . ."?

Millicent was a strange woman. She resembled her mother and I believed she would be capable of a great deal before which others would quail.

I felt myself turning cold with horror. Could I be in the presence of one who had tried, if not to kill me, to maim me for life? Did she know that it was in truth Billy Grafter who had been on the bridle path that day, because it was she who had laid the trap for me? Had she been watching in the bushes for me to fall? And if so, what did she know of Billy Grafter? And having made one attempt and failed, would she try again?

We came into the house together and I went to my room.

I was dreadfully uneasy and it was difficult to act normally. My mother, I had thought, was the only one in the house who would believe that I had actually seen Billy Grafter. I had to talk to her.

She was very upset. "If only Dickon were here," she kept saying.

"Maman," I said, "someone here . . . not far away, helped Billy Grafter to get away. Someone removed the rope from the bushes. That person must be looking after him. He was hurt, I know."

"Who, Claudine, who?"

"I don't know, but I have sent a message to Jonathan. He will come back with all speed when he receives it, I am sure."

"Let's hope he comes soon. That rope . . . why was it there?"

"I think . . . to catch me."

"Do you really believe that?"

"I must. It was the way I came . . . regularly. It was only by a fluke that I stopped to look at Jeanne's materials and Billy Grafter got there first."

"Oh, Claudine, I am afraid for you."

"I'll be all right. I've been warned now. And Jonathan will be home soon."

"Shall I send for Dickon?"

"I think Jonathan will manage it. Wait and see what he has to say."

"In the meantime . . . you must take the utmost care. I was thinking all last night of the things that have happened: those people coming to the house pretending to be Dickon's friends; the kidnapping of Jessica; then returning her and . . . now this. What does it mean? Where is all this leading? Promise me you'll take care."

"I will. I will. Maman, do you think Millicent knows anything?"

"Millicent! I shouldn't think so for a moment. She's very preoccupied with the prospect of becoming a mother. Why do you ask? Has she said anything?"

"No, but I just wondered."

"Well, promise me to take extra special care."

"I will."

Within two days Jonathan came back. I saw him arrive and waved from my bedroom window and immediately went down to meet him.

"Claudine!" he cried and kissed me.

"Oh, I'm so glad you've come."

"I want to know everything . . . now . . . at once. He's here . . . in this neighbourhood?"

"He must be."

We went into the parlour which led out of the hall and I quickly told him what had happened.

"Rope across the bushes," he said. "Whoever would have done that?"

"I think it was meant to catch me."

"Why? I am quite sure that Grafter and his associates would want to do such a thing—but if they did, how came it that one of their own fell into the trap?"

"I don't understand."

"It was somebody who wanted to harm *you.* I can't believe that those people would use such a method." He paused thoughtfully. "It would seem that there are two plots in progress."

I looked at him steadily and said: "There are some who know that you and I once met in Enderby. Someone was in the house when we were there . . . someone who spoke through the tube. Do you think it possible that that person could have told someone . . . someone who hates me for my part in it?"

"Millicent?" he asked.

"I can't think that she would do such a thing . . . but she does love you deeply and possessively, I think. She is an intense person. It is quite reasonable to suppose that she would therefore hate me . . . if she knew."

"All that was before my marriage."

"But she watches you . . . she watches me. I think we betray something."

He was silent for a few seconds, then he said: "The first thing is to get Grafter. He's here all right. He's in this neighbourhood. You saw him on the bridle path. How badly hurt was he?"

"I couldn't see exactly. He was lying there. He must have been unconscious."

"And then he was removed, but you had already let them know that you had seen Grafter."

"I thought there was no need to hide the fact, as they would all know when he was brought in."

He nodded. "Then there is this ghostly theory. That's good. That helps. You must take special care, Claudine. I don't understand why this clumsy attempt was made on your life, but I don't think it could have been Grafter's friends, for if it were they would never have gone into the trap. There is something very odd afoot, and I want you to be careful. I want you to watch everything with the utmost attention. But don't appear to be doing so. I've got to get Grafter. He's here. He can't be far away and he's useless to them now in London. They know we're looking for him. When I get him I'll find out where the rest are. Now don't forget, behave as though nothing had happened and appear to believe that you have had an experience of the occult."

"I will," I said. "Now you must wash the stains of your journey from your person, and it is nearly time to eat."

"I'm hungry," he said, and smiling at me with the mischief in his eyes which I knew so well, he added: "For many things."

As we came out of the room Millicent was in the hall.

"Hello, Jonathan," she said.

"Ah, here is my devoted wife."

She ran to him and embraced him. Over his shoulder she looked at me and I could not understand the expression on her face.

I was determined to carry out Jonathan's instructions and behave normally.

He himself was very merry and few would have guessed that he was engaged on an important mission. He chided me for seeing a ghost.

"Really, Claudine, I should never have believed it of you."

"It was an extraordinary experience," I replied.

"I wonder if you were looking into the past or the future. I believe that is how these things are supposed to work."

Then he began telling ghost stories and in such a manner as to make them ridiculous.

David was a little put out because he thought Jonathan was mocking me; but I smiled at him to assure him that I did not mind in the least.

"Perhaps," I said, "Jonathan will see a ghost himself one day. Then he won't be so sceptical."

The next day I went to see Aunt Sophie.

She had heard the story of what was now called "Mrs. Frenshaw's vision" and was very interested in it.

"It was the ghost of that poor young man who was murdered with Alberic," she said. "They were both murdered, poor innocent boys. Those are the people who come back . . . those who die violently. And they come back because they want their revenge."

Dolly Mather was there listening intently. Aunt Sophie addressed her now and then: "Dolly, bring another cushion for me, dear child." "Just put my footstool a little nearer and ring and tell them we want some coal on the fire."

Dolly obeyed these instructions willingly, even eagerly.

I asked about her grandmother and Dolly said she was not really well. She just wanted to be by herself all the time.

"It's very sad," said Aunt Sophie, with that relish she always had for misery. "But Dolly comes to me very often, don't you, child?"

Dolly answered: "I don't know what it would be like if I couldn't come here."

I left at the usual time and when I came to the bridle path I dismounted and walked my horse. There was a deep silence and the darkness gave the place an eerie aspect. If I had not known that Billy Grafter was at large and that he had certainly fled from London, I could easily have been convinced that I had seen a ghost.

On the second day when I was about to call on Aunt Sophie I met Dolly on the way and I had a feeling that she had been waiting for me, which proved right.

"Oh, Mrs. Frenshaw, I was hoping to see you. Mademoiselle d'Aubigné is not well today."

"Oh, isn't she? What's wrong?"

"It's nothing much. She's just tired and wants to sleep all the afternoon. Jeanne said if I saw you would I tell you not to call this afternoon. I haven't seen Mademoiselle today. When I went Jeanne said come tomorrow."

"Oh, I see."

"Mrs. Frenshaw, I'd like to talk to you. Would you . . . come for a little ride with me?"

"But of course, Dolly." I was rather pleased. I had always found it difficult to talk to her. I was sure she brooded a great deal, and I had often said to David that if only she would talk we might be able to help her. So now I welcomed the opportunity.

We turned our horses away from Enderby and I said: "Where shall we go?"

"Evie and I used to love to ride by the sea."

"Perhaps you'd rather not go that way now then."

"Oh, I would, I would. I often go there."

So we turned our horses in a southerly direction.

"It's wonderful for me to be able to go and see Mademoiselle."

"It's good for her, too. I think she's really fond of you, Dolly."

A flush suffused her cheek. "Oh, do you really think so, Mrs. Frenshaw?"

"I do indeed."

"She's taught me a lot. French . . . and everything. It has been wonderful to go there . . . especially after I lost Evie."

"I understand," I said.

"She's so sympathetic. After all . . . terrible things happened to her too, didn't they?"

"Yes."

"Can you smell the sea, Mrs. Frenshaw?"

"Oh yes. I just got a whiff. I always like that . . . when you know it's not far off."

"Evie used to like it, too."

I was wondering what it was she had to tell me, but I decided to leave it to her to do it in her own time and her own way. I fancied she could easily return to the secretive Dolly I had always known.

We broke into a gallop and went like the wind over the green fields. Dolly was a good rider and she seemed to gain confidence in the saddle.

Then we saw the sea. It was a grey, quiet, November sea with hardly a ripple on the water and not even the slightest breeze in the air.

"Shall we go down to the beach?" she said. "I love it there."

I followed and as our horses' hoofs touched the sand I saw the boat lying there on the beach.

"Oh look," said Dolly. "Shall we go and see the boat?"

We galloped across the sand to where the boat lay.

Dolly turned and looked at the boat house.

"Oh, I think someone's there."

"The owner of the boat perhaps," I said.

"Shall we go and see? Let's tie our horses there . . . on the rock. That's where Evie and I used to leave ours when we came here."

"All right," I said. I dismounted and tethered my horse. Dolly was already making her way to the boat house.

"Is anyone there?" she called.

There was no answer.

"I did think I saw someone," she said. "Let's take a peep inside."

Cautiously she pushed open the door and went in. I followed.

The door shut suddenly and I was in darkness. Something had been put over my head. I felt a sharp blow on the head and then there was darkness.

When I opened my eyes the first thing I saw was Dolly. She was sitting on a three-legged stool watching me.

I was lying on the floor; I felt dazed and there was a pain in my head. My wrists and ankles were firmly tied together.

"Dolly . . ." I stammered. "What . . . what's happened?"

She said: "You'll soon come round. It's ten minutes since we came in here. I've brought you here to kill you, Mrs. Frenshaw."

I should have thought she was being ridiculous if she had not been holding a gun.

She saw my eyes on it and said: "I know how to use it. It's one of the things I've been taught."

"Dolly! What is this? Some game?"

"Oh no, it's very serious. Death is."

"Do you really mean . . . ?"

She said: "Oh yes. You've got to die. You murdered Evie and you're going to die . . . as she did."

"You're mad. Nobody murdered Evie. She killed herself."

"She killed herself because others made her. That's murder . . . and murderers have to die."

"Dolly, try to be sensible. Talk to me. What do you mean? What is all this about?"

"I'll tell you. We've got time because I'm not going to kill you until Billy gets here. That's part of the contract."

"Billy? Billy Grafter?"

"Yes, Billy Grafter."

"So you and he are friends."

She nodded. "Well, he was Alberic's friend, wasn't he?" She smiled. "You can't move, can you? You're well tied up. Billy did that."

"He's here?"

She nodded. "He's going to get him. That's what he's going to do. And I'm going to get you. He helped me . . . and I'll help him. You don't understand, do you? Billy will be here in a moment. Then we'll just go ahead."

She caressed the gun and I thought: She really means it. She's mad. "Why should you go free with your sins . . . when my sister Evie . . ." Her face puckered as though she was going to cry.

"Dolly," I said, "let's talk."

"We are talking, aren't we? You see, you committed adultery. You broke the seventh commandment. You were married to the nice one and you committed adultery with the wicked one. It was in Enderby when it was empty before Mademoiselle came in. We knew you were there with him. We frightened you, didn't we, when we spoke through the tube?"

"So that was you."

"Yes . . . Evie and me. You were so scared. We laughed about it. And then . . . Evie was in love, and she said that when you loved it was the most wonderful thing . . . and then she was going to have the little baby. I wanted that little baby, Mrs. Frenshaw. Oh, I would have taken such care of it. And then she killed herself."

"She should never have done that. We could have done something. We could have helped her."

"It was you, Mrs. Frenshaw. You started it and he finished it. You betrayed him and he shot him . . . and he was drowned. Between you you killed Alberic. Oh, you are puzzled, aren't you? You thought Evie's baby's father was Harry Farringdon. She never cared for him. It was our Granny who wanted that. It was Alberic for Evie. They loved each other and I loved them both. They were going to take me to France with them. I was going to look after the little baby . . . because they would be married and it was all going to be wonderful. Then suddenly it all changed. He went to London and when he came back in a hurry he told us that you'd seen him and you'd told that wicked Mr. Frenshaw, who was your lover, and Alberic said he had to get away quickly . . . because they were after him. He promised to send for us . . . Evie and me. He told us we were to go to France. We would have gone. We knew how to get there. We were up here . . . hiding when it happened. So we saw it all. You came along and that wicked man shot Alberic and Alberic drowned and everything was different after that."

"You must know that Alberic was a spy."

"Alberic was a wonderful man."

"It is men such as him who brought terrible trouble to France."

"That had to be. That was injustice. Alberic talked about it to us."

"And he was trying to do to this country what he had done in his own. He had to die, Dolly. He always knew that he was taking that risk."

"And my sister . . . my Evie . . . she killed herself. She couldn't face Granny. She was always on about Evie marrying well, telling her she really belonged at Eversleigh and how pretty she was and how she would get a rich husband. She said she didn't try hard enough for Harry Farringdon."

"Oh Dolly . . . what a tangle of troubles! It need not have been."

"Evie couldn't face . . . having a bastard."

"People do . . ."

"You did . . . perhaps."

"Dolly!"

"That makes you angry. Of course you're angry. It makes me angry. Poor Evie had to kill herself and you . . . you did the same . . . only you were worse because you had a good husband. Evie never had that. She had to die . . . and you're the lady at the big house . . . with everyone being respectable while my poor Evie . . ."

"Oh, Dolly, I'm so sorry. It's such a waste of a life . . . a waste of happiness . . ."

"Not for you. You get what you want and nobody knows."

"Did you take the baby from Eversleigh?"

"Yes. I was going to kill it."

I caught my breath with horror.

"Well, Evie's baby was killed wasn't it?"

"Oh Dolly." I felt quite sick thinking of that terrible time when Jessica had been taken from us.

"I kept her in my room at Grasslands. I was afraid someone might see her, but we managed. Then I knew I'd taken the wrong one. How was I to know which was which? There was all that fuss. I had her with me all the time. She's a lovely little baby." Her face creased into a smile. "She laughed at me and grabbed my finger and wouldn't let go. She was a *dear* little baby. I'm glad I didn't have to kill that one."

I said: "And the rope in the bushes?"

She nodded. "You always went that way. Why does everything go right for you? Why did Billy have to come along that path just then?"

"Rough justice," I said.

"I was watching. I shouted when I saw who it was but I was too late and I didn't have time to get him away when you came so I had to leave him . . . and the rope and everything."

"So you were watching?"

"I wanted to see you fall."

"I understand. And then after I'd gone for help you came out and took him away. You removed the rope . . ."

"It wasn't easy. I had to get him on his horse. Then I took the rope away and I took Billy to the boat house and looked after him. He'd cut his forehead but he hadn't broken anything. He'd fallen into the bushes and they'd saved him. He was all right after a little while."

"I had no idea that you could be so devious," I said.

She looked rather pleased with herself. "Billy said I was making a mess of it. He said it was too important to be managed by an amateur. He said he'd help me to do it in a better way. He'd show me how to get you and I'd help him get the man. You've both got to die . . . for Evie. He knows too much, Billy says. He's going to finish him and help me with you. When you're both dead we're going to put weights on you and throw you into the sea. You'll just be a mysterious disappearance."

"And you, Dolly, what are you going to do? How are you going to feel when you know yourself to be a murderess?"

"I'm an avenger. That's different. We're not ordinary murderers. I'm doing what has to be done for Evie, and Billy . . . he's doing his duty."

"I don't think a court of law would recognize it that way."

"Aren't you frightened, Mrs. Frenshaw?"

"A little. I don't want to die. And, Dolly, somehow I feel you weren't meant to be a murderess."

"I'm going to kill you," she said. "I wish I could do it now and get it over."

"You don't like the idea of it, do you?"

She said: "I've sworn . . . for Evie."

"Untie my hands, Dolly."

She shook her head. "That would spoil everything. I've promised Evie. I've promised myself. Why should you break the seventh commandment and get away free while my sister Evie . . . She didn't break the commandment because she wasn't married. It was only because she loved Alberic. They would have been married and lived happily ever after . . . and I should have been with them."

"You couldn't do this to me, Dolly. How will you feel when people are asking where I am? Suppose somebody saw you with me? They would say, 'The last time we saw her she was riding away with you.' "

"Nobody did see us."

"How can you be sure? And when they started asking you questions . . ."

"They wouldn't. Billy said it would be all right. You're trying to frighten me."

I laughed mirthlessly. "And what are you doing to me?"

"You deserve what you're getting."

"Whatever I've done I have not murdered . . ."

"Yes you have. You murdered Evie. My dear sweet lovely Evie."

"Evie killed herself."

"If you say that again I'll shoot you now. I won't wait for Billy."

"Why do you wait for him?"

"Because . . . because . . . You must not ask questions."

"You have already told me all it is necessary to know. I am sorry about Evie. It was such a cruel waste of life."

She turned away from me to hide her grief, and just at that moment I heard a shrill whistle.

"It's Billy," she said.

She went out and there followed the sound of voices.

I heard him say: "I'll keep an eye on her. She can't get away. Take something of hers . . . something he'd know. He's a suspicious devil and he's on the trail."

"All right," said Dolly.

She came back into the boat house. She was no longer carrying the gun.

"I want a ring or something . . . something he'd know," she said.

"Something who would know?"

"Your lover, of course. The one you met at Enderby, the one you broke the seventh commandment for."

"Why do you want this?"

"Because I'm going to take it to him and tell him where you are."

"Dolly!"

"Then he'll come, won't he? He'll come to rescue you."

"And then?"

"Billy will be lying in wait for him."

"Dolly, you must not do this."

"It's part of the plan. Billy and I are helping each other. It was his idea. That's why he doesn't want you dead till after he is. You get the idea. Billy doesn't trust me. He thinks that if I killed you I mightn't help him bring Mr. Frenshaw here. I would though . . . because although you're both Evie's murderers, he was the one who actually killed Alberic."

I was more afraid now. I saw the plan clearly. Jonathan would come riding onto the beach and Billy Grafter would be lying hidden waiting for him. Jonathan would be an easy target. It must not happen. I suddenly thought of a world without him and I could not bear it. If ever I knew that I loved Jonathan it was in that moment.

I began to plead for Jonathan's life as I had not pleaded for my own.

"Dolly, please . . . listen to me. You must not do this. Jonathan has done no wrong. He is working for his country. He had to kill Alberic. Alberic was a spy."

"Alberic was going to be Evie's husband."

"Listen, Dolly."

"I won't listen any more. Billy will be angry. He gets very angry. He wants me to go at once. I've got to bring him here. Now . . . give me something. That scarf. That'll do. Oh yes. It has your initials worked on it in silk. He'll know that."

"Dolly, please don't do this thing."

She laughed, and snatching the scarf, ran out of the boat house.

It seemed like hours that I lay there. There was a deep silence broken only by the gentle swishing of the waves as they ran lightly up the sand; and now and then I heard the melancholy cry of a gull.

What could I do? I was powerless. Must I lie here trussed up like a fowl for the oven, unable to move? I looked at my wrists which were firmly bound together and I wondered if I could hope to release them. If I could do that . . . unbind my ankles and get out of here . . . I could find a way. Billy Grafter was watching out there. He would be at some vantage point, ready to kill Jonathan as he arrived.

It was hopeless. My hands were firmly tied and I could not break free.

I thought: What chance will he have? He will walk straight into the trap.

I should have been more astute. I should have tried to find out more about Evie and her sister. I should have tried to discover who was watching me, who had tried to bring me down on the bridle path. It seemed that I had been obsessed by Jonathan and I had thought it was Millicent's jealousy when it had been a much more sinister cause.

What was the time? Would she find him? I knew that when she showed him my scarf he would believe that I had sent it. What would she tell him? Some plausible story. She was quite inventive. She would say that I was Billy Grafter's prisoner in the boat house, that she had seen him bring me here, that she had slipped in and been unable to free me and I had begged her to go to him for help.

I guessed that in the circumstances, because of his fear for me, Jonathan would not pause to consider the story closely. He would come at once.

How long had she been away? It must be more than half an hour. These could be my last minutes on earth. I had seen purpose in Dolly's eyes; she had loved her sister devotedly. Evie had been all that she was not . . . pretty, attractive—and she had lived for Evie.

Oh, I understood Dolly's motives, her feelings, her emotions. The sadly maimed one, taken care of by her beautiful sister, giving all the affection of which she was capable—and that was a good deal—to Evie. Then the chain of events . . . the coming of Alberic, the love between him and Evie, the consequences, and then the death of Alberic.

I could understand the heartbreak, the intensity of the sorrow she had felt. Yes, I could understand why Dolly had been thrown off balance. I could understand why she could contemplate murder. But she had been moved by Jessica. I could see that in her face when she had spoken of her. I trembled to think that it might have been Amaryllis. What if it had been? Oh no, that was too appalling to contemplate!

I tried to look into the future. Jonathan would come. He would be killed. Then Dolly would shoot me. Would they send us both to the bottom of the ocean?

An idea came to me which filled me with horror. We should both be missing . . . lying at the bottom of the sea, weighed down so that there was no danger of our bodies being washed ashore as Alberic's had been. They would say that we had gone away together. Millicent would recall her suspicions. And David . . . what of David?

I had not thought of that until this moment and now I was filled with wretchedness. This was what I could least bear. He would believe I had gone off with his brother . . . that I had deserted him and my child.

"Oh no . . . no . . ." I moaned.

I cared so much about David, and the thought of his believing this of me, of the wound it would inflict, hurt me more than anything else I could think of.

I was in a cold sweat.

I would implore Dolly not to do this. Let her kill me if she would . . . but not let it be thought that I had disappeared . . . with Jonathan.

She would never agree. How could she without implicating herself?

"Shoot me," I would plead. "But leave my body in the boat house. Leave me here with Jonathan . . . and Billy Grafter could get away in the boat . . . but leave us here. Let David know that I was not guilty of the ultimate betrayal."

An hour must have passed.

It could not be long now. I was straining my ears. Then suddenly I heard the shot and I knew that Jonathan had arrived.

There was another shot and another. The shooting went on for some seconds.

Dolly was in the boat house; her hair fell wildly about her shoulders; she was white-faced and she was staring at me madly.

She said: "Billy's dead. He's got Billy."

Great gladness seized me. I said: "And Jonathan . . . ?"

"Him too," she said. "They're both lying there. I've got to kill you now. It's your turn . . . and Billy's not here to help me."

I felt numb. Jonathan dead! I could imagine it. He would have come riding onto the beach, making for the boat house . . . and Billy was lying hidden. Billy would shoot, but unless he killed Jonathan with the first shot, he would not succeed. Jonathan would be ready . . . on the alert.

"Dead," I said. "Jonathan . . . dead."

"Billy too . . ." she murmured and she picked up the gun, and pointed it at me.

"There'll be blood," she said. "There is blood. Poor Billy. I don't like blood."

Then she dropped her gun and covered her face with her hands. "I can't do it," she said. "I thought I could but I can't. I couldn't kill the little baby."

"Of course you can't do it, Dolly. I understand everything. I know how you felt. Help me now. Untie these ropes. Let's go and see them. Perhaps they're not dead."

She looked at me and I saw the timid girl I had always known.

"They are dead," she said.

"They might not be. Perhaps there is something we could do."

She hesitated. I felt then that my life was in the balance. Everything depended on the next few seconds. Suddenly she nodded. She felt in the pocket of her gown and brought out a knife. She looked at it for a moment and paused. I thought she was going to change her mind. Then she cut the ropes.

I stumbled out of the boat house. I saw Billy Grafter first. He was lying on the sand, which was dyed red all around him.

He was undoubtedly dead.

And there was Jonathan.

I had never thought to see him so. He lay limply and his face was the colour of ivory. He looked like a different person . . . so quiet . . . so still. His horse was standing patiently by. He must have dismounted before he was shot.

I leaned over him. I thought I detected a faint flutter of breath.

"Jonathan, my love, don't die. Please . . ."

Dolly was standing beside me.

Hope had come to me. He was not dead. He might yet be saved.

"Dolly," I said. "Ride back to Eversleigh. Get help. Tell them there's been an accident. Tell them that Mr. Jonathan is very seriously hurt. Promise me you will do this. I will stay here with him."

She said: "I can't. What will they say?"

I took her arm. I wondered whether I should go. But I did not want to leave her here with him. I was still unsure of her. I kept telling myself that there was hope and I was desperately afraid to leave him.

I said very seriously: "This is a terrible thing, Dolly. We've got to save them if possible . . . him and Billy. You have played a part in this, but you are no murderess. If we can save their lives you'll feel so much better. You'll forget that you lured him here. Tell them quickly and get a doctor and a stretcher and bring them here quickly . . . Please, Dolly."

"I'll go," she said. "I'll go."

And I believed her.

I knelt beside him. "Jonathan," I said. "Oh . . . Jonathan. Please don't die. You mustn't leave me, you mustn't . . ."

His eyes flickered for a moment and his lips moved. I bent low to hear what he said. It was: "Claudine."

"Yes, Jonathan, my dearest. I am here with you. I am hoping to take you back to Eversleigh. You're going to recover. Yes, you are. I promise you."

"Finished," he whispered.

"No . . . no. You're too young. Nobody could do this to you. Not to you . . . Jonathan Frenshaw. You've always been the one who succeeded. You're not finished. Your whole life is before you."

His lips formed my name again.

"Remember . . ." he murmured. "Live . . . happily, Claudine. Don't look back. Secrets . . . best kept. Remember. For Amaryllis . . . remember. Ours . . ."

I kissed his forehead. He seemed to be aware of me, for something like a smile touched his lips.

He was still trying to say something. "Be happy . . ." I think it was, and I knew he was reminding me of his philosophy. I was to be happy, to make David happy. I was to keep our secret. Dolly shared it, but I had a feeling that she would never betray it. There were many things which she would want to forget.

"Don't go, Jonathan," I said.

"Do you love me?"

"I do . . . with all my heart."

His eyes flickered and there was that smile again.

"Jonathan," I pleaded. "Jonathan . . ."

But he was unaware and he spoke no more.

When they arrived he was dead.

October 1805

It was a long time since those agonizing moments on the beach when I had watched Jonathan die. Amaryllis and Jessica were now eleven years old. We had celebrated their birthdays this year—as we always did—simultaneously. They were growing up together, close—perhaps closer than sisters would have done. They were so different—Jessica a dark flamboyant beauty with a temper to match her looks; Amaryllis, fair as an angel with the sweetest of natures. They were the darlings of our household.

I had enjoyed a happiness with David such as I had not believed possible. It was not complete happiness, of course. How could it be? There were dreams when I thought I was in that room and I heard voices telling me that I had sinned—sinned against the one who had loved me so dearly, so tenderly. Sometimes during the day when I was laughing and so intensely happy, the voices would intrude, shattering my pleasure and my peace of mind. Then I thought of Jonathan and found a certain comfort in remembering his words. I must never make David unhappy by letting him guess that ours had ever been anything but the perfect marriage. My punishment was to live with my secret, and I would never be completely rid of my guilt. Always there would be the reminder like voices in a haunted room.

Life at Eversleigh goes on much the same as it ever did.

It could no longer be kept secret that Billy Grafter had been a spy for the French and that Alberic had worked with him; and this was why they had met their deaths. Jonathan was the hero who had brought them to justice—and lost his life in doing so.

I often wondered about Dolly. I saw her frequently and she seemed to have become quite fond of me. She was happier than she had been for a long time, and I think it was due to her grandmother. Evalina Trent had changed. I never knew how much she had been aware of, but she ceased to mourn so desperately for Evie and gave herself up to the care of Dolly. I think in a way she saw that her ambitions for Evie had been one of the main causes which had led Evie to take such drastic action. It must have been a sobering thought that she preferred a watery grave to her grandmother's wrath.

Neither Dolly nor I would ever forget that dramatic event in which we had taken part. Once I talked to her of Jonathan and told her how he believed that it was better to keep secrets rather than make confessions which were going to hurt people.

"I don't know whether he was right or not," I said. "Perhaps before I die I shall find out."

Millicent had been stunned by Jonathan's death. She had truly loved him.

She talked to me of him.

"I once thought there was something between you and him," she said.

"Oh?" I replied. "But David is my husband."

"That is not always a deterrent. I don't think it would have been with Jonathan. I was not sure with you. Jonathan was the most attractive man I ever knew . . . or ever will. He was perhaps irresistible. He was not a good man . . . as David is. There was adventure in him. He would have his way, and he didn't always consider other people. But he died for his country."

I agreed with her—and so we accepted our lives, as we needs must.

When her child was born she became absorbed in him. He was her delight. She called him Jonathan, and that other Jonathan lived again for her in him.

She was happier now—and so was I. I had David; I had Amaryllis; we were a united family and I was grateful to be a member of it.

One day we had an unexpected visitor who came from the Continent. He had met Charlot, who had begged him, if he returned to England, to take a message to my mother. Both Charlot and Louis Charles had married and left the Army. They now had their own vineyard in Burgundy; and the message was that when there was peace between England and France we should all meet again. My mother's happiness was great. Only then did I realize how deeply saddened she had been by the loss of her son.

We had lived through stirring times. We had seen Napoleon become the Emperor of the French, with almost the whole of Europe under his control.

We had shivered with apprehension when he had turned his acquisitive eyes on our island. We were to be the next, and the threat of invasion by those seemingly unconquerable armies hung over us.

But we had our great men. Lord Nelson was one of them. We had just had the news of Napoleon's defeat at Trafalgar Bay, and there was a lightness in the air; bonfires were blazing from one end of England to the other.

Nelson, the national hero, had died on his flagship and that flagship was symbolically called the *Victory*.

We were a large party that night and the conversation was all of the victory at Trafalgar, which had removed the threat of invasion and stopped the conqueror in his uninterrupted progress through the world.

My mother proposed a toast to Lord Nelson, the dead hero.

"And there is another I should like to include," she went on. "Jonathan Frenshaw. It is because of men like these, who give themselves, that we may enjoy our peaceful lives. They are the real heroes."

And we drank to that, for it was true.